By H. P. Mallory

THE JOLIE WILKINS SERIES
Fire Burn and Cauldron Bubble
Toil and Trouble
Be Witched (e-original short story)
Witchful Thinking

THE DULCIE O'NEIL SERIES
To Kill a Warlock
A Tale of Two Goblins
Great Hexpectations
Wuthering Frights

H. P. MALLORY

The Witch Is Back

A JOLIE WILKINS NOVEL

BANTAM BOOKS
NEW YORK

The Witch Is Back is a work of fiction. Names, characters, places, and incidents are the products of the author's imagination or are used fictitiously. Any resemblance to actual events, locales, or persons, living or dead, is entirely coincidental.

A Bantam Books Mass Market Original

Copyright © 2012 by H. P. Mallory
Excerpt from *Something Witchy This Way Comes* copyright © 2012 by H. P. Mallory
Excerpt from *Be Witched* copyright © 2011 by H. P. Mallory

Published in the United States by Bantam Books, an imprint of The Random House Publishing Group, a division of Random House, Inc., New York.

BANTAM BOOKS and the rooster colophon are registered trademarks of Random House, Inc.

ISBN 978-0-345-53156-8
eBook ISBN 978-0-345-53157-5

Cover design: Eileen Carey
Cover illustration: Anne Keenan Higgins

This book contains an excerpt from the forthcoming book *Something Witchy This Way Comes* by H. P. Mallory. This excerpt has been set for this edition only and may not reflect the final content of the forthcoming edition.

Printed in the United States of America

www.bantamdell.com

9 8 7 6 5 4 3 2 1

Bantam Books mass market edition: August 2012

For My Readers: Thank You

ACKNOWLEDGMENTS

Thank you to my mother and husband for all your help and support.

To my editor, Shauna Summers, thank you for your guidance with this book.

Thanks also to my agent, Kimberly Whalen.

And thank you to all my readers for helping to make my dreams come true.

The Witch Is Back

One

When the phone rang at ten minutes to seven, I wasn't surprised. Nope, I figured that Sinjin Sinclair, the most handsome and charming man who had ever stepped into my life, had probably just come to his senses and realized he didn't want to take me out for dinner after all. Maybe he'd suffered from a slight brain freeze the night before when he'd been awaiting roadside assistance at my tarot-card-reading shop, and that was why he'd asked me out.

So when he phoned to say he was lost, I was surprised—not so much that his navigational skills were lacking but that he actually wanted to go through with this. Okay, I know what you're thinking—that I must look like a troll, or something equally heinous ... Well, I'm not a troll by any stretch of the imagination, but I'm also not the girl who stands out in a crowd. I'm more the girl next door—or at least I live down the street from the girl next door.

Okay, I'm probably being a little too hard on myself because I have been told that I'm attractive and I know I'm smart and all that stuff, but I'm still nowhere near Sinjin Sinclair's league.

But back to the phone call. After Sinjin said he would be at my door shortly, I hung up and then stood in the center of my living room for a few minutes like a space cadet, gazing at the wall until I'm sure I looked like a complete and total moron.

But while it might have appeared that nothing much was going on in that gray matter between my ears, appearances can be deceiving. Thoughts ramrodded my brain, slamming into one another as new ones were born . . . *What am I doing? What am I thinking? What do I possibly have to talk about with a man as cultured and refined as Sinjin Sinclair? Moreover, how am I going to eat in front of him? What if I choke on an ice cube? Or I sneeze after taking a mouthful of salad and spray carrot chunks all over his expensive clothes?*

Jolie Wilkins, calm down, I finally said to myself, closing my eyes and taking a deep breath. *You are going to go on this date, because if you don't, you're never going to forgive yourself. And, furthermore, Christa will most definitely murder you.*

I inhaled another deep breath and forced myself out of my self-inflicted brain coma, staring toward the mirror as I took stock of myself for the umpteenth time in the last hour. Christa, my best friend and self-proclaimed fashion advisor, had left twenty minutes ago after chastising me about my current getup. Yes, she'd tried to force me into what amounted to shrink-wrapping, complete with stiletto heels that were so narrow they could double as weapons. Then, after that attempt had failed, she'd tried to get me to go with a flame-red corset dress that was so tight, I couldn't walk—and breathing was out of the question. So yes, I'd defeated the raunchy-clothing demon but I couldn't say I felt very good about my victory.

I sighed as I took in my shoulder-length blond hair and the fact that the curl Christa had wrestled into it only minutes before was already gone. It could be described as "limp" at best. My makeup was nice, though—Christa had managed to talk me into a smoky eye, which accented my baby blues, and she'd also covered the freckles that sprinkled the bridge of my nose while playing up my cheekbones with a shimmery apricot blush. She'd lined my decently plump lips in a light brown and filled them with bubble-gum-pink lipstick, finishing them with a pink gloss called "Baby Doll."

There was a knock on my front door, and I felt my heart lurch into my throat. I took another deep breath and glanced at my reflection in the mirror again, trying not to focus on the fact that I was anything but sexy in a black amorphous skirt that ended just below my knees, black tights, and two-inch heels. Even though my breasts are decently large, you couldn't really tell in my gray turtleneck and black peacoat.

Maybe I should have listened to Christa . . .

Another quick knock on the door signaled the fact that I was dawdling. I pulled myself away from my reflection and, wrapping my hand around the doorknob, exhaled and opened it, pasting a smile on my face.

"Hello," I said, hoping my voice sounded level and even-keeled, because the sight of Sinjin standing there just about undid me. A tornado was rampaging through me, tearing at my guts and wreaking havoc with my nervous system.

"Good evening," the deity before me spoke in his refined, baritone English accent. His eyes traveled from my eyes to my bust to my legs and back up again as a serpentine smile spread across his sumptuous lips.

"Um," I managed, meaning to add a *How are you?* to the end of it, but somehow the words never emerged.

Sinjin arched a black brow and chuckled as I debated slamming the door shut and hiding out in my room for the next, oh, two years, at least.

"You look quite lovely," he said, with that devilish smile as he pulled his arm forward and offered me a bouquet of red roses. "These pale in comparison."

My hand was shaking and my brain was on vacation as I reached for the roses, but somehow I did manage to smile and say, "Thank you, they are really beautiful."

The beauty of the roses didn't even compute, though—my overwhelmed mind was still reeling from the presence of this man. *Man* didn't even do him justice; he seemed so much more than that—either heaven-sent or hell's emissary.

He was wearing black, just as he had been the night before. His black slacks weren't fitted, but neither were they loose—in fact, they seemed tailored to his incredibly long legs. And his black sweater perfectly showcased his broad shoulders and narrow waist. Even though his body and intimidating height would have been worth writing home about, it was his face that was so completely alluring.

Sinjin's eyes should have been the eighth wonder of the world. They were the most peculiar color—an incredibly light blue, most similar to the blue-green icebergs you might find in Alaska or the Alpine waters of Germany. They almost seemed to glow. His skin was flawless, neither too pale nor too tan, without the kiss of a freckle or mole.

His hair was midnight black, so dark that it almost appeared blue. Tonight it looked longer than I remembered. The ends curled up over his collar, which was strange considering I'd only met him the day before and I could have sworn he had short hair. But the strangest thing about this enigmatic man was that I couldn't see his aura . . .

I've been able to see people's auras for as long as I can remember. An aura is best described as a halo-type thing that surrounds someone—it billows out of them in a foggy sort of haze. If someone is healthy, his or her aura is usually pink or violet. If someone is unwell in some way, yellow or orange predominates. I had never before met anyone who didn't have an aura at all or whose aura I couldn't see. And what surprised me even more was the fact that I hadn't noticed his missing aura the first time I'd seen him . . . Of course I had been pretty overwhelmed by his mere presence—and that dazed feeling didn't seem like it was going to go away anytime soon.

"May I escort you?" he asked as he gave me another winning smile and offered me his arm.

I gulped as I tentatively wrapped my hand around his arm, trying not to notice the fact that he was really . . . built. Good God . . .

"Thanks," I said in a small voice as I allowed him to lead me outside.

"Are you forgetting something?" Sinjin asked as he glanced down at me.

"Um," I started and dropped my attention to my feet, attempting to take stock of myself.

Shoes are on, purse is over my shoulder, nerves are present and accounted for . . . the only thing I'd forgotten was my confidence, which was currently hiding beneath my bed.

Sinjin stopped walking and turned around. I followed suit and noticed that the door to my modest little house was still open—gaping wide as though it was as shocked as he was that I'd forgotten to shut it.

"Oh my God." I felt my cheeks color with embarrassment. It had to be pretty obvious I'd completely forgotten how to function in his presence. I separated myself from him and hurried back up my walkway, shaking my head at my inattention. Anxiety drumming through me, I closed and locked the door behind me.

"Shall we try this again?"

I jumped, shocked that he was suddenly right beside me. I shook the feeling off, figuring that he must have been trailing me all along. But still, there was something . . . uncanny about it, something that set off my "Spidey" senses. I blamed it on my already overwhelmed nerves.

"Yes," I said with an anxious laugh as he offered his arm again and I, again, took it. This time we made it to the curb, where a black car awaited us. So angular it almost looked like a spaceship, it was the same vehicle he'd been driving the night before when he'd gotten a flat tire and had asked to use my phone. He opened the door for me and I gave him a smile of thanks as I seated myself, glancing over at the steering wheel where I recognized the emblem of a Ferrari.

A Ferrari . . . seriously?

I had to pinch myself. This just wasn't real—it couldn't be real! I mean, my life was composed of TV dinners and reruns of *The Office*. My only social outlet, really, was Christa. Men like Sinjin Sinclair with their impeccable clothes and stunning good looks, driving their Ferraris, just didn't figure into the Jolie Wilkins equation. Not at all!

"I hope you do not mind that I made reservations at Costa Mare?" he asked with a boyish grin.

Costa Mare was renowned for its Italian food and even more renowned for the fact that it took months to get a reservation. "You were able to make a reservation there?" I asked in awe, my mouth gaping in response.

Sinjin shrugged. "As a rule, I never take no for an answer." Then he chuckled as if he was making a joke. But you know what people say about jokes—there's always an underlying element of truth to them. It would not at all have come as a surprise to me to learn that Sinjin Sinclair was accustomed to getting his way.

For the next fifteen minutes, we made small talk—discussing things like the weather, his flat tire, and the history of my friendship with Christa. Before I knew it, we'd pulled in front of Costa Mare and Sinjin was hand-

ing his keys to the valet. Sinjin shook his head at the
doorman who attempted to open my door, insisting that
he would do it himself. I couldn't remember the last time
a man had opened a car door for me. The guys in LA
weren't exactly gentlemen.

I took Sinjin's proffered arm and allowed him to escort me into the restaurant, where the staff seemed to
fuss over him like he was some great messiah. They led
us through a weaving path of tables, sparkling marble
flooring, and dim candlelight, finally designating us to
an isolated table in a corner of the room. Potted bam-
boos acted as a screen from the rest of the restaurant.

"Where would you prefer to sit?" Sinjin asked me
with a polished smile.

"It doesn't matter," I answered as I waited for him to
pull out my chair. He chose the seat with the best view
of the restaurant, but I hadn't been lying—I really didn't
care.

The host, a rotund, short man, who was probably in
his late forties, offered us our menus, placed our nap-
kins on our laps, and left us to our own devices.

"A man should always choose his seat wisely," Sinjin
commented, glancing at me with a smirk.

"Why is that?" I asked, wondering what he was getting at.

He nodded as if he was about to divulge a long and
interesting story. "In times long past, it could mean
death if a man's back was to his enemies."

"And you're still practicing that, I see?" I asked with
a smile, suddenly feeling comfortable with him. It was
strange because I wasn't a person who was, in general,
comfortable around anyone I didn't know.

"It is my duty to ensure your safety, poppet."

I wasn't sure why, but the word *poppet* seemed so familiar to me, even though I was pretty sure I'd never
heard it before. It was a sudden moment of déjà vu, of

that feeling that somewhere, sometime, I'd experienced this exact moment. It made no sense, but I couldn't help but feel haunted by it all the same.

"Well, I'm sure things are safer in this day and age," I said, trying to shake off the weird feeling. It wouldn't budge. There was just something so . . . familiar about all this. I took a deep breath and started perusing the menu, hoping to banish my wayward thoughts. Feeling as if Sinjin was staring at me, I glanced up and found his eyes fastened on me. He didn't even try to hide the fact, and when I caught him, he smiled.

This one was smooth.

"Have you selected your supper?" he asked, his mouth spreading into a wide smile as if he was in on some inside joke that I wasn't privy to.

I swallowed hard, suddenly more than aware that this whole date might just be the setup for a one-night stand. That was when it struck me—that's *exactly* what it was. Sinjin was traveling from Britain, and he probably wanted to taste everything the United States had to offer, including its women. Well, unluckily for him, I wasn't on the menu. I felt my lips tightening into a line, and I tried to keep my cool. But inside I was fuming— mainly at my own idiocy. Had I really been out of the game so long that this hadn't dawned on me from the get-go?

"I think so," I muttered and concealed myself with my menu.

"What is on your mind?" Sinjin asked as he pushed my menu down with his index finger, forcing me to look at him. I could feel my cheeks coloring. He had nerve . . .

"Nothing," I answered and dropped my eyes.

"Please, Jolie, do not insult my intelligence."

I took a deep breath. If he wanted to know what was on my mind, he was about to get an earful. "I'm not into one-night stands," I said stiffly.

Sinjin narrowed his eyes, but the smile on his lips revealed the fact that he was amused. "A wise policy."

So he was still playing this game, was he? "Well, I think you should . . . be aware of that . . . in case you . . . in case you . . ."

"In case I what?"

I could feel sweat breaking out along the small of my back. He was forcing me into a corner, and that damn smile was still in full effect. "In case you . . . were, uh, looking for that . . . that sort of thing."

He didn't drop his attention from my face. If anything, his eyes were even more focused, challenging. "Is that what you imagined I was in search of?"

So he was going to make this tough on me, was he? He was going to make me spell it out for him and embarrass myself? Well, I might not be in his league, but I wouldn't be made a fool of. I was way too smart for that. "Without a doubt."

"And what, pray tell, gave you that impression, if I may be so bold as to inquire?"

"I . . . um." I cleared my throat and forced myself to look him straight in the eyes. "I couldn't figure out why else you'd be here with . . . with me tonight."

Sinjin took a deep breath, and it seemed to take him forever to exhale it. "I see."

"So, if you are . . . expecting that, you might as well take me home now . . . no harm done," I finished and held his gaze for another three seconds before I picked up my ice water and began chugging it.

"Very well," he answered, and his voice was tender.

I dropped the menu and reached for my purse, feeling something icy forming in my gut as I readied myself to leave. I wasn't angry, no, but I was humiliated. Strangely enough, though, relief was beginning to suffuse me . . . relief at the fact that I could end this farce and lick my wounds in the comfort and serenity of my house. After collecting my things, I stood up and noticed that Sinjin hadn't moved an inch.

"What are you doing?" I demanded.

"Perhaps I should ask the same of you?"

I swallowed hard. "I thought we were leaving?"

"Why would we be leaving? We have not even ordered yet."

"But I thought," I started before my voice was swallowed up by the fact that I was at a complete loss.

Sinjin smiled up at me and shook his head, pulling out my chair. "Please have a seat, love," he said. "You misunderstood my intentions."

"But you said 'very well,'" I started, even as I sat down and pulled myself to the table again.

"I was simply agreeing with your assessment of the fact that you are quite opposed to 'one-night stands,' as you so fittingly termed them." He smiled again, cocking his brow. "And while I find you to be quite a delectable package, poppet, I am afraid I quite agree with you regarding the more intimate side of our association . . . for the time being, at least."

So he wasn't looking for a one-night stand? Or maybe he was so smooth, he was just faking it and he'd put his plan of attack into action once I was no longer suspicious. I took a deep breath and lifted my menu again, wishing I'd never agreed to this date in the first place. "Oh."

"Would you be averse to the notion of . . . starting over?" he asked and leaned back into his chair as he studied me.

I felt an embarrassed smile pulling at my lips even though I still wasn't sure what his intentions were. Well, either way, it took two to tango and my tango shoes were in a box in my closet, covered with dust. "No, that sounds good."

"Very well," he said again and called the waiter over. "Ms. Wilkins," he started.

"Please, it's Jolie."

He smiled languidly. "Jolie, what would you care to drink?"

I faced the waiter and smiled. "Do you have any Riesling?"

The waiter nodded. "Yes, ma'am."

"A glass of that, then," I finished.

"And you, sir," the waiter asked, turning to face Sinjin.

"The same please," he responded.

"Are you ready to order?" the waiter asked us both, his pen poised above the pad of paper as if he were about to start a race or something.

Sinjin glanced at me and I nodded, having already figured out what I wanted. "I'd like the sea bass, please."

The waiter scribbled down my order before facing Sinjin. "And you, sir?"

Sinjin shook his head. "Nothing for me, thank you."

"Sinjin," I started, shocked that he wasn't ordering anything. "You aren't going to make me eat alone, are you?"

He smiled. "I apologize, love, but my stomach is a bit finicky at the moment. Would you mind terribly?"

How was I going to say no to that? I shook my head and the waiter nodded, disappearing into the kitchen moments later.

"We can go if you aren't feeling well," I offered.

Sinjin waved away my concern with his long fingers. "I have a bit of a stomach condition, and it plagues me every now and again. Nothing to concern yourself with, love." He studied me for a moment or two and smiled again. "Where were we?"

"Um, I think we had agreed to start over."

He chuckled. "Ah, yes, starting over." His voice

trailed as he apparently searched for a new topic. "Tell me about your tarot-reading business."

I sighed and glanced down at my ice water. The ice had melted into tiny lumps, and I submerged each one with my straw as I thought about his question. "Well, as you know, I'm a psychic," I said. Whether he even believed in that sort of thing was anyone's guess—it wasn't something we'd established the night before.

"Have you always known this about yourself?" he asked, just as the waiter returned with our wine. Sinjin raised his glass. "Prost!" he said and brought his glass to his lips as I downed a swallow of my bitterly sweet wine. Before he took a swig, he set his glass back on the table and glanced over at me again. "Well?"

I smiled. "Um, yeah, for as long as I can remember. I could always see things and I just seemed to know things about people. Stuff that I shouldn't know." I wondered if I'd said too much. Usually men didn't react well to my day job—thinking I was either a charlatan or a nut job.

But there was no sign of judgment on Sinjin's handsome face. Instead, he just nodded. I couldn't tell if he thought I was full of it or not.

"I know the feeling."

I faced him, my eyes wide, as I wondered what he was admitting. "Are you psychic?"

He shook his head. "No, but I have had my dealings with the otherworldly."

So he didn't think I was a liar or a Looney Tune. I breathed out a sigh of relief. And as the relief washed over me, a feeling of disappointment surfaced. Sinjin might understand me, but it wasn't like he was going to stick around. I mean, he was traveling here on business or vacation or something.

"What about you," I started. "You're here for work?"

His eyes were still fixed on mine and there was something in their depths. Something untold, something hidden. I could tell that this man had his own skeletons hanging in his closet. "Yes, quite so."

"What do you do?"

He shrugged and finally averted his eyes, lifting his glass of wine as he trailed the rim of the glass with his finger. "I own my own company."

"Ah, what type of business?"

"Finance," he said quickly, somewhat dismissively, and then leaned forward, seemingly uncomfortable about discussing the specifics.

"And you're here for just a little while, then?" I hoped I didn't sound apprehensive. Still, I was all too aware that this charade probably wouldn't last longer than tonight. Not when he had a whole life waiting for him in Britain.

God, what if he's married?

He didn't respond right away, just continued looping his finger around the rim of his glass. "I am considering opening an American branch of my company. That is why I am currently here." He stopped talking for a few seconds and then smiled at me. "Perhaps I will not return to Britain—for the foreseeable future, at any rate."

I felt something happy burst within me even though it made no sense. If Sinjin decided to stay, that didn't mean we'd necessarily see each other again. And if we did see each other once, twice, or even multiple times, he'd still have to return to Britain eventually. And where would that leave me?

I shook the feelings of elation right out of me. I was getting way ahead of myself. And truly, I was just being silly, setting myself up for disappointment.

Two

"Wow, so was he just as hot last night?" Christa asked as she leaned against the counter in my store and watched me sweep.

"If you actually want to earn your keep, why don't you grab a trash bin?" I asked her with a smile. God forbid if my business ever went under and Christa found herself in need of a real job.

She made no motion to get the bin, which didn't surprise me. "Answer the question, Jules."

I paused from my sweeping and leaned against the broom as I considered it. Was Sinjin as hot as he'd been when Christa and I had first met him? *Hmm . . . those ice-blue eyes, black hair, broad shoulders, and massive height? That devilish smile . . .* "Hotter."

"Hotter?" she said with a huge smile as her eyebrows reached for the ceiling. "Hot damn!"

Yes, Sinjin Sinclair was most definitely hotter than he'd been when I first met him, but what was more surprising was that he'd asked me for a second date. And he'd asked to see me for that second date tonight. Even though I was pretty dumbfounded, I'd agreed. I was still trying to figure why exactly I'd agreed because I was most definitely out of my comfort zone.

"So this is the third time in three days that you're going to see him?" Christa continued, that smile still plastered on her fuchsia-pink lips. I just nodded. "Wow, he's pretty eager."

"He's probably just bored," I answered and shook my head as I tried to find the missing piece in the puzzle titled: *Why in hell would such an amazing man want to go out again with Jolie Wilkins?* It really didn't make any sense at all. But then, do men ever make sense?

"He's not bored, Jules," Christa said, the smile dropping from her lips. "When are you going to realize you have a ton to offer? You're pretty and sweet and you're the most generous person I know. And sometimes you can actually be pretty funny."

"Thanks, Chris," I said, not really sure how to take that last bit—I thought I was decently funny all the time.

"And the fact that he's a ten out of ten should be reason enough to be excited," she finished.

I cleared my throat and shook my head. "That's where the problem is. He's too hot and it isn't helping my nerves at all. Every time I see him, I feel like I'm about to have a heart attack or, at the very least, vomit."

Christa waved away my concerns with her perfectly manicured, flame-orange nails. "Puh-leeze. This is good for you, Jules." She brought her nails to her mouth and narrowed her eyes as she studied me. "In fact, the arrival of Mr. Sexy Bitch is the best thing that's happened to you in the last five years, at least."

I laughed; I couldn't help it. "Mr. Sexy Bitch?"

But Christa didn't respond right away. Instead, she continued that narrowed-eye expression as a lascivious smile stole across her mouth. This meant only one thing—she was thinking about sex.

"Don't even go there," I said, shaking my head. Conversations with Christa about sex were never fun.

She pushed away from the counter and walked over to me, snatching the broom from my hand. She made no attempt to start sweeping, though, so she must have just done it for dramatic effect. "You realize you're going to need to give it up eventually, right? I mean, it's been like forever since the last time you had sex."

"Give what up?" I asked, even though I knew exactly what she was talking about. I was just trying to delay the inevitable.

"The Jolie love flower," she answered with a straight face.

"Where the hell do you come up with this stuff?"

She frowned. "Doesn't matter. What does matter, though, is the fact that you're about to get some action for the first time in I don't even know how long."

It had been over a year since I'd had sex, but who was counting? "I'm not going there with him, Chris," I said, reaffirming out loud what I'd been telling myself since our date last night. Sex with Sinjin Sinclair was most definitely a bad idea.

"Yes, you are. If you get one thing out of that hot-ass man, it's going to be a sexfest."

"Sexfest?" I sighed, long and hard, not even finding the energy to laugh. "I really don't want to go there." I folded my hands across my chest and tried to stop myself from squirming. Squirming was just so high school and I *was* twenty-eight years old, for God's sake!

"Why?"

"Because I think that's all he's after."

She studied me for a second or two and then shrugged. "Who cares? I mean, when you get down to it, that's what all men are after. The sooner you realize that and go with it, the more fun you're going to have."

But I wasn't like Christa. I couldn't have sex without feelings getting in the way, and the last thing I wanted was that empty feeling when you liked someone more than they liked you. And sex with Sinjin would basically guarantee that I'd fall head over heels for him, probably at the same exact moment that he boarded a return flight to England. "I'm just not like you, Chris."

"With some training you could be," she said with a knowing smile.

But I wasn't even sure I wanted to be like Christa. I enjoyed my life as it was—predictable but happy.

"So you really like this guy then?" she asked, handing the broom back to me and starting to bite her cuticles.

"I've only had one date with him," I shot back, as much for myself as her. "How much could I possibly like him?"

"Let me repeat myself . . . so you really like this guy then?"

I ran a hand through my hair and exhaled a pent-up breath of frustration. "I had a nice time on our date."

And that was the truth. I'd lost track of time just as easily as I'd lost myself in Sinjin's incredible eyes. We'd talked and laughed so much, it almost felt like we were long-lost friends—I was just so comfortable around him. It was a weird feeling, almost like we'd known each other in some other place and time. I never really put much stock into the idea of reincarnation, but now I found myself second-guessing it—I mean, who knew, maybe in another life Sinjin and I had been acquaintances. Stranger things have happened, right?

Er, maybe not?

I had to shake these thoughts right out of my head—I mean, this was ludicrous! I'd only met the man two days ago!

"Jolie, whatever happens, there's a reason Sinjin walked through our door."

I faced her, startled by her insight. I wouldn't characterize Christa as an especially intuitive person, but there were moments when she surprised me. "You think?"

"Yeah, and you know it as well as I do. If you ask me, the reason is getting you to put yourself back out there and start dating. You need to leave yourself open to the opportunity of falling in love."

I inhaled sharply. "Sometimes you say things that I just can't argue with, Chris," I admitted finally as a huge smile pasted itself on her face.

"And when you finally admit I'm right, it surprises the crap out of me!"

I'm not sure why I thought it would be a good idea, but I'd suggested to Sinjin that we see a movie for our second date. In general, I didn't like going to the movies on a date because isn't the whole purpose to get to know the other person? Well, in this case Sinjin asked what I wanted to do and "let's go see a movie" just spurted from my mouth, seemingly of its own accord.

So here we were, sitting in the twentieth row and waiting for the horror movie, *Fear's Door,* to start. It's not like it had been on my list of must-see movies, but it was the only one that was playing at the right time. As we sat in the theater, waiting for the atrocities to start on-screen, I found myself nervously stuffing my mouth with popcorn.

"Had I known you were hungry, I certainly would have provided something better than that," Sinjin said with a laugh and a raised brow as he observed my munching with distaste.

I felt a kernel stick in my throat and after experiencing a coughing fit, in which Sinjin patted my back in mock aid, I wedged the popcorn container below the seat next to me.

"Are you all right?" Sinjin asked.

I took a few huge sips of Sprite and nodded, feeling the flush of embarrassment heat my cheeks. Guess I wasn't the poster child for femininity. Yes, I probably could have used an etiquette lesson or two from Audrey Hepburn. As it was, my etiquette coach had been Christa, and consequently I was dressed up like a two-bit whore. While I'd fought the metamorphosis into a prostitute the previous evening, this time I'd given in. Mainly because my nerves were on full-steam-ahead and I didn't have the wherewithal to fight multiple battles.

But now I was wondering if I should have been more selective with my chosen battles because Sinjin was eyeing me as if I were a freshly baked chocolate chip cookie and he was the Cookie Monster.

"You appear quite . . . different than you did last night," he said with a smile. "For my benefit, I hope?"

I suddenly wished I had lots more in common with a turtle so I could suck my head and legs into the protection of my shell and not have to witness the amusement in Sinjin's eyes. "Um, my best friend dressed me up like this."

He chuckled. "I did not imagine it was your idea, poppet."

I swallowed hard and looked at the movie screen, wishing I could actually focus my attention for long enough to read the words in what appeared to be a trivia question. As it was, I was so mortified that I'd actually allowed Christa to choose my clothes and, worse, that I'd willingly gone out in public, that I couldn't even concentrate on the sentence long enough to read it.

"Yeah, it wasn't my idea," I managed and reached for my Sprite again, sucking so hard on the straw that my entire mouth filled up with soda. Swallowing it, I started coughing again.

"You look very lovely," Sinjin said, but it was almost an afterthought—like he felt bad about the fact that I was dressed like a floozy and, consequently, was now choking on my soda.

I glanced over at him and shook my head. "I never should have let her talk me into it."

I couldn't help looking down at myself. And I immediately regretted it because Christa's red mini skirt was barely covering my upper thighs and the black fishnets that were beneath it hardly helped. The five-inch stiletto heels on the black leather boots I was wearing made walking a near impossibility, but it was my top that was causing me the most chagrin. My bust is much larger than Christa's, but she'd insisted on forcing me into a size small tube top that had fallen so far down, I could see the sides of both of my breasts.

And my cleavage looked like a butt.

The lights suddenly dimmed and the ads on-screen faded away into blackness as the movie started. I suddenly felt Sinjin's hand on mine and I turned to look at him, surprised by how cold he was.

"May I?" he asked with a sweet, boyish smile.

I just nodded and watched him fold his fingers over my hand, suddenly feeling as if I wanted to pull my hand away because his was icy cold. "You're freezing," I said softly. It wasn't the type of cold that came from being outside in the snow. No, this coldness felt like it was radiating from inside him.

He loosened his hold on my hand for a second or two and then tightened it again, as if he were startled by my comments. He dropped his eyes to his lap, then brought them back to mine with a deep sigh. "I suffer from a rare condition called Raynaud's disease."

I frowned, suddenly feeling like a total asshole for drawing attention to the fact that he was suffering from some disease. Talk about putting my foot in my mouth. "I'm so sorry. I've never heard of it."

He nodded as if my reaction wasn't unusual, but he didn't seem embarrassed. "Raynaud's is a disorder that affects the blood vessels in the skin."

"And it makes you feel cold?"

He brought his attention to the screen, where the opening credits were scrolling. "Yes. The blood vessels shrink and limit circulation to my extremities. I believe it is also to blame for my stomach issues and why I am quite often not hungry." Then he faced me. "Does it bother you?"

I shook my head, still feeling like a total jerk. And I didn't even really notice how cold his touch was anymore anyway—it was almost as if my body heat had warmed him up. "No, it doesn't."

He smiled and faced forward again as the credits faded and the movie started. I wasn't sure why but I squeezed his hand. Maybe it was just to let him know that I was okay with the fact that he wasn't perfect, that I accepted him the way he was. He glanced down at me and smiled, lifting my hand to his lips, which were just as cold as his hand. He kissed the top of my hand and brought it back to his knee again.

I faced forward and tried to get involved in the movie, but I couldn't stop thinking about Sinjin—how close he was to me, how wonderful it had felt when he kissed my hand, how something was stirring deep down inside me for the first time in so long, a kind of stinging at the thought of the other places he could kiss.

God, I'm as bad as Christa!

I forced the thoughts out of my head and mandated my attention to the screen. Some unfortunate half-dressed woman, complete with one ridiculously large boob hanging out of one side of her tank top, was running through a forest, apparently trying to get away from a madman wearing a mask made out of skin. Why the man was after her or how she'd ended up in such a dire predicament, I couldn't say. And I wasn't sure if that was because I hadn't been paying attention or the audience simply wasn't privy to the information.

Either way, it looked bad for the woman. I mean, how could she outrun a crazy guy when the two buoys on her chest had to weigh at least ten pounds apiece?

I reached for my popcorn again, feeling anxiety bubbling up inside of me. I glanced over at Sinjin, who
didn't seem to be affected by the woman's fear in the
least. Instead, he just watched the movie in a detached,
indifferent sort of way.

Raynaud's disease? The fact that Sinjin wasn't quite as
perfect as I originally imagined only endeared him to me
more. Just as I had my own Achilles' heel to bear in the
form of my self-confidence (or lack thereof), so did
Sinjin. Maybe we had more in common than I thought?
I mean, maybe most women didn't respond well when
he told them about his condition—maybe he was as nervous about it as I was about dating in general. Maybe I
wasn't as alone as I thought.

Sinjin's hold on my hand tightened but it wasn't an
intimate squeeze, it was more a reaction born from
something else . . . adrenaline? I glanced at the screen
and noticed that the woman had been stabbed and was
now dying on the forest floor, while the man in the meat
mask stood over her. There was blood everywhere.

"Are you okay?" I asked Sinjin with a small smirk as
if I expected that the big tough guy was actually afraid
of this corny and ridiculous movie. The smirk fell right
off my face when I looked at him.

He was paler than I'd ever seen him and he appeared
to be panting, his breath coming in short, quick gasps.
But his eyes were what threw me the most—they were
lighter than usual, almost white, and it seemed like he
was transfixed by the screen. His lips were drawn tightly
closed, almost as if he were forcing his mouth into
some unnatural grimace. Meanwhile, his grip on my
hand was actually becoming painful.

"Um, Sinjin?"

At the sound of my voice, he dropped his gaze from
the screen and immediately released my hand. A smile
claimed his lips and he shook his head with a laugh.

"Did I ever tell you that I am quite a coward when it comes to scary flicks?"

I smiled up at him and shook my head. "You looked like you'd seen the proverbial ghost."

He ran his hand through his hair and faced me again, not saying anything, just looking at me. His eyes were as blue as they'd always been. It must have been the light from the movie that had made them appear white . . .

"Do you . . . you mind if we leave?" he asked, seeming somehow flustered.

"Sure, I didn't know horror movies bothered you so much," I said, laughing lightly. "You should have said something before you agreed to go."

He stood up and shook his head, revealing an embarrassed smile on his lips. "I did not want you to think me a coward."

I took his proffered hand and followed him through the aisle of seats and into the hallway. He pushed open the door for me and I blinked against the bright lights of the theater, shielding my eyes with my hand.

"What do you want to do?" I asked him once my vision had adjusted. Sinjin didn't seem affected by the sudden transition from dark to light and watched me with an amused smile.

"Perhaps there is a park or a place we could sit down and get to know each other better?"

"Well, I'm not sure how great a park would be at night, but there's one by my house," I suggested, suddenly worried that Sinjin might think I was extending an invitation to my house simply because the park was so close in proximity. That was the last thing I wanted him to think and I really didn't want to give him the wrong idea. "I don't mean that we would . . . um . . . go back to my house, if that's what it sounded like."

"Poppet," he said, bringing a finger to his lips in the universal sign of *shut the hell up*. "I understand."

I managed a cheese-ball smile.

"Shall we?" he asked, offering his arm. I took it and allowed him to escort me to his Ferrari. He opened my door for me and made sure that I was comfortably seated before he got in on the other side. The drive to the park was maybe ten minutes and we spent it making small talk about the horrible movie.

"So tell me about you," I said as he parked and turned the engine off. He unfastened his seat belt and opened the door, appearing by my side just moments later. He was incredibly quick, so much so that he must have sprinted around the car.

"What would you care to know?" he asked as I took his arm and he beeped the car locked behind me. We started down the cobbled drive that led into the grassy expanse of the park. A lone bench sat at the end of the grass, surrounded by massive eucalyptus trees.

When we reached the park bench, I was about to sit, but Sinjin's grasp on my upper arm tightened and he shook his head. "It is damp," he commented. I glanced at the bench and spotted the condensation of the heavy dew. Sinjin wasted no time in removing his black wool jacket and placing it on the bench.

"You didn't have to do that," I said in surprise, wondering what this man would pull out of his pocket next. He was just so . . . unpredictable. "I hope the moisture doesn't ruin your jacket."

Sinjin smiled and gently pressed my shoulders down to indicate that I should sit. I did. "Material artifacts, love. They hold no value for me."

Well, he certainly was an enigma, but I wasn't about to argue with him. He took a seat beside me, very close beside me, I might add. But that was probably owing to the fact that his jacket wasn't large enough to accommodate both of us along with our personal space.

Getting uncomfortable with the awkward silence, I

tried to remember where our conversation had been headed. "Where in England are you from?" I asked, finding my train of thought.

He glanced down at me and raised his brows as if the answer should be obvious. It was a strange reaction. "London."

"Is that where you live now?"

"One of the places."

I felt surprise echo through me. "You live in more than one place?"

"*Live* is a complicated word," he offered with a smile. "I own homes in various countries, yes."

Wow, he really had to be loaded. If the Ferrari wasn't a clue, the fact that he owned homes in more than one country was a pretty good indicator. "May I ask where?"

"Yes, of course you may ask."

When he made no motion to answer the question, I realized he was making a joke. "Ha ha," I said with a smile. I boldly gripped his arm and pulled myself into him while he chuckled down at me. He lifted his arm from my grasp and wrapped it around me, folding me into the cocoon of his embrace. It was just as chilly as his hand and lips had been. But this time I knew better and I didn't say anything.

"London, Paris, and Lucerne."

"Lucerne?" I asked, trying to remember where that was.

"Switzerland."

"Ah, yes," I finished with an embarrassed smile. I'd never been much of a wiz at geography.

"I had fun with you tonight," I said with a nervous smile, my eyes focused on my fidgeting hands.

"As did I, poppet." He wrapped his other arm around me and pulled me into him, kissing the top of my head while butterflies began swarming in my stomach. "I find I always enjoy our time together."

I didn't say anything, just nodded and smiled up at him, probably looking like a lovesick dog. And before I could even comprehend what was happening, Sinjin bent down and, tightening his hold on me, kissed me. It was a light kiss and his lips were incredibly full, soft. I closed my eyes, feeling my heartbeat ricocheting through me until I started to feel dizzy, which immediately made me worry that this might be a huge mistake. Maybe it was all happening too quickly—I mean, the last thing I wanted to do was lose control.

Jolie, just go with it! I chided myself. *Just keep your eyes closed and stop thinking!*

But when I felt his tongue entering my mouth, something inside me ground its hooves into the dirt. A voice of reason suddenly came through loud and clear over the PA system in my brain, emerging from the swirling mass of my thoughts.

What if this is the lead-in to sex? Are you ready for that?

No, of course I'm not!

And furthermore, how are you going to feel when you're completely caught up in him and he goes back to Britain or France or freaking Switzerland?

"I . . . I'm sorry, Sinjin, I can't do this," I started as I pulled away from him.

He glanced over at me with a sweet but sad smile. "Why not?"

It wasn't a question I was expecting, so it sort of threw me for a loop. I mean, wasn't it obvious? It should have been crystal clear—Sinjin and I were from completely different worlds and things would never work out between us. "Um, because I don't know where this is going and I don't know when you're going to leave." I didn't want to sound pathetic or desperate, but I had the feeling that I sounded both.

"Ah," he said, nodding as if I had a point. I felt my

stomach drop in disappointment and I started to get angry with myself. I'd known this would happen from the get-go. I'd even told Christa that Sinjin was just after me for sex! So why did I feel so disappointed?

Before I had the chance to further lambaste myself, Sinjin turned his intense gaze to me. "As to the question regarding where our friendship is going, I cannot answer that, but would it help to know that I have no intentions of leaving America? Not for a long while at any rate?"

I faced him in surprise, holding back the onslaught of hope that was now pushing doubly hard, hell-bent to get inside. "You're staying?"

He nodded and glanced down at his shoes for a moment, a boyish twinkle in those beautiful blue eyes. "Do you recall how I told you I was considering opening an American branch of my business?"

"Yes."

"I have decided to move forward with it."

At first optimism flooded me, but then it was replaced with doubt. "Yeah, but for how long?"

"It would be quite a long-term move, as it would take years for me to ensure the success of the American branch and making sure it becomes profitable."

I nodded and, feeling like I'd just made an ass of myself, smiled up at him shyly. "I'm . . . I'm sorry I freaked out."

He shook his head, and the expression on his face said that he wasn't concerned with my freak-out. "I had hoped to ask you for a favor this evening," Sinjin continued, his left eyebrow elevated.

"A favor?"

He chuckled slightly, probably at the shocked expression on my face. Hey, I hadn't been expecting such a quick change in topic. "Yes, I was hoping you might be able to help locate a more permanent arrangement for

me since I will be staying here for quite a while. The
Four Seasons is becoming a bit . . . tired."

"You want me to help you find somewhere to live?" I
asked, wishing I didn't sound so doubtful or so excited.

He chuckled again. "I know it sounds bizarre and perhaps too forward, but I find myself so absorbed with
work during the day, I have not had time to put any
energy into house hunting."

I nodded. "Sure, I'd be glad to help you."

"Thank you, poppet," he said and ran his long index
finger down the side of my face.

"Where would you like me to look? What areas?"

"I will leave that up to you, love. The very best areas
and please spare no expense."

Why did I have the feeling that this was going to be
lots of fun?

"Oh, and of course I will compensate you for your
time."

I shook my head. "It would be my pleasure, Sinjin, and
I wouldn't accept anything from you. I mean, of course,
I'll have to do it in my off time, when I'm not with cli-
ents."

"Yes, of course." He smiled and his teeth glowed
white in the moonlight, his incisors looking incredibly . . . sharp. "And there is one other detail."

I cocked a brow and frowned up at him, deciding to
try my hand at flirting. "Oh yeah, and what's that?"

"I am quite clueless when it comes to furnishings."

I shook my head in mock pity and then smiled as I
thought about how entertaining this little errand was
going to be. "I can help you with that too."

He smiled again. I'm not sure why, but it somehow
appeared to be an expression of victory.

*
 *
  *
Three
 *
*
 *

I awoke out of a dead sleep and, glancing over at the clock on my bedside table, realized it was two in the morning. Lying back down, I tried to figure out what had woken me up. Had I heard a sound? Had I been having a bad dream? But I couldn't remember anything—it was as if my mind were a blank slate.

I closed my eyes and tried to quell the sudden misgivings that rinsed over me. There was nothing to be afraid of. The fact that I was agitated just because I'd woken up for no reason was ridiculous. I was twenty-eight years old, not a three-year-old afraid of the dark.

Jolie.

I sat bolt-upright and felt my eyes go wide. I'd heard the voice as clear as day. "Who's there?" I demanded.

There was nothing but quiet and it was suddenly deafening, eerie in its hollowness. It was as if the house were hiding something in its walls, playing with my sanity. My cat shifted from her prostrate position at the end of the bed and stretched in the moonlight, meowing up at me curiously.

"I heard someone say my name, Plum," I said in response, needing her to believe I wasn't completely losing my mind, needing someone to believe it because I was seriously doubting my sanity. The cat said nothing, of course, not even a purr, but jumped onto the floor, starting for the hallway. Her little paws made a soft plodding noise and before I knew it, I was completely alone.

I glanced over at the clock again and realized two minutes had gone by.

I heard something. I know I did, I told myself, shaking my head in wonder.

Just go back to sleep, came the indifferent response from that side of myself I mostly didn't care to hear from.

Where are you?

It was the voice again. Glancing around in the darkness, searching for a corner where someone could be hiding, could be concealed by the night, I suddenly realized that the voice was coming from my head. Granted, I had the habit of talking to myself—usually arguing with myself—but this was different. This was clearly a man's voice and, what was more, it had an English accent.

WTF?

I will find you, Jolie, the voice continued.

I wasn't sure if I should respond, thinking it would seem completely crazy for me to do so. I mean, the fact that there was a random, disembodied voice floating through my head was probably reason enough for most people to commit themselves to the local loony ward.

Can you hear me? the voice asked.

I didn't respond, didn't want to encourage the ravings of my lunatic mind. My heart was now pounding through me and sweat was beading along my forehead.

Jolie? Can you hear me?

I clamped my eyes shut tightly and shook my head, telling myself not to respond. Nope, instead I would just ignore the voice and it would eventually go away and I could get back to sleep.

Just ignore the voice and go back to sleep. It sounded like the perfect prescription.

Jolie?

Maybe the voice wouldn't quit, wouldn't give up until

I acknowledged it. And then the hope struck me that maybe in admitting to the existence of the voice, my frazzled mind would be satisfied and give me a break.

Yes! Yes, I can hear you, I thought the words finally, my tone panicked at the same time that it was anxious.

I'm coming for you soon, the voice continued. *So please don't worry.*

You aren't real. I thought the words, shaking my head again, as I tried to convince myself there wasn't a ghost in my room, or in my head. No, I'd just eaten something the night before—something that was bad and was now giving me hallucinations. *You're just a figment of my imagination.*

The voice didn't respond right away. It was as if it was thinking, pondering what to say next.

This is ridiculous! I thought to myself. *The voice can't think! And moreover, it's not like it's someone else's voice in your head. That's impossible. It's your stupid brain making you think it's someone else's voice in your head. God, you must be losing your mind!*

I'm sorry I upset you, the voice responded finally. *Of course you don't remember what's happened. I don't know what I was bloody well thinking.*

What is wrong with me? I thought and dropped my head into my hands, a sob tearing at my throat. "Stop talking!" I yelled at myself, begging the voice to recede, even as I wondered how my brain had concocted something so real, so believably British.

There's nothing wrong with you, Jolie. This is just a dream. Close your eyes and go back to sleep and when you wake in the morning, you won't remember any of it.

Something funny happened then. I felt my eyelids go heavy, as if the voice had issued a command that my body couldn't help but obey. I suddenly wanted nothing more than to lie down, to lose myself to sleep.

Who are you? I said the words in my head, even as I

closed my eyes and felt the satin of the pillowcase beneath my cheek.

Sleep, Jolie, and forget this ever happened.

At the end of the following Monday, I managed to locate a real estate agent, and by the middle of the week, the agent and I had narrowed down the list of housing possibilities for Sinjin to two houses and a condo, all of which seemed promising. All three properties were maybe five minutes from my house, which had been entirely by chance rather than design . . . no, seriously, I mean it.

I was exhausted after viewing so many places but also pretty excited about the remaining three choices. I had to imagine that Sinjin would be too. Speaking of Mr. Tall, Dark, and Mysterious, I hadn't seen him since Saturday. And now that a few days had passed, I found myself wondering what he was doing, when I was going to see him again. He called me every day, mostly to say that he'd been overwhelmed with work, which was completely understandable. I had my own business to tend to, even though I wouldn't exactly say that I felt overwhelmed by it. Unfortunately for me, the job of a psychic resembled a roller coaster—some days I had as many as seven clients and other days, not even one.

By the time Wednesday rolled around, bringing with it only two walk-in appointments, I was more than ready to go home and plan the evening's festivities because Sinjin was coming over—I had invited him for dinner.

And no, I hadn't changed my mind—no way were we going to get hot and heavy and possibly even have sex. I just wanted to show him printouts of the properties I'd selected for him. Sex didn't figure into the equation at all . . . no, seriously, I mean it.

As I stood in my kitchen and stirred a pot of spaghetti sauce so it wouldn't boil, I found it difficult to focus on anything but Sinjin. I just felt so incredibly alive lately—

well, ever since Sinjin had entered my life. It was as if he'd filled a void that I didn't even know existed, like he was my proverbial prince and he'd kissed me back to consciousness. And really, our little break over the last few days had been good for me. I'd needed space to think about the fact that it seemed I was headed into a—dare I say it?—relationship. No, Sinjin and I had never discussed anything close to the possibility that we might be embarking on that path, but I couldn't imagine what else it could be. I mean, we talked to each other every day and I was helping him find a place to live, for God's sake!

But while I was incredibly excited and happy to have Sinjin in my life, my feelings weren't all smiling cherubs. In fact, I'd been feeling a niggling sense of doubt ever since Sinjin had first asked me for a date. It just didn't make sense that Sinjin wanted to be with me. Leaving looks outside of it, Sinjin was cultured, well traveled, refined. I was an ordinary girl who hadn't really gone anywhere, other than moving to California from Spokane, Washington. I was just a simple woman with ESP, which was hardly enough to separate me from the masses.

God, Jolie, how did you get to be like this? a voice inside me inquired, a voice that originated from the depths of my soul. *Why can't you just accept this situation for what it is? Why can't you just be happy, knowing that Sinjin likes you as much as you like him? Why do you always have to overanalyze everything into the ground? Just let it be!*

There was a knock on the door that precluded further mental debate, which was probably just as well because the optimistic side of me wouldn't like hearing what the cynical side of me had to say.

I started for the door, surprised by the fact that Sinjin was early. I thought I'd told him eight and, according to the clock on my living room wall, it was only seven thirty. But the sun had already set, making it feel much later.

My cat meowed and interlaced herself between my legs, making it difficult for me to get to the door without stepping/tripping over her. "What's with you, Plum?" I asked as I glanced down at her. "I already fed you."

"Meow" was her unsatisfying answer.

I unlocked the door and opened it, remembering too late that I was still wearing my apron. And there was Sinjin, dressed to the nines in a black suit. "Wow, nice suit," I commented mindlessly.

"Poppet," Sinjin said with that devilish smile as he took me in from top to bottom. "I am coming from work and had a business meeting," he answered in response to the fact that he was definitely overdressed for a house call.

I didn't have the chance to respond because the cat suddenly completely lost her mind and leapt away from him, arching her back, every hair on her body standing on end. Her ears drew back, and a low gurgling sound erupted from within her, becoming an all-out hiss after a few seconds. With her claws extended, she took a few steps toward him, only to lash out and hiss again.

"Plum!" I yelled, gently nudging her away from slashing Sinjin's slacks with my foot.

"It appears your cat does not approve of me," he said with a smile, narrowing his eyes at her.

Plum continued to hiss at him, her ears flat on top of her head. I picked her up and took her to the back door, where I deposited her at the top of the stairs, outside. "Go find something to do, rude cat," I scolded, giving her a little shove with my toe.

Heading back into the kitchen, I noticed that the front door was still open and Sinjin hadn't yet stepped inside. "Come in," I said. "Make yourself comfortable."

He nodded and flashed me a handsome smile before

stepping inside my house. I found myself watching him as he inspected my humble abode, no doubt taking in the Pottery Barn furnishings and the earth tones of the walls that, when paired with the warm oak floors, gave the whole place a comfy sort of coziness.

"Very impressive," he said finally.

"Well, it isn't much, but it's mine," I answered with a smile before remembering the spaghetti sauce, which was now boiling. "Oh, shoot!"

Sinjin chuckled and turned to watch me run full-bore for the kitchen. "Have you burned our supper?"

I grasped the spoon and thrust it into the pot, stirring like I've never stirred before, only then realizing that I should probably just turn down the burner. "Well, if I have, it would be your fault," I said with a smile.

"My fault?"

I shrugged. "Yeah, because of you, I wasn't paying attention."

Sinjin smiled as if he was absolutely unconcerned about the spaghetti. He strode into the kitchen, his steps purposeful. He'd apparently seen enough of my house.

"Have you missed me?" he asked with a boyish grin.

Before I could respond, he wrapped his arms around me from behind, burying his face into the nape of my neck. I felt myself recoil from the coldness of his embrace, but a few seconds later the feeling of iciness disappeared; suddenly he was just a man and I was just a woman. The thought made me shiver.

"Mmm," Sinjin moaned as he inhaled the scent of my hair. "I have missed you, my little poppet."

I closed my eyes and forced myself to go with the moment, to try to accept the fact that Sinjin wanted me as much as I wanted him. "I've missed you too," I whispered.

And that must have been enough for him because he whirled me around to face him, and there was something in his eyes—something dark and passionate. I wasn't sure why, but the urgency of his expression frightened me.

"Let me kiss you," he breathed.

"Sinjin," I started, doubt creeping into my voice as my body went stiff. I couldn't drop my defenses long enough to let him in. I just wasn't totally comfortable around him. And that was when it was plainly obvious to me that, for whatever reason, this was not going to work.

Well, it had been fun while it lasted. I pulled away from him and wrapped my arms around myself.

"What is the matter?"

I couldn't hold his gaze—his eyes were too demanding and their intensity seemed to strip me, piece by piece, until I felt as if I were standing naked at the moment of judgment. "I just . . . I just . . ." I couldn't even get the words out.

"You just what?"

"I just don't understand how this can work," I managed finally.

"How what can work?"

I sighed, not anxious to say the words. It was so . . . humiliating. "You and me, us, this."

"What is there to work or not to work?"

Why were men such simple creatures? Why did they only deal in black and white when, for me, there were about five million shades of gray? "You and I are from completely different worlds, Sinjin," I started.

He looked surprised—like I'd unwittingly figured out some deep dark secret. "Elucidate, please."

"That's just it," I said with a half smile that wasn't really a smile at all because it was sad. "You use words like *elucidate*. I don't. You drive a Ferrari and you have houses in three countries. I have a cat that doesn't like you, I drive a Jetta, and I'm nowhere near getting my mortgage paid off."

"These are mere trivialities that do not concern me. I am quite a bit older than you and, therefore, have had many more years to build my empire."

I frowned, shaking my head at how he described his business as an "empire." But what baffled me more was that he couldn't have been a day over thirty-five. Where was he getting off saying he was so much older than I was? "Sinjin, you're what . . . thirty-four?"

"Close enough."

"You're barely older than me."

"Than I," he corrected me with a little smile.

"Ugh," I grunted and shook my head at his cocked eyebrow. "Age isn't what matters anyway."

"Was not that the point you were just attempting to make?"

"Well, now I've changed my way of thinking," I said in an irritated voice.

"Then what does matter, poppet?" Sinjin asked, his tone trying to hide the fact that he found this whole thing extremely entertaining. Well, it was good that he was trying to mask it, because I found it anything but.

"This is never going to work, that's my point," I finally said. "You and I are just too different and as I said before, I'm not looking for casual sex."

He studied me in a detached sort of way for a couple of seconds, then took a few steps away before turning to face me again. His lips were tight, his jaw even tighter. Gone was that look of amusement. "Insecurity does not suit you."

"Suit me?" I repeated, surprised. Yes, I guess I must have been at the end of the line when God was handing out self-confidence, but insecurity not suiting me? I had no idea where that came from.

He narrowed his eyes as he studied me, crossing his arms against his great expanse of chest. "It does not suit you because it is not who you are."

Why was it that Sinjin sometimes did or said things that made me feel like he knew me—that I knew him? That we'd known each other forever? "As if you know the first thing about who I am." I started stirring the spaghetti sauce again, needing something to focus on other than the fact that I was definitely destroying whatever there was between us. I'd come this far, though, and I couldn't back down now. Not when he was professing to know me better than I knew myself. I mean, that was ludicrous!

"I know you better than you might imagine."

"And how the hell is that possible?" I demanded in a small but angry voice. I stopped stirring and glared up at him. "You've known me for all of a week!"

"Time is a mere insignificant detail where you and I are concerned," he retorted, and when I made the mistake of looking at him again, I noticed that his eyes were hard, determined. They were the eyes of someone who rarely lost an argument, someone who had gotten his own way for a very long time.

"Is that so?" I started, wondering how we'd gotten into an argument so quickly. He hadn't even been here for five minutes! Was this really how our relationship, for lack of a better word, was going to end? Was this really how it was going to go down (to paraphrase Justin Timberlake)?

"Yes, that is so," Sinjin said in a serpentine sort of way. I could feel him right behind me. Refusing to turn around, I started cutting up the sausage to go in the spaghetti sauce.

"I know you are capable of many astounding things," he whispered into my ear, and I felt my heart stop. He was so close that the iciness of his breath fanned across my neck. And suddenly I urgently needed to turn around and kiss him. My desire was almost suffocating.

"And how the hell do you know that?" I repeated, my

tone increasing in anger—I mean, anger toward my traitorous body, which wanted nothing more than to feel him pressed against me. Meanwhile, my brain still reeled at his familiarity, at the feeling that he was right, that we were more to each other than we had any right to be. I still refused to even glance at his hands, which were now on either side of me, resting on my hips.

"Let us call it an uncanny ability to simply know things."

"You said you weren't psychic."

He turned me around so that I was facing him and then stared down at me with eyes that dared me to argue with him. I swallowed . . . hard.

"I am not."

"So this is just a pep talk?"

He was quiet for a few seconds, and then a broad smile brightened his beautiful face. "Ah, there is the poppet I know so well." He paused for a second or two, then tipped my chin up when I tried to look away. "May I make a request of you?"

"What?"

"Can we have another do-over?"

I felt a smile pulling at my lips and allowed it to take over my face. I shook my head and gazed up at him in admiration. "I bet you could sell a bicycle to a fish."

"Perhaps, although I do not care much for merpeople as they are quite underhanded."

I felt a laugh escape my lips and I nodded. "Yes, you can have a do-over." Feeling uncomfortable under his scrutiny, I pushed away from him and turned around to attend to my dinner preparations again. "I found three places I think you might like."

He made no move to back away and, instead, continued hovering over me like my long-lost shadow . . . my long-lost sexy shadow that I now desperately wanted to jump.

"Three places?"

I turned around and smiled in an embarrassed sort of way, realizing I hadn't exactly been clear, that my change of subject had been abrupt. "Sorry, I meant three places to live." At the expression of pleasure on his face, I felt myself suddenly develop diarrhea of the mouth. "I got a real estate agent like I told you the other night, and for the last few days we've been looking at lots of places. I narrowed the search down to three and I have pictures of each of them to show you." Then I took a breath. "Two are houses and one is a condo. The first house is three stories and the other is a ranch-style, but it's huge and has vaulted ceilings. The condo is a two-story. Well, it's really more of a town house, I suppose—"

"Poppet," he interrupted with a shake of his head. "All very good," he said and nodded, pretending to be interested. "Thank you for your help, love."

"You're welcome." I paused and then smiled up at him. "Thanks for the pep talk."

He chuckled and shook his head as if he just didn't understand me. I turned back to the task of cutting the sausage and felt a shiver run up my spine as he began playing with my hair, which was pulled back into a low ponytail. He shifted his finger from my hair to my neck, and I felt my skin tingle in response.

"I hope you like spaghetti with meat sauce?" I asked, my voice coming out breathy as I searched for anything to concentrate on other than the feeling of his fingers running on my skin.

He sighed and stilled his movements. "Ordinarily I love it, yes. But my stomach is a bit . . . upset this evening."

I couldn't help my disappointment. I'd slaved over dinner and now I'd be the only one to eat? If I'd known that was going to be the case, I would have just heated up a Healthy Choice. What a bummer. I lifted the knife over a piece of sausage, ready for my next bout of chopping, but I paused first and glanced back at him with a smile. "I understand." As soon as I turned back around, I pushed the knife down and felt a surge of pain well up from my index finger. I pulled it back immediately, the knife clattering against the cutting board. "Damn!"

I glanced down at my injured finger and noticed blood welling up from the shallow slice. Even though it hurt like a bitch, it didn't appear to be very deep. Blood started pouring from it, though, beading down my hand.

"Are you all right?" Sinjin asked in a voice that sounded tight, almost pained.

"It looks worse than it is," I mumbled as I raised my eyes to look at him. He seemed completely transfixed by the sight of my blood. He was staring at it as it dripped from my hand and landed on the floor, forming a small puddle. "Can you hand me that dish towel next to the oven?"

But he did nothing of the sort. Instead he just stood there, eyes penetrating my wound. Eyes that were now . . . white?

"Sinjin?"

"Yes, yes," he said absentmindedly, and his mouth formed a line as he tightened his lips in the same expression he'd had during that awful horror movie. He must have had a real aversion to the sight of blood.

"The dish towel?" I prompted when he continued to just stand there, as if my request had gone in one ear and out the other.

But he did exactly nothing, seemingly immobilized. I watched as he clenched his eyes tightly shut, his hands turning into fists at his sides. "Are you okay?" I asked as I sidestepped him and reached for the towel myself. But I never made it. Instead he grabbed me in a split second and pulled me to him, his eyes wide and most definitely white.

"Your eyes," I started.

And then fear took hold of me. I pulled away from him and was surprised when he released me.

"I . . . I must go," he said and headed for the door without waiting for my response. I wasn't so much concerned that he had to go as I was with the state of my sanity—because I could have sworn his incisors were lengthening before my eyes—they were long enough to indent his bottom lip when he spoke.

I said nothing, just watched him as he sprinted to the door. He pulled it open at the same exact moment that Plum came inside. Once she recognized him, she reared back and hissed, her ears pressed to her head and her fur and tail standing on end.

"I . . . I am sorry," he muttered as he sidestepped the cat, closing the door behind him. Once he left, Plum looked up at me with her green eyes and meowed, as if her outburst had never happened, as if she were happy to return to her role of lazy house cat. But I couldn't say I was so easily relieved. No, I was wondering what the hell had just happened—and more important, what the hell was Sinjin Sinclair?

It was two hours later and I still couldn't stop thinking about my bizarre evening. The spaghetti stood uneaten in the pot, now cold and sticky, and the sausage still sat on the cutting board. The only thing I'd managed to do was bandage up my finger and clean the blood off the floor.

And it was impressive that I'd been able to accomplish anything given what had happened with Sinjin. It made me doubt my own mental faculties, and even to question reality as I knew it.

Why? Because I was convinced that Sinjin Sinclair was a vampire.

I shook my head at how completely inane it sounded—how Halloween and storybook idiotic. But every time I tried to find another explanation, I came up empty-handed. And if it looked like a vampire, acted like a vampire, and felt like a vampire . . . it most probably was a vampire, right?

Okay, so how can you prove it, Jolie? I asked myself. *Well, let's see:*

1. *I've only ever seen him at night.*
2. *I've never seen him eat.*
3. *He has no aura.*
4. *He doesn't speak like normal people do. His vocabulary and delivery are like something from a book . . . an old one. I mean, he's self-admittedly older than I am . . . but how much so? That's the question.*
5. *He freaked out at the sight of my blood and the blood in that movie. Freaked out doesn't really capture it . . . he looked hungry.*
6. *Plum flipped out when she saw him and she's never done that before.*
7. *His body is freezing.*
8. *He moves incredibly quickly.*
9. *He didn't come into my house until I invited him to . . . holy crap, I invited him in!*
10. *His eyes turn white.*
11. *He has fangs.*
12. *And most important, he grabbed me when there was blood spurting from my finger and it wasn't to try to stop the blood flow. He had the look of a starved man.*

Any way I looked at it, I couldn't escape the inevitable. Sinjin was concealing something—a huge secret.

And that secret was that he was not what he appeared to be. No, he was something far more sinister.

Four

I felt like a zombie over the next few days, because I just couldn't seem to sleep. I mean, how could I sleep when all I could think about was Sinjin? I knew in my heart of hearts that he wasn't what he appeared to be. Nope, as much as my logical mind still refused to accept it, I was convinced he was a vampire. After replaying our every moment together, what else could I think? And his claim that he had Raynaud's disease? It didn't match up—Sinjin possessed too many vampiric traits that had nothing to do with Raynaud's. Nope, Raynaud's was just a handy little way to explain why he was so cold. It was an excuse and nothing more.

"Okay, what's going on with you?" Christa asked as she leaned against the front counter in our store, busily texting one of her many boyfriends. It was a wonder that anything ever got done around here.

I hadn't exactly decided whether or not I should tell her about my little hunch about Sinjin, but I figured I'd really lose it if I didn't tell someone soon. Aside from my cat, who already knew that Sinjin was otherworldly, the only other person in my small circle was Christa. And if you couldn't tell your best friend your innermost secrets, what good was having a best friend?

Sitting on a stool next to Christa, I stared at the cursor as it relentlessly blinked on my laptop screen. I couldn't even remember what I'd been doing. I eyed Christa, debating over whether or not I should tell her about Sinjin. I mean, she usually didn't react well in times of panic. 'Course, this wasn't really an instance of panic, but I also didn't expect her to be rational about it. On the other hand, what was there to be rational about? We were talking about vampires!

She placed her phone on the counter and faced me with an expression that read: *Spill the beans, pronto*. There was something inside me that desperately wanted to tell her while urgently hoping that she wouldn't think I'd completely lost my mind. I just needed some kind of validation that I wasn't headed for the loony bin.

"Okay, Chris, if I tell you something, you have to promise me to have an open mind about it," I started, already regretting it.

"You finally had sex with him?" she asked as a slow smile spread across her face. "I know you probably feel like you shouldn't have, but this was a long time coming, Jules. So was it good? Did he totally rock your world?"

I shook my head and couldn't help but feel irritated. God, if only my problem was as simple as feeling like a floozy 'cause I'd had sex with Sinjin too soon. "No, that isn't it at all," I answered and then shushed her when she started to say something else. I took a deep breath and faced her again, wondering where I should even start. "What I'm about to tell you is going to make you seriously question my sanity."

She frowned, puffing out her lower lip. "Jules, I would never question your sanity."

I laughed, but there wasn't anything happy about the sound because I'd been questioning my own judgment for the past three days—three days, I might add, during which I'd completely ignored all of Sinjin's phone calls and messages on my answering machine. "Remind yourself of that in a few minutes."

She crossed her arms over her chest. "Okay, what do you have to tell me that could possibly be so bad?" Her eyes widened. "You didn't kill someone, did you?"

"Oh my God, no!"

"Well?"

"Maybe you should sit down?" I asked, pointing to the couch in the corner of the room, which served as our waiting area. I walked over and sat myself down, patting the open space next to me encouragingly.

"This has got to be pretty big news," she said, her eyes beginning to brighten with interest. Christa loved gossip above all else, and I could just imagine how she was eating this up.

"Huge," I muttered and waited until she was sitting beside me before I took another deep breath and faced her. "Chris, you have to keep this to yourself, okay?" I couldn't imagine Sinjin would want any of this out in the open. Furthermore, there *was* the question of my own safety. Shoot. I hadn't actually thought about self-preservation in all my many hours of brooding about Sinjin. Mostly because I hadn't felt threatened by him at any point. Even when he'd grabbed me after I'd cut my finger, he'd restrained himself. I'd never felt like he might become out of control or . . . dangerous. That was probably just as ludicrous as believing he was a vampire, because what do vampires do?

They eat people.

"Do you believe there are things out there that defy explanation?" I started.

She frowned at me. "Of course . . . I work with you! Hello?"

That was true: She did believe in psychic abilities as well as ghosts. We were off to a good start. "Okay, good point," I started. Then my voice trailed away as I tried to think of how to broach the topic without sounding like a total whack job. "Um, Chris, what do you think about witches, vampires, and werewolves?"

She shrugged. "I think they're cool, I guess. I mean, I really liked the *Twilight* movies. Edward is super-hot, but Jacob's body . . ." She started fanning herself. "Someone call the fire department because I think I'm *en fuego.*"

Okay, she wasn't getting it. I obviously needed to be more direct. I grabbed her hands to get her to stop day-dreaming about Jacob's chest, never mind the fact that he was like twelve or something. "Chris, I'm not talking about *Twilight.*"

"What are you talking about then?"

I sighed. "Do you believe that those . . . creatures could possibly exist?"

She was quiet as she thought about it, tapping her red fingernails against her lips. Then she cocked her head to the side and shrugged. "I mean, I guess they could. I don't really see why they couldn't if things like ghosts are real, you know? And my cousin who lives up in the mountains swears that she sees Bigfoot every year right around Christmastime. She even knitted him a scarf once."

Well, if she believed in the existence of Bigfoot, vampires weren't that much of a stretch, right?

I nodded, knowing I needed to just come out with it, because claiming to see Bigfoot every Christmas was a far cry from admitting that your boyfriend had a thirst for blood. "Chris, I think Sinjin is a vampire."

She didn't say anything for a long moment, just stared at me blankly. Then her mouth dropped open as if I'd sprouted another head. "Oh. My. God."

Neither of us said anything for at least four seconds. We just sat there gaping at each other as she tried to persuade herself that I had not lost my mind.

"You're being serious, aren't you?" she said finally.

I sighed and nodded, dropping my eyes to my lap. "Yes, I'm being completely and totally serious, although I wish I weren't."

"Jolie, that's a really big thing to accuse someone of."

"I know." I took a deep breath. "And believe me, I've tried to talk myself out of thinking it, but all the evidence points to it, Chris."

"Hmm," she started.

"I know I sound completely insane."

"I don't think you're insane," she interrupted and smiled at me reassuringly. "But maybe you just made a mistake, that's all. I mean, maybe there is a logical reason behind the fact that he seems to be a vampire."

"I doubt it."

"Why do you think he's a vampire anyway? Did he like try to bite you or something?"

I shook my head, although I hadn't forgotten the way he'd lunged at my bleeding finger. Then again, he hadn't forced my finger in his mouth or anything like that. "No, he hasn't."

"So what makes you think he would?"

What made me think he was a vampire? I glanced out the window, trying to get my thoughts into some sort of order. Then I faced her again and held out one finger. "He's incredibly cold." Second finger. "I only see him at night." Third finger. "Plum freaks out whenever she sees him." Fourth finger. "He moves inconceivably fast." Fifth finger. "It's like he gets transfixed over the sight of blood." Sixth finger. "I've never seen him eat." Seventh finger. "He has no aura."

"Wow," she said, her eyes growing wider.

"There's more, but I can't think of all of it right now." Then I took a deep breath and faced her, wondering what she was thinking. "I know this sounds weird, Chris."

She nodded, but didn't say anything for a while. "The night he came here, it was pitch black."

"Yeah."

"And when he took the phone from me, I brushed my finger against his hand to flirt with him and I remember thinking he was freezing. But I figured it was just because he'd been outside," she finished. I could see the wheels turning in her head. "He isn't super-pale, though."

"Well, maybe not all vampires are?"

She nodded. "And Plum freaks out when she's around him?" Before I could respond, her mouth dropped open and her eyebrows reached for the ceiling. "Oh my God, Jules, did you invite him inside your house?"

I swallowed hard. "Yeah."

She shook her head. "That isn't good. Not at all."

"That thought crossed my mind."

She tapped her fingers against her knee and then faced me. "Jules, we need to find out where his daytime resting place is and we need to stake him."

"Oh my God!" I said and stood up, aghast that she would even think such a horrible thing. "We are not staking him!"

She stood up and grabbed my shoulders when she realized that I was about to walk away from her. "Jules, think about it. He has an open invitation to your house. That means he can come in whenever he feels like it."

"Then I'll just take the invitation back or I'll stay with you."

"Those are short-term solutions."

I crossed my arms over my chest, completely in denial that we were even having this conversation. There was no way in hell I would even consider stabbing . . . er, staking Sinjin. It was just insanity. "Chris, we are not freaking Van Helsing! We don't even know for sure that he's a vampire!"

She frowned and refolded her arms over her chest as if to say, *Two can play this game.* "You were just trying to convince me that he was."

I sighed. "Okay, you win that argument, but I'm not about to go and kill Sinjin with you! He hasn't done anything to hurt me!"

"Yet."

So she wasn't going to back down. I eyed her and said nothing for a few seconds. "Chris, do you really think we'd be able to take down a vampire? You and me?"

She cocked her head to the side and was quiet for a few seconds before she finally sighed and shook her head, dropping her shoulders in resignation. Thank God. "No, probably not."

Phew. "Okay, so . . ."

"But we can find someone who can," she insisted and started for the counter, where she grabbed her purse. "In the meantime, we need to go to Ralphs and buy all their garlic and then we need to go to Target and buy all their crosses."

I sighed deep and hard, wondering why I had to put up with this crap. Yep, it had been a bad idea to tell her. Dammit. "They don't have crosses at Target."

"Then we need to go to a religious store," she said and started chewing on her lip, as if trying to bring to mind a religious store close by. I didn't even know what that meant—or if "religious stores" even existed. "On the way back, we can stop off at my mom's church for some holy water. But I can't be gone too long because I have a date with Richard tonight."

Before Christa could continue plotting Sinjin's assassination, we both turned at the sound of the door opening. A man entered carrying an enormous flower arrangement, swaying with the weight of it. The arrangement was so massive that it dwarfed him entirely; all I could see were his jean-clad legs.

"Delivery for Jolie Wilkins," he said as he wrestled with the arrangement, finally setting it down on the counter before he stood up and stretched out his back. I heard an audible crack. "Damn thing is heavy," he muttered.

"I'm Jolie," I said, walking up to him. He handed me a receipt and motioned for me to sign it. I did and received a quick smile before he raked Christa up and down (she, of course, smiled flirtatiously at him).

"Hope you enjoy them," he said, throwing Christa a wink. She didn't respond, but she watched him slam the door and disappear into his delivery van.

"He was kinda cute," she said, but I wasn't paying any attention. Nope, I was focused on the mammoth bouquet. I made no attempt to approach it.

"Well, you have to find out who they're from," Christa said.

"I already know," I answered. My stomach had fallen to the floor. But queasy stomach or not, I couldn't help admiring how exquisite the arrangement was, with enormous white lilies hovering fragrantly over crimson roses. There had to be more than seventy-five roses.

Christa reached for the card. I didn't try to stop her, so she broke the seal and pulled the card out, clearing her throat as she did so. "Please forgive me," she read, then dropped her hand and shrugged. "That's all it says."

But I didn't know if I could forgive Sinjin because it wasn't a matter of anything he'd done. It was a matter of something that he was.

Six hours later, I was still in my store. I hadn't had one client all day. Ordinarily, I would have packed up and gone home, but an hour or so earlier, someone had called and begged to come in for a reading. Figuring my wallet could certainly stand to benefit, I'd consented. Christa had already left to prepare for her date, but I wasn't too concerned. I usually let her go home early when it was slow anyway.

At exactly four p.m., I heard the door open and I glanced up from where I was sitting behind the counter. I started to smile in greeting, but the smile was immediately wiped clean off my face. For the second time in the course of a week and a half, I was struck speechless by a handsome man. The first time, of course, had been when I met Sinjin. And this time . . . I glanced down at my logbook to where I'd haphazardly scribbled down his name.

This time, it was . . . Rand.

"Hi," I said, jumping down from the stool, and circling the counter to meet him. I gulped hard, wondering why I was suddenly being tormented by incredibly striking men. Men who exceeded the most admirable qualities of humanity.

This guy didn't say anything right away. Instead, he just stood there—all six-two, maybe six-three of him—and seemed to stare through me, almost as if I were transparent. He was broader than Sinjin, but also shorter by a couple of inches, if I had to guess. His hair was wavy and chocolate brown, the exact shade of his eyes. He had a strong, tan face, sculpted with broad, masculine angles, and a cleft in his chin.

"Um, are you Rand?" I repeated, beginning to feel uncomfortable under his silent scrutiny.

A huge smile softened his face, bookended by two dimples. He was simply magnificent, and I felt myself swallow hard. "I apologize for zoning out," he said as he shook his head in apparent embarrassment. He spoke with an English accent, and his voice seemed suddenly so familiar. I shook the feelings right out of my head and focused instead on the fact that he was British. What was it with me and gorgeous Englishmen lately?

Oh my God, what if he's a vampire too? The thought

tore through my head and I felt myself unwittingly re-treating because it suddenly made perfect sense. Maybe this was a friend of Sinjin's—or worse, maybe an enemy? 'Course, then the fact that this guy actually had an aura—and more so, that said aura was bright, electric blue (like nothing I'd ever seen before)—caused me to recon-sider. Maybe it was just Sinjin who didn't have an aura? Maybe other younger, lesser vampires did? I remained on guard.

"Thank you for seeing me on such short notice," the man continued, moving forward to fill the space that separated us. He thrust out his hand with a large smile. "You are?"

I gulped but didn't back away. I didn't want to give him the advantage by appearing nervous or by letting on to the fact I knew he was something extraordinary. "Jolie . . . Jolie Wilkins." I glanced down at his hand and, figuring this would be the true test of whether or not he wanted to dine on me, clasped it.

He was warm. Thank God.

But before I could revel in any feelings of relief, a surge of energy traveled directly up my arm from his hand. I pulled away from him in an instant, rubbing my hand against my pant leg as I stared at him in wide-eyed shock.

"Must have been static energy from my shoe brushing against the carpet," he offered with an apologetic smile.

"You felt it too?" I asked, feeling the relief return-ing. He just nodded and I shook my head, laughing slightly. "That was some serious static cling!"

"Well, it is very nice to meet you, Jolie," he said, and I could tell that he wasn't just going through the stan-dard protocol you follow when you first meet someone. No, he said it like he meant it, like he was incredibly pleased to make my acquaintance, like this was the best moment of his whole day. It was definitely true what they said about the English—they were damn polite!

"It's nice to meet you too," I said and motioned him toward the back room, the hair on the back of my neck still on end even though we were no longer touching. I just couldn't shake the feeling that there was something . . . different about him. And of course I had to wonder what he wanted from me. Best to just keep my guard up, give him his reading, and send him on his merry way.

When he made no motion to follow me, I glanced up at him questioningly. He seemed to have completely forgotten why he was here and just kept staring at me in that off-putting way. It was almost as if he recognized me, or thought he did. It made me uncomfortable.

"You're here for a reading?"

"Yes, yes," he said, and nervously ran his hand through his hair. "Apologies, I've had quite a long day." Then he laughed.

I just smiled back at him before turning to walk into my reading room, which was at the rear of my store. I was eager to get through this appointment so I could go home and figure out what I was going to do next about my little problem known as "the guy I'm dating is a vampire." A part of me was nervous about being home alone considering I *had* invited Sinjin over; but if what I knew about vampire lore was true, I could just as easily uninvite him if he threatened me. Yes, Christa had told me that I could stay with her, but I could already see that ending badly when she came home with her flavor of the night and had really loud sex in the room next to mine.

Yeah, no.

"How have you been?" Rand asked, and when I glanced up at him, he seemed nervous. "Er, how has your day been?"

I studied him for a second or two, finding it odd that

such a handsome man seemed . . . nervous around me. *Nervous* wasn't even the word for it, actually. It just seemed as if he knew something I didn't. Of course, it didn't make sense, but that seemed to be the theme of my life lately. "Um, it's actually been pretty slow."

He nodded but didn't say anything more, just continued watching me as if he was more than content to stare at me all night. I smiled up at him, really not knowing what else to do, and took a seat at my reading table, motioning to the empty seat across from me. He nodded and pulled out the chair, seating himself so that he faced me. I reached for my cards, which were on the table, but he suddenly moved his hand on top of mine, preventing me from grabbing them.

There was that weird feeling of energy reverberating from his hand again, though it wasn't anywhere near as strong as it had been the first time we'd touched. Given the Santa Ana conditions lately, I guessed there were lots of electrons in the air. But really, I knew I shouldn't have been focusing on the static electricity buildup in my store—my attention should have been on this man who had come in for a reading . . .

"I thought you wanted me to read your cards?" I asked, my tone dubious.

"Can you read me without the cards please . . . Jolie?"

It was the way he said my name. He seemed familiar with it—as if he'd said it a million times. And that bothered me and not just because I didn't understand it. I'd never told him I could do anything besides reading cards . . .

"I never said I could do anything beyond reading tarot cards," I said in an even voice, which was a feat of itself considering how hard I was shaking inside. It was becoming apparent that this man was here for another reason.

"In the phone book you're listed as a psychic," he answered in a matter-of-fact sort of way. "Psychics can do more than read cards."

I gulped. Okay, he had a good point. But that didn't keep me from feeling freaked out and unable to relax. "I can try to read you without the cards, but my visions aren't very reliable," I said in a small voice.

"I have faith in you," he answered, smiling, but I was past smiles. At this point, I just wanted to get through our appointment so he could go on his merry way. I motioned for his hands, and when he placed them on the table, I clasped them in mine. Then I closed my eyes.

And nothing happened, which was normal. Being psychic wasn't something that came easily—visions usually appeared to me when I least expected them. When I actually tried to drum them up deliberately, they were as recalcitrant as stubborn goats.

I opened my eyes and found him staring at me. I suddenly felt extremely uncomfortable again—like this man had an agenda and he wasn't about to divulge it anytime soon. "I'm not getting anything," I started. "Maybe we should reschedule for another day."

"Do you mind trying again?"

I sighed. "It's probably useless. My visions come and go as they please." Neither of us said anything for a few seconds. "Are you sure you don't want a card reading instead?"

But before he could respond, I was suddenly struck by a series of images that unfurled behind my eyes. It was as if someone had unlocked a drawer full of angry wasps. Pictures circled through my head like a twister. I clenched my eyes tightly shut and felt my hands tighten over his. Channeling psychic information was never easy, and it usually took an emotional toll on me. And given the fact that so much information was spiraling through my brain at the moment, I had a feeling I'd need a long nap after this meeting.

"What's happening?" he asked in a concerned voice.

"I see something," I whispered. The sensation of pure energy seemed to vibrate through my entire being. He might not have been a vampire but he was definitely something otherworldly. If his crazy electric blue aura hadn't convinced me before, I was convinced now.

I swallowed hard and forced myself to focus, to absorb the darkness behind my eyes—to allow it to take me where I needed to go. I felt the visions begin to slow down and I reached out for one, plucking it with my mind's eye. What I saw surprised me, and the surprise slowly gave way to fear.

"What do you see?" he asked, a note of hope in his voice.

But I couldn't respond. I was too busy choking on the fact that what I was seeing defied everything I knew.

Five

"I don't understand," I finally said, shaking my head. I'd automatically pulled my hands free of Rand's as soon as the first confusing images had reached my delirious mind. I just didn't want to see any more.

"Don't understand what?" he asked, leaning forward as he offered me a sweet smile that was probably meant to be encouraging. But I couldn't take encouragement from anyone or anything at the moment—the visions I'd seen had completely blindsided and dumbfounded me.

I stood up abruptly. Rand stood too, but he didn't move. Instead he stared into my eyes, his gaze intense and piercing. "What did you see?"

I knew I couldn't tell him—I mean, he'd be as shocked as I was. Somehow I'd managed to drum up a bunch of ridiculous fluff in my brain—what I'd seen could hardly even be considered a vision. It was more like the wiring in my mind had short-circuited and cooked up a ridiculous concoction of absurd images. Why? Because my brain was on overdrive lately, trying to deal with the disturbing realization that things like vampires actually exist. So really, there was no point in sharing any of it.

"I didn't see anything that would interest you." I took a deep breath, my hands shaking as I sidestepped my chair and started for the door. He made no attempt to leave so I figured he just wasn't getting it. I looked up at him again, offering an apologetic smile. "I'm sorry but sometimes my visions don't make any sense."

"I understand, but perhaps they might make sense to me."

I swallowed hard; he was bold. But he was also mistaken. "I . . . I didn't see anything of a psychic nature," I managed and rubbed my forehead, trying to dispel the remnants of the wayward "vision." All the while, I found myself wondering what the hell was wrong with me, and whether I was slowly but surely losing my mind.

"Jolie . . ."

It struck me again, the way he said my name—like we'd been friends for twenty years. But I'd only known him for fifteen minutes, give or take. And now I'd had enough.

I started forward again, but he reached out and touched my upper arm, stopping me.

"Please," he said, and there was something in his eyes that pulled at me, something that made my stomach do a funny little flip because I suddenly felt it too . . . the sense that I knew this man, that I'd known him for a long time.

This is completely implausible, I told myself. I clenched my eyes shut tightly against the headache that had just started pounding behind them. *I've never seen this guy before in my life. This must just be déjà vu—it's the only thing that makes sense because there's no way I know him and no way he knows me.*

"I don't know what I saw," I snapped dismissively, and pulled away from him, hell-bent for the door. "I . . . I need to get going."

He caught up with me easily, and before I could comprehend what was happening, he'd pushed me up against the wall by my shoulders, not in a rough sort of way but passionately . . . I felt the air catch in my throat as he stared down at me, both of us breathless. Even though I knew I should be afraid, I wasn't. Instead, I was wholly transfixed by the beauty of his eyes. They seemed to be a darker brown now, as if their ordinarily rich color had been dipped in dark chocolate.

"Jolie," he said again and his tone of voice and his expression promised me I wasn't in any sort of danger, that I could trust him. Something in me responded, quelling the fear that I should have been feeling.

This makes no sense! I berated myself. *What is wrong with me? Why aren't I resisting him? Why am I acting like this?*

And all of a sudden I was suffused with the absolutely insane need to kiss him. I couldn't tear my gaze away from his sumptuous lips, though I didn't understand why I wanted, no needed, to feel his lips on mine.

This just isn't who I am! I am not a sexual person—I don't think of strangers like this!

Something was most definitely wrong with me . . .

"I don't know what's going on here," I started, my voice wavering, fear now taking charge. And it was about time.

He shook his head, and I could feel the frustration seeping off him in rivulets of electric charge. He was holding back—it was obvious by the tightness of his shoulders, the way he dropped his gaze to the floor and shook his head. There was something he knew, something he wanted to tell me. He returned his attention to me, staring at me as if he was waiting for me to reach some sort of epiphany, for me to do or say . . . something.

"I didn't mean to frighten you," he started. I wanted to insist that he wasn't frightening me but I wasn't exactly a good liar.

"Please tell me what you saw," he insisted, his gaze searching. Before I could even think, he brought his face closer to mine until maybe an inch separated us. That burning need to taste him suddenly overwhelmed me. I felt my eyes begin to drift closed and forced them open again.

"I . . . I . . ." I couldn't even finish the thought. Instead, I stared at him, dumbfounded. I could swear he was about to kiss me!

"Please tell me, Jolie," he whispered and his breath was warm as it fanned across my neck. I could feel my heartbeat thundering through my ears. He was going to kiss me. I could see it in his eyes, which were fixed on mine. They were burning a hole through me, as if he could see down to my very soul.

"Let go of me." I was surprised to hear the words come from my mouth because my body was singing another tune.

"Jolie . . ."

"Take your hands off me right now," I said again when he made no attempt to release me. But there was a force within me that was rallying. It was something strong and something angry.

He took a deep breath and stepped away from me, as if he was suddenly realizing that he'd just accosted a relative stranger in a dark room. He dropped his attention to the floor before returning it to me. "I apologize."

"I have to go," I said, starting for the door again, this time anxious to get away from him.

But maybe there's something he needs to tell you, that insane voice inside of me piped up. *Maybe there's more to this than you think. Maybe he could make sense of the vision you had?*

I swallowed hard. *It wasn't a vision. My brain was just tripping over itself because I can't deal with everything that's been going on lately.*

"Jolie, please tell me what you saw," Rand said, his voice husky. I didn't know why, but I stopped walking—it was almost as if my feet were sunk in cement. I didn't turn to face him. I couldn't understand why I hadn't already run out to the front room and grabbed the phone to call the police. But that strange voice inside me told me not to—it told me I could trust this man, that I was safe.

It was absurd.

"Please leave," I said, shaking my head as tears of confusion began to well inside my eyes. Something was very wrong with me, but what that might be was anyone's guess. I felt as if I'd just boarded a runaway train and had no control over any part of me anymore, certainly not my thoughts and emotions.

"Not until you tell me what you saw."

I frowned and felt my lower lip quivering. "I didn't see anything," I said, turning to face him.

His lips were tight and his eyes narrowed as he approached me again, this time without touching me. His body was a mere gasp away from mine, so close that I could smell him. And he smelled incredible—a clean, spicy scent that was purely masculine. As preposterous as it was, I felt as if I'd be able to recognize that smell anywhere—like it had taken up permanent residence in my mind.

"I find that hard to believe," he said with a frown.

"I don't care what you believe," I said as I looked up at him, feeling fury radiating from my eyes. And that was when he did it. He leaned down and grabbed the back of my neck, pulling me into him. Suddenly his mouth was on mine. His kiss wasn't soft. It was hard and demanding, zealous, as if he couldn't control himself, as if he'd been resisting the urge to kiss me ever since he walked through my door.

And what was even stranger was the fact that I didn't fight him. Instead, my body went into autopilot and I felt myself looping my arms around his neck. I leaned into him and moaned when I felt his tongue enter my mouth.

What about Sinjin? a tiny voice welled up from within me, but it was suddenly overpowered by a chorus that sang: *This feels right! This just feels so right!*

Jolie Wilkins, what the freaking fuck is wrong with you? my inner voice thundered through me. I forced myself to pull away from Rand, if only to stop this idiocy.

I wiped my arm across my face as if I could erase the memory of his sweet lips just as easily. "If you don't leave now, I'm going to call the police."

But he refused to back down; he reached out, lifting my chin up. "Jolie, don't be afraid." His voice acted like a command, because any fear I was feeling suddenly vanished. He continued to stare down at me and his lips began moving in time with his thoughts. It almost looked like he was chanting something in his head. His electric blue aura vacillated this way and that, erupting in spires of royal purple . . .

"Let go of me," I said, my voice rough.

He dropped his hand from my face; he seemed surprised, like he hadn't expected such resistance from me, especially after we'd shared such a heated embrace. But his expression also revealed disappointment. Whatever he'd just been doing had not had the desired outcome.

"Jolie . . ."

It was pretty obvious he wasn't going to go away if I didn't tell him what the hell I'd seen. Well, fine, let *him* make sense of it.

"I saw what looked like a battlefield and it was dark out, nighttime I guess. People were fighting and I could feel death all around." I took a deep breath; this next part caused a lump to form in my throat. "But the part that doesn't make sense to me is that you and I were both there." I glanced away, feeling like an idiot for disclosing such outrageousness. But when I focused on his eyes again, they looked victorious, smoldering.

"Go on," he said softly.

I couldn't look at him. "I could feel pain burning my insides and when I looked down at myself, I realized I'd been stabbed."

He nodded and sighed sadly, as if he was reliving this story as I was telling it—as if he'd been there. "Was there any more?" he asked.

I couldn't help it, so I looked up at him again. He was still wearing a small, triumphant smile. It made no sense. Why wasn't he insisting I was a charlatan, that I was full of it? "You were crying," I finished in a small voice, crossing my arms over my chest. "You were holding me and crying." I shook my head, suddenly exhausted. "It makes no sense to me and you shouldn't even consider it a vision. It's just a bunch of mumbo jumbo." I brought my gaze back to his and sighed. "Are you satisfied now?"

He didn't say anything; he just stared at me for two seconds before nodding. His hands twitched at his sides as if he wanted to reach out and touch me, but he restrained himself. "I am. Thank you."

But his lack of surprise suddenly bothered me, worried me. "Does that make any sort of sense to you?" I inquired, wondering why he was acting relieved by what I'd told him.

He started to answer, but then stopped himself, his striking eyes softening with his smile. God, why did he have to be so completely beautiful? And why did I need to fight my feelings for him? Why did part of me want nothing more than to be close to him? Maybe he'd bewitched me? Maybe he was some sort of witch doctor or wizard or magician or something equally crazy.

"No," he said almost sadly as he shook his head. "No, it doesn't make any sense."

But somehow I didn't believe him. "Why are you here?"

He seemed surprised that I had asked. "Isn't it quite obvious?"

There was no point in holding back now. I'd already demonstrated the fact that I was anything but sane by relating the whole bizarre vision to him. I might as well complete the lunacy by asking him what the hell he was. "No it's not obvious at all. Why is it that when you touch me, I feel this energy traveling through me? Why do you have an electric blue aura? For that matter, why is it that I seem to have no willpower whatsoever when you're . . . close to me? You must have some sort of psychic power?"

He smiled but said nothing. I didn't get the chance to further question him, though, because he suddenly stepped away from me, like he was finally ready to leave. "Thank you for your time, Jolie."

I didn't say anything, figuring he was going to walk out of my life just as quickly and easily as he'd walked into it—and if this was one mystery that was never solved, I was fine with it. I mean, I already had enough weird and random stuff going on in my life; I really didn't want to make room for more. So if he was determined to walk right out of my life, I wasn't about to stop him. I watched him smile almost apologetically as he turned and walked out of the reading room, opening the front door and disappearing down the street.

At the end of the following day, I drove the fifteen minutes from my store to my house, still constantly replaying last night's strange events in my already muddled head. If I didn't have a stroke soon, it would be a wonder.

Sinjin is a vampire, and the man I met last night, Rand, must be something otherworldly too.

It was the only way I could make sense of how I'd acted like a complete and total Froot Loop around him. He must have bewitched me; that's all there was to it.

I mean, I kissed him! A complete stranger!

I inhaled deeply and then exhaled the pent-up frustration inside me, wondering what the hell had become of my life. In less than two weeks, everything I knew had been completely turned on its head and I was acting like a crazy person.

I pulled into my garage, put the car into park, and turned off the engine. I didn't move, though. Instead, I just sat there, staring at the wall in front of me as I tried to figure out what the hell I was going to do.

Why did Rand show up at my store? What does he want from me? What is he after? And why did that so-called vision seem to please him so much? And furthermore, why did I meet Sinjin the week before? Why are supernatural beings suddenly seeking me out?

There were just too many unanswered questions and I instantly felt like I was going to be sick. I opened the car door, then reached over to grab my purse. Glancing up, I saw Sinjin standing in my driveway, bathed in moonlight.

My heart climbed into my throat.

"Poppet," he said with a wickedly sexy smile. And if I'd never appreciated how incredibly gorgeous he was before, it now hit full-force over my already aching head.

He was dressed in black as usual, but with the moonlight glowing around him, he almost looked angelic. Of course I knew better. This was no angel I was dealing with.

I felt my hands go clammy as my heartbeat started racing. I unfastened my seat belt and stood up, taking a few steps from the car. "You stay away from me," I said, throwing myself forward and slamming the button on the wall that closed the garage door. But just as I'd expected, Sinjin moved much faster than the garage door did and before I knew it, he was standing right in front of me. The door closed on us both and we were bathed in darkness.

"I know what you are," I said, but my voice was shaking. I started feeling along the wall for the door that led into the house, suddenly remembering how I could save myself. "I withdraw your invitation to enter!"

Sinjin chuckled heartily, but I didn't give myself time to consider his reaction. Instead I found the doorknob and opened it as quickly as I could, the light from my kitchen cutting through the darkness of the garage. Sinjin was suddenly standing directly in front of me, maybe two inches of air separating us. I screamed and threw myself into the kitchen, tripping over the step I'd forgotten about in my haste. Hauling myself upright, I turned around, watching him to see if my annulled invitation had prevented his entry.

"Poppet," he started and shook his head like the joke was on me. Then he took a deep breath, which I assumed was for show because vampires can't breathe, since they're dead, right? I didn't have much time to debate that fact because Sinjin stepped into my house, just like that.

He didn't do anything right away. I wasn't sure what I was expecting—maybe that he would dissolve into my floor or burst into ash right in front of me? But no, that didn't happen either. He just continued staring down at me. A few seconds later, he threw his head back and chuckled. And that was when I realized I was as good as dead.

"Why didn't it work?" I screamed and started to back away.

"Because it is a fallacy that the vampire requires an invitation to enter someone's home, love," Sinjin replied and stared down at me with a twinkle in his eyes, which were now fully white. His fangs lengthened as I watched, gaping up at him.

At the mention of the word *vampire,* something inside of me burst. I was filled with fear and anger.

I won't go down without a fight. I won't let him kill me without at least trying to do some damage of my own.

I took a deep breath and then lunged for my kitchen counter, reaching for the knife block. I wasn't sure what I was thinking because, of course, Sinjin was much faster. He bowled into me and knocked me off balance, grabbing me around the waist to keep me from falling over. Holding my hands at my sides, he turned me around until I was facing him.

He smiled and cocked a brow. "I am impressed, little poppet."

"Stop calling me that," I said as I tried to keep the tears at bay, my heart thundering in my ears. I would not allow myself to cry. This bastard could torture me and kill me but I wasn't going to give him the benefit of my tears.

"I can smell your fear," he said. I could only imagine the perverse pleasure he was taking in this whole situation.

"Let go of me," I seethed. I pulled against his stranglehold on my arms, but it was useless. I was beginning to regret the fact that I hadn't taken Christa up on her offer to stake him.

"I must admit I expected it to take longer for you to sort out exactly what I am."

I shook my head and glared at him. "Well, you underestimated me."

He shrugged and appeared indifferent, bored even. "Perhaps I did, love."

I suddenly felt a wave of panic wash over me and the

tears were building in my eyes again. "Whatever you're going to do to me, please make it quick," I said in a small voice, hoping he wasn't going to take some sort of sick joy out of draining me, eating me.

There was a sudden expression of surprise on his face. "Do to you?" he repeated and then shook his head. "Are you suggesting I would harm you?"

"Um, yeah," I said with a frown. "Isn't that . . ."

"I would never hurt you," he said, as if the mere thought angered him.

"Don't play games with me, Sinjin," I yelled at him. "Respect me enough not to play games with me!"

He grabbed the back of my neck and forced my head upright, making me look into those eerie white eyes. "I am your protector, poppet. I would kill any man or creature who ever threatened you."

"But you . . . you're a vampire?" I said.

"Yes."

"Vampires eat people," I finished, swallowing hard.

He chuckled. "We do not eat people as you would suggest, love." Then he smiled down at me in a sweet sort of way, which sounds ridiculous because he was a monster and could easily have ripped my throat out. "We drink from donors, yes."

"Donors?" I repeated. "People willingly . . ."

"Quite so. A vampire's bite is not necessarily painful." The way he said it caused shivers to run up my spine. But not from fear.

"It wouldn't hurt?"

He shook his head and smiled. "It can be a quite . . . pleasurable experience, pet."

The last thing I wanted to think about was pleasurable experiences. Not when I still hadn't quite come to terms with the fact that (1) Sinjin really was a vampire, and (2) he didn't appear to have any plans to kill or maim me, at least not for the time being.

"Unless the donor in question is a witch, in which case, it can be quite painful," he added with a grin that said he thought the whole conversation was comical.

But I wasn't concerned with witches and painful vampire bites at the moment. Instead, I was concerned with the more important thing. "You promise you won't hurt me?" I asked again, trying to decide whether I was truly safe.

"Of course not!" he said with another chuckle, as if he was thoroughly amused by the whole exchange.

"I . . . I don't understand," I said, my voice breaking.

He pulled away from me and allowed me to find my balance. "What is there to understand, love? I am a vampire, yes, but no, I would never harm you. And as to drinking from you . . ." He smiled that devilishly handsome smile and looked me up and down. "I would only do so if you asked."

I exhaled a pent-up breath of anxiety and tried to make sense of everything he'd just said. "Why are you here?"

"I came to inquire as to whether you received the bouquet I sent."

I shook my head. "No, I mean, why are you in my life? I can't imagine that you walked into my store by sheer accident."

He smiled down at me and shook his head. "You are quite observant, my love."

"Answer the question," I insisted, feeling a new wave of courage growing inside of me, probably given the fact that I was no longer worried about being Sinjin's dinner.

He nodded. "I cannot explain everything at the moment, poppet, but I will tell you that you are correct. I did not happen upon you by chance."

"So?"

He ran his fingers through my hair. There was something in me that still wanted to shrink back. Maybe it was just because he was a vampire, the cat to my mouse.

"I am your sworn protector."

"My sworn protector?" I repeated, shaking my head in doubt. "Why would I need a protector, Sinjin? What would I possibly need protection against?"

His jaw went tight. "You have many enemies."

I dropped my head into my hands, frustration eating me from within. "Enemies?" I asked, finally looking up at him. "Sinjin, I barely even have friends!"

"I know this is difficult to grasp, poppet, and you do not realize your own abilities yet, but in time, you will."

"My own abilities?" I couldn't stop repeating every thing he said. An ache began throbbing behind my eyes, promising a migraine. I needed nothing more than an early night and a few Tylenol PMs. A sworn protector who also happened to be a vampire did not figure into my plans. "Abilities in what sense?"

Sinjin sighed as if he didn't have the patience to explain. "You are a witch, love."

"A witch?" My voice broke into an acidic laugh. And at that exact moment I realized that I wanted no part of this. Witches, vampires, men who seemed to radiate energy . . . I wanted nothing to do with any of it. Instead, I wanted my life to go back to how it had always been— predictable, yes, but also stress-free.

"Poppet," Sinjin started.

"No!" I interrupted and stepped away from him. "I want you to leave and never come back again, do you understand?"

"Love . . ."

I shook my head and crossed my arms against my chest. "I'm not a witch and I never will be. That's all there is to it."

"Do not fight what you are," he said, and his eyes were narrowed, angry.

"I don't ever want to see you again." I headed for the front door and pulled it open, signifying that I wanted him out of my house and, more pointedly, out of my life.

Sinjin frowned, but he started for the door. Instead of leaving, he paused at the threshold to turn and face me again. "I will leave you this evening because I believe there is much on your mind."

"Never mind what's on my mind. This ends here and now."

He cocked an irritated brow and was quiet for a few seconds before he finally spoke again. "When you are ready for my assistance, I purchased the home you found on Potter Street." He paused for a second or two. "I believe you know the address."

I was surprised that he'd already bought a home. I mean, it had been only a few days since I'd given him all the information on each property. But that really wasn't my concern anymore. "Fine. Good. Now I want you to leave."

He didn't say anything more, but he nodded and disappeared into the darkness.

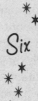

Six

"So he didn't try to attack you?" Christa asked. Her mouth had been hanging open ever since I told her that Sinjin had shown up at my house and admitted that he was a vampire. Sitting on the stool behind the counter, she watched me as I paced back and forth.

"No, he didn't attack me," I said, feeling my heartbeat escalate as I dredged up the memory. "He said he would never hurt me and that he was my protector or some crap."

Christa smiled dreamily. "That's so romantic."

I eyed her dubiously and shook my head. "You're insane. A few days ago you wanted to stake him."

"I'm over that," she said dismissively before her eyes lit up again. "Really, Jolie, it's not every day a girl gets an incredibly hot man, er vampire, who's also her sworn protector." She paused for a second or two, as if she was imagining what she would have done in my position, then faced me again. "Why did you tell him to leave?"

I frowned at her. "You're seriously asking me that, Chris?"

Christa shrugged. "Vampire sex sounds like it could be super-hot."

"Oh my God, that's all you think about," I said, striding from the front door back to the reading room door, only to turn around and repeat.

"Sounds to me like there was nothing to be worried about and you got rid of a perfectly good man."

I stopped pacing and threw my hands onto my hips. "Vampire, Chris, he's not a man. He's a vampire."

She waved away my concern with nails that were now polished lilac. "He said he was your protector—I mean, what more do you want? If you ask me, you shouldn't have told him to leave. There's obviously a reason he came into your life."

I'd also reached the same conclusion last night after Sinjin left but I still wanted nothing to do with any supernatural creatures, no matter how appealing they might be. "Chris, who could he possibly protect me against? Who could be after me and for what? For not feeding my cat on time or for watching too many reruns of *Lost*? I mean, seriously, I have no life!"

Christa shrugged and raised her brows, offering me a wounded expression. "You don't have to yell at me, Jules, jeez."

I took a deep breath. "I'm sorry. This whole thing is just incredibly frustrating and I have no idea why it's happening to me or what I'm supposed to do about it. I just want it all to end so my boring-ass life can return." I took a deep breath and faced her with a smile. "FML, Chris," I muttered. "Fuck my life."

She laughed, no doubt pleased that I'd stolen her phrase. "Well I guess you put the kibosh on the whole thing by telling the hot vamp to take a hike, so end of story, right?"

I sighed and glanced over at her, nodding as I considered it. "Yeah, I guess I did."

"No harm, no foul."

I frowned. "I guess so." Then why did I have the feeling that this wasn't nearly over yet? And furthermore, why was I suddenly depressed by the idea that I might never see Sinjin again? What in the hell was wrong with me? FML and then some.

"So can I have the flowers?" Christa asked, motioning to the colossal bouquet, which I'd relegated to the farthest corner of the room. Apparently it wasn't far enough, because the store was still drenched with the scent of lilies. Not only that, but I found myself constantly gazing at them, which made no sense because I was firm in my conviction: I wanted Sinjin out of my life. I had made the right decision in telling him to beat it . . . hadn't I?

"Sure," I said, eyeing the arrangement forlornly before shaking the feelings of dejection right out of my ridiculous mind. "I have no need for them."

"Awesome, thanks." She trained her eyes on me for a few seconds, her mouth turning up in a smile.

"What?" I demanded.

She shrugged. "Maybe Sinjin was right. Maybe you are a witch."

"Oh my God, Chris, seriously?"

She shrugged again. "Think about it—you can read tarot cards, see visions, and read people's auras. You've always known things about people when you first meet them. You've been different for as long as you can remember. Why is it so far-fetched to think you might be a witch? I mean, vampires exist, right?"

I sighed, figuring I couldn't argue with that. But I still wasn't convinced—I hadn't really ever done anything that seemed in any way witchy. "I'm a psychic, Chris, not a witch. And there are lots of people out there just like me."

She glanced over at me and frowned as if to say she wasn't buying it. Luckily, though, she didn't get the chance to argue more because my ten o'clock appointment arrived.

Old Mrs. Rose Pierson came religiously every week,

hoping she'd make contact with her dead lover, George, who had passed about two years ago. And every week, I told her the same thing: "Sorry, Mrs. Pierson, but I didn't make a connection with George." Still, it wasn't like I hadn't managed to contact anyone for her. One time, her mother had come through, then a little boy she used to babysit and also her husband. As you can imagine, that one hadn't gone over too well. Hopefully, Old Mr. Pierson wouldn't make a return visit today because my drama limit had been surpassed and was now approaching implosion levels.

I took the old woman's arm and led her into the reading room while she chirped on about the dreams she'd been having about George. She felt sure he would make contact with us today, and for her sake I hoped she was right.

Christa shook her head in apparent sympathy as I opened the door to the reading room, closing it behind us. The only light in the room, a red bulb from the ceiling, cast an eerie sort of brightness, something I'd never really considered macabre until now.

"Please focus very intently now, Jolie," Rose said in her rickety voice as I assisted her into the chair across from mine.

"I will, Rose," I answered. "But I can't promise you that George will make contact."

"Oh, I am quite certain he will, dear."

I just smiled, although I very much doubted it. Since he'd never shown up before, I was sure that George had found his place up in the sky, and that he liked it well enough not to want to return to this plane. Or maybe he'd never really been that into Rose Pierson from the beginning. I mean, wasn't that how relationships usually ended anyway?

Bad-mood check on aisle five! Jeez, I really needed to snap out of it.

I motioned for Rose's hands, and she gratefully encapsulated them in mine. Then I closed my eyes and tried to summon up an image of George, based on the photo that Rose showed me nearly every time she came.

"Do you need to see his photograph again, dear?"

I shook my head. "No, I remember it."

I focused on the image of the old man in the blue sweater who had a Homer Simpson hairline and a donkey's smile. But of course, nothing came. I was about to say as much to Rose when a tingling at the nape of my neck suddenly grabbed my attention. I cinched my eyes closed and waited for something to appear. I could see the faintest outline of a person, but the image was blurry. I focused more resolutely, clenching my eyes shut even tighter.

"Are you getting something, dear?" Rose asked, her tone hopeful.

"I think so." Whatever I was receiving, though, had started to fade. "Please don't say anything, Rose, because I'm losing whatever it was."

I tightened my grip on her hands and begged the vision to return, to delineate itself more clearly. I focused on the darkness of my eyelids. Suddenly a jolt ricocheted through my body. Stunned, I opened my eyes. When I did, I was traumatized to discover that Rose wasn't sitting in front of me anymore. In fact, I wasn't in my reading room or even in my store. Where the hell I was and what the hell had happened was anyone's guess because I'd never experienced anything like this before.

I didn't recognize my surroundings, but I couldn't help noticing that everything seemed so three-dimensional, so real. I could reach out and touch the walls next to me. Generally my visions were cloudy, making it difficult to figure out just what was going on, but this one was something entirely different. I reached out for the marble pillar that stood in front of me and when I felt the cold penetrate my hand, I pulled it back in shocked surprise.

I was inside my vision! The thought caused panic to start in my stomach.

Completely shaken and frightened, I turned to face my surroundings—a great expanse of white marble flooring, complete with Corinthian columns lining the walls and ornate tapestries. I was inside some sort of mansion.

I glanced to my left and noticed a floor-length mirror. The reflection I saw in it scared the hell out of me. I was looking at myself, only I was dressed in the costume of a fairy, which made no sense at all because I would never be caught dead in such a ridiculously short getup. I mean, the skirt ended about mid-thigh and my breasts were busting out of the top, not to mention the fact that I was wearing ridiculously high heels, as in teetering over five inches.

But my outfit really wasn't what concerned me. Usually, when I received a vision, I either shared the perspective of the person involved—that is to say, I became them—or witnessed the events as if I were watching a movie. Or, most commonly, I was just able to converse with the deceased.

In this vision, though, I was myself, but I was no longer in my shop, and that had never happened before.

I couldn't help but notice the sounds of music and laughter as I moved along. The room flared into a giant receiving area that showcased a wide set of stairs. Swallowing hard, I started up the steps. At the top of the stairs, I found myself facing a ballroom. A satiny white baby grand piano played itself, and Louis XIV armchairs and love seats lined the expansive room. But the people in the room were what arrested my attention—mostly because they were floating in the air, dancing as if they were on clouds. I shook my head, trying to clear the ridiculous vision, but it refused to budge, stubbornly persuading my mind to believe what I knew to be a lie.

Whose mansion it was I had no clue, and why I was

here was an even bigger mystery. In the back of my mind, though, I hoped George was well-to-do and threw lots of Halloween parties.

"Hello, poppet."

Sinjin.

I turned to face him, in complete shock. He was dressed in the costume of a vampire . . . How fitting.

"I did not intend to frighten you," he said in his cultured English accent.

"You didn't," I heard myself respond. It was as if my voice spoke of its own accord. The words didn't enter my head at all—they came out of my mouth like someone else had spoken them. Wondering how much control I had over the vision-me, I glanced down at my hand, willing myself to raise it. Nothing happened. So I couldn't control my voice, or my body. Guess I was just along for the ride as a passive spectator. Great.

Sinjin reached for my hand, smiling as he took it in his, and brought it to his lips. "Pleased to make your acquaintance, Miss—?"

"Wilkins."

He swept his black cloak forward and bowed theatrically. "Ah, Miss Wilkins, you are ravishing, if I may say so."

"You can call me Jolie," I felt myself answer as I tried to understand what this vision meant. In it, I was obviously meeting Sinjin for the very first time, and yet this wasn't at all the way I'd met him in reality. He'd come into my store, needing to use the phone due to his flat tire, right? What, then, was the meaning of this?

"Ah, the witch Jolie, now I am even more pleased to make your acquaintance."

Witch? What was with the witch business again? I felt my mouth open as I asked, "And who might you be?"

He bowed again. "You may call me the Count."

The vision-me laughed. "Nice costume. You look the part."

"Do not be frightened, I mean you no harm," Sinjin said.

Before I could comprehend what was happening, the vision faded away. I was about to release Rose Pierson's hands when another jolt flashed through me, identical to the first. As soon as I could open my eyes, I found myself in a moving car. I glanced down, realizing I was in my own body again, and when I looked to my right I saw Sinjin behind the wheel. The last that I'd checked, the driver's seat was on the left side in the United States, which could only mean one thing . . . We weren't in the United States.

"Are you still angry with me, love?" the vampire asked as he looked at me.

As in the last vision, I felt myself respond automatically. "It's difficult to stay angry with you."

He smiled eagerly. "Good, I do not like it when we quarrel."

I turned my head back to the window as I studied the passing lights. I had no idea where this vision was taking place, but I didn't recognize any of the scenery. 'Course, it didn't help that it was dark. But since the wheel was on the opposite side of the car, maybe we were somewhere in the UK? That thought caused a flurry of disquiet in my stomach because, again, it made no sense. I'd never traveled abroad and had no immediate plans to. My thoughts were interrupted because I was suddenly overcome by a feeling of emptiness. Something deep inside me was worried, anxious—terrified, in fact. And I had no idea why. My stomach suddenly cramped violently and I thought I might be sick. The vision-me grabbed the car's armrest, leaning forward and hyperventilating. I tried to resist the feelings, realizing that it wasn't really me who was experiencing them, but it was no use.

"Jolie?"

"I . . . I can't breathe," the vision-me blurted.

I felt the car pull over and come to an abrupt stop. Sinjin lurched from the driver's side and threw open my door, fumbling with my seat belt before he managed to undo it and haul me out of the car and into his arms.

"Breathe, love. You are having a panic attack."

I tried to make sense of what was happening—why I was with Sinjin in the first place, where we were going, why I couldn't breathe—but of course nothing was explained. I was just witnessing a moment in time, a moment that had yet to come.

"Jolie, look at me," Sinjin said, holding me at a distance. "Focus on the black of my eyes."

"I . . . I . . ."

He shook me. "Focus on the black of my eyes!"

I felt myself concentrating on him as he held me.

"Just breathe. You and I are going to get through this, do you understand?"

The vision-me nodded dumbly as my breathing became more regular.

"Take another breath for me, love," he whispered. "There's my good girl."

I inhaled deeply and felt myself collapse against Sinjin's chest, wrapping my arms around him. He rubbed my back in large circles, reassuring me.

"What is the matter?" he crooned against my ear.

"I'm so afraid, Sinjin," the vision-me said, and there was something in me that was chilled by the notion that I could ever be this frightened. Sinjin's claim—that he was my protector—came back to haunt me. Was it possible that he had been telling me the truth? Was something bad going to happen to me? Did he know something I didn't? Judging by this vision, I have to say the answer was an alarming yes.

"There is nothing to be afraid of; I will not allow you to come to harm."

And that was when the second vision left me and I opened my eyes. I couldn't speak for a few seconds. I wasn't sure what to say or do, and half of me was terrified that I'd be racked by another jolt and sent God only knew where else.

What had just happened? I had no clue. But I'd never before experienced visions so real, so defined, so exact. What was more, I felt like there was no way I could discount them as hallucinations from a tired and jumbled brain. No, these were the most three-dimensional visions I'd ever had.

"What did George say?" Rose Pierson asked finally, as if she was still afraid her voice might dispel any messages I was receiving.

I glanced at her and immediately knew that I couldn't tell her the truth; but she also wouldn't believe me if I told her that I hadn't seen anything at all. "Yes, it was George, Rose." I felt bad as soon as the words left my mouth. But I had nothing else up my sleeve, and the poor old woman wanted so desperately to think George had a message for her . . .

She smiled. "I knew he would come through, eventually."

I tightened my hold on her hands and smiled reassuringly. "He wanted to tell you that he loves you and wants you to continue enjoying your life. He is in a happy place, Rose."

She nodded, and there were tears in her eyes. "Thank you, dear." She shook her head and cleared her throat, apparently trying to get control of her emotions. She faced me again and smiled. "I always believed in you. I hope you realize what a gift you truly have."

I just watched her as she stood and left the reading room. I debated with myself about my gift. Could it be possible that I really was more than just a psychic? I mean, did witches see these sorts of things? I shook my head and forced the thoughts from my mind, knowing that the second I admitted to myself I might be more than I was, the floodgate on my questions and concerns would be opened—and I couldn't say I was ready for that.

But while I wanted to refuse to believe I had anything in common with Broom Hilda, it was harder to argue that maybe Sinjin wasn't going to play a bigger part in my life. And, what was even more interesting, I might even need him.

"So when are you going to call him?" Christa asked. It was lunchtime and I'd just finished up with my second client of the day.

I glanced up at her, chewing a bite of my turkey sandwich as she used her chopsticks to gingerly place an enormous piece of California roll into her mouth. Her lips wrestled with the huge mouthful as they tried to stretch tightly closed to spare me the inner workings of her mouth, thank God.

"Well, he obviously won't answer the phone during the day," I said and raised my eyebrows as I watched her continue to macerate the colossal wad, only to wash it down with a healthy swig of iced tea.

"Ah, that's right. I keep forgetting all his vampire idiosynchronyms."

"You mean idiosyncrasies?" I asked with a laugh.

"Yeah, that's what I said." She reached for roll number two. I was about to comment when I caught sight of someone just outside our store windows. Looking up, I felt that bite of turkey I'd just swallowed work its way back up my throat.

"Son of a freaking . . . ," I started and bolted upright, slamming my sandwich on the counter as I ran to the door.

"What? What happened?" Christa exclaimed, but I didn't bother to respond because I wanted so much to reach the door before the person on the other side did—reach it, so I could lock it.

But it was no good. He was already inside by the time I got there.

"You aren't welcome here," I started, my body shaking with anger and . . . fear. I didn't understand what he wanted, why he wouldn't leave me alone, and, furthermore, what he was. His bright blue aura seemed to blaze up at my outburst, flaring this way and that.

Out of the corner of my eye, I noticed that Christa was sitting up straight and hiding the remnants of her lunch. She'd no doubt just realized how shockingly attractive Rand was. Still, he was also so shocking in general that I wanted nothing more to do with him.

"I need to speak with you," he said, and his voice warned me not to argue with him—something major was weighing on his mind.

But I was beyond the stage of arguing. "I want nothing to do with you. Please go find another psychic."

"I need to speak to *you*, Jolie, not someone else."

I wasn't screwing around this time—no, I was not about to let him start all that mumbo jumbo stuff that made me feel like I'd known him forever and made me want to kiss him all over . . . a feeling that was already beginning to rear its unwanted head, dammit to hell.

I turned to face Christa. "Chris, call the cops."

She frowned at me, but reached for the phone anyway. As she was picking up the receiver, Rand faced her, his eyes narrowing.

"Stop," he said, and what happened next not only scared the crap out of me, but challenged everything I knew . . . and defied logic. Christa completely froze, her hand suspended in midair and an expression of surprise pasted on her face.

"Chris," I said, my voice betraying my concern. My mouth dropped open and I turned to face him. "What the hell did you do to her?"

"She will be fine," Rand said in a soft voice, holding his hands up as if to say he was completely harmless and I was safe. But I was hardly stupid enough to buy any of it. He was as harmless as a pissed-off rattlesnake. Crap and a half, where was Sinjin when I needed him?

"You get the hell away from me," I cried out as he started to approach me.

"I'm not going to hurt you, Jolie," he said, but there was no way in hell I believed him.

"What are you?" I demanded as I backed up, feeling myself hit the wall. I was cornered. Turning to my left, I armed myself with a broom that was leaning against the wall. Yes, it was ridiculous, but it was the only thing I had so I went with it.

"I am a warlock," he answered matter-of-factly.

"A warlock!" My voice broke over the word. "As in a male witch?"

"Yes." He nodded and stopped approaching me when he was oh, a broom's length away.

"And I suppose you're going to insist I'm a witch too?" I yelled at him.

That caught him off guard. He stopped whatever he'd been about to say and just stood there for a second or two, studying me carefully. "How did you know?" he asked finally.

"Because I'm not as ignorant as you would like to think and I . . ." I racked my brain, trying to find something that I could use against him—something to wave in front of his face that might get him to leave me alone. And of course, the only thing that came to mind was my vampire, Sinjin. "I have a protector, and one you won't want to mess with."

"A protector?" he repeated as his eyes narrowed.

"Yes," I insisted, and as ridiculous as it was, I pushed the broom out, catching him in the middle of his waist with the scratchy end.

"And who is this protector of yours?" he demanded.

"None of your damn business!" I railed back at him, suddenly wondering if it would be smart to throw around Sinjin's name. I mean, I had no idea if Sinjin would consider this guy a friend, a nemesis, or a nobody. Better to keep that information to myself. But I would tell him what was most important. "He's a vampire and he could kill you just as easily as look at you."

Well, I hoped that last part was true, at least. Judging by the look on Rand's face, the threat had done its job.

"I've come too late then," he said, and his voice had a strange quality to it—something that sounded sad and hollow. "He's already found you."

I had no idea what he was talking about, but I thought it would be smart to run with it. "Yes . . . Yes, he has."

"Jolie," he started again, his tone urgent this time. He took a step closer. What happened next completely baffled me. I jammed the broom at him, hitting him in the stomach with it. At the very instant that the broom hit his mid-section, I felt something like energy leave my body and travel the length of the broom. It hit him in a huge burst of bright blue light and sent him sailing through the air. He landed maybe three feet away, on his back.

"Oh my God!" I screamed, covering my mouth in shock as I took a step forward and then stopped, reminding myself that I was protecting myself against an intruder.

He sat up and shook his head, apparently trying to shake off my Wonder Woman impersonation. Then he simply stood up, took a deep breath, and turned around, exiting through the door. He slammed it shut behind him.

Seven

The following evening, I found myself driving to Sinjin's new house. I parked in front, took a deep breath, and stepped out of my Jetta—then suddenly felt like my feet were mired in quicksand. There was a part of me that was nervous about dropping my guard and getting close to Sinjin. I mean, he was a vampire for crying out loud! Granted, we'd established the fact that he was apparently my guardian and, as such, wouldn't be sampling my goods, but there it was—he was a bloodsucker and I was, for all intents and purposes, a blood bag.

Maybe if that brush with Rand at my store hadn't happened, I would have been less eager to seek Sinjin out. But now something inside me felt panicked, something that demanded action urgently. I was overflowing with questions—*Why have both a vampire and a warlock entered my life? And what is a warlock anyway? What other powers does Rand possess? Is he bad, for lack of a better word? And finally, why do both Sinjin and Rand think I'm a witch? Most important, how in the hell could I, boring Jolie Wilkins, zap a powerful warlock across the room with my bare hands—well, with the help of a broom?*

Speaking of the warlock, Christa had instantly become reanimated after he left the store—as if someone had turned her switch back on. She had seemed a little confused, maybe—looking around herself as if she'd misplaced something, which turned out to be her sushi. But after finding it, she'd acted as though nothing strange had ever happened. She didn't even recall Rand's visit, and I wasn't about to remind her, afraid that she'd really freak out.

I, myself, was relieved that my best friend had been restored to me and that she apparently hadn't fared any the worse for her brief mental vacation, but that relief was short-lived. Why? Because Rand was a wild card. I didn't know what he wanted, why he continued to harass me, or what he was capable of.

I was now incredibly frightened about the path my life was taking. It felt as if everything I knew had been ripped out from underneath me and I was spiraling out of control in a twister of doubt and confusion. It was time for answers. I wanted—no, needed—to understand what was happening.

So tonight would be the night . . . I planned to spill my guts to Sinjin about all of this in the strained hope that he could provide the missing pieces and fill in the gaps. And while there was a part of me that demanded answers, there was also a part of me that was rejoicing over the fact that I would see Sinjin again. As much as I didn't want to admit it to myself, I'd missed him . . . a lot.

A cold wind picked up and wrapped itself around my ankles, reminding me that I couldn't just stand out here on the curb forever. I needed to make a decision. I needed to either face Sinjin or get back in my car and go home. I swallowed hard and moved forward.

It felt like it took me two years to make it onto the walkway that led to Sinjin's house—a three-story Spanish villa, complete with an expansive front yard filled with fragrant olive trees and Mexican sage. The sage plants hugged the lighted walkway, their long purple blooms dancing back and forth as the wind whipped through them. I followed the undulating path as it snaked back and forth toward Sinjin's front door. Funny how the first time I'd taken this same walk, I hadn't had any of the feelings that consumed me now. Instead, I'd cheerfully followed the real estate agent up to the house, asking myself if Sinjin might like this property, without even the slightest idea that he might be a vampire.

There was a lone light coming from the dining room, but other than that the house was dark, making me wonder if Sinjin was even at home. Maybe he was out hunting for prey? I felt my feet fumble over each other and steadied myself against the huge pepper tree that stood in the middle of the path, trying to imagine what it meant for Sinjin to drink blood.

Was it painful for the victim? Or was it sexual, plea-surable, like Sinjin had implied? And that part about it being painful for witches, was that something I'd have to now consider? I shook my head, still not completely accepting the fact that I might be able to add "witch" to my list of credentials. But back to the victims of Sinjin's bite . . . did he tell his prey the truth about what would happen to her or did he merely glamour her into accep-tance? Was the person actually injured afterward or even dead? I shook my head, unable to believe that Sin-jin was a killer. He just couldn't be—not when he was so convincing about being my protector. How could he protect me and still be a murderer?

Because he's a vampire, you dumb-ass, my brain re-plied loudly.

I gritted my teeth, not allowing my wayward thoughts to get the better of me. I was here for a reason—I had a purpose and I was ready. It was now or never.

I stalled in front of the dark, wooden, double doors that led into the mansion. I raised my fist, about to knock, when I noticed the doorbell off to one side. I rang it once and listened as the sound echoed throughout the house, reminding me of the sad tolling of bells in a belfry—the music of the cemetery, of the dead.

Jeez, Jolie, snap out of it, I reprimanded myself. *It's not like Sinjin's dead . . .* But then I had to stop and ponder on that a bit longer. *Oh my God, is he dead?*

He's a vampire, he must be dead.

But he's animated—it's not like he's some corpse, rotting away.

A corpse? Ew, that's so gross.

I closed my eyes and told the voices in my head to take a permanent hike. I didn't have the strength or the wherewithal to argue with myself any longer. Instead I focused on the fact that Sinjin didn't appear to be home. Pivoting on one foot, I turned around and walked right into someone, my nose banging into his chest.

"Agh!" I yelled, bracing my hands against the broad, cold chest in front of me. Sinjin grabbed my hands and held them as he smiled down at me. I struggled to free myself, suddenly breathless, winded, and nervous. "How long have you been standing there?" I demanded.

Sinjin smirked that incredibly sexy grin of his and arched a brow, regarding me with amusement and, more obviously, patience. He released my hands suddenly and I nearly fell backward, but I managed to regain my balance. As I looked up at him, I was irritated with my racing heart. I was nervous around Sinjin and yet he was as comfortable and carefree as ever. He had the eternal look of someone who never let anything bother him. It also seemed like he had nowhere to go and nothing to do but all the time in the world to do it in. Given the fact that he was a vampire, my observation was probably spot-on.

"How old are you?" I added, my voice a mere whisper.

"Which question would you prefer I answer first, love? My age or how long I have been standing here?"

I frowned. "The age one."

"I am six hundred," he replied in a matter-of-fact sort of way, then cocked his head to the side, as if judging my reaction. I felt my jaw drop, and he calmly reached across and closed my mouth by lifting my chin.

"Six hundred!" I squeaked, shaking my head in shock. "You are six hundred years old?"

"Yes, love, I was not referring to moons."

I busily did the math. "So you were born during the fourteen hundreds?" I asked, feeling like I might pass out right there.

"Yes, the exact date of my birth now escapes me, but I am at least six hundred."

For the first time in my life, there was not even a single thought in my mind. It was as if I'd just been frozen, like Rand had done to Christa. The man standing in front of me had lived through the reign of Henry VIII, Queen Elizabeth, the American Revolutionary War, the Civil War, Hitler . . .

"And to answer your first question, poppet," Sinjin continued, "I have been behind you from the moment you started up the drive."

"Why didn't you announce yourself?" I snapped, but I was secretly pleased that he'd given me something to focus on besides his age. He hadn't made so much as a sound when he was following me, proof that he was well versed in the supernatural and incredibly powerful, probably more powerful than I could even imagine. I mean, he'd had centuries to hone his craft—to practice, to learn from his mistakes and become stronger, faster, smarter, and . . . better. This realization made me all too aware that he and I were as different as day and night. If I'd thought Sinjin could snap me like a twig before, now

I wondered if he so much as glanced at me with foul intentions, would I cease to exist?

He shrugged. "I enjoy observing you when you think you are alone." He paused a moment or two. "I can see the real you—natural, uninhibited."

I didn't know what to say, so I stayed quiet. I could feel goose bumps starting to form on my skin. I wasn't sure if they were due to Sinjin's proximity or the cold night air. Maybe it was both.

"Shall we?" he asked as he sidestepped me, reaching for the front door.

"Where were you?" I didn't mean to sound so . . . interested or hopeful.

He turned around and paused, his hand on the doorknob. "I was taking a walk."

"To drink someone's blood?" I didn't want to think about Sinjin feeding—though surprisingly enough, the image of that didn't really bother me. I didn't want to admit it, but it was more the thought of him being so intimate with someone, especially a woman, that made me . . . jealous!

Swimming in a sea of unanswered questions, I was absolutely certain of one thing—I had completely lost my mind.

He smiled. "To enjoy nature." Then he opened the door without even unlocking it.

"You just leave your doors unlocked?" I asked, suddenly grateful for the change in subject.

Sinjin turned around to face me and grinned widely. "I welcome intruders."

Which made total sense. "They should fear you," I mumbled.

He chuckled and stood aside, holding the door open for me. "Please come in."

I nodded and paused only momentarily, thinking that I was placing my trust in someone who could easily kill me. But what choice did I have? I needed answers, and the only way I was going to get them was to trust this man. Really, I had no one else I could turn to. I mean, I supposed I could turn to Rand, but in my heart of hearts I didn't think that was a good idea. I didn't know why, but my instincts usually don't steer me wrong. I stood up straight and marched through the double doors.

"I have a lot of questions for you, Sinjin," I started, my voice sounding loud and almost abrasive as I tried to hide the underlying nervousness that was gnawing at me.

He strode inside behind me and leaned against the wall, crossing his arms against his chest. He watched me as if completely indifferent to the fact that I was so nervous. I, on the other hand, felt like I might be sick.

"All in good time," he said in that deep voice of his, which was currently causing shivers to snake up and down my spine. "I would prefer to give you a tour of my new home first, if that pleases you?" He closed the door behind him.

I couldn't keep a smile from my lips. Somehow, I just found it incredibly cute that he wanted to show off his house—a house that I'd found for him. "Sure."

He pushed away from the wall and offered his hand, expecting me to take it. I hesitated only momentarily before doing so. He instantly pulled me into the cocoon of his body, wrapping his arms around me.

"Sinjin," I started, tremors in my voice. I just wasn't good with this one-on-one, flirty stuff. Truth be told, I felt like an idiot—I didn't know what to say or do with myself.

"I have missed you, my pet," he whispered into my ear. His heady scent seemed to fill my entire being. I closed my eyes and told myself to go with it, not to fight the feelings that were welling up inside me. I leaned my head against his shoulder, inhaling deeply. I *wanted* to be close to him, to feel his arms around me. Yes, they were cold at first—he was cold at first. But, as with the last time I'd touched him, the cold began to fade away, almost as if his body was absorbing the heat from my own.

"Sinjin, is it true that vampires can bewitch people?"

"Yes," he whispered into my hair as he ran his index finger up and down my naked forearm, causing me to squirm against him. I wanted him! And as much as I tried not to, it was useless because I craved him, needed him. "We refer to it as glamouring our . . . prey."

"Your prey," I repeated and felt a shudder of fear. I pulled away from him and forced myself to hold his gaze, to understand what that meant. "Is that what I am to you?"

He looked down at me and shook his head, his eyes narrowing as he cupped my cheek. "No. Never. You do not realize what you are to me yet, love, because you do not yet understand who and what you are."

I swallowed hard. "A witch?"

He nodded. "You are extremely powerful, poppet. And, as such, my powers are useless against you."

But I couldn't focus on the idea that I was supposed to be a witch and a powerful one at that. The concept was just too foreign, too weird. Instead, I found myself dwelling on the idea of a vampire's power of persuasion, because that could possibly explain a lot—like why I felt the way I did about Sinjin. "So never in the course of our . . . friendship . . . have you ever . . . glamoured me?"

He smiled at my use of the term *friendship*. "Never."

Well that put me right back to square one. I had to accept that I was lusting after Sinjin of my own accord. And I hadn't wanted to address the whole "you're a witch" conversation before, but I couldn't avoid it any longer.

"Sinjin," I started. "How do you know all this about me?"

He glanced over at me. "Perhaps it is a hunch, love."

I shook my head—it wasn't a hunch. He could read me like a book. It was as if he knew things about me he shouldn't have. As a psychic, I could have believed that he was something similar—some sort of sensitive who could see someone's past just as I could see someone's future. Maybe that was my answer, but somehow I couldn't shake the feeling that I was duping myself—that there was more to this picture than met the eye. "You act like we've met before?" I suddenly remembered the vision of him at the masquerade party—it had felt so real, so tangible. Was it possible . . .

He smiled that sexy grin of his and shushed me with his finger. "I will answer all your questions, love, but first our tour. Come." And he started forward, tugging me along.

"Sinjin . . . ," I began to argue.

He gave me a stern expression that told me the issue was not open for debate, so with a frustrated sigh I followed. Easier to give in now and get my answers later.

We began our tour in the dining room, and I was soon surprised to discover that in the course of just a week or so, Sinjin had completely furnished the entire six-bedroom, four-bathroom house. After seeing the dining room and living room, I had to admit his style appealed to me. His couches were sumptuous, each easily accommodating five grown men. I could only imagine how small I would look on them, like a little child lost in the dark black leather. On either end of the couches were stainless-steel tables that matched an enormous steel coffee table in the center. With the black leather of the couches and the sharp lines of the tables, Sinjin's living room was a vast expanse of modernity and hard angles. Of course, he'd also invested in the best gadgets that technology had to offer—including what appeared to be a state-of-the-art surround-sound system and a TV that took up half of one wall.

"Apparently sucking blood is healthy for your pocket-book," I grumbled.

Sinjin chuckled and started for the staircase, so I followed him. "I am very pleased with this home, poppet. Thank you for your assistance."

I couldn't help but beam inside. When the real estate agent had taken me through this house, I'd somehow known it would be his favorite. I'd been able to picture Sinjin here—with the dark wood floors and the incredibly high ceilings, the openness of the floor plan and the views that overlooked the valley. Somehow it all just seemed to fit him.

"Thank you," I said in a soft voice, reminding myself to keep from falling for Sinjin. I could feel . . . my attraction to him in my very core, but something told me it wasn't a good idea. I mean, I was on the precipice of something huge here. It was a feeling that I had in the depths of my soul. Something was about to happen to me, something big. I assumed that Sinjin would be the person to hold my hand and guide me through that something. It just wasn't smart to get attached to him, to have feelings for him. Especially given how old and powerful he was. Nope, it wasn't a good idea at all.

Yet I also couldn't help but feel I'd issued this warning to myself too late. Because the stupid truth of the whole situation was that I was falling for Sinjin—I could feel it by the way my heart sped up whenever he looked at me, how I longed to feel his skin against mine, and how, whenever I was apart from him, he occupied my thoughts.

"And this is my bedchamber," Sinjin announced as he opened the double doors. I was confronted with the most enormous bed I'd ever seen.

I gulped hard. I couldn't help it.

"Come in," he said, walking to the far end of the room, looking around himself as if he were taking in the room for the first time. "What do you think of it?" He appeared proud.

I took a deep breath and followed him in, pausing once I reached the center, afraid to go too near the bed and equally afraid to get too close to Sinjin. I mean, we *were* in his bedroom . . .

I nervously looked around, taking in the stone fireplace that dominated the corner of the room, the many large-paned windows where the moonlight threw strange reflections against the pool in his backyard. My gaze drifted back to that *enormous* bed . . .

"Um, I really like it," I said, feeling my cheeks coloring. God, I needed to focus on anything but that bed, but the carnal activities that could go on there . . . "Where do you sleep during the day?" I asked breathlessly.

"In the wine cellar below the house," he answered and eyed me in such a way that I knew that he knew exactly what had been going on in my head.

But I refused to grant another second to the nervousness that was still consuming me. Instead, I focused on the wine cellar. While I was looking at real estate for him, I hadn't realized how important it was for there to be a dark underground space—his decision to buy this property now made even more sense. It was the only one of the three that had a basement, a sanctuary from the marauding sunlight.

I nodded and felt my eyes return to the bed. I mean, it was hard not to focus on it considering how much its vastness dwarfed the rest of the space. I could now feel my blush spreading from my cheeks to the tips of my ears.

Sinjin chuckled. "I wonder what is going through that

beautiful head of yours, poppet." And he took a few steps toward me.

"Why?" I asked, probably too quickly, as I took a few steps back.

"Your heartbeat is escalating."

Stop beating so hard, heart, I begged, wondering if there was any way I could calm myself down. But it seemed like the harder I tried, the more urgently my heart thumped . . . and the more Sinjin smiled.

"Are you nervous, love?" he asked.

"Yes," I admitted, figuring I had no reason to lie to him. More important, he'd be able to tell a lie from the truth.

"And what is making you nervous?"

I swallowed hard. "You."

He chuckled, but somehow the laugh never reached his eyes. No, those eyes were fixed on me—just as they'd been since we had entered his bedroom. They seemed predatory, hungry . . .

"And why is that?"

"Because you're a vampire."

He didn't say anything for a while, but he crossed his arms against his chest, his eyes still trained on mine. "It is more than that."

"I don't know what you want from me," I finally admitted, unable to hold his gaze. I dropped my focus to my shoes and felt the sudden urge to flee.

"You are a strong woman, poppet," he began, and I glanced up at him, surprised. "You must never drop your eyes from your opponent."

"Are you my opponent?"

He didn't answer, just continued to stare at me. I held his gaze. The seconds snailed by, and I wanted to look away, but I didn't. Nope, I knew better. This was a test—for what, I wasn't sure, but it was a test all the same.

A huge smile suddenly broke across Sinjin's face and I

felt myself inhale deeply without being aware of it. I'd been holding my breath the entire time during our little stare-down.

"Very good, little poppet, very good." He smiled again, his canines lengthening into fangs. My breath caught, and I backed up until I was pressed against the wall. "Do not be afraid," Sinjin said, his eyes glowing white. "I will never hurt you."

"But . . . your fangs," I started as I eyed the door, judging the distance.

"You would never make it in time," Sinjin said with a quick smile. "Rule number one, never run from a vampire."

But the last thing I wanted to think about was running from him. I was still transfixed by his fangs and his eyes, which were now totally white. "Sinjin, why are your eyes white and why are your fangs so long?" Fear was pumping through me.

He took two steps closer to me. "I desire you."

"I thought you said you would never think of me as . . . food."

"Not that type of desire, poppet," he said, closing the distance between us.

"W . . . What type then?"

"The type where a man desires a woman, desires to know her intimately." He smiled. "I desire nothing more than to know you intimately, love."

I gulped, knowing where this was headed, what he wanted, and what I wanted. My body was screaming for it, for him, and I only hoped he couldn't read me. "I'm not good at this stuff, Sinjin," I said and shook my head, suddenly more afraid than I'd been at the prospect that I was going to be his main course for the evening.

"That is your insecurity speaking, poppet. Silence it."

"I can't," I started, but he shook his head, interrupting me.

"I know you." He brought his finger to my chest and pointed at what I imagined was my heart. "I know who you are inside, and that is the Jolie I want."

"How can you know me, Sinjin? It hasn't even been a month yet," I said, trying to make a point to myself as much as to him. *It hasn't even been a month yet! So how the hell could I feel like this, how could I be so into someone I haven't even spent that much time with?* "You're talking like a crazy person."

"I know you better than you can imagine," he said, and that determined look was back in his eyes.

"But how could . . ." Then I remembered again my vision of Sinjin in that mansion, of me in the fairy costume. I felt a cold sweat break out across my forehead. Why did that vision keep rearing its head? Why wouldn't it just die away? Because maybe there was a kernel of truth to it . . . Maybe there was more to this picture than met the eye? "Sinjin, where did we first meet?"

He stopped moving toward me, pulling back as shock pasted itself on his face. In a split second, the expression was gone and he was back to his calm and collected self. "Why do you ask?"

"Answer the question."

He smiled a smooth, practiced grin. He'd had six hundred years to perfect his skills—if he wanted to keep the truth from me, he could do a damn good job of it.

"We met in your store, of course, silly poppet. What a strange question."

I sighed, part of me relieved by his answer. The other part, however, couldn't let go of the surprised look I saw in his eyes when I asked the question in the first place.

Eight

Half an hour later, our tour was over. Now it was time for Sinjin to explain just what the hell was going on— why vampires and warlocks were suddenly infiltrating my life and why both he and Rand seemed to believe I was a witch or, at the very least, something powerful. Now was the time for answers.

As I followed Sinjin into his living room, I couldn't help but take in his perfect body—how long his legs were and how the softly flowing fabric of his pants did nothing to hide the sleek lines of his butt. His shoulders appeared even broader from behind. With his narrow waist, he had the physique of a swimmer.

"Please have a seat," he said, turning to face me with a devilish smile. He motioned to the two empty couches as well as the two club chairs on either end of them. There wasn't any shortage of seating options.

I offered him a quick and nervous smile, then sat in the middle of one of the couches. I felt the expensive leather embrace me as I sank into the down pillows. Just as I'd imagined, the enormity of Sinjin's sofa dwarfed me and made me feel like a small child. My feet actually dangled off the edge. I was just missing a gigantic lolli-pop to complete the image of a five-year-old.

Sinjin chuckled to himself, shaking his head in apparent admiration. "You are such a delectable little package, my pet."

The way he watched me caused a flurry of butterflies in my stomach. Again, I had to remind myself that he was a vampire and I was completely at his mercy, but somehow I still wasn't frightened. For whatever reason, I truly believed in my heart of hearts that Sinjin would never hurt me.

He rested one arm on the fireplace mantel and scrutinized me as I bounced my feet nervously, my hands clasped in my lap.

"Are you hungry, little poppet?" he asked, his voice breaking the silence in the room.

I could feel my eyes growing wide at the mention of hunger. "No, and I hope you aren't either."

Sinjin dropped his head back and laughed heartily before focusing on me again. "Fear not, love."

I took a deep breath, trying to calm my nerves and figure out how to best handle the situation. I could feel the seconds ticking by, the quiet of the room pounding in on me. I had so many questions swimming through my head, all straining for the opportunity to be first, that I didn't even know where to begin.

"Your silence surprises me, love."

I glanced up at him and nodded, surprised by my own silence. The entire time he'd dragged me on the tour of his home, I hadn't been able to keep the questions at bay—and now my brain was suddenly silent. "I'm not sure what to ask first."

The incredibly handsome, even sexier vampire nodded and smiled. "Perhaps you would like to inquire about my species?"

"Sure, that's a good place to start."

He moved away from the fireplace and approached one of the floor-to-ceiling windows, where the moon was wrestling with the clouds, fighting to bathe him in its beauty and make his already luminescent magnificence shine even brighter. He rested his long, refined fingers against the windowsill and drummed them back and forth, as if he were playing a piano.

I swallowed hard at the sudden thought of those fingers on me, touching me, *playing* me as expertly as any instrument. I shook my head, irritated with myself. It was like I suddenly turned into a cat in heat whenever Sinjin was anywhere near me. He made me lose sight of who I really was.

Or does he bring out the real you? I argued with myself. *Maybe you've been suppressing this side of yourself for so long, you didn't even know it was there. Maybe Sinjin's just woken you up, allowed you to feel again?*

Uncomfortable with the thoughts, I focused on the conversation. "Um, were you going to tell me about vampires?" I asked, standing and smiling nervously up at him. I wanted to touch him. I could feel the need radiating through my fingers, but I was suddenly afraid to. Not so much because he was a vampire, but because he was a man.

"Ah, yes, your nearness threw me off track," he said, grabbing my hand. He held it to his face and, staring at me all the while, brought my palm to his lips and kissed it. I swallowed hard in response. "Your skin is delightfully soft," he whispered, kissing my hand again, his eyes boring into mine.

"Sinjin . . . ," I started, trying to focus on the reason I'd come here tonight—getting my questions answered.

He smiled apologetically. "As I have already told you, poppet, I am six hundred years old," he said, as if he was beginning a story.

I shook my head at the reminder, still unable to fathom exactly what that meant—living through so much history, experiencing such pain and happiness. "I still can't believe you're that old."

"Believe it, love." He smiled at me again, but this time his smile seemed sad somehow, pained. Or maybe I was just imagining it. "Because of my age, I have become one of the strongest vampires. I am referred to as a master vampire."

I nodded to emphasize the fact that I was following his story, but feelings of intimidation began to bubble up inside of me. A master vampire?

"So what does that mean exactly?" I asked, now even more keenly aware of Sinjin's power.

"The Underworld is made up of hierarchies, love," he started before I cut him off.

"The Underworld?"

He nodded and smiled encouragingly, as if realizing it was going to take me a while to fully grasp all of this.

"The Underworld is a federation of all otherworldly creatures, my pet. We have our own government, and we abide by our own laws."

I closed my eyes, trying to make sense of this. Logic and reason just had no place in this conversation—well, really, in my life as of late. And the sooner I accepted that, the sooner I could see the world as it really was. I opened my eyes again and focused on him. "So this Underworld has existed for . . ."

"Centuries," he finished. "We have always lived among humans undetected, in the shadows."

"And no one knows? How have you been able to keep yourselves hidden?"

He smiled at me boyishly, which seemed like such an oxymoron because Sinjin was anything but a boy. "It hasn't always been easy, love, but suffice it to say for now that our community is a secret one. There have been breaches and betrayals throughout the years— hence the stories that humans create about our kind. Luckily for us, though, humans are a rather skeptical species, and they invariably talk themselves out of believing there could be . . . others, non-humans, sharing their world."

"What sorts of creatures are we talking about?" I asked, almost afraid to get an answer.

Sinjin shrugged. "All sorts: vampires, werewolves, the fae, witches and warlocks . . . demons."

"Speaking of warlocks," I started, purposely ignoring the part about demons; I just wasn't sure I could handle discussing them at the moment. I cleared my throat as my brain conjured an image of the only warlock who had ever played a role in my life. As thoughts of Rand entered my mind, I was suddenly consumed by feelings of warmth and adoration. I shook them off angrily and glanced up at Sinjin. His eyes had narrowed on me, like a falcon's on a field mouse.

"Yes?" he asked impatiently.

"Um, I met someone who called himself a warlock." I fumbled over the words, feeling unexpectedly nervous because of the heated expression on Sinjin's face.

His eyes instantly turned icy white, and his hands fisted at his sides. His jaw was tight and I could see indentations on his lips suggesting that his fangs were present and accounted for. So I was right! Rand, the warlock, was no friend of Sinjin's, which ultimately meant he was no friend of mine.

"When did this meeting occur? And where?" Sinjin asked in a matter-of-fact, deadly serious tone.

I took a deep breath, intimidated by the look in his eyes. "I don't know, a few days ago at my store."

"Did you get his name?"

I nodded. "Rand."

At the mention of Rand's name, Sinjin bashed his fist into the windowsill. The entire wall shook. It was a wonder the glass didn't break. I felt myself jump in shock as my heart started beating wildly. Why was Sinjin so upset by this? Who was Rand to him and what did this mean?

"How many meetings have you had with him?"

I shook my head, finding it difficult to concentrate. I just hadn't been expecting Sinjin to react with such vehemence to the mere mention of the warlock. I could only wonder what had happened between the two of them. "Why are you so upset, Sinjin?"

"How many times have you seen him?" he repeated while his eyes burned with anger.

"I don't know . . . Twice, I think," I spat out. "The second time I forced him to leave." A flashback of the last time I'd seen Rand came on with a vengeance. I looked up at Sinjin, my eyes going wide. "I . . . I touched him and something happened, Sinjin. There was like a bright burst of light and the next thing I knew, he was sailing through the air. I . . . I have no idea how it happened."

Sinjin nodded as if it were no surprise at all, as if he weren't in the least alarmed by my ability to defy the laws of gravity. "Did he hurt you?"

I shook my head and in a blink Sinjin was standing before me, holding both of my hands in his. I gasped, shocked by his speed. He smiled apologetically, as if he'd just realized that I wasn't exactly used to his vampire quickness.

"He is a dangerous man, poppet. You must avoid him at all costs. Do you understand?"

I nodded, feeling like I could lose myself in the whiteness of Sinjin's eyes, the beauty of his face, and the caress of his skin against mine. Then the image of Rand intruded on my thoughts. "Why is he dangerous?"

"He is a warlock, love, a conjurer of dark magic." Sinjin took a deep breath, which I knew was all for show, and turned away from me. "He wants to possess your power, poppet. He wants to control you."

I nodded, thinking about Rand's visits, how emphatically sure he was that I was something other than what I thought, how he and Sinjin had that in common. "Yes, he insisted that I was a witch."

The narrowed, calculating expression returned to Sinjin's eyes. "What else did he say?"

I closed my eyes, trying to remember what had happened during my meeting with Rand, but was flooded by feelings instead. Memories of Rand's touch, the way he looked at me, how I'd felt so connected to him . . . I faced Sinjin. "There was something about him . . ."

"Yes?"

I shook my head, unable to put my finger on it. "I just felt like I'd met him before, a long time ago, as crazy as that sounds. I felt like we'd known each other all our lives and . . ."

Sinjin's jaw became even tighter as he crossed his arms against his broad chest. "That is his magic, love, nothing more. It is an artifice, a lie to manipulate you."

I faced him and took a deep breath. "He glamoured me, then?"

Sinjin nodded. "Something quite similar. He bewitched you, my little poppet. He bewitched you into believing that the familiarity between the two of you was real. He wanted you to trust him, to feel safe with him." He approached the fireplace and leaned on the mantel, quiet for a second or two as his gaze seemed to focus on the floor. Then he faced me again. "You must believe none of it."

"Why did he come after me?" I asked, my stomach sinking at the thought that my feelings for Rand were fake, not to mention designed to take advantage of me. Who knows what would have happened if I hadn't zapped him across my store?

Sinjin ran his hands through his hair and studied me for a moment or two, as if he were trying to memorize my features, line by line. "Because, little poppet, you are the missing puzzle piece."

"I don't understand," I said and shook my head. "You're going to have to explain better than that."

"Sit," Sinjin said as he escorted me to the couch. I took a seat and he knelt in front of me, pushing his body between my legs. He took each of my hands in his and smiled up at me while my stomach dropped. He was just so . . . close, and now he was kneeling between my . . . legs.

"You are more than a witch, love. Your power is unrivaled, and has never before been seen in any single creature of the Underworld."

Okay, I could admit that this whole role of witch was starting to grow on me—maybe I was just getting used to the idea. I mean, everyone I seemed to encounter was convinced I had lots in common with Glinda, the Good Witch of the North. So the witch part wasn't what struck a note of discord. But the fact that Sinjin seemed to think I was incredibly powerful? Me? Someone who couldn't even command my visions? Nope, power and me were definitely not bedfellows. "Why do you think I'm powerful?" I demanded.

Sinjin shrugged. "I do not think. I know."

"But how?"

He didn't miss a beat. "Let us just say it is a feeling, a strong one."

I wasn't satisfied by the fact that it was just a hunch. I mean, it was difficult enough to wrap my head around being a witch, but now the idea that I was even more than that . . . I couldn't really comprehend it. What did that even mean? What was more powerful than a witch? A different creature altogether? A harpy maybe? I shook my head. "It just sounds really far-fetched, Sinjin."

"That is because your powers have not realized themselves yet, love. You will come to see in time."

I seized his mention of the Underworld. "You're saying I'm part of the . . . Underworld?"

"Yes. Although not yet formally, of course. My duty is to prepare you, to teach you."

I was still having a difficult time grasping it. "Prepare me for what?"

"Your place, love, exists in the Underworld, with your people, and it is my responsibility to ensure your continued safety."

"My people?" I repeated.

"Yes, love, I will answer all of your questions in time. But what is most important for you to know now is that you have a purpose, a calling."

"But—" I started.

Sinjin held his hand up. "In time," he answered simply.

Figuring I'd make no headway on that front, I focused on another. "You make it sound as if you were assigned to me."

He shook his head. "As I mentioned earlier, I am a master vampire . . ."

"You're in charge then?" I interrupted.

"I answer to no one, love." He smiled with fangs as if he relished the fact that he was a free agent.

"Is that what it means to be a master vampire?"

"Not necessarily," he replied. "Master vampires are merely the oldest of our race, and therefore the strongest and the most powerful, but that is not to say that they do not come under the authority of others."

So how come he didn't answer to anyone? "Then you must be the oldest of the master vampires?"

He shook his head, and the smile died from his lips and eyes. "No, there is one even older than I am."

"Then why don't you report to that vampire?"

He cocked his head and smiled, his eyes raking me from head to toe. I felt myself begin to blush, but I forced my attraction to Sinjin aside. This was not the time for that—I needed to understand what I'd gotten myself into, and what it meant to be a member of this so-called Underworld.

"Are you going to respond?" I asked.

"At one time, I did answer to a vampire older than I, love; but I was granted autonomy by someone very special to me, and now I answer to no one but myself."

I gulped, not liking the part about the person special to him, and liking even less that I was getting jealous. "And this person who granted you autonomy . . . Was it a woman?"

He smiled even more broadly. "Yes."

I nodded, deciding I didn't want to hear any more. Sinjin and other women was not a subject that interested me. Instead, I wanted answers about how and why Sinjin had orchestrated our first meeting. "So you never really had a flat tire, did you?"

He shook his head. "Oh yes, it was flat."

"But?" I prodded.

"I flattened it."

Even though I had every right to be annoyed—Sinjin had basically created the circumstance that led to our introduction—I wasn't. Go figure. "How did you know who I was?"

"You are part of the prophecy, love, of the Underworld."

"The prophecy?" I repeated, dubious. "What does that even mean?" I shook my head, wondering why I was believing any of this. "God, I feel like I'm stuck in *Lord of the Rings* or something."

Sinjin chuckled. "You are meant to unite the creatures of the Underworld, little poppet."

"Unite them?" I repeated, wondering when Frodo or Gandalf would be making an appearance. Gollum I was less enthusiastic about. "Unite them against what?"

He sighed but apparently realized he needed to tell me just what was going on. "Unite us against a threat that will wipe us out."

"What?" I asked, rather eloquently.

"They are called Lurkers," Sinjin clarified. "I, myself, think of them as the others—those who are underworldly but do not associate with the creatures of the Underworld kingdom."

"Who are they?"

"They were once humans," he said and tapped his long fingers against his thigh. "By ingesting vampire blood, they gained the extreme strength and speed of the vampire but none of our weaknesses. Thus they can go out in the daylight."

"And they want to destroy you?" I asked, not understanding why that would be. I mean, it sounded like they were cut from the same cloth.

"Yes, they want to destroy all creatures of the Underworld. I suppose you could say they have a vendetta against us."

"Why?"

He shrugged. "No one knows for certain."

"And you think it's my duty to bring the creatures of the Underworld together so they can fight this threat?"

He nodded.

"The creatures of the Underworld don't get along?"

Sinjin nodded again. "Quite disparate factions of creatures make up the Underworld, my pet. It is your duty, your calling, to ensure the Underworld is not divided against itself so that we can defend ourselves against the threat of the Lurkers."

"Great," I muttered and shook my head, deciding to shelve this newest information for now. Otherwise, I thought I might have apoplexy.

"I have searched high and low for you," Sinjin continued, his voice deep, sexy.

"Do you have some sort of witch-tracking device?" I persisted, feeling as if there were something he was leaving out, something he wasn't telling me.

He chuckled and shook his head. "It is very complicated, love; but it took me years to locate you, and now that I have, I remain your faithful and loyal servant, as well as your teacher and protector."

"What does that mean?"

"I will help you perfect your abilities, poppet. I will introduce you to the right people, mentor you, protect you, and essentially help you grasp who and what you are."

I swallowed hard as all of this sank in. And then something occurred to me.

Sinjin has never been romantically interested in you! It was all a front, just a show.

It felt as if the air was constricting my lungs as this newest discovery began to unfold within my mind.

Oh my God, it's so obvious, Jolie! His goal this entire time was to ensure your role as "she who will unite the Underworld." He's known all along who and what you are, and his goal has always been to train you to fulfill this role.

You don't know that for sure, I started to argue with myself, too ashamed to face the truth in my thoughts.

God, you are so stupid! All along, Sinjin's objective has been to get you to yield to him, to accept him as your mentor, and you stupidly fell for it, wanting nothing more than to believe he actually had the hots for you!

Well, you don't have all the pieces to the puzzle yet. You don't know for sure what his intentions were.

Puh-leeze, Jolie, he's been playing you all along, bending you to his will as prettily as you please. You've felt it too—that he was completely and totally out of your league.

I suddenly felt sick to my stomach over my own stupidity. Sinjin must have thought this whole charade was so simple. Lure in the naïve girl with your incredible good looks and charm, and once she chomps on the bait, reel her in bit by bit until you have her flopping back and forth in your hands.

"Poppet, you appear upset. What is stewing in that lovely head of yours?"

I faced him as anger and humiliation took over. "I just realized what a complete idiot I've been."

"Idiot?" he repeated.

"This was just business for you all along."

"Business?" he repeated, sounding confused, even as I realized I'd used the wrong word. "I am afraid I do not follow."

I felt something simmer within me that was about to start boiling and blow its top. "What I'm trying to say is, you came into my life with an agenda. It was never for . . . it was never because . . ."

I couldn't finish the sentence, afraid I sounded too much like a lovesick dumb-ass. I couldn't deny I was now head over heels for this man, who saw me as nothing more than a duty. It was crushing, not to mention humiliating. Actually, the whole thing was mortifying.

And that was when I realized I wanted nothing more than to escape, to stop this from gathering steam and turning into a huge cluster fuck. I took a deep breath and started for the door.

"Where are you going?" he demanded.

"I'm tired," I said and glanced back at him. "And this conversation is too much for me at the moment." I started for the door again.

I didn't even have time to expel my breath before I felt a rush of air against my face and found myself in Sinjin's arms. I pulled away, glancing up at him in shock.

"You do not realize my feelings for you. You never

have," he said. His hold on my upper arms tightened, but I didn't feel threatened. It just seemed like he wanted to feel me against him, to be close to me.

Yet there was no way in hell I was falling for it. Not again. "Fool me once, shame on you . . . fool me twice . . . No, I won't be fooled twice."

"Poppet, you do not understand."

I shook my head, rage still rampaging through me. "I understand perfectly well." I dropped my gaze to the floor and exhaled. "God, I'm so dumb."

"Jolie," he insisted and tipped my chin up with his long index finger. When I made the mistake of glancing into his eyes, I felt the breath catch in my throat. His expression was determined, angry even. "I will not allow my feelings for you to be trampled so."

I swallowed hard. What did that even mean? "But you . . . You just said there was a reason you came into my life . . . You made it sound like the whole thing was orchestrated."

He nodded and never dropped his gaze from mine, taking both my arms prisoner in his large hands. "When we first met, love, I had one goal in mind—to mentor and teach you, to help shape your powers. But sometime during the course of our acquaintance, our friendship, you have grown to mean much more to me."

And I wanted to believe him so completely. Yet there was part of me that was still holding back, that wouldn't surrender to his words.

He glanced down at his hands and immediately released me, as if realizing how tightly he was holding me. "I apologize," he said quickly as he studied my arms, presumably to inspect them for bruises. "Sometimes I hardly realize my own strength. I hope I have not harmed you?"

I looked down at myself and saw the imprints of his fingers on my skin. I rubbed my arms up and down but didn't notice any pain. All I noticed was a hollow sensation inside me at the prospect of the distance Sinjin was now putting between us. Although I hated to admit it, I wanted nothing more than to feel his arms around me again.

"I'm fine," I said dismissively and then eyed the door again. I just felt overwhelmed, not sure what to think or what to feel anymore. I needed to retreat to the solitude of my little house and be alone.

"You are still leaving me then?"

I sighed. "I want some alone time," I said, feeling exhausted. "I just need to think about all this, to make sense of it all. I'm . . . I'm overwhelmed."

Sinjin nodded. "Very well. I will call on you tomorrow."

I took a few steps forward then, and with my hand on the doorknob, glanced back at him. "Thanks," I said and walked out.

*
 *
Nine
 *
*
 *

The next day was pretty busy at the store. By the time I returned home, I found myself counting the minutes until the sun set. I couldn't stop thinking about the fact that I'd really screwed up with Sinjin the night before. It wasn't right that I'd let my own feelings of insecurity cause me to lambaste him. It would be shocking if he wanted anything more to do with me after I'd acted like such a terrified and insecure idiot.

I just didn't know what to make of Sinjin. Truth be told, I was still having trouble believing that he and I were in an actual relationship, that we were some sort of couple.

But you have to get over that, Jolie! I chided myself. *And you need to apologize to Sinjin for being such a Froot Loop!*

Yes, I'd made up my mind to try to fix whatever damage I'd done. As the sun started its final descent, I got dressed for the evening, deciding to put some extra attention into my hair by curling it. After spending the next ten minutes on my makeup, I emerged from my bedroom and caught my reflection in the mirror that hung over my couch. I looked halfway decent.

I was surprised by a knock at the door, but it was only the UPS man dropping off a box. I opened the door and waved hello to him as he climbed back into his truck and disappeared down the street. Glancing down, I eyed the small rectangular box before picking it up. There was no return address.

I closed the door behind me and placed the box on my kitchen table, reaching for the scissors to open it. Inside there was another box—a white gift box. I opened it and found a small green box with fake peonies affixed to the top, a little hummingbird on top of the flowers. It was charming to say the least. Untying the purple ribbon that held the box together, I pulled off the top and glitter exploded all over my living room floor as if the contents had been under pressure.

"Dammit!" I said as I thought about the fact that I'd now have to vacuum. Needless to say, cleaning wasn't one of my favorite occupations.

But before I had a chance to whip out the old Hoover, the glitter on the floor started moving like a mini twister on my living room carpet, hoisting the glassy specks into a whirlwind.

And then before I could take another breath, the glitter formed into the outline of a person, which gradually evolved into a hologram of Rand standing before me.

My first thought was to put the top back on the box, in the hope that it would undo everything that had just happened, but when I did Rand and the glitter remained. I was thinking of trying the vacuum on the hologram when it started speaking.

"Because you won't let me anywhere near you, I recorded this message so that I could explain some things to you," he began.

Even though it was just a recording and Rand wasn't really standing in the middle of my living room, I still felt on edge. I crossed my arms against my chest and continued watching, reminding myself that I was safe.

But are you really safe? my inner voice piped up. *Rand's a warlock, so who's to say you didn't just release a spell?*

Well, if I had just opened Pandora's box, there wasn't

much I could do about it now. And as far as I could tell, nothing of a worrisome nature was happening. I mean, I didn't feel as if I were on the receiving end of a spell, and it wasn't like anything threatening or dangerous had come out of the box. Instead I just focused on the hologram of Rand.

"You won't be able to turn this off until I've said everything I need to say," he continued. "It's up to you whether or not you listen to any of it."

"Fine," I said, but then I realized it was ridiculous because I was essentially talking to myself.

"Jolie, you need to know the truth. There is a whole history you're missing, a history between you and me." He took a deep breath. "And that history is why you can feel that there is an incredible bond between us. I feel it too, and even if you don't want to admit it to yourself, I think you know it's real and valid."

The visual of Rand faded and was replaced with what appeared to be images cycling in the mini twister of glitter. I took a few steps closer, not quite able to make out the dancing pictures from where I'd been standing. Once I came closer, the cyclone began to slow and a picture began to take shape, delineating itself into something I recognized. It was the inside of a mansion, the same one I'd seen in my visions of the masquerade party when I'd supposedly been contacting Rose Pierson's boyfriend. I watched an image of myself, again dressed in the garb of a fairy, walking into a ballroom, only to be greeted by Sinjin, dressed in the costume of a vampire.

"This is how it truly happened, Jolie," Rand narrated over the images before me. "You met Sinjin two years ago at a masquerade party held for the creatures of the Underworld."

I shook my head, not wanting to believe a word of it. I had no memory of this, nothing that would in any way help me believe it. It was just Rand's artifice again, his powers of persuasion.

That image of the mansion died away, only to be replaced with one of Christa and me standing in the living room of a house I didn't recognize.

"This is Pelham Manor, my home in Alnwick, England. You and Christa moved here with me so I could act as your protector and tutor," Rand continued as the image of his living room died away, replaced with pictures of verdant forests and open pasture where bubbles of light frolicked in nature. "You learned from the fae, Jolie. They taught you everything you know."

I shook my head, not understanding how any of this could be true. I didn't even know what fae were. Fairies, I guessed.

"I know you don't know what to think," he continued. "That all of this sounds crazy to you and you have no memories of it."

I seconded that. I didn't know what to think. I didn't want to believe it, couldn't imagine how it could be true—and if it was true, what did that mean about Sinjin?

It means he's been lying to you all along, I answered myself.

How, though? You know you first met him when he had a flat tire (even if he orchestrated the flat tire) outside your store.

"I know this is going to sound absurd, Jolie," Rand continued. I couldn't really imagine anything sounding more absurd than what he'd already concocted. "This is all possible because time was altered," he finished.

"What does that mean?" I demanded, even as I realized he couldn't hear me. I was merely talking to a projection of him. 'Course, he was a warlock, a practitioner of magic, so maybe he could hear me.

"I am certain you have questions about all of this and

I can answer all of them, Jolie. We need to meet in person."

Well, that figured.

"I just need you to trust me, Jolie," he continued. "Everything you think you know isn't real. This wasn't the way it was supposed to happen. Time was manipulated and this is the outcome."

I still didn't fully grasp what the hell he was talking about. What was the difference between time travel and time manipulation? Was I supposed to believe that Sinjin—or was it Rand—had stepped into a local time machine and pulled a Marty McFly on me? Not likely.

"I just hope you will be open to the possibilities, Jolie."

The images died away then and the image of Rand returned. He seemed pensive, as if he were pondering his next words. He glanced up at me and amazingly seemed to make eye contact with me even though he was just a hologram. It was eerie and sort of spooked me out.

"I never meant to frighten you," he said and then paused, sighing. "Nothing has worked out the way I hoped it would so far. I would never hurt you, Jolie. Please believe that."

And then the vision blinked a few times and disappeared into the air as if it had never been. I glanced down to see that the glittery particles were also gone. All that remained was the little green box with the peonies and the hummingbird.

And as for me? I was at a complete loss. I just didn't understand how any of this could be true, how Sinjin could have actually met me in a situation I didn't remember, wasn't familiar with. Or how I had apparently spent so much time with Rand, when as far as I was aware, I'd only met him a few days ago.

The answer is time travel, a voice rang out within me.

This is ridiculous! I thought back. *I can't believe I'm even entertaining the possibility.*

Well, you believe in vampires, warlocks, and witches, right? What's a little time travel then?

I shook my head. *No, I don't believe it, I won't believe it. Nothing that warlock said is true. Sinjin said Rand is only trying to control me, that he's dangerous and I should stay away from him.*

And that was when I made up my mind not to put any trust in Rand.

I was agitated, nervous about the fact that Rand knew where I lived. How he'd gotten my address was anyone's guess, but it made me feel like I wasn't safe in my own house anymore—that any moment he could drop by in person.

Hurrying to the Jetta, I buckled up, started the car, and backed out of my garage, heading for Sinjin's. I needed to see him, now more than ever before, needing the strength of his embrace. And, furthermore, he would know what to do.

I drove the five minutes to Sinjin's house in silence. Well, the radio might have been on but I couldn't say I noticed it if it was. Instead I was trying to construct an apology for Sinjin, trying to think of a way to say I knew last night had been my fault, that I'd overreacted and, consequently, been a dumb-ass.

What if he doesn't accept your apology? I asked myself.

I took a deep breath. *That's a risk I'm going to run, I guess.*

At his house I didn't bother with parallel parking on the street out front. Instead I pulled into the driveway, hoping Sinjin wasn't planning on leaving anytime soon because I was completely blocking the garage.

Maybe he isn't here, I said to myself.

Well, there's only one way to find out.

I opened the car door and stood up, holding my head high as I steeled myself for what I was about to do.

Without waiting any longer, I closed the car door and strode up Sinjin's walkway, not pausing as I reached for the doorbell and pressed.

There was no answer, so I rang it again.

I was convinced he wasn't home, and had started to leave when I heard the door open. Feeling my heart in my throat, I turned to face Sinjin, my heart now racing.

"My pet?"

"I, uh, I came to tell you a few things," I started.

Sinjin just smiled at me languidly, as if he had no idea how stunningly handsome he was in his black shirt and slacks. "Oh?" he asked.

I cleared my throat, wondering where the speech that I had planned to make had gone. It was like it was hibernating and now I had only my nerves to rely on. "Yes," I said.

Sinjin chuckled and held the door wide. "Come in, my love, I do not like to see you shivering in the cold night air."

I didn't say anything but nodded and entered his house, trying to get my nerves in order.

"Come," he said and took my hand, leading me upstairs.

"Where are we going?" I demanded, all too aware that Sinjin's bedroom was upstairs.

"To my bedchamber," he answered nonchalantly. "I was repairing a faulty light switch."

I smiled at the thought of Sinjin repairing anything. He didn't really have the essence of "handyman."

"Okay," I said as I followed him up the stairs and into his bedroom, my heart in my throat the entire time.

"I am pleased to see you, love," he said. "I did not care for the way our last visit ended."

I swallowed hard. "About that," I started.

But then Sinjin turned his attention to me and smiled sweetly. He opened his arms and I smiled in return, falling into them. I rested my head against his chest and toyed with the buttons on his shirtfront.

"I am waiting," he said with a chuckle, his breath tickling the top of my ear.

I glanced up at him. Time for my apology. "I'm sorry I freaked out and stormed out of here," I said with a guilty smile. "This is all just pretty new for me and I guess I'm having a hard time with it."

Sinjin nodded. "Apology accepted."

I laughed and shook my head, pleased and relieved by the fact that Sinjin never seemed to take things too seriously, that he could find it in himself to see beyond my issues. "Thank you."

"And I would like to apologize as well, poppet."

I glanced at him curiously. "For what?"

"For leading you to believe that I do not care for you," he said, his eyes pools of concern. "The truth is very much the opposite."

I frowned. "I'm not sure you did lead me to believe that. I think it was just a conclusion I reached all on my own."

"I—hm." He cleared his throat and then smiled over at me as if he hadn't been about to just say something.

"You what?"

He swallowed hard and stepped away, turning his back on me as he faced the window. That was when I realized Sinjin may have been an all-powerful master vampire, but he had his own fear—showing emotion. It was as obvious as the tightness in his shoulders, the rigidity of his whole body.

"Finish what you were going to say, Sinjin," I said, wanting—no, needing—to hear the words from him.

Instead of turning to face me, he stared out at the clouds that were obscuring the moonlight. It made the dark night sky a fuzzy haze. It looked like the backdrop to a horror movie.

"I am not a man who confesses love," he said and turned around, facing me. His lips were tight. "It is not in my nature."

"I never asked for that, nor would I," I said immediately, thinking it ludicrous that he'd even brought the L-word up.

"The truth is that I have wanted to make you my own from the moment I met you," he said quickly, his eyes penetrating me to my core. He took a step closer. "I have lusted after your body, yes, but my need to possess you did not end there." He shook his head and continued inspecting me. "There is something about you that fascinates me." He paused for a few seconds. "You have always fascinated me."

I shook my head, refusing to allow my heart to rejoice because there was a time-line issue here—something that waved a red flag and prevented me from succumbing to the beauty of his sentiments. "You act as though we've known each other for a lot longer than we actually have."

"Perhaps that is because we have known each other in ways time cannot specify," he said simply. I felt my stomach drop. The vision of Sinjin at that masquerade party suddenly reared its ugly head again.

"What do you mean?" I demanded.

He shrugged, and whatever he was going to admit died on his tongue. "A day, a week, a month are mere moments of time, love. They mean nothing in terms of the soul's understanding. How can you qualify or, for that matter, quantify my feelings for you based on that?" He shook his head. "You cannot."

I couldn't argue with that, so I chose another tack. "Then what are you saying?"

He took a few steps closer to me until we were face-to-face, er, face-to-chest. "I am doing a rather poor job of explaining my desire to be your mentor, teacher, and protector. More urgently, my desire is to be your lover, the one man to capture your heart." He suddenly grabbed both of my arms, pulling me into him. He was going to kiss me; I could see it in his eyes. "I want to be the man who haunts your dreams and thoughts, the man whom you cannot live without."

I wasn't sure when it happened, but at some point during Sinjin's admission, I simply stopped breathing. Suddenly light-headed, I remembered my respiratory system and tried to take a deep breath but, before I could get a word out, Sinjin's mouth was on mine. His tongue immediately entered my mouth and I was shocked to find my body's response dominating my brain's. My tongue met his fervently and I felt myself lapping at him, wrapping my arms around his neck so that I was as close to him as possible. He pulled me even tighter to him with a moan, and I responded with feelings of lust that I'd kept bottled up for too long. Now they were refusing to be quelled until they were satiated.

And instantly everything was crystal clear.

I wanted Sinjin to make love to me.

I wasn't sure why I'd suddenly decided to seal the proverbial deal with a vampire, with Sinjin, but there was no going back. It was as if my body had suddenly tasted filet mignon after months of Spam.

I pulled away from his embrace and looked into his eyes, wondering how such an incredible man had arrived in my life, how I had been so lucky. But there was also a part of me, in true Jolie Wilkins form, that wanted to prevent myself from moving to Heartbreak Avenue. I couldn't allow those feelings of doubt to penetrate me now, though. Not now when whatever I was feeling for Sinjin seemed to be natural, right.

"Sinjin, swear to me that everything you said is true," I whispered, knowing that whatever we did here tonight was going to change everything. Yes, I was attached to

Sinjin now. But I also knew myself well enough to know that if I had sex with him, I would become even more attached, and if our relationship failed, my anguish would be all the worse.

Anguish if it fails . . .

Who am I kidding? Sinjin is a vampire; of course it will fail!

But there was something in me that wanted to take the leap anyway, to believe in what could be. *And, really, who's to say that a vampire can't sustain a healthy emotional relationship?*

Um, he's been around for six hundred years, so chances are he's going to get bored with you in, oh, I'd say a week—max. I mean, come on, he's got 572 years on you! What could you possibly offer him? How could you even hope to prolong his interest?

Shut up, you stupid voice!

"Poppet," Sinjin started, tearing my attention from my mental debate and refocusing it on the beauty of his ice-blue eyes. "Sometimes I marvel at the thoughts going through that brain of yours," he finished and chuckled, shaking his head in apparent wonder.

I smiled, embarrassed. "Sorry . . . I, uh, sometimes get into arguments with myself."

"Why does that not surprise me?" His archangel's grin combined with a cocked eyebrow told me he was nothing if not amused. But a few seconds later, the look of delight was replaced by a solemn expression. "Everything I have told you is true, love, and it reflects my innermost feelings." He studied my face and became silent as he secured a stray tendril of hair behind my ear. Then he added, "You have certainly burrowed your way into my heart—something I never imagined could happen."

I felt warmth penetrating me at his words, and even though something inside me still doubted them, and must have recognized the fact that I was walking out on an emotional limb, I didn't care. I had never pursued a man before, and it was time for me to step out of my comfort zone. I knew I would never forgive myself if I didn't. Sinjin Sinclair was not the type of man who came into your life every day. He was a once-in-a-lifetime prospect, and I wasn't about to let him get away. "Sinjin, I want to know that this will be lasting . . . something long-term."

He stayed silent but continued gazing at me. Something in his expression, however, seemed out of place—a triumphant gleam just beyond the ice-blue veil of his eyes. "It will last as long as you will allow it, love." He took a deep breath that, once again, was only for show. "I have always been by your side, poppet, and so shall I always remain."

I could feel the smile spreading across my lips, involuntarily echoing the joy that was blooming within me. "Then you aren't opposed to a real relationship?"

He smiled. "Nothing would please me more."

And that was enough for me. Without another word, I tightened my hold around his neck, pulling him closer to me. I closed my eyes and felt his lips on mine, and this time, his kiss was hungry, needy—seemingly insatiable. He pulled me into him, and I could feel his hardness beneath his pants. I felt the flame of excitement radiate through my entire being as a sense of weightlessness flashed through me.

Somehow—and I wasn't sure what I'd done to warrant the gift; this incredible man, this exquisite (dare I say it?) *vampire*, had fallen for me . . . Me! It was almost too good to be true. Thankfully, I was beyond the point of self-doubt now. No, I was a new Jolie Wilkins—like a phoenix rising from the ashes of the old wallflower. Someone who now acted without doubt, someone who was going to blaze her own way in the world and stake her claim.

I caught my breath, surprised to discover that I was panting. I had to tell him what I wanted—no, needed. "Sinjin, I want you to make love to me."

He said nothing, merely stared at me for a few seconds, a smile on his lips. Then he hoisted me into his arms and started for the bed. I couldn't breathe—couldn't force myself to inhale or exhale. "You do not know how I have longed to hear those words, love," he said in a deep, throaty voice.

But I couldn't take my eyes away from his fangs as a tremor of fear and excitement erupted through me. "Are you going to bite me?"

"Only if you want me to, but as I mentioned, it would be painful as you are a witch."

Somehow the idea of Sinjin feeding from me was the most enticing, erotic thought possible. I couldn't even fathom the idea of pain. I didn't even hesitate. "I want you to."

He chuckled heartily and, standing above me, eyed me up and down with approval.

"Sinjin?" I started.

"Shh." He shook his head as his gaze raked me from head to toe. "I want to paint every moment with you into my memory, poppet."

"I had no idea you were such a poet," I said with a nervous laugh.

How are you going to go through with this? You aren't like Christa, Jolie. You haven't had sex in . . . how long?

Shut it!

God, you can't even remember because it's been so long. What if he thinks you're a total bore in the sack? What if . . .

I closed my eyes and shook my head, ordering those damn voices in my brain to take a hike. Then I remembered I wasn't alone and my eyes shot open as I focused on my incredibly handsome bed partner.

He smiled down at me, seemingly unaware of the debate going on inside me. "You incite the poet within me."

I didn't say anything more—I just watched him watching me, not sure what I should say or do. Sinjin didn't seem concerned, acting as if he had all the time in the world to do nothing but stare at me.

"Please remove your blouse, love," he said at last in a husky voice. He stood at the foot of the bed, his feet shoulder-width apart and arms crossed against his chest. He looked every inch the dark rogue, his longish hair mussed and falling forward, one lock obstructing his right eye.

Sinjin Sinclair was the absolute epitome of God's gift to women and I couldn't stop gloating over the fact that I was the woman lucky enough to have him. Then a realization dawned on me and I had to correct myself—God had nothing to do with the creation of Sinjin Sinclair. But for some reason, that thought didn't scare me.

I gulped down the sudden embarrassment that overtook me at the thought of undressing in front of him. But with Sinjin in attendance, there was no room for modesty or shame. I glanced down at the white, long-sleeved, button-up shirt I was wearing and my fingers suddenly felt like they had weights attached to them as I fumbled with the buttons. Eventually, I managed to undo one and then two, and before I knew it, I'd reached the final button. I glanced up at Sinjin to find his gaze wholly fixed on me, and somehow the intensity of his stare gave me the strength to let the blouse fall off my arms. I glanced down at my white lace bra and back up at Sinjin again.

"Take it off," he said.

Ten

I flushed at Sinjin's straightforward and commanding words. Reaching behind me, I unhinged the clasp of my bra and pulled slightly, the straps loosening and tumbling down my shoulders. I felt a blush steal over my cheeks, but I ignored it and allowed the bra to fall on the bed and took a deep breath.

Sinjin's eyes focused on my bare breasts, a smile spreading across a face that had to be sculpted by the devil himself.

"How stunning you are," he whispered. "As I always knew you would be."

I stood up and started approaching him, but he held me back with the palm of his hand. "No," he said firmly. "I want to watch you."

I stopped and glanced down at my jeans and wedge sandals. When I kicked them off, my height dropped about three inches and I felt the cold hardwood floor against my bare feet. I returned my eyes to Sinjin almost as if I was looking to him for direction. His gaze was steadily fixed on my face and I could tell that he was recording every second of this, permanently imprinting it into my memory.

I smiled as I unzipped my jeans, then I pulled them down the sides of my hips and allowed them to crumple at my ankles before stepping out of them. When I faced

Sinjin again, he was staring at my black lace panties—thong panties. Thank God I'd at least taken one lesson from Christa in the sexuality department and traded in my granny panties for one of Victoria's secrets.

"Turn around," he commanded.

And suddenly I was overcome with the feeling of supreme control, of power. The need and desire in Sinjin's eyes were overwhelming, and the idea that I was causing his disquiet was something that wholly appealed to me. This was an example of the age-old battle of the sexes, and at this point, I thought I was winning.

So I turned around slowly, allowing him to admire my backside as much as he appreciated my front. When I faced him again, he said nothing, merely stared at me with those pale blue eyes that were now on fire, a subtle reddish glow behind his pupils.

"Your eyes," I started.

"Remove your panties," he interrupted, obviously not concerned about his eyes.

I slid my fingers beneath each side of my panties and pulled them down, saying a silent prayer that I wouldn't pass out. I stepped out of the black lace thong, steeling my courage, and glanced up at Sinjin. He was staring at me with an intensity I'd never seen before.

"I have dreamed of this moment for what seems an eternity, love," he said as the fire behind his eyes continued to burn.

Before I could respond, he was instantly beside me, using his incredible vampire speed to meld with the air, only to be spat out a moment later. I inhaled sharply as he pulled me to him and I felt the coldness of his body against me. But after a few seconds, his body temperature warmed to mine.

He kissed me and splayed his hands across my back, grabbing my butt and pulling me into him so I could feel his obvious excitement for me. I looped my arms around his neck and met his tongue, feeling consumed by an incendiary need, burning with a passion the likes of which I'd never known.

Sinjin broke away and observed me with an expression I'd never seen from him before. If I didn't know better, I might have said it resembled . . . love? But, no, that was my female brain speaking. Sinjin had made it very clear that he didn't have it in him to fall in love—or at least, that he'd never admit to it. I wasn't sure why it had seemed okay at the time, because now, the thought bothered me. It bothered me because I knew I could fall in love with him. That is to say, if I weren't already . . .

"I will never disappoint you, poppet," he whispered and tilted my chin so I could see the promise in his eyes. "I know you cannot understand our connection yet, but you will, in time."

I said nothing—simply nodded, letting him finish.

"I will remain your protector and destroy anyone who would cause you harm. I will be, first, foremost, and forever, your loyal subject, and I will stop at nothing to bring a smile to your beautiful face."

"I don't want you to be my subject, Sinjin," I started, frowning. "I want us to be equals. As much as you want to do for me, I want to do for you."

But Sinjin just chuckled as if he knew more than I did, as if there was more to this picture than I could possibly grasp. I didn't respond. I just held his gaze instead as the smile ran away from his face. He pushed me toward the bed and I acquiesced, lying down as he stood above me and watched me, his gaze penetrating my body from head to toe. He pulled his black V-neck sweater over his broad shoulders, followed by his black T-shirt. I felt myself smiling as I admired the ridges and valleys of his bare torso.

"I thought vampires were supposed to be pale?" I asked, appreciating his tan skin.

He laughed. "We remain exactly as we were at the time we were changed."

"I see," I said as I focused on his pants. Then, in my best Sinjin voice, I added: "Remove your trousers."

He chuckled and shook his head, smiling down at me and said: "I have missed you." He started unbuttoning his pants and I didn't even have time to wonder what he meant by missing me, because before I knew it, he was standing in front of me completely naked.

And I was in . . . awe. "Wow," I said, smiling, not even bothering to pull my attention away from his erection, which was, in a word . . . sizable. "Um, I haven't been with anyone in a really long time, Sinjin," I started, worry squeaking in my voice.

He arched a brow and smiled at me. "I will take my time."

I just nodded and said nothing more as I watched him kneel down and grab each of my knees, pulling me to the end of the bed. He pushed my legs apart.

"What are you doing?" I started, my tone betraying my concern.

"What I have wanted to do since we met," he answered with a mischievous smile as he pressed his face between my legs. My pelvis shot off the bed as soon as I felt his tongue lapping at me, and it took me a good few seconds to calm down. Once I did, I felt my body begin its own rhythm as Sinjin's tongue worked to bring me to climax.

I wasn't sure what to expect regarding the prowess of my six-hundred-year-old lover, but he definitely understood how to pleasure a woman. He was experienced and then some. But the last thing I wanted to think about was Sinjin's sexual conquests. Instead I focused on the sensation of his tongue as I gripped the sheets—hard. When he pulled away from me, I opened my eyes and looked at him with confusion.

"I want to hear you, love," he groaned out, the blue of his eyes eclipsed by white. I heard myself gasp, but I wasn't frightened. I just nodded dumbly and watched him resume his place between my legs as he started licking me again, still looking up at me. I dropped my head back and closed my eyes, feeling my body begin to convulse as an orgasm shook me. I opened my mouth and moaned, my hips undulating against him.

He pulled away from me and chuckled, staring down at me with a hungry expression. He spread my legs farther apart and positioned himself between them, rubbing me up and down with one finger before plunging it deep within me. I arched up against him, gripping the sheets again, and closed my eyes, filled with anticipation.

Then I remembered. I glanced at him and smiled. "I want you to drink from me, Sinjin," I said in a breathless voice.

He was already on top of me and I could feel his penis at my entry, as if it was waiting for permission to impale me. He smiled broadly and bent down, kissing my neck as he did so. His hips ground against me, promising what was soon to be. I gripped his back and hugged him tightly, wanting nothing more than to feel him thrust inside me.

"Remember what I told you earlier? Because my glamour is useless on you, my bite will cause you pain," he whispered into my ear. "But you possess the ability to ignore the pain by way of your magic."

"Ignore it?" I repeated, utterly confused.

He drew up from me and nodded, his gaze riveting, beautiful. "You are a powerful witch, my little poppet. You must bewitch yourself into enduring my bite without suffering my sting."

"How do I do that?"

"Close your eyes and focus," he responded matter-of-factly, like it was no big deal.

"I don't even know what that means," I muttered, wondering if this whole Sinjin-drinking-from-me thing was going to pan out.

"Close your eyes," he said softly, so I did as he commanded. I could feel his lips on my neck again, kissing a trail down to my breasts. "Focus now, love, order your body to numb itself, not to feel the pain of my bite."

"But I want to feel you," I argued.

He chuckled. "You will feel me, love; of that I have no doubt. But you must free yourself of the pain. If you were a mere human, I would glamour you myself."

And suddenly the idea of being a mere human held lots of appeal. "How do I convince myself not to feel pain?" I asked, my eyes still closed.

"Concentrate," he answered. Before I could insist on a better answer, I felt him thrust inside me. I arched against him, a moan escaping my lips as his mouth moved to my breasts, sucking and toying with my nipples. I squeezed his back more tightly, opening my eyes to find his riveted on me.

"Are you in distress, love?" he asked, smiling down at me.

"No," I managed to say between rapid breaths as I pushed my pelvis forward. "I want all of you."

He chuckled again and drove deeper as my grip tightened and I could feel my nails burrowing into the soft skin of his back. I moaned as he pushed inside me still harder. Before I knew it, he was fully ensconced within me, thrusting inside me even faster.

I glanced up at him and saw that his fangs were fully distended—white, sharp, and long. I wanted nothing more than to feel them puncturing the virginal skin of my neck. I wanted them sinking into me as Sinjin lapped up my blood.

"I want all of you," I repeated, hoping he understood my intentions.

"Love, not if you are not prepared," he started.

I shook my head. "I don't care. I want to feel you."

He didn't say anything more, but he continued to watch me as he thrust inside me and pulled all the way out again, teasing me torturously.

"This moment belongs to me and I will never forget a single second of it," he whispered, staring at me with unbridled passion.

"I want to feel your bite," I repeated, not allowing him to change the subject.

He smiled at the same time that he thrust into me again and I arched up to receive him more deeply. I was on the brink of another orgasm—I could feel it in the distance, just slightly out of reach. Then Sinjin's fingers landed on the sensitive nub between my thighs, and something blossomed inside me, spreading throughout my core as I began moaning uncontrollably with pleasure. And that was when he did it.

I felt a burning pain when he sank his teeth into my neck. I couldn't even register it, though, because my body was showered in the most intense orgasm I'd ever experienced. Sinjin's timing had been impeccable. He pulled his fangs out as he began sucking at my wound. His fingers dug into the linens as he continued driving his shaft into me, his rhythm becoming more and more urgent. Each thrust was stronger and faster than the one before.

"Yes, Sinjin, yes!" I ground out between clenched teeth, reveling in the feel of his body as he quenched his thirst on me. He lifted his face and I could see the red of my blood spilling from his mouth. He closed his eyes, and his head dropped back as he swallowed. When he faced me again, the stain of my blood was on his lips. But there was nothing in me that was frightened or turned off. Instead, I cherished the fact that I could provide his sustenance, that I was sharing myself with him in the ultimate fashion.

His eyes were on fire again, no longer white but a burnished red, like embers. "You taste," he began and then shook his head as if he had no words. He opened his eyes and before I could respond, he dropped his head to my breasts, taking one in his mouth. He sucked and teased my nipple ruthlessly before sinking his fangs into the soft flesh above it. I squirmed beneath him, at the pain as well as the sensation of his fingers stroking between my legs. I hadn't even realized he'd pulled out of me until he entered me again and began pumping inside me as he sucked savagely at my breast.

I felt another orgasm seize me. I grasped the back of his head, pushing his mouth against me harder and allowing the orgasm to crest to its peak as I screamed out his name. He drove into me with renewed zest only to pull his face away from my breast at the same time that he withdrew from me. Then he sank his teeth into the soft skin of my inner thigh. He pushed two fingers inside me and I was suddenly struck with the realization that my vampire had an insatiable libido.

"I have to feel you inside me again, Sinjin," I managed, beginning to smart from the pain of his bite. As long as he was inside me, the pain didn't register.

"As you wish, love," he said with a smile and pushed into me with one quick stroke, making me gasp beneath him in response. He made no motion to bite me again, but he continued to watch me with spellbinding eyes. His jaw tightened and his eyes narrowed, which had to mean one thing.

"I want to watch you," I whispered to him, wanting to witness his orgasm. "Do it for me, Sinjin."

He said nothing; he just closed his eyes and continued to pump hard and fast into me. A few moments later he threw his head back, fangs fully extended, and moaned loudly. Then he opened his eyes and focused them on me again.

"Wow," I said with a smile.

He pulled himself out of me and collapsed on the bed beside me. I rolled onto my side so I could face him. He looked at me and smiled. "That, poppet, exceeded even my expectations."

I felt myself flush as I realized just how happy I was. I could honestly say I was happier than I had been in years. "Thank you," I said in a soft voice.

"Thank you?" he asked with surprise.

"You've renewed my hope in men," I said with a little laugh. "I never imagined in my wildest dreams anything could be this . . . perfect."

He chuckled and ran his fingers down my face. "Thus begins day one, little poppet."

I laughed and relaxed against him, relishing the feel of his naked body pressed up against mine. I felt his fingers as they caressed my upper arm, lazily drawing loops. I couldn't imagine a time when I had felt this content, this complete. I wasn't afraid of warlocks, I wasn't concerned with what it meant to be a witch, and I was also amazed to find that my thoughts weren't revolving around indecision and doubt.

I just was.

And it was a feeling that I loved wholeheartedly, a feeling that Sinjin had allowed me to achieve.

No, this is your doing, Jolie, this is the person you were meant to be, that inner voice piped up.

Sinjin opened my eyes, he is responsible for bringing me out of my solitude, I argued.

Sinjin might have acted as a vehicle but you're responsible for your own actions. He might have helped you to find your way but everything you are today is due to the choices you've made, Jolie.

Hmm, I like that.

The more I thought about it, the more I realized that I truly had shaped my own destiny, merely because I'd been open to it. Yes, Sinjin had given me the opportunity, but he hadn't imbued my powers within me. That was purely 100 percent Jolie Wilkins, and for the first time in a long time I was proud of myself.

But of course Sinjin played an enormous role in this metamorphosis of self. It was almost as if Sinjin had warded all those negative feelings of doubt and fear away, as if merely being with him kept my bogeymen locked in the closet. I glanced up at him and smiled, rolling over onto my side again so I could gaze at him, overwhelmed by his beauty and perfection.

"What are you doing, love?" he asked, a chuckle in his tone.

"I just want to look at you," I whispered and traced the outline of his face, running my fingers over his lush lips and losing myself in the vibrant blue of his eyes.

"Are you happy?" he asked. I didn't answer right away, instead pondering the question.

Yes, I was happy. Absolutely happy. Happier than I had been in a very long time. I'd thought I was happy while living my solitary and lonely life with only a cat and Christa to call my friends. But the truth was I'd been fooling myself—I hadn't really been living, just going through the motions day after day but not allowing myself to experience true life, afraid to witness pain and disappointment so I shut out all emotions, including love, excitement, adventure.

"I can't remember the last time I was this happy," I said softly. "I feel alive, Sinjin, almost like I've been asleep for the last ten years or so and I've suddenly woken up."

"My sleeping beauty," Sinjin whispered into my ear.

I nodded. "Yes, that's what it feels like. I just never

knew there was such an amazing world out there, complete with incredibly handsome and sexy vampires," I finished and giggled as he cocked a brow, obviously amused.

"I cannot tell you how much that pleases me to know." His eyes were sharp, as if they could look right through me. "I want nothing more than your happiness."

"I . . ." But he never let me finish, interrupting me instead.

"I hope you will always remember, poppet, that everything I said or did was only to ensure your happiness."

I swallowed hard, finding it an odd thing for him to say. "You have done nothing but support me, teach me, and look out for me. Of course I'll always remember that."

"Very good," he said with a smile.

And then it dawned on me that it could have been Rand who walked through my store before Sinjin ever had, given how determined he had been to find me. I could have succumbed to Rand's treachery, and had the so-called wool pulled over my eyes. I sighed heavily as I thought about it, so relieved that things had worked out the way they had, that Sinjin had beaten Rand to the punch. "I'm so glad you found me," I said. "So happy it was you and not Rand."

And that was when I remembered Rand and his little gift. I felt the smile drop off my lips.

Sinjin sat up instantly. "What is wrong?"

I took a deep breath and frowned. "I forgot to tell you my other bit of news."

"What, poppet," he said and took my hand, squeezing it in his own.

"I received a package," I started and then told him the story about the box, the glitter, the holographic Rand and the images he'd sent me. The entire time Sinjin's mouth was tight, his composure clearly strained. "I don't understand it, Sinjin," I finished. "What was he talking about with the time-travel stuff?"

"Nothing," Sinjin replied quickly and shifted uncomfortably. "It is nothing but bunk, drivel. As I mentioned before, the warlock wishes only to gain your confidence, your trust. He recognizes your abilities, and he seeks to control them and you." He took my cheeks between his hands and turned my face toward his. "You must believe none of it, my love. He wishes only to undermine me, to turn you against me."

"I will never be turned against you, Sinjin," I said softly.

Sinjin nodded and cupped my chin, smiling down at me. "I will never allow anyone to harm you, Jolie," he said and kissed my lips.

Eleven

A few hours after our marathon lovemaking session, I found myself alone. Sinjin had announced that the dawn was coming and he would have to leave me for the day. That was when it hit me. Sinjin and I would never witness the beauty of a sunrise together, never see the world bathed in that beautiful nascent pink. We would never spend the day at the beach, watching children play in the waves under an August sun. And speaking of children, Sinjin and I would never have any—vampires were unable to procreate. The more I thought about it, the more it bothered me.

Is everything in life a trade-off, then? I asked myself. Sinjin was basically the perfect guy in every way but one . . . he was a vampire. And even that was arguable, because there were aspects of his vampirism that could definitely be considered benefits. His incredible strength and speed, for one, and the fact that he could live forever . . .

Yeah, but you won't live forever.

I felt my breath catch, and I had to ask myself why this had only just occurred to me. I mean, the realization that I would grow old while Sinjin remained just as gorgeous and young as ever should have been one of my first thoughts after I'd discovered what he was.

I don't care, part of me declared. *Sinjin is everything I could ever want in a man. He's funny, kind, thoughtful, and extremely intelligent. He's protective, not afraid of commitment, financially well off, and incredibly attractive. And he's amazing in bed! I mean, what more could a woman want?*

Jolie, stop kidding yourself—you've always wanted a two-story house with a picket fence and two kids running through the yard.

But Sinjin was the only man I'd ever met whom I'd even consider as a possible partner for my "two-story with a picket fence" scenario. How cruel fate was, offering me someone so perfect when there was no chance of us having a real future together.

Besides, he's made it pretty clear that he isn't the fall-ing-in-love type. I felt my heart sink.

Although it seemed as if Sinjin was falling for me just as, er, well, almost as quickly as I was for him, I still couldn't ignore the fact that he had *purposefully* an-nounced he wasn't into admitting to any sort of love.

And, really, where did that leave me?

Don't give up on him, my optimistic side said. *Don't give up on him, because you are already in love with him.*

I took a deep breath at the very thought that I could be in love with Sinjin. Was I? Could I be? The more I considered it, though, the more I had to admit to myself that I absolutely was head over heels in love with him. I mean, really, how could I not be? He was basically like a knight in shining armor: someone who had ridden into my life and opened me up to a world I never knew ex-isted, helped me see truths about myself I never would have otherwise known. There was a whole new world waiting for me, complete with creatures that had previ-ously only existed in my dreams . . . or nightmares. And while that realization was frightening in itself, knowing that Sinjin would serve as my teacher and guardian somehow made it seem a little less daunting.

Sinjin Sinclair was my sworn protector, teacher, friend, confidant, ally, and lover. And I was in love with him—it was as obvious as the fact that he was a vampire.

Then why should it matter that you won't be able to have his children? I asked myself.

Hmm, I guess maybe it doesn't matter . . .

And furthermore, what do you care if you never watch a sunrise or sunset with him? Sunlight isn't all it's cracked up to be anyway, you know. It's responsible for freckles, sunburns, skin cancer . . .

Okay, okay, I get it. I paused at the realization now dawning within me. *I guess I'm okay with loving Sinjin and seeing where it will go.*

But what about my getting older while he stays young?

Hmm, that was a problem that I couldn't discount quite so easily. But I also didn't need to solve it today.

I climbed out of Sinjin's bed and took a deep breath, looking down through the window as the sun's beams glittered on the pool's surface, looking like thousands of diamonds. I turned back to the king-sized bed; half the linens were twisted up on the floor, and the fitted sheet hung off one side of the mattress. I smiled to myself and set about making the bed, almost regretting the fact that I was destroying evidence that I'd had the best sex of my life last night. I couldn't help the flush that stained my cheeks. According to Sinjin, he'd never forget our first night together; I knew I wouldn't either. It was chiseled into my memory, and I already looked forward to re-playing it endlessly.

I scanned the room for my clothing and I found the garments strewn around as haphazardly as if a hurricane had blown through the room. Still in a sex fog, I dressed slowly, and once I was decent, I opened the door,

a small piece of paper on the floor taking my attention.
I picked it up and unfolded it, reading:

My lovely little poppet,
   Your breakfast awaits you in the kitchen.
   Last evening was magical and I am most excited to
repeat it this eve.
   I will dream of you.
                 ~ Sinjin

I couldn't help the smile that curled across my lips.
I folded the note into a small triangle and put it in
my pocket, knowing that I'd refer to it countless times
today—to reread it and to admire the neat curlicues and
flourishes of Sinjin's calligraphic handwriting.

I took the stairs two at a time and entered the kitchen,
where a bouquet of red roses was sitting in a vase of
water on the black granite countertop. Beside that was a
plate full of croissants, biscuits, muffins, and Danishes;
beside those was a bowl containing a mound of melon
slices, grapes, strawberries, and bananas.

"Wow, Sinjin," I whispered with a smile as I plopped
a few grapes into my mouth, helping myself to a croissant. I took a seat on one of his bar stools and leaned
over to smell the roses. This whole thing was just so
unbelievable—such a perfect fairy tale. Wasn't this exactly what every woman dreamed of—a man, er, a vampire, as amazing as Sinjin in the looks department who
was also just as caring?

And suddenly I was angry with myself—angry that I'd
ever doubted the future of a relationship with Sinjin in
the first place. He was just so incredibly sweet and . . .
good. And what was more, he made me happy. In fact, I
couldn't remember the last time I'd been this completely
content, this thrilled with my life.

After finishing the croissant, a handful of strawberries, and a few melon wedges, I couldn't eat any more. I got off the stool and searched through the kitchen drawers, looking for some Saran Wrap, but found them completely bare. Reluctantly, I put the uncovered bowl of fruit in his fridge, which was just as empty as the rest of his kitchen, and, grabbing the bouquet, started for the door. I made up my mind to stop off at Bed Bath & Beyond on the way to my shop and get Sinjin all the accoutrements of a well-stocked kitchen. Granted, he probably wouldn't ever use any of them, but I would.

Beeping my Jetta unlocked, I closed Sinjin's door behind me before having second thoughts and locking it. I mean, it was daytime, after all, and Sinjin couldn't protect himself. As soon as that thought dawned on me, I felt bogged down with worry. Sinjin was basically as helpless as a turtle on its back during the day. Hmm, we would have to have a discussion regarding his safety this evening . . .

I jogged across the street, got in my car, and started it as I glanced at the clock.

"Shit," I said, remembering that my first client of the day was due in twenty minutes. My trip to Bed Bath & Beyond would have to wait until my lunch break.

I peeled out into the street and gunned it, happy to find that I didn't hit any red lights on the way. When I pulled up to my store, I noticed Christa's red Camaro in front and breathed a sigh of relief that she'd managed to open the store on time. Her punctuality was usually fifty-fifty. I parked behind her, grabbed the bouquet, and sprinted to the front door.

"Ahem," she said as she glanced up at me, an irritated frown marring her pretty and otherwise perfectly made-up face. I handed her my purse, which she accepted and put underneath the counter, where we both kept our bags. "Did someone forget it was a school day?"

I smiled guiltily. "Um, yeah, sort of lost track of time."

She narrowed her eyes on me and cocked a brow as her gaze dropped to my neck. "Looks like Mr. Vampire got a little carried away."

My hand immediately rose to my neck, where I felt the two telltale punctures. I hurried to the bathroom and looked in the mirror, turning my head to the side to see how bad the damage was. The two bite marks were red and raised, looking swollen and irritated. "It's bad," I said once I noticed Christa behind me.

She handed me the pink scarf I insisted she keep in the drawer underneath the cash register. Why? Because Christa had come into the store more than once with hickeys all over her neck. Luckily for me, the hickey wrap was now going to come in very handy.

"Did it hurt?" she asked.

"No . . . well, maybe a little but I barely noticed because we were . . . doing other things."

She sighed and shook her head, crossing her arms against her chest. "So he finally got some vag?"

I glanced over my shoulder at her and frowned. "Oh my God, Chris, do you have to be so . . . so gross?"

She sighed. "Okay, so he finally got to lick your cupcake?"

I laughed. I couldn't help it. And then, remembering the moment when Sinjin devoured my so-called cupcake, I smiled, feeling a blush steal across my cheeks. "Yeah, you could say that."

"And you didn't even call to tell me?" she demanded, following me into the front of the store. I glanced at the clock on the wall and noticed we had five minutes until my client was due.

"Well, I didn't really have time to call you, Chris." I shot her a look over my shoulder. "I mean, I am late this morning, in case you didn't notice."

She muttered something unintelligible, but I couldn't say my mind was on her. Instead, I couldn't help but

focus on the beautiful woman who had just walked
through my front door.

With her arms crossed against her chest, she didn't
look happy. Well, happy or not, she was unarguably
stunning. She looked like one of those femme fatales in
the James Bond movies—perfect hourglass figure, large
breasts, tiny waist, and generous hips. Her oval face
finished in a square jaw and extremely high cheekbones, which emphasized her incredibly shapely, full
lips. Her hair had a reddish tinge but was overall dark,
and she had to have the most beautiful skin I'd ever
seen. She was dressed in fitted black slacks and a low-cut,
ivory satin blouse with heels that were so high, she appeared to be over six feet tall.

But despite her incredible beauty, there was something
hard about her, something bitchy.

"Which one of you is Jolie Wilkins?" she asked, glancing between us. She had an American accent, which surprised me; her looks gave her a certain foreign vibe.

"Um, that's me," I answered and stepped forward.

She arched a brow at me, taking me in from head to
toe and frowned, seemingly unimpressed. "Sinjin sent
me."

"You know Sinjin?" I asked, feeling my heart plum-
met to the floor. Almost immediately, jealousy began to
well up within me.

*How does she know Sinjin? And furthermore, why
is Sinjin carrying on with such an incredibly beautiful
woman?*

They must have been an item in the past.

Who knows, maybe they're an item now?

*Don't think that or you'll just drive yourself crazy.
Besides, it isn't fair to Sinjin to just make assumptions.*

*Remember what happens when you assume. You make
an ass of u and me.*

I shook my head, forcing the voices to shut the hell up.

"Yes, I know Sinjin," the mystery woman said hurriedly, like it was a given since she was here and he'd apparently sent her.

"Who are you?" I asked, not liking the fact that she knew who I was and yet I had no clue who she was or why she was here. "And why did Sinjin send you?"

She glanced at me and then at Christa, as if she wasn't sure if she should say certain things in front of my friend.

"Whatever you have to say to me, you can say in front of her," I managed.

The woman narrowed her eyes. "I'm Bella Sawyer, and I'm here to perform a protection spell on you."

"You're a witch?" Christa piped up, sounding like a five-year-old, excitement brewing in her tone.

Bella faced her but said nothing, merely scowled. It was pretty apparent she was a witch, and just then, I registered her electric blue aura, which I hadn't even noticed. No, I'd been too busy sizing her up and feeling dejected and jealous all at the same time.

Apparently dismissing Christa as unimportant, she faced me again. "Sinjin told me about your little visit from the warlock, which is why I'm here."

"Rand," I said. She nodded, taking a few steps closer to me as she eyed the surroundings of my store and frowned with distaste.

"Yes. Apparently Sinjin doesn't want a repeat of Rand's last visit. That's why he called me."

"When you say a protection spell . . ." I started.

She huffed, apparently annoyed that we weren't getting down to business. But before anyone put any sort of spell on me, I had to understand just what that meant.

"Think of it as a magical restraining order. The warlock won't be able to get within twenty feet of you."

I felt myself sigh in relief, grateful that Sinjin seemed to think of everything. Just as quickly as the relief overwhelmed me, another feeling reared its unwanted head, which was hard to describe. It was maybe something of a cross between regret and sadness. I trampled the feeling down, though, because it was ludicrous. Rand wanted to control me. Sinjin had said so himself. I glanced at Bella as it suddenly occurred to me that maybe I shouldn't be so trusting of her either. I mean, how did I know Sinjin had sent her and not Rand? Maybe this was some sort of setup, and she was really going to drug me with her witchcraft. Who knew where I'd end up? "How do I know you are who you say you are or that you were really sent by Sinjin?"

Bella frowned and glanced at her watch, obviously wanting to get the message across that she had places to go and people to bespell. Well, join the club. I still had a client who was probably going to walk in any second.

"Check your cell phone," she ordered. "You should have a message."

Surprised, I glanced at Christa. She reached for my purse underneath the counter, handing it to me. I fished through it until I found my cell phone. I clicked the voice-mail button and listened.

"Good morning, my love," Sinjin's voice rang out. "A witch under my employ, Isabella Sawyer, will be visiting you today. I apologize for not giving you adequate notice but I am worried by the warlock's visits. Isabella is a very capable witch and will ensure your protection. I apologize that I could not introduce you both in person. I do hope you understand." He paused for a second or two. "Last evening was magical, little poppet."

He hung up and I turned the phone off, facing Bella. "I didn't know he'd called."

She frowned again. "He contacted me early this morning before the sun came up. Apparently you were sleeping." Then she eyed me up and down again, her expression one of repugnance, as if she were beholding Jabba the Hutt. She was, no doubt, shocked that girl-next-door me was now Sinjin's newest flavor. At that moment I knew Bella Sawyer and I would never be friends. And it was also at that moment that I realized that she realized Sinjin and I were sleeping together. I couldn't seem to find it in myself to be embarrassed.

She clapped her hands together as if we were now moving to step two.

"Do you believe her?" Christa asked me, reminding me that she was still in the room. She was eyeing Bella with daggers.

I smiled at Christa, appreciating the fact that my best friend was so protective. Then I glanced at Bella and nodded as I approached her. "We can go in the reading room."

"Um, you do have another client coming in soon," Christa announced.

I gulped and nodded, thinking this might be an issue. "Can you just have him or her wait for a few minutes?"

"Her," Christa corrected.

"Maybe offer her some coffee and make small talk," I finished.

Chris nodded and glaring once more at Bella, returned her attention to the *Vogue* magazine that was spread out on the counter.

I started for the hallway, Bella just behind me.

"I'll be out here if you need me," Christa called.

"Thanks, Chris," I answered as I faced the reading room. When I opened the door, the darkness seemed to accost me; it took a second or two for my eyes to adjust to the red lightbulb that fought against the otherwise pitch blackness. Approaching the reading table, I pulled out the chair for Bella as I took a seat on the opposite side.

She motioned for my hands. "I need to touch you in order for the spell to work."

I nodded, giving her my hands. I felt a slight pinch of

electricity flow through me, which automatically reminded me of the first time I'd touched Rand—how his
electricity had jolted through me and how overcome I'd
been by my feelings toward him.

Do you think this could be a mistake? I heard my
inner voice.

*No, Rand wants nothing more than to control me,
and who knows how desperate he'll get. Who knows
what he's capable of.*

*But what if what he said was true? What if you really
should trust him? What if those feelings you get around
him are valid?*

They aren't. Now stop talking, stupid voice!

"So Rand won't be able to ever get near me again?" I
asked, suddenly impatient to get this show on the road.

Bella closed her eyes and nodded. "That's the plan."

"How foolproof is this?" I continued, worry lacing
my voice. Hey, it wasn't like I'd ever been on the receiving end of a spell before . . .

She opened her eyes as she dug her nails into my
hands. "I am an extremely powerful witch," she barked,
clearly offended. "It's foolproof."

I swallowed hard. "I didn't mean to insult you."

"Close your eyes," she said, obviously still affronted.
"And focus on receiving my power."

"How do I do that?"

She shook her head and grumbled something unintelligible. "Just clear your mind, and for God's sake, stop
talking."

I frowned but closed my eyes and did my best not to
think of anything, which was damn hard to do. My
brain instantly switched into overdrive with thoughts of
everything from what I was going to eat for lunch to
what relationship this woman had with Sinjin. Finally I
was able to focus on the blackness of my eyelids.

"It's done," Bella announced and dropped my hands, standing up.

I glanced up at her in surprise. "That's it?"

"Yes," she said impatiently.

"I didn't feel anything."

"You weren't supposed to."

Somehow I just couldn't fathom that there hadn't been any sign at all that I'd just been bewitched. I mean, she hadn't even chanted or done anything resembling hocus-pocus. "Are you sure you did it right?" I asked and then gulped at her expression of pure hostility. "There wasn't anything I was supposed to say or you were supposed to say or some potion I should have drunk?"

She started for the door. "I hope Sinjin knows what he's doing," she said and turned to face me, scowling as she exhaled her pent-up frustration. Then before I could respond, she walked out of the reading room. Moments later I could hear the sound of the front door closing behind her.

If I'd thought my dealings with Bella Sawyer were over, I was sorely mistaken. That evening marked meeting number two, and to say I was disappointed was an understatement.

After getting off work, going home and showering, feeding the cat and myself, I headed for Sinjin's. I wanted to throw my arms around him and forget the stresses of the day in his embrace. So you can imagine my frustration when he announced we were due at Bella's house momentarily. He escorted me to his Ferrari and, once we were en route, glanced over at me with that winning smile of his.

"Isabella is going to act as your teacher, love," Sinjin responded when I gave him a pouty face that said just how much I was looking forward to this.

"I thought you were my teacher," I replied.

He chuckled and shook his head. "There are only so many subjects I can teach you, my pet. Unfortunately witchcraft is not among them."

I just nodded but didn't say anything more. I glanced out the window, getting lost in the scenery as it blurred past, and wondered about my life. It was like I'd just woken up one day and everything was turned upside down. Well, more like inside out.

I felt Sinjin's hand on my thigh and glanced up at him. He smiled over at me as his attention moved from my face to my bust and down to my legs. "I dreamed of you today, poppet," he whispered.

"I didn't know vampires could dream," I said.

He just nodded. His eyes seemed to glow with the whiteness that meant that he was either angry or aroused. "I dreamed of being inside you, feeling you writhing beneath me."

I swallowed hard and damned Bella to hell for even existing. "Why do you have to talk like that when we aren't going to be alone anytime soon?" I demanded grumpily.

Sinjin chuckled. "All in due time, my pet, all in due time."

Before I could say another word, he pulled up in front of a plantation-style three-story home that looked like something out of a magazine. "Is this where Bella lives?" I asked, shocked.

"It is," Sinjin said as he turned the car off and opened and closed his door, materializing in seconds at my side. He opened the car door for me and helped me up, offering a chaste kiss on my lips as he closed the door behind me. "We will not tarry long."

I just frowned and accepted his arm as we approached the front door. He rang the bell and Bella opened it instantly, pasting on a smile as soon as she saw him. Once she saw me, her smile dropped.

"What a pleasant surprise," she said in a way that made it pretty apparent there was nothing pleasant about the surprise at all. Well, about the me part of the surprise anyway.

"How did the spell go?" Sinjin asked and helped himself into her house. She stepped out of the way and looked pissed off.

"Do you doubt me?" she asked, obviously miffed.

He faced her and smiled. "Of course not." Then he turned to me and motioned for me to come in. "Poppet, stop lolling about."

I didn't say anything but nodded a small greeting to Bella and stepped into her vestibule, craning my neck as I took stock of my surroundings. She breathed out what sounded like irritation and started forward, Sinjin just beside her and me bringing up the rear. We walked into her living room and she took a seat on her sofa, crossing her legs seductively as she stared up at Sinjin. I couldn't catch his reaction since his back was to me, so instead I turned to take in the room's furnishings. The ceilings were incredibly high and with the white tile floors, white slip-covered furniture, and bright white walls, the whole place felt like a hospital—antiseptic and cold.

"Isabella, I want you to cast a spell in order to judge the Lurker threat," Sinjin said, all matter-of-fact and businesslike.

"And how do you propose I do that?" she demanded and stood up as if shocked by his request. "The spell requires more than one witch."

Sinjin smiled and glanced at Bella furtively. "One," he started and then turned to me. His smile broadened. "Two."

"She's hardly a witch," Bella said and harrumphed.

"She has more power than you could dream of," Sinjin responded, his tone icy.

Bella scowled at him and turned to face me. "Do you even know who and what the Lurkers are?"

I nodded, feeling like I was a student on the receiving end of a quiz. "Yes, they are humans with vampire powers and they want to kill all of you."

"Succinct," Bella said with distaste, as if I were a complete and total idiot. "Give me your hands."

I obeyed and awaited more direction.

"Because you cannot visualize a Lurker, given that you have never seen one, all I need from you is your energy," Bella started. "I want you to close your eyes and funnel your power, your energy into me. I will do the rest." Then she turned to face Sinjin. "We will see if she has enough power within her."

Sinjin said nothing but glanced at me with a wink.

"How do I funnel my energy into you?" I asked, facing Bella.

"Each witch has her own way of channeling her power. I find it easiest to imagine pulling my energy from all parts of my body into my center. Then allowing it to spill out into whatever requires it, filling up a void." She narrowed her eyes at me. "Do whatever feels natural."

I nodded and closed my eyes, imagining any power that might actually be within me pulling into my center. It felt as if energy was suddenly springing up from my fingertips and feet, like tiny pricks all over my skin. It was akin to when your foot falls asleep and you have to shake out that feeling of pins and needles. I continued to imagine that energy moving to my middle; when I felt the busy hum of bees in my stomach, I then concentrated on sending the energy to Bella, bathing her in it.

I clenched my eyes shut as I felt the energy leave me— then I could suddenly see Bella before me, in my mind's eye. There was a cord of white light joining us, which I imagined was my power going into her. Even though my eyes were closed, I could see her as clearly as if they were open, which was odd to say the least. How that was even possible I wasn't sure, but I was also past the point of asking how and why. I mean, I *had* sort of accepted the fact that I was a witch. When my energy hit her, she jumped slightly and I could hear her intake of breath.

"I can see them, the Lurkers," she said in an awed sort of voice.

"How many?" Sinjin demanded.

"It is difficult to say but perhaps hundreds. They are building their numbers, concentrating only on replenishing their army."

"How are they building it?" Sinjin probed.

In my mind, I could see Bella shake her head.

"Dig deeper," Sinjin demanded. "Find out how they are adding to their battalions."

Bella nodded. "I need more power, more magic."

I figured that was my cue, so I focused even more resolutely, scraping up every last inch of whatever it was inside me that was fueling her abilities and sent it over to her. The white light around her glowed even more brightly.

"By way of magic," she said, sounding surprised. "It appears they blend magic with their own blood in some form of ritual."

"Are the victims taken by force?" Sinjin asked.

I felt myself swallow at the term *victims*.

"I can't tell," Bella answered. "I just have this feeling that there are many of them and they choose not to attack us because they are focused on growing their numbers first." She paused for a moment or two, then took a deep breath. "I believe there will be a battle, and it could be devastating for our kind."

Then she dropped my hands and I suddenly felt like I

was going to pass out. I started to swoon and Sinjin immediately caught me. I blinked a few times, trying to clear the stars from my vision, and gazed at him in shock.

"Are you well, my pet?" he asked.

I nodded. "I think so. I just feel a little light-headed and weak."

Bella glanced at me and frowned. "It is to be expected. You just gave me all your power. It will take a few hours for it to return. Eat a large meal."

Frowning over the fact that I probably wouldn't be acquainted with a large meal in a long while, I tried to focus on the conversation and not the fact that I felt completely wiped out. "We will need to locate the prophetess," Sinjin said as he took a seat on her sofa, with me in his arms. He ran a hand through my hair as I relaxed against his chest, still feeling like I wanted to pass out.

"The prophetess?" Bella repeated, obviously surprised. "Impossible."

"Not impossible," Sinjin replied, smiling down at me as he did so.

"There are those who doubt her very existence," Bella continued.

Sinjin finally glanced up at her and there was impatience in his eyes. "I am not one of them."

Twelve

The next day, I was back to feeling like myself—aka not about to pass out from sending all my life energy to the bitch, Bella. After we'd left Bella's, I'd questioned Sinjin about this so-called prophetess, but he hadn't admitted to much—just that she was some sort of super-witch and we needed her talents to help us combat the threat of the Lurkers. He'd also said that contacting her would be a feat and I wasn't up to it just yet: I'd need more lessons with Bella. So for the time being, I wasn't supposed to be concerned with prophetesses or Lurkers.

I took a deep breath as I stood behind the counter of my store while Christa prattled on about her last date and what a disaster it had been. I actually had been paying attention to her until I caught sight of a woman walking down the street. Ordinarily, I wouldn't have looked twice at a passerby, but this woman seemed out of place somehow, dressed in a white-and-yellow dress that skimmed the ground, the high collar and wrist-length sleeves looking like something out of *Little House on the Prairie*. Her incredibly long, flowing silvery hair seemed just as odd. She appeared to almost float down the street even though she looked old and frail, like she was in her eighties. The closer she came, the more I realized her aura was beaming out of her in an exquisite bright blue. That had to mean one thing . . .

"Oh, fuck," I said under my breath.

"Are you listening?" Christa persisted as she took a seat on the stool behind the counter and stared at me with irritation on her face.

"No," I said rather absentmindedly. My mind, instead, was wholly focused on what to do about this woman. She was clearly a witch, or something similar. Her aura was the same color and intensity as Bella's and Rand's.

Rand.

Something warm flowered within me at the mere thought of his name. It was a feeling I couldn't categorize and didn't have time to, because the witch opened my front door.

"Hi, are you . . ." Christa glanced down at my appointment book, tapping her long, fake orange nails rhythmically. ". . . Mathilda?" she finished with an expectant stare.

The old woman nodded with a sweet smile at Christa before her gaze fell on me and she smiled even more broadly. I saw something like recognition passing through her intense green eyes. "Yes, I am," she said in a soft voice, the cadence of which sounded like the trilling of bells.

All at once the panic that was welling up inside me evaporated, leaving me with nothing but a feeling of complete trust. I felt sure this woman would never harm me. 'Course, by now I was also well aware that anything I might be feeling could be due to her witchcraft.

"Hi," I said, sounding a bit too harsh. I decided right then and there, however, that I didn't want this Mathilda woman to know that I knew what she was. Better to play it safe; and by *safe*, I meant dumb. "Are you ready for your reading?" I asked in a much friendlier, softer voice.

She nodded and offered me a charming smile. I forced

a smile of my own, but all the while, anger was bubbling up inside me as I wondered what in the hell she wanted from me. All I knew was that I had to remember every second of what happened here today because I would report it back to Sinjin tonight.

I led her into the reading room and wondered if I should alert Christa to the possibility that this might turn out to be unpleasant. But then I thought better of it. It wasn't like Christa could do anything to help me; furthermore, I could be endangering her. No, I was just going to play it cool—find out what this woman wanted and send her on her way.

Once we entered the reading room, I shut the door behind us and lost sight of everything in the darkness for a few seconds until the glow of the red light overhead illuminated our surroundings again. I motioned to the small table in the center of the room and said, "Have a seat."

"Thank you," she responded, pulling out the chair. Her gnarled hand confirmed that she had to be pretty old. It was strange, though, because despite her advanced years, she appeared so statuesquely beautiful and serene. It was almost like her age made her more beautiful.

"Is there a particular person you were hoping to make contact with? Or did you want a card reading?" I asked as soon as we were both seated comfortably.

She smiled at me. "I was interested in you reading my cards."

Hmm . . . That surprised me but whatever. Besides, reading cards was way easier than trying to make contact with the dead. I grabbed the stack of tarot cards, unwrapped the red silk scarf from around them, and handed her the stack. "Please shuffle the cards, then choose seven of them, and hand them to me."

She nodded and separated the deck between her gnarled hands, carefully shuffling them four times. She cut the deck and then shuffled them another four times as if she had OCD or something. Then she removed two cards from the top, cut the deck again, and removed four cards from the middle, then the remaining card from the bottom, before handing them back to me.

When her skin touched mine, I felt a wave of electricity course through me, much like what I'd experienced with Rand. I abruptly pulled my hand back and realized I'd given myself away.

"I am not going to harm you, child," she said in a soft voice as she stared at me with her beautiful green eyes.

"Then what do you want?"

Her gaze didn't waver. "I am here to inform you that Rand is not your enemy."

"Oh my God!" I felt my face go white with fear as I realized she was one of Rand's emissaries. "So, what, he got too freaked out when I zapped his ass across the room and now he's sending his grandma to retaliate?" I wanted to throw her off the scent of the truth, which was that Bella's spell was protecting me. The less Mathilda knew, the better. Although, I had a mind to yell at Bella for not ensuring that all witches had to keep their distance from me. 'Course, then that would include her as well, I supposed. And maybe me too, for that matter. And how the hell would that work?

Never mind, Jolie! I yelled at myself. *All that matters is this woman! Find out what the hell she wants and get her out of here!*

"No, that is not why," she said simply.

"Let's stop beating around the bush then. What the hell do you both want from me?"

She took a deep breath like the answer was going to be long and complicated. "We want you to know the truth."

And then I remembered how anxious Sinjin had been when I told him Rand had come into my store and sent me that package—how he'd warned me that Rand was dangerous. I mean, Sinjin had taken major steps to ensure that Rand would have to keep his distance from me. So, as far as I was concerned, this woman might be equally dangerous. "You can leave now." I stood up, but she made no motion to follow suit.

"You need us," she said simply.

"I want nothing to do with you and I want nothing to do with that warlock. Do you understand?" I said, my voice deadly serious. "Now if you don't leave, I'm going to call the police."

She took a deep breath and rose from the chair, wobbling as she did so. I had the sudden urge to help her but another part of me wouldn't allow it. She was a witch or something magical—all of this was probably just a game, something meant to evoke my sympathy. Well, I wasn't going to fall for it.

"The vampire is not telling you the truth, child," she said in a soft voice.

I shook my head, although her comment made me apprehensive. Still, as soon as the worry reared its unwanted head, I shot it down. I just couldn't believe it—wouldn't believe it. Sinjin wouldn't lie to me. He was my protector, my teacher. He was the one person who had promised to guide me into this Underworld. He was the only one I could turn to, the only one I had.

And suddenly it seemed readily apparent that Rand had sent this old woman to shake my foundation regarding Sinjin. Her whole purpose was to weave lies and cause me to distrust him. Rand and this old woman wanted to woo me to their dark side. Well, I wasn't going to fall for any of their Jedi mind tricks. Yoda be damned. "Leave him out of this," I warned and started for the door. "And neither you nor the warlock is welcome in my store or anywhere near me ever again."

She reached out and touched my hand when she

brushed past me. I felt my knees buckle, then I hit the ground hard. I had no time to even wonder at what the hell had just happened because her voice was suddenly in my head.

You must trust Rand and me. We are here to help you.

I tried to fight against her but she was too strong and the control she had over my mind and body was too powerful. I grabbed my head between my hands and closed my eyes, trying to force her out of my head. At the same time, I willed my legs to move, to stand up, but it was useless.

Everything you see around you is a farce, she continued. *It was never meant to be this way. The vampire broke the rules, Jolie.*

Images swarmed through my head like a hive of agitated bees. Images of Rand, of me in his arms, us kissing, dancing . . .

I shook my head, trying to clear the ridiculous visions because I knew they weren't real. How could they be? I'd never done any of these things! They were mere hallucinations—the work of a powerful witch—she was trying to implant memories into my subconscious that weren't real, memories that were fabricated by her.

"Stop!" I finally screamed, when I found my tongue again. But the sound came out as a weak whisper.

"Do not resist me," she said, softly placing her hand on my shoulder. As soon as she did, I felt myself surrender to her, suddenly weak. The images in my head slowed down, allowing me to focus on only one.

The vision appeared as any other, only the images were much more delineated and sharp. It took me a second to adjust, but once I did, I recognized my store. It was dark outside, the streetlamps already glowing yellow against the otherwise black night. I heard a sound to my right and glanced over to see myself as I busily readied the store for the next morning. So I was the omniscient eavesdropper in this vision? I didn't have time to further ponder it because the door opened. And that was when I saw him.

Rand.

I felt something catch in my throat and didn't want to even acknowledge it. But something like happiness filled me as soon as I saw him. Yet the feeling made no sense since Rand was my enemy.

I shook the feeling off and forced myself to concentrate on the vision. I watched myself greet him as if this were the first time we'd ever met. I wasn't afraid of him, which of course made no sense. This wasn't the way our meeting occurred at all. I mean, for one thing Christa had been there and it had been midday . . .

This is how it truly happened, Jolie, Mathilda's voice announced in my head. *You were destined to meet Rand first, not Sinjin.*

I wasn't able to argue with her. It was as if she were controlling my mind, showing me what she chose to. And there was nothing I could do to fight it. Instead, I watched myself unwittingly take Rand to the reading room. We sat down and I started to pull out the tarot cards, but he stopped me and asked me to read him instead. As soon as I touched his hands, that surge of energy coursed through me. I watched myself pull back in shock.

"I know all of this seems impossible," Mathilda said, her voice gentle. "But what you are seeing is real, and everything you know now is not as it was designed to be, Jolie."

I watched the vision fall apart before me and then I was back in my reading room, sitting on the cold floor. "That doesn't make any sense," I said, shaking my head.

Mathilda nodded. "Rand is the one who trained you to become a witch, child, who introduced you to this life," she continued. "He is not your enemy."

I shook my head. "So you're saying Sinjin is my enemy?"

She stepped back as I righted myself, leaning against the wall for fear I might topple over again. After a long moment of silence, I glanced over at her.

"Yes," she finished.

I shook my head, refusing to accept any of it. "I know what you're trying to do and it won't work. I will never, for one minute, believe any of this shit. Sinjin is not my enemy."

"He has brainwashed you to believe his lies," she argued.

"He hasn't brainwashed me into anything. He warned me about Rand. He told me how powerful and dangerous he is, so don't think I'm going to fall for your tricks."

She seemed surprised at that information and was quiet for a second or two. I, on the other hand, was another story—*how dare she come here and try to convince me to believe her lies! And, furthermore, how dare Rand send her here!* I needed to nip this right in the bud, if only to ensure I wouldn't receive any more visits from Sinjin's enemies.

"Sinjin and I are together and I trust him," I said. "So I suggest you and Rand don't ever come near me again or you'll have Sinjin to deal with."

She nodded as if she understood.

"Please tell Rand exactly what I've said to you," I finished.

"I will," she said softly. Before she left, she turned to face me again. She simply smiled and reached out, grabbing my hand. I flinched, and immediately tried to pull away, but her grip was too strong.

"See me not as I am and remember nothing," she said, and I struggled even harder. She released my hand and I suddenly felt myself falling backward.

It was like I blacked out or something. I shook my

head and found myself on the floor of my reading room, looking around in bewilderment as if I'd just awoken from a cold faint.

"Are you well, dear?"

I glanced up at the face of the woman who had come into my store, looking for a reading. She offered her hand, as if such a frail creature could even hope to pull me to my feet.

"I . . . I think so," I said. "What . . . what happened?"

"You do not remember?"

I shook my head and felt slightly nauseous.

"You tripped, dear," the old woman said as she smiled down at me again. I stood up and leaned against the wall for support.

"Are you feeling okay now?" she asked again.

I nodded, not wanting to worry her. She held my hand and led me out of the reading room and back to the front room, where Christa looked up from buffing her nails.

"Your friend had a nasty fall, dear," the old woman said to Christa.

"Jules?" she asked and came around the counter. "Are you okay?"

I just nodded and allowed the old woman to lead me to the couch, where I sat down, still feeling woozy but more scared. It just wasn't like me to black out. God, what if I'd had a mini stroke or an aneurysm or something?

"What happened?" Christa asked as she took a seat beside me and held my hand. "Do we need to take you to the hospital?"

"No." I shook my head. "I'm fine, really. I think I just passed out."

I glanced up to thank the old woman but she was already gone. I looked to my left and right, but she was nowhere to be found.

"Where did she go?" I asked, baffled, a headache already starting between my temples.

Christa looked around herself and then shrugged, seemingly unconcerned. "She must have left, I guess." Then she faced me again. "Jules, are you sure you're okay?"

But I couldn't answer because I honestly didn't know.

The rest of the day went pretty much slower than a snail's pace and I couldn't wait to tidy up for the night so I could spend the evening with my vampire. Although, I had to admit that I needed to find a happy medium where sleep was concerned, because I was exhausted. Staying up all night and all day was too much for me to function properly.

Even though I felt like a sleep-deprived zombie, I couldn't hide the excitement coursing through me as I pulled up to Sinjin's house. I parked the Jetta in his driveway and glanced at my reflection in the rearview mirror, taking in my pink lips and shadowed eyes. Yes, I'd taken a few courses in the art of wearing makeup from Christa; we'd even paid a visit to the M•A•C counter in Macy's, where I spent way too much money. But there was now a part of me that wanted to look feminine and sexy. I shook my head, allowing the large blond waves to bounce around my face. Yes, I'd even gone so far as to curl my hair. Where the old Jolie Wilkins had retreated to was anyone's guess.

I unbuckled my seat belt, catching sight of my short, brown corduroy skirt, under which I'd worn tights with knee-high brown leather boots. And on the top? A skintight, camel stretch turtleneck that made my natural C-cup boobs look like D's. Or maybe that was just the Wonderbra.

I stepped out of the car and marveled over how much I'd changed. Two months ago, I wouldn't have been caught dead wearing this. Not that my outfit was too revealing or anything—it was just fashionable. And fashion and I had never been friendly. Well, I guess I could say we were now.

I opened the rear door and pulled out my overnight bag, a smile gliding across my lips at the thought that I had packed an overnight bag for Sinjin's. It just made things between us seem so . . . official—like we were definitely an item, boyfriend and girlfriend. Yep, I was going to spend the night with my boyfriend and we were going to make love all evening. I was so giddy, I felt like I might throw up all over my brand-new boots.

I slung the bag over my shoulder and, after beeping the car locked, I made my way to Sinjin's front door. Taking a deep breath, I glanced down at myself to make sure nothing was out of place. Then I ran my fingers through my hair once more, giving it an extra fluff before ringing the doorbell.

A few seconds later, the door opened to reveal my incredibly handsome vampire.

"Poppet," he said with that mischievous grin that characterized him so well. He was dressed all in black, as usual, his long-sleeved T-shirt doing nothing to hide the swells of his biceps or the mountains of his pecs. God, he was just so beautiful.

I stepped inside his house, dropped my overnight bag, threw my hands around his neck, and rose on my tiptoes so I could kiss him. He seemed taken aback at first, but then chuckled and draped his arms around my waist, sliding his tongue into my mouth. I groaned against him and met his tongue, thrust for thrust. I could feel him stirring beneath his pants and wondered if we might not even make it to the bedroom. But that thought was cut short when I heard the sound of someone behind me clearing her throat.

I squealed in shock as I pulled away from Sinjin and spun on my heel to face the intruder—Bella Sawyer! Son of a . . .

"Isabella," Sinjin said and smiled at her as if it didn't matter to him that she had just walked in on us in a passionate embrace. Based on her expression, she wanted to kill me right then and there. Hmmm . . . She was definitely jealous.

God, why can't I get away from this blasted woman? I asked myself. *And the bigger question—what is she doing in Sinjin's house?*

Actually, the bigger question is what's the history between them? That other voice reared up.

Do you think they used to date?

Oh my God, what if they're dating now? What if this is like that movie Dangerous Liaisons?

Well, Jolie Wilkins, you're definitely not killing yourself!

Despite the irritation snaking through me, mainly at Sinjin for having this awful woman in his house when he hadn't, at the very least, warned me, I remembered my manners and smiled. "Hi, Bella, it's nice to see you again." I mean, the American way was innocent until proven guilty, right?

Her feeble attempt at a smile came out as more of a sneer. "Hello again."

Not knowing what else to say or do, I faced Sinjin. "So, you never did tell me how, uh, how you two know each other?"

Sinjin closed the front door, drawing my attention to the fact that it had been open the entire time without me realizing it. As he walked back toward us, I noticed he was wearing black pajama pants and no socks or shoes. I gulped hard as images of the two of them in bed came crashing down on me. I pushed the images away, though, trying to force myself to be fair to Sinjin. Just because this hideous woman was in his house and he was in his jammies didn't mean he'd just screwed the hell out of her . . . Right? I mean, she was fully dressed, for crying out loud. Granted, her skintight, dark purple dress only went to her mid-thigh and was cut so low, I could see her navel, but still. I didn't even want to focus on her incredibly high, pointed stilettos; added to her already long legs, they made her look like she was descended from a gazelle.

"Isabella Sawyer and I go back many years, do we not, love?" he asked as he offered Bella his devil's grin. I felt myself swallow down a lump of resentment. I wasn't sure if the resentment was reserved for their long history or that he referred to her by the same name that he called me . . . *love*. Maybe it was both.

Bella sort of "hmmphed" at him and then nodded, her lips tight. "I suppose you could say that."

I tried to keep my temper under check, not wanting to paint this whole situation in a bad light, but little by little my patience was wearing thin. I mean, really . . . Why was Bella dressed so slutty and standing in Sinjin's house? With him in his pajamas! "I wasn't aware that Bella was visiting."

Sinjin took my hand and the cold of his skin surprised me for a moment or two, until his temperature warmed up to mine. "I invited Ms. Sawyer over this evening, poppet, to train you."

"Train me?" I asked, having momentarily forgotten that Sinjin had said Bella would have to train me in order for us to locate that supreme witch person.

"Yes, we have much work to accomplish if we are to locate the prophetess," he responded. Ah, that was it— the prophetess. "Isabella needs to teach you everything she knows—how to cast spells and do charms," he continued.

"Tonight?" I asked, aghast at the very thought. I'd

been hoping for a quiet, romantic evening alone with my boyfriend and now Bella had been thrust into the mix? Really?

Sinjin pulled me closer to him, laughing into my neck as he did so. I watched Bella's hands fist at her sides and had never felt more uncomfortable in my life. Was Sinjin so unaware that this woman obviously had it bad for him? Or was he just playing with her heartstrings? I had to hope for the former because I couldn't imagine my caring vampire would sink so low as to toy with a woman's feelings. Either way, he definitely wasn't making it easy for her to like me.

"Shall we get started, then?" Sinjin asked with a large grin as he clapped his hands together and started down the hall. I noticed her raised-eyebrow expression as she apparently sized me up and found me lacking. She was quick to follow behind him as I took up the rear.

And just like that, my hopes for an awesome evening were crushed.

Sinjin led us into his living room, where I noticed he'd moved all of the furniture to the perimeter of the room. I was just waiting for him to bust out a pool filled with mud and tell us to go at it.

"Um, why did you clear everything out?" I asked dubiously, turning to face Sinjin.

"Because you, my dearest little poppet, are about to learn how to command your inner beast."

He might as well have been speaking Swahili for all the sense he made. "My inner what?"

He chuckled then, as if the whole thing were a big joke that I, stupid and uninformed Jolie Wilkins, didn't get. I exhaled a pent-up breath and felt my lips tighten as I watched Bella saunter toward us, hips swaying seductively. She stood very close to Sinjin—as in shoulders-touching close. I felt like I was playing the part of the third wheel, and doing a damn good job of it.

"Poppet, every witch has a wild beast within her that she can call upon when required," Sinjin explained.

"I still don't understand," I said, feeling my lower lip pout like a child about to have a temper tantrum.

"Witches can turn into animals," Bella finally said, sounding exasperated.

I looked at her like she'd just sprouted another head. Then I laughed, figuring the joke was totally and completely on me. People turning into animals . . . yeah, right. Yes, I had come to grips with the fact that witches and vampires weren't just the stuff of Halloween cartoons—but people taking the shape of animals? Then it occurred to me that werewolves probably also existed in this strange new world I called my life. "Um, so you're what, also a werewolf?"

Bella looked at Sinjin as if she was anything but amused, as if being called a werewolf was like being called a bitch or something. He just smiled at her, shaking his head. "Perhaps you should demonstrate?"

Bella's lips curled malevolently into what I suppose was the closest to a smile she could achieve. It was, however, dripping with something that was far from sweet. She then stepped away from Sinjin and walked to the center of the living room, swaying her hips like she thought she was Marilyn freaking Monroe.

"Remember your tail this time, love," Sinjin said, and chuckled to himself at what I imagined was an inside joke. I swallowed hard, not wanting to admit that there was nothing worse than an inside joke when you weren't on the inside.

I crossed my arms against my chest and watched Bella, hoping she would turn into some slathering, furry, flea-infested beast. I felt Sinjin come up behind me and wrap his arms around me, but I didn't change position. No, at this point, I was too pissed off. None of this made any sense. If I'd had any real balls, I would have just turned around and left when I discovered her here.

'Course, I was interested in what Bella planned to turn into, so I suppose my deciding to remain there was purely in the interests of curiosity. I watched her walk the perimeter of the room—and then she did something that defied logic, something that I don't even know how to begin to describe. She dropped to her hands and knees and, in a split second, became a lioness. There was no scrunching of bones, no snarling or sweating or anything that seemed to characterize the shape shifters you see in the movies. She was a woman one second and a lion the next. Her purple dress lay in scraps at her feet, obviously having not fared well in the transformation.

"Oh my God!" I screamed, not waiting around to decide if my eyes were deceiving me. Instead, I looked for the nearest exit. Sinjin laughed behind me and pulled me tighter into his chest.

"Shhh, my pet," he crooned into my ear. "She will not harm you."

I looked down at the lioness in front of me. She sliced the air with her paw, missing my leg by a few inches. Then she growled, so fiercely that I found myself climbing up Sinjin to escape. "She's going to kill me," I protested as I tried again to run away, but Sinjin held me in place, chuckling all the while.

"Come," he said to Bella, the lioness, and she purred immediately, allowing him to stroke her between the eyes. I wasn't sure if I should be jealous or not, considering they looked like Siegfried and Roy, but somehow jealousy did enter into the equation.

"I believe she is ready for instruction now," Sinjin finished.

With that, the lioness trotted back into the center of the room and lay down on the floor. Then, just as miraculously as before, she transformed, only this time it wasn't quite as spontaneous. Her long caramel-colored tail shortened into her backside while her claws recessed into human fingertips. Her rib cage decreased in size, now revealing only the outline of her ribs. Her two perfectly matched, very large breasts (D's by the look of them) were perky and completely real. She stood up and faced us both, naked.

In her nudity, she was absolutely magnificent. Great, just great.

"Um," I started, not really sure where to look. By the expression on Bella's face, she wasn't exactly shy when it came to standing completely naked in front of Sinjin or me. 'Course, I couldn't say any of this was for my benefit.

"Well done," Sinjin said, and I felt myself coloring. Whether or not he was getting pleasure from the sight of her flawless body was anyone's guess, but I wasn't a total moron so I had to imagine he was.

"Poppet, now it is your turn," he said as he pushed me away from him.

That was when I lost my temper. "If this is some plan you've concocted to have some freaking, weird three-some animal-style, I'm not into it at all." Then, feeling a bit more bravado after my outburst, I threw my hands on my hips and glared at Sinjin. "In fact, I've seen enough. So you two just party on down, but I'm leaving." Then I made for the nearest exit.

I heard the sound of Bella snickering, which was just as well. I wanted nothing more than to escape—to lick my wounds in the comfort and privacy of my own little home, to bemoan the destruction of my relationship with Sinjin. I hurried down the hallway, grabbing my overnight bag from the corner, and was about to throw open the door when Sinjin materialized instantly in front of me. I walked headlong into his chest and sucked in a surprised gasp of air.

"Get out of my way," I said.

"Is my little poppet jealous?" he asked with a big smile.

I felt something in me breaking. So he was going to tease me about this, was he? "I don't want to talk to you anymore, Sinjin. I want to go home."

"Please," he started.

"No, this whole thing was shitty on your part." I tried to sidestep him but he grabbed both my arms and wouldn't let go.

"I apologize for offending you, love."

"Stop calling me that."

"I do not understand," he said.

So I decided to make him understand. I dropped my bag and stepped back, away from his hold. Surprisingly, he released me. "Let me help you then. First off, it's not okay that you surprise me with that awful woman in your house and especially"—I glanced down the hallway to see if we were alone, which we were—"especially when she's dressed like that and you're dressed like that!" I motioned to his pajama bottoms. "Second, you should have warned me ahead of time that Bella was going to be here because that was just incredibly disrespectful, not to mention suspicious. And third, it is totally not okay that she's parading around completely naked and, even worse, that you seem to be enjoying it!"

He smiled slightly, as if my little freak-out session amused him, but when I bent down to pick up my overnight bag, his smile disappeared. "Please accept my humblest apology, love," he started. "And for the record, I cared no more for her demonstration than you did."

I looked at him in disbelief. I'd have to be the biggest idiot in the world to be buying any of this bullshit. "Please. I'm smarter than I look." Then it dawned on me that he'd just called me "love" again. "And I don't want to hear you call me 'love' ever again, when it obviously doesn't mean anything!" I railed against him, feeling my voice choking with tears.

"Calm down, poppet," he whispered and pulled me into his chest. "I see now where I went wrong and I cannot express how sorry I am. Please believe me that Isabella means nothing to me. We are merely old friends."

"You really expect me to believe that?" I asked incredulously.

He nodded. "Yes, because it is the truth. You are the only woman for me, Jolie." The way he said it screamed of honesty. There was no smirk on his face, no arrogance in his eyes, nothing. "You have always been the only woman for me."

I faced him and sighed, my guilt reminding me that acting the part of the jealous girlfriend was probably unwarranted.

No way, Jolie, jealousy was most definitely warranted here, and you did the right thing, I corrected myself. But somehow my anger had managed to simmer down. Maybe it was due to his confession that I was his only one. "Sometimes you say things that I just don't know how to argue with."

"How can I make this situation more comfortable for you?" he asked with sincerity. I knew he was being straight with me; his eyes showed no deceit or subterfuge. "We need Isabella, poppet, to instruct you; but I understand your reservations."

"Well, for starters, you can tell her to put some clothes on," I said angrily, but my slight smile softened the bite of my bark.

He chuckled and threw his arm around my shoulders, grabbing my bag and looping it over his opposite shoulder. Then we sauntered into the living room again where Bella was sitting on the couch and dressed in a tight black mini skirt and a plunging red halter top. She had magicked the outfit, if I had to guess—I hadn't seen her with a change of clothing.

"Is your little outburst over?" she asked with a sneer.

"Isabella, we shall have no more of your foul mood," Sinjin said with authority. Bella turned a surprised expression his way but said nothing.

"What does turning into a beast have to do with finding the prophetess anyway?" I asked grumpily.

Sinjin glanced down at me and smiled reassuringly. "They are not necessarily related, love, but you will need to hone your magic, cultivate it, in order to attempt to locate the prophetess. This is just one avenue to allow your magic to grow, to encourage it and strengthen it so you will be prepared when the time comes."

"I have places to be so let's get this over with," Bella announced as she glared at me and stood up.

"Fine by me," I grumbled.

She approached me, and her eyes raked me from head to toe. "You honestly believe she has it in her?"

Sinjin tightened his hold around me. "Without a doubt," he said sternly. "And I do not recall asking you for your opinion."

Bella looked at me, her jaw tight. "Let's see if you truly are such a powerful witch. All you need to do is focus within yourself and draw your sister beast to the forefront. She will choose you."

I glanced at her and then at Sinjin before my mouth dropped open. "What does that even mean?"

Sinjin looked down at me, a sweet smile on his beautiful face. "Your magic works only if you concentrate on it, love. You must guide your power, tell it what you expect of it."

"Okay," I said, still not sure what I was doing. Did everything have to be so esoteric where magic was concerned?

"Close your eyes," Bella snapped and I obeyed. "Now imagine a field full of animals, as many as you possibly can."

I exhaled as I debated about inquiring whether I should be selective in my imagining the animals. But deciding Bella probably wouldn't react nicely, I just went with my gut and imagined an enormous pasture, like what you'd see in the farmlands of the Midwest. Then I pictured an elephant dropping from the sky and landing with a thud on the ground. He wasn't hurt, though. The next animal up was a hyena, who landed a few paces behind the elephant, followed by a yak and then a dog that looked like Lassie.

"Are you done?" Bella insisted.

I clenched my eyes even more tightly closed and realized I only had a dozen or so animals in my pasture. "How many do I need?"

Bella grumbled something that I couldn't make out. But she didn't say anything else so I continued imagining animals dropping from the sky until it looked like I had the best-ever petting zoo.

"K," I said, finally satisfied.

"Now, without losing your focus, tell the animals to come forth and claim you."

"Okay," I whispered and imagined myself walking into the pasture. Then I cleared my throat and said in my best authoritative voice: *Please come and claim me.*

And nothing happened. So I said it again. Still nothing.

"Um, nothing's happening," I said aloud, being sure to keep my eyes shut.

"It may take a few moments, but eventually, one will," Bella responded.

I shut my eyes even more tightly and focused on the animals that were now surrounding me—an elephant, tiger, all sorts of birds, an alligator, various rodents, anything I could think of. Then I said to myself: *Please se-lect me. Whoever you are, please select me.*

Then a funny thing happened. An elephant and a monkey stepped forward at the same time, followed by a puma and coyote, as well as a red-tailed hawk that soared overhead. "Um," I started.

"What?" Bella snapped.

"What is bothering you, poppet?" Sinjin whispered.

"What do I do if more than one animal comes for-ward?" I asked, still keeping my eyes clamped shut, afraid the animals might disperse if I opened them.

"There can't be more than one," Bella said, her tone dismissive and impatient. "There will be only one."

I looked at the animals that were now circling me. Yeah, there was definitely more than just one. "Um, are you sure?"

"Just choose one!" Bella snapped.

I looked around me again. The elephant sidled some-what closer but, figuring an elephant would do a num-ber on Sinjin's living room, I turned to the monkey. After Bella's little sexy-lioness show, however, the last thing I wanted to do was show up as a freaking chimpanzee or baboon. I continued until my eyes rested on an animal that would certainly give Bella's lioness a run for her money. A tigress.

And then a feeling of lightness descended on me—as if my soul were floating to the very top of my head. I opened my eyes and found myself on all fours. I glanced down and noticed the stripes of the tiger coloring my paws, which were in a word . . . huge. So this could only mean . . . I'd done it! Somehow, and I had no idea how, I just managed to magick myself into a tigress.

Holy crap! I am a witch!

And that was when I realized for certain that I was something more than I'd ever thought I was or could be. It wasn't really so much that I'd turned myself from human girl into wild cat; more that I'd been able to control whatever power existed within me to actually be able to do something so completely . . . impossible. At that moment I felt a huge outpouring of emotion toward Sinjin. He'd been right all along—I was far more than I thought I was and it was because of him that I'd been able to cultivate my abilities, to hone my powers. Sinjin was my teacher, my mentor, and what was more, he had never stopped believing in me. Even when I doubted myself.

You will never doubt yourself again, Jolie Wilkins, I thought firmly.

Taking a resolute step forward, I focused on my surroundings. Everything appeared almost colorless, and distorted—as if I were looking through a bottle. I looked up at Sinjin and felt my heartbeat increase. He was just as stunning as always, but his eyes were bright red. The way he shifted looked as if he were moving a million miles a second, and strangely enough I could see every fraction of his movement. It wasn't just a blur.

I took another few steps, feeling wobbly on my new legs. I glanced up at Sinjin again and tried to say something, which only came out as a growl. He approached me, kneeling until we were eye level.

"You are stunning, love," he whispered.

At the word *love,* I growled at him again and he chuckled, as if he understood. Then, just as quickly as the bizarre sense of light-headedness had overcome me, it started again. I shook my head and found myself suddenly lying in Sinjin's arms. I glanced down and felt my cheeks flush as I realized I was completely naked, just as Bella had been.

"She is a tigress, as I knew she would be," Sinjin announced to the room, pulling me closer. Apparently realizing I wasn't as comfortable as Bella with public shows of nudity, he tore off his shirt and slid it over my head and arms. It fit me like a dress. And of course I didn't miss the display of his incredibly muscled chest, which caused a hiccup in my heart rate.

"Very good," Bella said in a hurried, dismissive sort of way. "I imagine we will be in touch."

He smiled at her courteously and kissed the top of my head. She stormed out of the room. Judging by the fact that I heard the front door slam shut behind her only moments later, I had to imagine she'd seen herself out.

"You share an unusual friendship," I started.

He nodded. "Truly we are not friends."

"Then why?"

"She owes me," he interrupted. "Speak no more of her, poppet. I am much more interested in you."

I imagined this was his line to move us into the bedroom. I smiled up at him. "Interested in me?"

"You had a multitude of animals to choose from, you said?" he asked. I felt my hopes deflate. I mean, how hard was it for a girl to get a little action?

"Yeah, I think so."

"Can you demonstrate?"

I took a deep breath and figured there was no point in arguing with him. Besides, I *was* curious as to whether or not I could become another creature. I closed my eyes and was surprised to find it took no time at all for all the animals to assemble around me again. This time my attention centered on an eagle, perched in a nearby tree. I focused on the gallant raptor and the same feeling of light-headedness began to fill me. Then, in the span of a blink, I was in Sinjin's kitchen, standing on the counter and glancing down at the room while an array of colors reflected back at me. The brightness of the colors astounded me—they were like nothing I'd ever seen before. I guess it made sense because a bird's vision included a much broader spectrum of colors than a human's.

I heard Sinjin chuckling but couldn't seem to focus on him and realized my eyes were now on the sides of my head. I hopped around, turning my head in order to see him. The scratching of my talons against his granite countertops scraped in my ears and I had to hope he wouldn't be concerned about me damaging them. When I turned my eagle head, I could see him out of the corner of my eye. He was entirely black, like a shadow.

"Can you fly, poppet?"

I lifted my arms—er, wings—and flapped a few times before kicking off with my legs to find myself airborne. But I never had the chance to fully experience the rush of flying, because seconds later the dizziness from before returned. My heartbeat escalated at the thought that I was midair and resuming my human body. I didn't have much time to worry, though, because the next thing I knew, I was falling.

"Sinjin!" I screamed out and felt the air stirring beneath me as Sinjin materialized just in time to catch me in his large arms. I glanced down at myself, to find I was naked again. When I looked up at Sinjin, he was grinning from ear to ear.

"You do not realize the immensity of the gift you have," he said softly, his eyes running down my naked body as his fangs began to lengthen.

"Gift?" I asked with a smile, loving the expression of pride in his eyes. "Well, one thing I can say is I'm pretty convinced that I'm a witch."

He chuckled deeply, heartily. "You are much more than a witch, my pet."

"More than a witch?"

He nodded. "I have never known of any witch or warlock with the power to transform into more than one creature, poppet." He shook his head in apparent surprise. "You are an anomaly."

An anomaly? I wasn't sure what to make of it. I was

having enough trouble just coming to terms with being something super-human. After everyone else decided I was a witch, I sort of figured there must have been some truth to it. But to be something more than a witch? I didn't even know what that meant, or could possibly mean . . .

Thirteen

The next evening, I found myself sitting on my couch, bobbing my leg anxiously as I tried to watch television. I actually had no idea what program was on because my mind was wholly absorbed by Sinjin. We planned to have dinner in at my place (well, dinner for me, anyway) and a nice, relaxed, romantic evening with just the two of us. The night before had been anything but relaxing, what with the Bella drama, so Sinjin had promised to make it up to me tonight.

Speaking of my last meeting with Sinjin, I still didn't quite know what to make of everything. Really, for the first time since Sinjin entered my life, I found myself concerned about what was becoming of me. I felt different down to my very core. Yes, I looked different because I was paying more attention to my outward appearance, but the changes within me were much more significant. I was not the same woman today that I had been two months ago. And truth be told, I was struggling with those changes, not the least of which was my ability to morph into two animals. I had no clue what had made that at all possible. How could I, Jolie Wilkins, now turn myself into a tiger and an eagle?

My mind had been stretching in order to make room for the reality of vampires, witches, and warlocks. It only continued to stretch with the sure knowledge that I was included in this much-esteemed company. Yet I felt as though I'd just about reached my limit after the events of last night. It was almost as if my mind refused to accept any more. What if I *had* completely lost my mind and was now living in some parallel universe, fueled purely by my imagination? What if Sinjin and Rand were entirely made up? In that case, maybe the lion, tiger, and eagle transmogrifications were hallucinations too? I mean, that would make a hell of a lot more sense than actually accepting the fact that I was still a perfectly sane woman.

I glanced up at the clock on my wall and noticed it was seven p.m. Sinjin wouldn't be arriving for at least another thirty minutes. Out the window the sun was on her way out, bathing the world in a darkish rose hue. I never wanted the sun to go down faster than I did now. Although I didn't want to admit it, and definitely wasn't comfortable with it, the truth was that I yearned for Sinjin constantly. Whenever I wasn't with him, he was the only thing on my mind.

I smiled when I remembered last night—how Sinjin had made love to me repeatedly, how tender he'd been and attentive. He said more than once how terrible he felt about the whole Bella situation and how I had become the most important woman in his life. No one else mattered to him. Well, if Sinjin was just the creation of my befuddled mind, I'd done a damn good job, that was for sure.

My inner monologue was interrupted by a knock on the door. Puzzled, I glanced at the clock again and realized only ten minutes had elapsed. Looking out my window, I realized dusk had arrived, although it still seemed too light for Sinjin. But apparently I was wrong.

I stood up and glanced down at my skintight jeans and low-cut black, stretch T-shirt, imagining Sinjin would appreciate my cleavage spilling over the top. I ran my tongue across my teeth to ensure that my pink NARS lip gloss hadn't smudged and then fluffed my hair a few times. Finally, I felt a smile begin as I opened my front door.

And instantly my smile vanished.

My first instinct was to slam the door shut, but he was too quick and, instead, threw all his weight into the door, forcing it open. It was like time stood still as I tried to sidestep him, hoping I could make it through my kitchen to the back door, but he seemed to read my mind. As soon as I made a move for it, he thrust himself forward and knocked me on my butt. I squealed as I hit the ground, but immediately tried to stand up. He was too fast for me. In a split second, he slammed the door shut and threw his body back on me, forcing me down to the floor.

Bella's spell hadn't worked. Or maybe Rand's magic had been stronger, and he'd broken her charm.

"Get the hell off me!" I screamed as I pushed against him, but he was way too solid. He pinned my hands down on either side of my head. At his touch, that now familiar sense of electricity coursed through me and those ridiculous feelings of warmth began to well up inside me.

You are a freaking idiot, Jolie Wilkins! I chided myself. *This asshole is probably going to rape you and then kill you and all you can think about is his great energy and how he feels familiar!*

At the realization that I couldn't fight him, that I was now in serious trouble, I started screaming. He went for my mouth and tried to cover it with his hand but I threw my head left then right, screaming louder in the vain hope my neighbors would hear me.

"Jolie!" he yelled as he grabbed both of my cheeks with one large hand. "It's no use—I've soundproofed your house!"

I stopped screaming and tried to struggle from his massive hand, but of course got nowhere. Meanwhile, a continuous flow of terror was contaminating my insides at the realization that no one could hear me. "What the hell do you mean you soundproofed my house?" I finally demanded in a raw voice.

"Magic," he answered in a matter-of-fact sort of way. He breathed out a sigh of relief, probably because I was no longer thrashing against him or screaming.

Neither of us said anything for a few seconds. We just stared at each other as we both tried to get our breathing under control. Rand was the first to speak.

"I'm not here to hurt you."

I shook my head and laughed acidly. "I don't believe a word you say." And that was when it occurred to me. If I could just stall him long enough, Sinjin would arrive and there would be hell to pay. I also considered morphing into a tiger and mauling the shit out of him—but then I remembered that whole nudity bit once I returned to normal, and that part didn't sit so well with me.

"What do you want?" I demanded.

He swallowed hard. I couldn't help but notice how incredibly handsome he was with his chocolate-brown hair, now completely mussed, and his clothes all askew and rumpled. Well, gorgeous warlock or not, he remained dangerous. And that's what I had to keep in mind.

"Nothing could keep me from you."

"What?" I asked, gulping down the anxiety at the very thought that all this time, he could get to me, Bella's spell be damned. "How is that even possible?"

"It's a long story," he started and then sighed deeply. "And it's the reason why I've come here. Did you receive my package?"

I glared at him but nodded. "Yes, I received it."

"And did you watch the whole thing?"

"Yes but that doesn't mean I believed a word of it."

He sighed again, seemingly frustrated. "There's so much more I need to tell you, so much to explain to you, so you understand."

But I shook my head, not wanting to hear another word of his "drivel," as Sinjin had termed it. Then it suddenly occurred to me that I'd be putting Sinjin in a dangerous situation. I mean, he'd have no idea Rand was here or what magical abilities Rand had up his sleeve.

I would never forgive myself if something happened to Sinjin on my account. "I don't want to hear another lie from you," I spat back. "I want you to leave."

He shook his head and I could see his jaw was tight. "We can do this the easy way or the hard way. I'm leaving the choice up to you."

Sighing, I figured it was probably easier to persuade warlocks with honey than with vinegar. "What's the easy way?"

He shrugged. "We sit down, like civilized people, and you listen to what I have to say."

"So, after I listen to you, you'll leave?"

He took a deep breath and there was something in his eyes that looked hurt, painfully so. Or maybe I was just imagining it. "Yes."

I glanced at the clock and realized it was now seven thirty. It was also completely dark outside. Sinjin should be arriving any minute . . . "I . . . I have plans tonight but how about tomorrow?"

"Plans?" Rand's eyes narrowed, as he seemed to consider my offer. "And how can I be sure you'll actually show up tomorrow? You haven't exactly been accommodating thus far."

"Well, you know where I live so it's not like you won't be able to hunt me down." I frowned. "Something you've already proven you can do."

He seemed okay with a rain check and stood up, extending his hand to me as he did so, but I ignored it, pushing myself up and off the floor, dusting my jeans. I wasn't sure why, but for some reason I no longer felt afraid of him. It was almost as if his consenting to come back tomorrow negated all of my dread. It was weird and probably stupid, to say the least.

"What is this?" he demanded. Before I could stop him, he brushed my hair away from my neck, and his features contorted with anger when he saw Sinjin's teeth marks.

"That fucking bastard!" Rand yelled, his hands fisting at his sides. He turned around and I could see the rage in the tightness of his shoulders. Before I could even blink, he smashed his fist into my door.

"What is wrong with you?" I yelled, taking a few steps back, suddenly afraid again. Nothing like a pissed-off man unable to control his temper to jar me back to my senses. I mean, I knew he was a dangerous warlock. It shouldn't have taken an act of what appeared to be jealousy, strangely enough, to assure me of that.

He turned to face me and there was fury in his dark brown eyes, as well as a certain hollowness and pain. "I should never have let it progress this far," he said, mostly to himself. Then, before I could guess what would happen next, he lunged for me and grabbed my arm, pulling me toward the door.

"Let go of me!" I screamed, pulling against him.

"You're coming with me, Jolie," he said in a voice that brooked no argument. "It's for your own good."

I tried to extricate myself from him, but fighting him was useless. He was built like a mountain lion—sleek, yes, but also incredibly strong. "I'm not going anywhere with you!"

He instantly stopped dragging me and, instead, turned to face me. His expression was completely unreadable, but he didn't let go of my arm. "You will never forgive Sinjin for what he's done to you."

"What are you talking about?" I yelled as I struggled against him again, trying to pull my arm from his vise-like grip. He simply held me tighter. "You're hurting me!"

He let go of me then, as if I'd bitten him. I lost my balance as I tripped over my ridiculous wedge sandals and crumbled into a clumsy heap on the floor.

"This was never meant to happen, Jolie," Rand said as he approached me again, standing above me. I knew I wouldn't get far if I tried to bolt, so I stayed put.

"What was never meant to happen?"

He looked around himself and waved his hands as if to include everything—us, my house, my neighborhood, the whole world. "It was always you and me."

"Sinjin—"

"Sinjin never had a claim on you!" he interrupted. Then he shook his head as if this whole thing were a big misunderstanding and a damn shame at that.

"You aren't making any sense," I said, my voice softer as I realized I was dealing with someone who wasn't playing with a full deck. "There's nothing between you and me and there never was. I don't even know you!"

He shook his head and laughed but it was not a happy sound. "That's where you're wrong, Jolie. You and I have known each other for years. I taught you everything you know."

"But—" I started, shaking my head as I tried to comprehend his statement.

"The life you're leading now is a farce—it's all because that bastard Sinjin wanted you for himself and he knew the only way he'd have a chance in hell of wooing you away from me was to make contact with you first."

"That doesn't even make any sense!" I yelled at him again and stood up, wrapping my arms around myself protectively. "Look, I don't know who the hell you are . . ."

Then he was in front of me, grabbing my shoulders and holding me still. I could feel his breath fanning the naked skin of my chest and I closed my eyes. "Yes, you do, Jolie," he said softly, whispering as my breathing lengthened. There was just something so familiar about him, something that made me want to yield to him.

Resist the feelings, Jolie! I yelled at myself. *It's nothing but his warlock magic trying to charm you, making you feel like you've known him forever!*

It can't be. We're close—I can feel it in my blood, in the center of my being.

You haven't even known him two weeks!

Then why do I feel like this? I argued. *I know this man. I've known him for a long time. I can feel it. And you can't deny it either.*

"It's impossible," I said out loud and shook my head, opening my eyes and focusing on the dark chocolate pools of his.

"What's impossible?" Rand asked, his eyes searching, pleading.

"I. Don't. Know. You."

He took a deep breath and shook his head, even as I fought the need to believe everything he said. "You know me—deep down, I know you do."

But I refused to give into the part of me that wanted to believe him. Instead, I forced myself to consider how absurd the whole thing was. I had only just met him when he walked into my store. He and I meant nothing to each other; we weren't even acquaintances. "You must have me confused with someone else."

"No," he said, anger and frustration returning to his voice. He shook his head adamantly. "I have known you intimately, Jolie, I've known you like no other man ever could."

I swallowed hard. I knew he meant in more ways than just sexually, but it was the sexual connotation that made me blush right down to my feet. I dropped my gaze to my shaking hands, trying to figure out my next course of action, inventing a plan of escape.

"Look at me," he said, and I wasn't sure why, but I acquiesced. When I did, I felt the urge to believe him grow stronger. I felt that same sense of familiarity welling up inside me all over again.

"Stop doing that," I whispered, afraid because I could feel myself succumbing to the power he wielded over me. As strange as it sounded and as much as I didn't want to admit it, there was still something in me that needed to believe him, and to accept him.

"Doing what?"

"Making me feel things that aren't real."

He chuckled then, heartily. "It is real, Jolie. Whatever you're feeling for me is real."

"No, it isn't." I paused, taking a deep breath. "It's your magic."

He pulled me closer to him, and I was surprised at my lack of resistance. It was the same as it had been when he came to my store—as if I dissolved into mush in his hands. "No it's not my magic—it's the connection between us."

I closed my eyes and shook my head, feeling as if everything I knew, my entire world, was now under siege again. "I met you only a week or two ago," I started, reminding myself more than him.

"Jolie, I walked into your store two years ago and I've loved you ever since."

I felt my eyes open wide as I tried to make sense of his words. "Loved me?" I repeated, shocked.

He nodded and smiled almost shyly. My entire body began to quake from the inside out, to shake with the need to touch him, kiss him. I forced the feelings down, straining to recognize them for what they were—the spell of a master magician and nothing more.

"You have been the only woman in my life and you will continue to be the only woman I could ever love."

And that was all it took—just a brief reminder of a similar sentiment from Sinjin—to remind me that Rand was not the one I was meant to be with, that everything he was telling me was a lie. I loved Sinjin, that's all there was to it. "You need to leave," I said frigidly.

"Don't fight this, Jolie." He looked into my eyes, and I couldn't pull my gaze away. "God, you are so beautiful," he said and I felt my heart flutter at his words. "You have no idea how worried I've been about you, how much I've missed you."

Then his lips were on mine and I was shocked and disgusted with myself when I did nothing to fight him. In fact, I welcomed his lips and encouraged his tongue to find entrance into my mouth. He ran his hands through my hair and I felt myself melt against him.

"My, my! Such a happy little couple."

I heard Sinjin's voice. I pulled away from Rand and turned to Sinjin in the doorway, but he didn't seem upset in the least. Rather, he appeared merely entertained. He was wearing that smirky smile, but when I looked at his eyes I realized he was livid.

"Sinjin. I . . . I don't know what happened," I started, realizing how completely horrible this situation looked. He'd basically just walked in on me kissing another man.

He faced me, shaking his head. "Do not apologize, little poppet. The warlock's coercive powers were too much for you to fend off."

I glanced at Rand and didn't know what to think. Had it been his magic all along that caused me to feel and act this way? Maybe, but there was definitely something inside me that felt as if I were right where I needed to be—in his arms. I almost felt as if I'd come home.

"Come," Sinjin said to me. Still in a fog of confused emotions, I pulled away from Rand and walked closer to Sinjin, all the while fighting the need to return to Rand's arms. Sinjin grabbed me and pulled me close to his chest, never dropping his eyes from Rand's. "She is mine, Balfour. The sooner you realize that, the better." Then he smiled, his eyes narrow. "You have been spurned."

Rand was fuming—I could see it in the red of his cheeks, his shallow breathing, his chest rising and falling. "You've gone too far this time, Sinjin," he managed to spit out. Then he faced me. "Step away from him, Jolie."

I glanced at Sinjin as though I were seeking his permission, or at the least, to get a clue of what was happening. He merely smiled down at me and nodded, pushing me slightly from him. "Randall . . ."

But he never finished his sentence. Instead, I watched, horrified, as Rand lunged for him and threw him to the ground. Rand pulled his arm back and pummeled Sinjin's face as the vampire held up his arms to protect himself. In a split second, Sinjin disappeared from below Rand and reappeared behind him. But Rand was prepared, seeming to fly off his feet, pivoting around. He ducked in time to miss Sinjin's blow and delivered his own series of jabs into Sinjin's stomach. All in all, it seemed as if they were pretty evenly matched.

"Stop!" I screamed and, not even thinking, rushed over to the two of them. I threw myself onto Rand's back, toppling over a table just beside the door in the process. But I wasn't concerned. Instead, all my distress was reserved for the fight that was in the process of blowing up between the two men. Grabbing Rand's forearms, I screamed again. "Stop it!"

Rand merely shook me off and dived for Sinjin. "You will pay for what you've done, bastard!" Rand yelled. The vampire chuckled and sidestepped him, giving me the opportunity to wedge myself between the two of them.

"I love him!" I screamed at Rand, not even realizing what I was saying or what I was admitting in front of Sinjin. I'd promised myself I wouldn't (well, not until he admitted it to me first). But the time for regrets was over. "Whatever you think we share isn't real!" I continued, tears flooding my eyes.

Rand stood stock-still, his shallow breathing betraying his exhaustion. But I couldn't look away from his face. He was devastated. He continued staring at me, pain and betrayal in his eyes. But I didn't care. If his relentless hunt for me was based on unrequited love, I needed to nip it in the bud . . . now.

"If you truly care about me, then you'll leave us alone!" I screamed again, tears streaming down my face. "Because I love Sinjin."

"Jolie," he started, taking a step toward me.

I held him back with my hand. "No," I said, my voice cracking with the effort. "Whatever you think we have, it's nothing more than a delusion."

"Just listen to me," he said.

I shook my head. "I have nothing more to say to you."

He took a deep breath and ran his fingers through his hair as he shook his head but said nothing more. He walked past me and hesitated only momentarily. Once he approached Sinjin, though, he stopped and faced him with hatred flashing from his eyes.

"This isn't over, Sinclair," he said. "I will never stop until she understands what you did to her."

Smiling, Sinjin threw his arm around my shoulder and pulled me close to him, kissing the top of my head. Rand's lips were tight as he turned around and disappeared out my front door. For some strange reason, and I wasn't sure why, there was something within me that felt numb, something hollow and sad, that I hadn't felt before.

I pulled away from Sinjin, my head ready to explode, there were so many thoughts and questions running through it. I immediately noticed that any damage Rand might have inflicted on him had already healed.

"What was he talking about?" I demanded.

Sinjin shook his head. "The nonsensical ravings of a madman."

I didn't say anything right away but, somehow, I knew he was lying to me.

Sinjin has no reason to lie to you, Jolie, part of me argued. *Rand has just completely lost his mind and must think you're someone else. Or he's just trying to manipulate you into believing there's something between you.*

That may be, my other half replied, *but I also think Sinjin's holding out—that he knows more than he's letting on. He just makes everything seem so simple and I know well enough that that is never the case.*

"Did I meet Rand . . . before? Like, a long time ago?"

Sinjin faced me with a smile. "Poppet, that is a question only you can answer. I know of no affiliation between you and the warlock."

I shook my head, trying to understand how any of this made sense, trying to fill in the pieces. "I met him in my store not long ago, like I told you."

"Then you have your answer."

"But why does he seem to think . . ."

"He is mad, love," he said simply. "If you remembered the moment you met him accurately and it truly was only a week or two ago, as you claim, then that can only be the truth, correct?"

I nodded, relieved that it made lots more sense to just

trust Sinjin. That part of me that insisted I could only have known Rand for a matter of days had to be right. I mean, what more could I go on? It's not like I could remember meeting Rand earlier. The whole thing was completely absurd.

I faced him with a smile and nodded. "Yes, you're right."

"Poppet," he started and approached me with a twinkle in his eyes.

"Yes?" I responded.

"Did you mean what you said?"

I gulped hard, realizing he was referring to when I basically yelled at Rand that I was in love with Sinjin. Well, no use in denying it now. The cat was already way out of the bag. I dropped my eyes to the ground and felt my cheeks flush. "Yes."

Instantly, he was before me, tilting my chin up so I could gaze into his face. There was a passion in his eyes I'd never seen before. He just stared at me for a few seconds, and when he spoke his voice was deadly serious. "You do not know how I have yearned to hear those words."

Fourteen

My eyes flew open, my heartbeat pounding away in my chest. I took a deep breath and tried to calm myself, trying to persuade myself that whatever nightmare I'd just awoken from was just that—a nightmare, nothing more. Staring at the dark ceiling of my bedroom, I realized night was still upon me. I turned my head to the side, the clock on my bedside table glowing two thirty in the morning. Sitting up, I rubbed my eyes. Somehow I just couldn't shake off the feeling of dread instigated by the dream—it was still eerily haunting me.

Jolie, it was just a dream, something you completely made up in that ridiculous head of yours! I tried to reassure myself. But it was one of those nightmares where you can't really stop thinking about it—despite knowing that you're safely ensconced in your own bed, in your own house, and whatever evils your brain created aren't real and can't hurt you.

This nightmare wasn't so much about the visuals, though, as the feelings it drummed up within me—anxiety, hopelessness, dread . . . familiarity. It was as if I'd seen it all before, that uncanny déjà vu everyone experiences sometime in his or her life. The strangest part about the whole thing, though, was that although the images of the nightmare were macabre, they meant nothing to me. I lay back down again and closed my eyes, trying to go back to sleep, but all I could focus on were the visions that had just faded—from a nightmare that made no sense at all . . . So why couldn't I shake it?

The dream began with scenes of open land that was devastated and barren, like a bomb had gone off. But the lumps on the ground were what grabbed my attention. They were people lying facedown in muck, people who were also very much dead. Almost as quickly as the vision upset me, it receded into the distance of my subconscious and another one replaced it. This dreamscape centered on a throne that was vacant. A scepter and a crown stood at either side of a golden chair. Then, just like that, the image of the chair was ripped away, replaced by a battle scene. I saw creatures I knew— witches, warlocks, and vampires—as well as others that I didn't recognize. They all displayed extraordinary powers as they battled one another, fighting to the death. The term *Lurkers* entered my mind, and seemed to eat through my body like cancer. Just as quickly as the image of the combative creatures vanished from my unconscious mind, the image of the throne returned. This time, however, the crown and the scepter began melting into the base of the golden chair. And that's what woke me up, now a frantic mess in a cold sweat.

As I lay in my bed and coaxed my mind to rest—to ignore the meaningless dreamscapes—I started to feel an overwhelming sense of exhaustion, almost of nausea. What did it mean that the word *Lurkers* was in my dream? I remembered Sinjin telling me about the Lurkers, how Bella had cast that spell to learn what they were up to. I shook the feelings of dread aside. It was merely my subconscious playing tricks on me, bringing to light subjects from my conscious mind. Still, mind trick or not, I suddenly didn't want to be alone. I was cross with myself for telling Sinjin I needed to be alone tonight, that I had to sleep. Really, that was never the truth. Instead, I'd been so bothered by his exchange with Rand, I felt I needed some "me-time" away from the imposing, larger-than-life vampire.

Yes, I loved Sinjin, but I couldn't deny that there was something within me that didn't entirely believe him, not 100 percent, anyway. So, seeking some elucidation, I opted for a night on my own. I hoped that with some time to think about everything that had happened, I could figure out what to make of the whole ordeal. Well, that was then. Now I would have gladly traded in the me-time for some Sinjin-time. I just felt strangely feeble—like an incredibly rapid illness had started consuming me, draining me of strength. Of course, that was ludicrous—it wasn't like dreams could cause illness.

I tossed and turned for a few more minutes, unable to get comfortable. After another ten minutes, during which I counted 150 sheep, 70 horses, 54 chickens, and 20 rabbits, I decided to give up. I sat up and took a deep breath, fighting the realization that I truly wasn't well. The more I fought it, however, the more I knew I had just contracted a case of the most contagious flu known to man. I brought the top of my hand to my forehead and checked my temperature the old-fashioned way.

I was definitely feverish.

Then, deciding not to rely on such a non-scientific test, I pushed the bedclothes aside and forced myself up. Instantly, I felt light-headed and almost dazed. I managed to make it to my bathroom where I turned on the light and groped inside my top drawer for the thermometer. I stuck it in my mouth and waited. When it beeped its signal, I pulled it out and read it. I was running a temperature of 104.

"What?" I asked out loud. I shook it, thinking there must have been something wrong with the thermometer, and put it back under my tongue. A minute later it beeped again, revealing the same result. I was on fire!

Now really nervous, I threw open my medicine cabinet and searched for the Tylenol. I swiftly downed two of the gelcaps and glanced in the mirror, noting how pale my skin looked and damp my hairline was—from sweat.

"What is wrong with me?" I asked my reflection. As I hobbled back to bed, I felt pathetically feeble and frail. I sort of collapsed on top of it and managed to wrap the duvet cover over me, taco-style. That was when I knew something was seriously wrong. I'd never had a cold or a flu develop so quickly. What if I'd picked up a strange infection like *E. coli* or something equally unpleasant? What if I had flesh-eating bacteria? I felt my stomach suddenly recoiling at the thought and I had to wonder if the bacteria hadn't already invaded, devouring my stomach lining.

I reached for the phone beside my bed and dialed Sinjin's number.

"Poppet," he answered on the first ring. "Why are you awake at this hour? I thought you needed your rest?" His tone was jovial, as if he was delighted to hear my voice.

"Something's wrong with me, Sinjin," I said as I shivered despite myself. "I think I have that flesh-eating bacteria."

"Wrong with you?" he repeated, any joy now completely absent from his tone. "Flesh-eating bacteria?"

"Yes, I feel incredibly sick and weak."

"I will be there momentarily," he said and, before I could respond, he hung up. I placed the phone on the cradle and huddled in the fetal position, trying to will myself warm, but chills were now running up and down my body.

No more than five minutes passed between the time I got off the phone with Sinjin and his arrival at my house. I heard him try the front door and remembered I'd locked it. Then I heard his footsteps as he walked around the house, eventually finding his way to my bedroom window. I sat up and took a deep breath, unsure of how I would stand up and walk over to the window to let him in. I hobbled a few steps but suddenly felt light-headed, seeing stars orbiting around me. Leaning and off balance, I started to succumb to what I assumed was a faint and caught myself on my boudoir chair in the corner of the room.

At the sound of shattered glass, I didn't need to glance up to know Sinjin had just arrived. Within an instant, he was beside me, heaving me into his arms as he crunched on the glass underfoot. I couldn't find it within me to complain about my smashed bedroom window. I was just too tired, too sick to care.

"What is the matter, poppet?" he asked with visible concern. "What is wrong with you?"

I nestled my head against his broad chest and closed my eyes for a moment, relishing the fact that he was here, that he would take care of me. "I don't know," I whispered. "I just remember this weird dream and then, all of a sudden, I felt so weak and so . . . so sick."

He lay me down on my bed and I shivered as soon as he removed his hands. Strangely enough, considering how cold he was, I felt warmer in his arms. He wrapped the duvet around me and sat down close to me, stroking my hair like a mother would her sick child.

"Describe the dream."

I closed my eyes, wanting only to sleep off my feelings of exhaustion and weariness. But Sinjin tapped my shoulder as if to remind me that I hadn't answered him. I yawned and tried to remember the dream again. "It was just a bunch of images," I started. "The first was a battlefield of dead bodies. Then there was an empty throne with a scepter and a crown." I glanced up at him and saw him swallow hard. It was almost as if he could see the very scenes I was describing. Something in his eyes hinted at familiarity; he didn't seem shocked or surprised.

"Go on," he prodded.

"I remember the word *Lurkers* repeating over and over again through my head." I was quiet for a second or two as scenes from the dream returned anew. "But it wasn't even my voice in my head that was saying the word," I said, amazed by the sudden realization. "I think it was a man's voice that kept repeating 'Lurkers.' It was as if someone else sent the dream to me."

"And then what happened, poppet?" Sinjin asked, his tone purposeful, his eyes narrowed on me.

I shook my head, still fixated on the idea that the dream seemed forced—as if it hadn't really been mine. "Then seconds after I woke up, I had a fever and started feeling awful."

"I see." He glanced down at me with a fake smile, as if he was trying to hide what was in his eyes—could it be fear? "Perhaps you have caught the flu?"

I shook my head, refusing to believe that my current condition had anything to do with a virus. At this point, I'd also ruled out the flesh-eating bacteria. No, this was somehow connected to my nightmare. I was certain of it. "Sinjin, what does this mean?"

He shook his head, crossing his arms against his chest as he did so. "I do not know, love." But something in his expression screamed the opposite. After a few seconds of silence, he said, "Poppet, I think we should call Isabella."

"Bella?" I asked, as my stomach dropped to my feet. I felt like vomiting now more than ever before. The last thing I wanted to do was deal with that snobby bitch again, especially when I wasn't feeling my normal, patient, good-natured self.

He nodded and stood up, fishing his iPhone from his pocket. "I want her to . . . examine you."

I tried to sit up but found I wasn't strong enough. "Examine me?" I took a deep breath, suddenly finding it difficult to inhale as I was seized with a fit of coughing. Once I'd gotten myself under control again, I said, "I don't understand."

But he said nothing more as I watched him dial Bella on his cell phone. Then he turned his back on me as if he didn't want me to overhear their conversation. A few seconds later, he clicked off his phone, sliding it back into his pocket as he turned to face me with an artificial smile.

"Why are you acting so weird?" I demanded.

"Weird, poppet?"

"My dream didn't seem to surprise you at all."

He shook his head and sat down beside me, rubbing my shoulder as he gave me a reassuring smile. "It must be your fever speaking, love. I have no knowledge of your dream."

I figured it was useless to argue, especially when I was feeling so crappy. "Why does Bella have to come over?" I asked, turning to something else that aggravated me.

He sighed. "I want to be certain there is not more to this sudden illness of yours than meets the eye."

"Do you think it's magic-related, then?" I asked, feeling the tentacles of a headache starting between my eyes. I closed my eyes and purposefully willed the headache to go away. It surprised me when the pain began to fade away into nothing.

"Perhaps," he said simply before facing me again, compassion in his ice-blue gaze. "Poppet, you need to rest and conserve your strength to overcome this bug. Please no more questions."

I wanted to argue with him, to demand an explanation as to how and why he thought magic was involved, but he was correct, I did need to conserve my strength. I was now even more exhausted than before. It was as if the willpower to send my headache packing had zapped me of any remaining energy I possessed.

I closed my eyes and tried to sleep, but was unsuccessful. Instead, I listened to the sound of Sinjin cleaning up the broken glass from the window, and then his footsteps as he paced back and forth, obviously distressed by my condition. I found myself zoning out with the rhythm of his footfalls against my wood floor. I wondered why there were times when he didn't make a sound, and could walk up behind me without me ever hearing him. Yet at other times, he made as much sound as a regular person.

The next thing I knew, Sinjin was at my bedside with Bella. I didn't recall the sound of her knocking on my door, nor had I heard him leaving my room to let her in. So either I'd fallen asleep for a few seconds, or my fever was accompanied by delirium.

"What is wrong with her?" Bella demanded caustically, eyeing me with disinterest. I didn't get a good look at her but what I saw was enough. She was dressed in skintight black pants and a magenta sweater with a deeply plunging neckline. I bet this woman couldn't be casual if she tried.

I heard Sinjin inhale deeply before he told her, "I am not certain. However, I believe it to be a magical attack."

"A magical attack?" she repeated in an abrasive tone. "Who would possibly want to attack her? No one knows about her anyway." She sounded dismissive, not to mention irritated that someone would bother about me—since she saw me as just a nobody.

"I refuse to discuss the specifics with you, Isabella. Please use your powers to detect what has happened to her."

There was silence for a few seconds, but I could feel the tension in the room. It didn't take a genius to realize that Bella not only was unaccustomed to being spoken to in such a way, but really didn't like it. "I am not at your beck and call, Sinjin," she said flatly.

"You know why you are here," he countered. By the sound of his voice, he was just as irritated as she was.

"I understand we have an agreement, but—"

"Enough!" His angry tone caused my heart to race for a few seconds, and I felt a rush of pain in my head. The headache I'd just willed away moments before had returned with a vengeance.

"Put her on her back," Bella said in an aggravated voice.

I felt Sinjin's hands on either of my shoulders, and he smiled down at me almost apologetically as he gently rolled me from my side to my back. Then he pulled away and I was faced with Bella's beautiful but fuming countenance. She narrowed her eyes as she looked down at me and offered no form of a greeting. Instead, she held out her hands, palms above me, and closed her eyes. Her lips twitched as she seemed to recite some sort of chant in her head. But it was the space between her hands that had me enthralled as a light began to build between them. It was purplish and then began to morph into what resembled smoke, circling between her palms. She opened her eyes and brought her hands to my face, touching her fingers to my temples. At her touch, the smallest spark of energy—a gentle drumming that fizzed against my skin—ran through me. I could see the purplish smoke light cycling around my head now, right before my eyes. I glanced at Bella and noticed her eyes were shut again as she chanted something to herself.

She opened her eyes sharply and pulled away, dropping her hands from my temples. Immediately the swirling smoke dissipated. She faced Sinjin and arched her left eyebrow. "You're right. She has been the victim of an attack of magic through her unconscious mind," she announced simply.

"What does that mean?" I demanded.

She glanced in my direction. "It means that someone knew it would be easiest to plague you when you were sleeping."

"So?" I continued.

"So he or she infiltrated your mind with a dream, attacking you when you were at your weakest and leaving behind the sickness you're currently experiencing."

"So the dream was some sort of illness?" I asked.

Bella nodded. "Essentially, yes."

"Attack by witch or fae?" Sinjin asked, his voice laced with concern.

"I don't know," Bella responded.

"How advanced is her condition?"

She glanced at me again without even the slightest bit of concern in her expression. "It seems to be progressing rapidly."

"What can you do?" Sinjin insisted.

She shook her head. "I will need time."

"Time is a luxury we cannot afford," he barked.

Her jaw was tight. "In this case, you don't have a choice."

"What—" I started. "What is wrong with me?" My voice was rough as my heartbeat started escalating. I could feel my breath coming in short spurts.

"She should sleep," Bella said. "There is no use in keeping her awake."

"Charm her," Sinjin ordered as he turned to me again. He smiled sweetly as he held a hand to my forehead and ran his fingers down my temple to my cheek. Bella swallowed hard as she watched him, her eyes narrowing on me again.

She said nothing but faced me and never took her eyes

from mine. Then she held up her hands, a white light glowing from them, as she said, "Sleep now."

My eyelids were instantly heavy. I fought to keep them open, though, since I wanted to understand more about what was happening to me. I'd never been so sick, seemingly deathbed sick. But it was no use. I began to succumb to Bella's power, my body falling into a deep sleep. My eyes were the last to give in to her power, and before I closed them, I caught the image of Bella looping her arms around Sinjin's neck as she smiled up at him, asking him when it would just be the two of them, when she would have him to herself again.

I never heard his response.

I was dreaming, some part of me well aware that I'd been charmed to sleep. Another part of me, however, somewhere in the back of my mind, remained awake. But it really made no difference because most of me was already lost in dreams.

These dreams were much more welcome than the last batch I'd been unfortunate enough to endure. Now I dreamed of a man with wavy brown hair and eyes of the same color. I could see him above me as he smiled, his dimples giving him a boyish sort of grin. There was rough stubble on his cheeks and chin that tickled when he kissed me. I giggled against him, and when he pulled back, proclaiming I was the most beautiful woman he'd ever seen, I just laughed and wrapped my arms around his neck, pulling him down to kiss me again.

We were outside in the sunshine, rolling and laughing in a field of heather. There was a certain crispness to the air, a salty mist brought over from the sea.

"Come with me, Jolie," the beautiful man said and stood up, reaching down for me. I put my small hands in his, and as he pulled me upright, I glanced down at myself to find I was wearing a white eyelet dress that came to my knees. The sleeves were long but did nothing to keep me from shivering in the brisk sea air.

"Where are we going?" I asked, brushing my long golden locks over my shoulder to find they were decorated with bluebells.

"It's not safe for you here," he answered as he pulled me close to hug me and I wondered what he could mean.

Then my handsome man began to fade right in front of me, right there in my arms. Soon he vanished into the air as if he'd never been there at all.

"Wait!" I screamed after him, alone in the cold air that was now surrounding me. "Come back!"

I felt my eyes pop open as confusion muddled my mind. I was no longer in the meadow with the beautiful man. Instead I was in my bedroom, and the garish sun was forcing itself through my windows, blinding me with its intensity. I tried to identify the shadow of a person sitting in a chair beside me, blinking a few times against the intrusive sun, waiting for my pupils to constrict. When they did, I half wished they hadn't.

"Bella?" I asked, sounding puzzled.

"You've been asleep for half the day," she responded in her usual irritated tone.

"What are you doing here?" I continued in a feeble voice, feeling as if my head was going to split in two. Exhaustion and weakness were consuming me, just as they had the night before. I couldn't even lift my head.

"Sinjin put me on duty while he rests," she responded and began inspecting her nails.

I nodded and closed my eyes again, feeling even sicker than the night before. As soon as my eyelashes touched my upper cheeks, I heard something. At first it sounded far off and muffled, but the more I focused on it, the clearer it became.

Jolie.

It was a man's voice and a voice I knew, a voice that I

suddenly felt I had known forever. It was the voice of the man in the meadow, and I had to wonder if I were dreaming again. I opened my eyes to test the theory but found Bella sitting beside me, glaring at her phone as she texted someone. No, I definitely wasn't dreaming.

Yes, I thought the word, testing to see if it was in my head. *Who are you?*

Rand, the voice said and a flush of warmth crept through my body, overwhelming me with the sensations of safety and happiness.

He is your enemy, came my next thought but I shook it away as something within me, something bigger and stronger, insisted that Rand was not my enemy and never had been.

Listen to me, Jolie, his voice said. *You must trust me or you're going to die. I can heal you—I'm a warlock and I have that ability.*

But you're my enemy! You're dangerous.

You know that isn't the truth! Trust me.

How are you in my head? I asked, suddenly feeling even more exhausted.

It is the connection we share, one we've always shared. He paused for a second or two. *It's just a small link of our bond.*

I didn't understand what he meant so I didn't respond.

I can feel your weakness, Jolie. I can feel your illness.

I swallowed hard, not even bothering to wonder how that was possible, much less how we were having a telepathic conversation. I just chalked it up to my fevered mind, which was just as sick as my body. *I don't know what's wrong with me,* I answered in my mind's voice.

I am coming for you, he said. *We can heal you.*

I didn't have the strength to wonder who "we" meant and let it go. Instead, I felt relief flooding me at the thought of seeing him again, feeling his arms around me, knowing that I was safe.

Are you alone? he asked.

No, Bella is here.

There was silence for a moment or two, and I could feel the beginnings of anger welling up within me. A split second later I knew it wasn't my own anger I was experiencing but Rand's. It was, as he said, our connection.

You must send Bella away, Jolie. You must think up a diversion.

I swallowed hard but figuratively nodded.

When she is gone, contact me again, he finished.

How?

Just think the words, the same as you're doing now.

I breathed out a large breath and tried to imagine a way to get rid of Bella. What could possibly send her away? At first, I drew a blank; then it came to me.

I opened my eyes. "I feel something," I said, my voice hollow, pained.

"What?" she demanded with little or no interest, continuing to fiddle with her phone.

"Sinjin, I feel like there's something wrong with him," I finished and smiled inwardly once I realized I had her attention.

"What do you mean?"

I shook my head and sighed, feeling exhaustion beginning to claim me again. It took all the energy I had just to speak. "I don't know. I just . . . have a bad feeling about him. Can you . . . can you go check on him?"

She narrowed her eyes, but something in them hinted that my words worried her. "He told me not to leave your side."

"Please, Bella, I just feel something . . . bad about him, like something's . . . happened to him."

She stood up and threw her purse over her shoulder. "I'll be back," she said before disappearing into my hallway.

I smiled as I closed my eyes and reached out for Rand. *Rand! Can you hear me?* I thought the words.

Yes, I heard in my head. *Did you manage to get rid of her?*

She's leaving but you'll only have twenty minutes, at the most.

I am already on my way, he said, and then our connection was lost. I smiled to myself before clenching my eyes tightly as another headache hammered me.

It felt as if mere minutes had passed when I heard footsteps. I opened my eyes and found Rand before me. He was wearing dark jeans and a white T-shirt that contrasted against his tan skin, making him literally glow with healthiness. It was the same outfit, I suddenly realized, that he'd been wearing in my dream.

"Jolie," he whispered.

"I don't know what's wrong," I started but he brought his fingers to my lips and silenced me.

"You must sleep, Jolie. When you wake, everything will be fine again. I will see to it." His words must have acted like a spell because I suddenly felt myself falling back into the seas of sleep, cresting the waves of dreams.

Fifteen

"I think she's coming to."

There were voices—three of them, one woman and two men. And they all sounded tense. I could hear the sound of pacing—footsteps going to the far end of the room and back again, only to repeat themselves. I groaned as I opened my eyes and rolled my head to the side, feeling the prick of goose down from the pillow my head was currently lying on. I rolled my head upright again and spotted a thatched ceiling just above me. I had to still be dreaming.

"Jolie?" It was Rand's voice.

I turned my head and my focus went blurry as I tried to look at him. He hurried to me from across the room and I guessed he was the "pacer" I had heard walking back and forth when I woke up. He appeared as a brown blur at first, but after a few seconds, this delineated itself into the insanely handsome man I was coming to know. "What . . . what happened?" I asked.

He grasped my hand as he smiled down at me. His smile reminded me of the dream I'd had when we were kissing in the heather, feeling the sea breeze wrap around us and caring about nothing besides each other.

"We've healed you," he said softly before turning to face someone else in the room. "Mathilda?"

I glanced beyond him at the little old woman who was

now hobbling up to my side. There was something about her that was also familiar—something that tugged at my memory. She smiled down at me and held her hands above my face. I felt my eyes focusing on the lines etched in her skin, hinting at just how old she was. That was when it hit me. She was the same old woman who had come into my store. Just like the first time I'd met her, she was wearing the same ill-fitting, outdated long dress, and her hair was just as unruly in its extreme length. And she still possessed that same aura of age-old beauty.

"The block has been removed," she said simply as she dropped her hands, turning to take a seat just beside the bed.

"But . . . ," I started, still staring at her. "You . . . you were in my store."

"Yes, child," she said and smiled softly, her voice again reminding me of the ringing of bells. "Yes, that was I."

"You're a witch?" I asked as I focused on the blaze of blue light emanating from her. How had I missed it before? I tried to remember if there had been any indication she was otherworldly when I first met her. Try as I might, though, I could think of nothing.

She shook her head and Rand patted my hand, pulling my attention back to him. "No, Jolie. Mathilda is one of the oldest and wisest of the fae."

"The fae," I repeated, shaking my head as doubt seized me. "You mean, like a fairy?"

"Aye," a man's voice called from the corner of the room. I craned my head and swallowed hard at the vision of an incredibly tall, broad, muscular man who stepped out in front of me. "I am Odran," he said simply.

"Odran is the King of the fae," Rand said, smiling as I regarded the King of the fae with openmouthed aston-

ishment. He was just so . . . so . . . big! Big and beautiful . . . stunningly so. His long blond hair fell about him
in a mass of waves, pale against the bronze of his body.
His eyes reflected the tan color of his skin, flecked with
rays of amber. He was wearing nothing but a kilt, and
his chest, though riddled with muscles, was completely
hairless. His face and overall stature seemed reminiscent
of a lion.

And that was when feelings of dread descended on
me. I was completely at their mercy now. If Rand and
Mathilda had evil intentions where I was concerned, I
was as good as dead. God, I'd been so stupid. Why had
I trusted them? Why had I allowed myself to get into this
predicament?

Because you were dying and Rand saved you, my con-
science announced.

*So what, maybe he just saved me so he can kill me
later.*

You know that isn't true.

*Well, you can't tell me what the truth is so why listen
to you anyway? And dammit all, how is Sinjin going to
find me?*

I turned to face Rand again, needing to know where I
was and what was happening. "I don't understand
what's happened and where I am . . ."

"Ye are in oone ah me villages, lass," Odran responded
in a thick Scottish brogue. It was as if he'd crawled off
the cover of one of those Highlander romance novels
they sold at the grocery store.

"Jolie, I will explain all of this to you in time but suffice it to say you're safe now. No one can harm you."

I closed my eyes and swallowed down the relief that
suddenly washed over me at his words. Relief that was
immediately replaced with fear.

No one knows where I am.

I felt like I wanted to sit up again. Rand tried to hold

me down but I adamantly shook my head. Admitting I'd won the tacit argument, he assisted me. He pushed the pillow behind my back so I could prop myself against it. "Am I still in Los Angeles?" I asked, wondering where a fairy village could exist in the city.

Rand shook his head. "No, we're in the sequoia forest."

I swallowed hard. "The what?" I asked, thinking to myself that the sequoias had been a good four-hour drive the last time I'd ventured up there. And that had to mean that at least four hours had passed since I blacked out at my house . . . Oh my God. Four hours!

"All fae villages exist in forests," Rand continued, but I couldn't say my mind was on the habitation and villages of fae.

"How long have I been here?" I inquired, my voice laced with worry.

Rand nodded in understanding and when he spoke, his voice was soft, compassionate. "A day."

"A day?" I repeated, shaking my head. How could I have been out of it for a whole day? And furthermore, what was going through Sinjin's mind? He must be worried sick because as far as he was concerned, I'd basically vanished. I swallowed down the worry that suddenly plagued me and tried to think of a way back. "I've been asleep all this time?"

Mathilda nodded. "You had to overcome the magical block, child," she said.

"What is a magical block?" I demanded, feeling as if the weight of the world was now descending on my shoulders. I didn't know what any of this meant, nor what to make of it.

"Your sickness was of magical origins, Jolie," Rand explained, taking my hand and rubbing it as if that could help ease my frazzled nerves.

"Whose magic?"

"Well, we aren't exactly sure, just yet," he admitted. "All we know is that you had a magical block in place that made you very sick. We were able to remove it; but in order for you to regain your strength, you need your rest."

At the thought that they expected me to stay here and "rest," I started to freak out. I needed to get back to Sinjin, to let him know I was okay. "I can't stay here," I protested. "Sinjin . . ." But at the expression on Rand's face at the mention of my vampire, the words died right on my tongue.

Rand swallowed hard. "Jolie, you will come to realize that Sinjin is not the person you believe him to be."

I shook my head, not wanting to listen to Rand's words, refusing to believe there was any truth to them. He just didn't understand the connection between Sinjin and me—Sinjin was my protector, my teacher. "He has no idea I'm here."

Rand took a deep breath. "No, he does not."

Even though there was something within me that had let Rand in, and allowed him to come to my aid while I sat wasting away in front of Bella, I couldn't say that I trusted him. Not while my heart still belonged to Sinjin. Not while I still believed in Sinjin.

"I know this is a lot for you to take in," Rand started.

"I don't trust you. I don't believe that everything you say is true."

Rand was quiet for a second or two, and then I heard his voice in my head.

I don't know how I can prove anything to you, Jolie. But what I can tell you is that you and I have a long, shared history.

If that's true, I thought back, *tell me something about myself that you shouldn't know.*

He was quiet for a second or two and then smiled victoriously. *Your father is dead and you were never close to your mother. You once told me that she just didn't understand you—she never had, perhaps because she was too involved in religion to understand the fact that you could see things that didn't make sense. And you have been able to see auras since you were a small child.*

I took a deep breath but said nothing, stunned by his statement. Everything he'd just said was true. The only other person who knew any of it was Christa. True, he could have somehow bewitched Christa into spilling the beans, but I somehow doubted it. He just seemed so genuine.

"Please, Jolie, just trust me, this will all make sense to you shortly," he said. "For now, I need you to rest and regain your strength."

I was incredibly worried, especially as I thought about Sinjin waking to find me gone and not knowing where to even begin looking for me. Rand's words must have acted as some sort of magical command, though, because I felt myself suddenly relaxing, lying back on the bed. He helped me get comfortable, fluffing the pillow before I dropped my head on it. I took a deep breath, realizing I could breathe much more easily now. The headache had vanished. Even though I still felt tired, it wasn't the same sort of aching exhaustion I felt before with Bella. "What was wrong with me?" I asked, my voice already heavy with sleep.

"We do not know for certain, although we believe it was Lurker magic," Mathilda responded.

"Lurker," I repeated, starting to sit up as realization dawned on me. Rand immediately pushed me back down again.

"You need to rest, Jolie," he said softly.

"Lurkers . . . That was the word that kept going through my head during those dreams," I said as I battled with my heavy eyelids. "They are rallying, building their numbers. They're going to attack us."

"Dreams?" Rand repeated and glanced up at Mathilda, a question in his eyes. "That's how they must have attacked her."

"In exactly the same fashion they did the first time," Mathilda added.

"What first time?" I started just as I felt myself drop off only to wake up with a start a second later. "What are you talking about?"

"Jolie, tell me about this dream you had," Rand said. Then he added, "Awake unless I tell you otherwise."

The exhaustion that was relentlessly trying to claim me instantly vanished. I took a deep breath, thinking about the dream images, feeling fear begin to bubble up within me once again. "There was a battlefield with dead soldiers; and others who were still alive, in combat. None of them was human—they were witches, vampires, and the fae, I think. Then I saw a throne with a crown and a scepter. Both the scepter and the crown later melted into the throne." I glanced at Rand with an expression that said I was at a loss as to the rest of the images.

"I see," Rand said softly and smiled at me.

"What did you mean by the 'first time' I had this dream?" I asked, turning to face Mathilda.

She glanced at Rand as if seeking his approval to answer, but he shook his head. "We will explain everything in time, Jolie, but for now, I just want you to sleep."

Before I fell back into unconsciousness, I caught an expression of worry that passed over Rand's face as he eyed Mathilda and Odran.

"The dreams were one and the same" were Mathilda's last words before I lost the struggle and drifted to sweet sleep.

*   *   *

When I woke up, it was dark. I opened my eyes and saw the same thatched ceiling. Sitting up, I yawned with relief as I realized I felt completely healthy again. The intense sickness I'd experienced was now just a distant memory. Discovering I'd been left unattended, I stood up and stretched my arms over my head, wondering if the feelings of dizziness would return. But they didn't. Encouraged, I took a few steps, still testing my body. But I was fine. One hundred percent restored to my former self.

Glancing around, I took in my strange accommodations—there was a stone fireplace in one corner, with a little wooden stool placed before it, somehow welcoming in its austerity. Looking up from the fireplace, I noticed a circular window, complete with muslin drapes on either side. Outside the circular window were flowers of a species I'd never before seen. They were lemon yellow and as tall as me. I continued scanning the room, taking in the dirt floor, which was covered by a large rug that looked to have been woven of straw. The furniture in the room, including a bed and a table with two small chairs, was completely constructed of hand-hewn logs.

I heard the door open and turned to face my visitor, tension riding up my neck. When I realized it was Rand, the tension disappeared, replaced by relief. Well, that was until I remembered Sinjin had no idea where I was and that I was basically being held hostage. Yet something within me still didn't believe it—it felt as if I were right where I was meant to be. "You have a lot to explain," I said simply.

"Are you feeling better then?" he asked as he handed me a wooden mug of what appeared to be water. I accepted it but didn't bring it to my mouth, just swirled the contents around in the cup.

"I feel like I'm back to my old self," I announced and glanced up at him with a slight smile of thanks. I couldn't deny that I had a lot to thank this man for—namely for restoring my health.

Yeah, but you also have to think about the fact that you are now Rand's pawn, that he has you right where he wants you and Sinjin has no idea where you are, I reminded myself.

I dropped my gaze to the mug in my hands and studied the contents, wondering what he'd brought me.

"It's water," Rand said softly.

Suddenly feeling parched, I held the wooden mug to my lips and drank. It tasted strange—almost like well water, as if it hadn't been treated by any sort of plant, which I guess made sense since we were out in the boonies otherwise known as fae.

"I do want to explain everything to you, Jolie," Rand continued. "Are you feeling well enough to listen?"

I nodded and sat down on my bed, as if to prove that I was ready and willing to hear his side of things. I needed to understand what sort of threat the Lurkers were and what my dream signified. Rand took a seat beside me and smiled. It was strange, but I could suddenly feel the heat radiating from him, heat that was such a contrast with the coldness of Sinjin's skin. I had to swallow down the sudden urge to feel Rand's warmth on my skin, to taste him and experience for myself what it meant to be with someone supernatural who shared my own temperature.

"I can explain everything to you or I can do you one better," he started.

"What do you mean?" I asked as I eyed him suspiciously.

He chuckled at my expression and shook his head, never taking his eyes from mine. "With the help of fae magic, I can restore all your true memories to you, Jolie. Things can be as they were always meant to be." He paused. "Or as close as possible, given the circumstances."

"My true memories?" I started, already lost. "What true memories?"

He nodded and took a deep breath, as if realizing he needed to go back to the beginning. "Everything that you know is not how it really was," he started.

"You've said that before. I don't understand what you mean."

He nodded and was quiet as he apparently searched for the right words. "Jolie, Sinjin broke the rules—he altered history. He was never supposed to walk into your store that day. It was supposed to be me." Rand's gaze never left mine. "Jolie, I met you before Sinjin did."

I shook my head. He'd told me this before too. "But that isn't the truth!" I took a deep breath, trying to understand what he was telling me, and make sense of it somehow. "How? Explain to me how?" I insisted.

"Because Sinjin sent himself back in time to ensure that he would meet you first."

"How is that even possible?"

"I have learned to stop asking myself that question. We are creatures of magic, Jolie." He paused for a second or two and offered me an apologetic smile. "Anything is possible."

I took another deep breath. "So just playing devil's advocate here for a second, let's suppose that I believe you about Sinjin wanting to go back in time and meeting me before you ever got the chance to . . ." Was I really even considering this craziness? "What would be the reason? Why would he even bother in the first place? I mean, I can't imagine time traveling is as easy as getting on a bus or something?"

Rand shook his head. "You just don't get it, Jolie."

"Get what?" I asked and sighed. "What is there to get?"

He took each of my hands and stared at me. As much as I felt like maybe I should pull away, I couldn't. "Jolie, you are incredibly powerful. So powerful that all sorts of creatures want to control you or at least have you on their side."

I swallowed hard, anger and pain assaulting me at the same time. I tried to figure out where Rand was going with all this. "So you're saying Sinjin wanted to control me too?"

Rand frowned and dropped his gaze, as if he didn't want to witness the pain that I'm sure was building in my eyes. "I think so, yes."

If everything Rand had just said was true, it suddenly cast my relationship with Sinjin in a new light. It made me feel as if I might be sick. Why? Because it made total sense. I'd always wondered what Sinjin saw in me—the girl next door who definitely didn't stand out in a crowd. And he was so regal and handsome, so dashing and completely out of my league.

Or, on the other hand, this could be Rand's way of getting me on his side—weaving doubt about the truth of Sinjin's affections for me. Maybe I was playing right into Rand's hands by doubting the person who was my true protector, the person who had come into my life for the express purpose of keeping me safe.

I exhaled a pent-up breath of pain and frustration as I felt tears stinging my eyes. Which was it? Was Sinjin just using me or was Rand hoping to take his place?

"Sinjin was never good enough for you. He never deserved you," Rand said and placed his hand on mine, squeezing it reassuringly. Then he sighed. "I once promised myself that I would do everything in my power to ensure that Sinjin never hurt you, and I'm afraid I failed."

I swallowed hard, trying to fight the need to believe him, but somehow I couldn't. It was as if there was a crack in the foundation of my feelings for Sinjin and that crack was spreading, turning into a valley of doubt. I looked up at Rand, all the while aware that he was watching me. "How do we get my memories back?"

An hour or so later, I was standing in the middle of my cottage room surrounded by people—well, by the fae. Mathilda had instructed Rand that the spell would only work if there was enough magic.

I was nervous as I listened to the hushed voices of the twenty or so as they assembled in the room. It sounded like a hive of bees all nervously buzzing about. I felt an arm around my shoulders and glanced up to find Rand smiling down at me. I wasn't sure why but this time-traveling thing was beginning to grow on me. Maybe there was something to it. Maybe Rand had been telling the truth all along.

Well, whatever the outcome, all I knew was that I was fed up with all the second-guessing—of Sinjin, of Rand, even of myself. Maybe that was the reason I'd agreed to this so-called memory spell—I needed to know the truth, whatever it was.

"So what happens if this doesn't work?" I asked, feeling both agitated and frightened.

Rand shrugged. "Then I suppose it just doesn't work."

"This spell won't take my current memories away?"

He shook his head. "No, everything you know now will remain the same. All this is intended to do is return to you everything you knew before—all your experiences, your feelings, your memories."

I watched Mathilda enter the room and all the voices around us became silent as she parted the sea of fairies and proceeded toward Rand and me. I wasn't sure why, but at the sight of her, my heart raced. She reached for my hand and I willingly offered it to her. Then she smiled at me so serenely, I felt any nervous energy fade away.

"This should not take long, child," she said in her soft cadence. "And when it is done, you will understand everything . . . It will all be clear."

I nodded at her and thought how wonderful that sounded—how I wanted now, more than ever before, to no longer feel as if I were always the last to know, as if I'd been completely left out in the dark.

Mathilda turned to face everyone in the room and smiled broadly. "I thank you all for coming and for doing so on such short notice. I understand that many of you have traveled from Britain, as did our generous and kind King." Then she glanced at Odran and bowed. I looked at Rand and mouthed, "How did they get here so fast?" I mean, last time I checked, a flight from the UK to California took at least ten hours.

He just smiled at me and said—in my head, I might add—*Fairy magic—they can travel much more quickly than humans can.*

Oh, I thought in return and faced Mathilda again. I could feel Rand's gaze as it lingered on me. When I turned back to him, he just smiled in that handsome way of his.

"Please join hands," Mathilda said. Those in the room formed a circle around the three of us, each of them taking the hand of the person on either side of them. "This is one of the most difficult charms to perform," she continued. "It will require your absolute focus and strength. Please close your eyes."

Mathilda reached for my hand and Rand's at the same time that Rand reached for my other hand. I felt his familiar electricity course up my arm but it didn't cause me any discomfort. No, now I felt as if I was on the brink of something wonderful, of coming home again, as crazy as that sounds.

"Focus on sending all your magic, your power, into Jolie," Mathilda instructed, closing her eyes and tightening her hold on my hand. "Rand, I need your concentration the most," she whispered.

"Of course," he responded.

"Focus on your feelings toward her, on everything you have shared together, everything you have experienced. Think of emotions as well as actual events."

He just nodded. Mathilda opened her eyes, facing me. "You must open yourself, child, open yourself and accept all the power that is offered to you. Embrace it and make it your own."

I didn't know what that meant but nodded anyway, figuring I could just do my best. Mathilda closed her eyes again and started chanting something indecipherable, her mouth twitching with the effort. I looked at Rand and found that he too had his eyes closed tightly.

That was when it hit me. And it hit me like a truck. I suddenly felt as if my entire body were being swept up in a typhoon, my feelings and emotions battling one another, only to sink into my subconscious. It was like puzzle pieces circling before me in a great wind, some falling down to find their place in the puzzle that was beginning to take shape—the puzzle that reflected my life—a life that I had no clue ever existed.

As strange as it sounds, I felt like I was filling up. It was as if there were a void within me that was now growing solid. And while there was no pain, there was tremendous pressure on my very being, on my soul. Little by little, I began to fill up from the inside out. Thoughts and emotions ran through me that I didn't understand as experiences I had no familiarity with began to build within me.

I clenched my eyes tightly as images came, one after another. I watched Rand walk into my store that fateful day, just as he'd said. Then that memory was whisked away, to be replaced with Rand teaching me how to take the shape of the beast—but I was only able to assume the shape of a fox. Another vision dropped in front of that one, this one of Rand dressed in nineteenth-century garb—from a time when I'd traveled back to 1878 and fallen in love with him all over again. Memories continued to pummel me, images of Rand on the battlefield of Culloden in Scotland when we'd gone up against Bella's forces, Rand in the drawing room of my home in Scotland, Kinloch Kirk, where we'd planned my future as Queen, and Rand inside me when we'd first bonded . . .

I opened my eyes, my breathing elevated as my heart pounded in my chest. At the point when I felt I could handle no more, Mathilda dropped my hand. I glanced at her then, seeing her in a new light. I felt as if I had known her for years. She looked at me curiously.

"Mathilda," I said with a smile, tears glistening in my eyes.

She responded with a wonderful grin. That was when I remembered his hand still clenched in mine. It felt like slow motion as I turned around and my eyes settled on the one man whom I had loved so completely for the past two years—the one man who had made me what I was today.

"Rand," I whispered.

Sixteen

I felt as if I'd just awakened from an incredibly long and frustrating nightmare and finally landed in the realm of clarity. It was almost as if I'd been living in a hallway of closed doors, wondering at what could possibly be behind each one, and now every door was open, inviting me to explore.

It was just like Rand said it would be—I'd retained my most recent memories but now I had a whole shelf of memories layered above them, some complete contradictions, which I assumed were due to Sinjin's manipulation of time. Even though there were still unanswered questions, and I had to force myself to remember the truth in several events, I felt complete again. And that feeling of wholeness created a sense of serenity and contentedness within me.

"Jolie," Rand said, and I returned my attention to his beautiful face, his caring eyes and loving expression. I was faintly aware that he and I were now completely alone. I wasn't sure when it happened, but everyone in the room was gone, allowing us to rekindle our love in privacy.

"Did Mathilda's charm work?" he asked, his tone hopeful.

I simply nodded, smiling up at him. Her charm had worked, and then some. But while looking at him, I completely lost control of myself and felt a sob strangling my throat as my eyes unleashed a deluge of tears. Instantly, Rand's arms were around me and I buried my face in his shoulder, inhaling his clean, masculine scent. I held on to him as hard as I could, never wanting to let him go— never again wanting to think of him as my enemy . . .

My enemy.

I pulled away and looked up, into his beautiful chocolate eyes. "I'm so sorry," I started. "I'm so sorry for not trusting you, for not believing everything you said. I . . ." I shook my head, feeling so completely disgusted with myself for the way I'd treated this man. He was the one who cared for me so completely that he'd traveled through time in order to find me again. "I feel horrible about everything that's happened between us."

He shook his head, a smile claiming his sumptuous lips. "None of that matters now, Jolie," he said and held me closer. "You didn't know me from anyone and everything you did or said was completely understandable. And I'm sure Sinjin didn't help matters."

Ire began to grow inside me at how Sinjin had completely manipulated the situation: how he'd openly lied to me about Rand, declaring that he was dangerous and wanted only to control my powers, and ultimately me. I was suddenly able to see Sinjin for the absolute manipulative asshole he was.

Do you really believe that was all there was to it though, Jolie? my inner voice sounded. *Could there have been more to the role Sinjin played in all this?*

Of course I believe it! He changed the course of history to ensure his place next to the Queen.

But you've always known Sinjin had feelings for you. And there were moments when he seemed to genuinely care for you . . .

He's a good actor but that's it!

You know it's not as simple as that, Jolie. You know

Sinjin better than that. He wasn't always thinking about the throne. You're lying to yourself if you think Sinjin was just out for himself.

How can I believe for one second that I meant anything to him? All he wanted was to control me, with the ultimate hope of getting closer to the crown.

You can't believe that. You know he's more complicated than that.

Okay, so he also wanted a good romp in the sheets.

A feeling of sickness suddenly passed over me as the memory of having sex with Sinjin hit me like a bomb. And then the shock was replaced with fury. It was bad enough that Sinjin had ripped me away from Rand, had reversed the natural order of things for his own selfish reasons; this was the ultimate icing on the cake. He'd not only taken advantage of the situation, but he'd taken advantage of me, my heart and my body. He'd always wanted to know me as intimately as Rand had. Somehow this was the ultimate blow, making the pain inside me suddenly worse.

You're feeling this way because the pain is still so raw, that voice continued, driving me crazy with its need to defend Sinjin.

I'm feeling this way because I should be feeling this way! And regardless of what you think, what it comes down to is what Sinjin did wrong—he had no right to tear me away from everything I knew and loved. I can't see past that.

My other voice was finally silenced. Not that it mattered anyway because I was fully convinced that all my thoughts should be focused on Rand and how happy I was to be fully restored to him.

I laid my head against his chest as I listened to his heartbeat. He was so broad and warm. I just wanted to lose myself in the beauty of the moment. But I knew I couldn't, because so many questions were cycling through my mind—

there was just so much that had happened, so much I needed to better understand.

"Rand?"

"Yes?"

"How were you able to come back and find me?" I asked, remembering the last time I'd talked with him before this whole time-travel incident had happened. I'd been in my home, Kinloch Kirk, and Plum, my cat, had just squeezed through the door. I'd gone after her and, in the process, happened to glance down at the beach just beyond the cliffs of Kinloch. What I'd witnessed there not only shocked but profoundly disturbed me. Standing on the beach had been Sinjin and the prophetess, Mercedes Berg. But observing them wasn't the cause of the fear and angst within me. It was what Mercedes and Sinjin were in the midst of doing—an incantation. I recognized Mercedes' preparations for the spell immediately—mainly because I'd undergone the same one with her before, when she arranged for the two of us to leave 1878 and return to modern times. Once I'd realized what they were up to—time traveling—I'd used my telekinetic abilities to reach Rand and tell him exactly what was happening. I'd begged him to find Mathilda as quickly as possible. And that was all I remembered . . .

He was quiet for a few seconds as he took a deep breath. "When I found Mathilda and explained what Mercedes and Sinjin were up to, she was able to harness some of Mercedes' residual charm."

I shook my head, already confused. "What do you mean?"

"When a charm is performed, the molecules of energy that aren't utilized in the charm float away into the air. The farther they get from other charmed molecules, the less potent they become, eventually dissolving into nothing. Mathilda was able to weave a magical net whereby all the residual energy from Mercedes' charm was harnessed by Mathilda. That allowed us to return to this time and place, just as Sinjin did."

I nodded, thinking his explanation made sense. I sighed as I recalled the visual of Mercedes on the beach with Sinjin, trying to understand why she would have ever agreed to send him back in time. Mercedes was not someone I would consider my enemy—quite the contrary. She was my advisor in all things related to my kingdom. She was also my mentor, someone who helped me in my struggle to grasp my duties as Queen of the Underworld. I had relied on her, as well as valued and trusted her.

"Why would Mercedes do this to me?" I asked.

Rand cocked his head to the side and was quiet for a few seconds. "I don't know," he said in a harsh tone, betraying the fact that he held Mercedes responsible for everything that had happened. I couldn't imagine she was his favorite person at the moment. "I believe Mercedes, herself, is the only person who can answer that question."

One thing was certain—there was no way Mercedes had agreed to such a plan merely to grant Sinjin a favor. Sinjin meant nothing to her. I was fairly sure she didn't even like him. No, there had to be another reason why she'd done what she had . . .

"The prophetess should never be doubted." I heard Mathilda's voice from the corner of the room and felt my breath cut short. How long she'd been sitting there was anyone's guess—it was as if she'd just materialized from thin air because I was convinced Rand and I had been alone only minutes earlier. She stood up and approached us, wearing a placid smile.

"So you believe we should still trust her?" Rand asked with a frown. "On the face of it, it appears she has already teamed up with Sinjin."

Mathilda shook her head. "The actions of the prophetess

are much more black and white, Rand," she said softly. "The monarchy is the only priority the prophetess has. She exists only for the betterment of the Underworld society, and even though we may not comprehend her motivations, we must, nonetheless, trust in her judgment."

"Blindly?" Rand asked, his tone betraying the fact that he disagreed.

Mathilda nodded, flashing Rand a frown as her eyes burned. "The prophetess seeks to protect the monarchy, to protect the Queen," Mathilda finished. Hmmm, just as Mercedes existed solely to protect the kingdom, so Mathilda would always protect Mercedes.

"She has a damn funny way of showing it," I muttered.

"And Sinjin," Rand started, anger returning to his tone. "What do you propose we do with him?"

Mathilda's gaze focused on something outside the window, as if she were picturing Sinjin in her mind's eye. "The vampire should be punished."

"Punished here and now? Or when we return to our own time?" Rand persisted.

"Return to the present?" I asked, never considering until that moment what our plan would be. "Those molecules you collected—are there more?"

Mathilda smiled up at me. "Yes, they are forever ensnared in my magical web."

Then something occurred to me. "Would it be better to remain here?" I asked, just tossing the possibility up for consideration. "If anything, it would allow us more time to build our legions against the Lurkers." Another thought occurred to me. "And we could nip Bella's rebellion in the bud, stopping it before it ever got started."

And furthermore, I thought, I would never have to die on the battlefield . . . which also meant I would never find Mercedes . . . "We have to return to the present time because the battle with Bella has to occur, or Mercedes can never be freed from the year 1878."

Although speculation regarding the existence of the prophetess had always been alive and well throughout the Underworld community, no one had ever laid eyes on Mercedes. Why? Simply because she was trapped in time, in 1878, reliving each day because otherwise she'd be killed off by Lurkers, according to a vision Mercedes had had.

In the war against Bella's forces, while I lay in Rand's arms dying, Mercedes had usurped control of my own magic, thus saving me at the same time that she brought me back to 1878. And once there, through the use of our mutual powers, we had been able to travel back to the present time, saving Mercedes from a fate at the hands of the Lurkers.

"We must return," Mathilda said flatly, staring at Rand. "And we must bring the vampire."

I swallowed hard at the mention of Sinjin, thoughts of hurt and disappointment returning once again, pricking me just as freshly as they had the first time.

"Sinjin should be staked," Rand said with finality.

"No." I heard the word leave my mouth without being aware I said it. But there was something within me that rebelled at the thought of killing Sinjin—making him pay the ultimate price for his offenses.

Rand faced me with a frown but was spared the obligation of responding when Mathilda cleared her throat, shaking her head. "We cannot condemn him as we know not what motivated him. And until we do, we must avoid making judgment."

I said nothing more, although inside my emotions were in an uproar. Of course, I didn't think Sinjin deserved to be killed—he hadn't done anything that unforgivable. And as far as anyone knew, he'd acted with Mercedes' support. No, I didn't believe he should be put to death for his transgressions. But I also couldn't help my feelings of devastation, not wanting to admit that even though he'd wronged me, I was still very much in love with him. That was the unfortunate part about retaining all my most recent memories. Of course, now that love was also being mitigated with anger and distrust. But there was no point in crying over something that was never anything in the first place. No, I would shelve all the pain and the anger and move on. Even though I still stupidly loved Sinjin, I also couldn't deny that I was deeply in love with Rand. And Rand was the right choice, the only choice.

I glanced over at Rand and smiled, reaching for his hand. He folded mine in his and smiled back down at me. I felt a shard of guilt. How could I ever have been able to love another man when Rand was my true heart's connection? I took a deep breath and shook thoughts of Sinjin right out of my head. There was no use in focusing on him ever again, nor wasting any more of my energy. I mean, I'd already wasted more than enough of myself on Sinjin. Now I would, instead, focus on the issues at hand.

I took another deep breath, turning back to the laundry list of items to discuss. This time I glanced up at Rand. "I was able to take the shape of more than one animal when I called on my sister beast," I started.

"You called your inner beast?" Rand reiterated as worry began to well up behind his eyes.

And so I explained it all to him, which led to a discussion about just what I was if I wasn't a witch. And of course that conversation really led nowhere because no one had a definitive answer for me. So I just figured it would go unanswered at least for the time being.

Another mystery I was able to put to bed was how Mathilda had been able to restore my full memories to me. When we'd attempted a similar charm in 1878,

Mathilda had only been able to restore feelings rather than actual memories. The answer was that Mathilda hadn't been the fairy then that she was now, because "one never stopped learning, and one's magic never stopped advancing." And that made sense. Her magic must have grown by leaps and bounds in over a century.

"I think you should rest for a bit, Jolie," Rand suddenly announced. "You have been through a great deal and we have all the time in the world to answer your questions."

I shook my head, feeling as if there was just so much I needed to know, not to mention the catching up I needed to do. But Rand faced me and his lips were firm. It was the expression he wore whenever he didn't want me to argue with him.

"If you are going to attempt to help us travel back in time, you will need your strength," Mathilda added with a nod of her silver head.

"When are we even going to attempt this?" I asked, glancing first at Rand and then at Mathilda.

Mathilda was quiet for a few moments, presumably considering the question. "We have many preparations to make ahead of time. First, we must locate the vampire."

"Why?" Rand demanded. "He existed in the present time, before we traveled to the past, so he should continue to exist when we return."

"It is not quite so simple," Mathilda responded. "If he remains here, he could wreak all kinds of havoc if left unattended." She stood up. "I grow weary and will now take my leave of you both."

I didn't say anything else but just nodded and watched Mathilda open the door to my little ramshackle cottage and close it behind her. Then I faced Rand, unprepared when he suddenly pulled me into his arms and kissed me. His kiss was demanding, passionate, and I met his thrusting tongue as I wrapped my arms around his neck.

He pulled away from me then and stared down at me,

his expression flustered as his breathing came in quick gasps. "I need to make love to you," he whispered.

I felt something catch inside me at his words and a fire began building. He brought his lips back to mine, kissing me as if it would make up for the multiple weeks when he must have been going out of his mind with frustration and disappointment.

I felt his hands beneath my shirt, squeezing my breasts. A groan rose up from his throat as he did so. He pushed aside my bra and found my stiffened nipples, pulling his lips from mine as he knelt and took one of my breasts in his mouth. I moaned against him just as the image of Sinjin intruded on my mind.

A shudder flashed through me.

"Rand," I said, suddenly feeling sick to my stomach. I pulled his face up from my breast and started to blush at what I was about to say to him. But there was no going back. I simply couldn't make love to Rand when my feelings were so chaotic and up in the air. I couldn't make love to Rand when I was still in love with Sinjin.

"I can't do this," I whispered.

"Can't do this?" he repeated, his tone revealing how thrown he was by my change of demeanor. Thrown and disappointed.

"I just . . . It's just too soon," I said and adjusted my bra back in place while I smoothed my T-shirt down, refusing to glance up into Rand's face. I was afraid of the disappointment and pain that would probably be in his eyes. Rand wasn't an idiot. He had to know where this was coming from.

"Look at me, Jolie," he said in a small voice. I felt my breath stop as I glanced up and caught his eyes. He gazed at me for a few seconds, as if he were trying to make sense of what I'd said. Then something made him glower and shadowed his mood and I knew he'd figured it out.

"Because of Sinjin?"

I closed my eyes at his words, hating to admit it—hating the fact that Sinjin owned a part of my heart, my soul. But it was, nevertheless, the truth. Until I could straighten out my messy emotional allegiances, I needed time to myself. I needed to retreat and heal. It wasn't right for me to give myself to Rand, not while I wasn't a whole person.

"I'm sorry," I said softly, reaching out to touch him as if that would make it all better. But he backed away from me, and my hand merely dropped to my side.

"Are you—" he started as he ran an agitated hand through his hair. "Are you in love with him?"

I took a deep breath, afraid to answer the question. But, finally realizing I had to answer it, I did. "Rand, I . . . I don't know what to tell you, what you want me to say. I love you just as much as I always have . . ."

"But you love him too," he finished for me and shook his head. "Even after what he's done to you?"

I took a deep breath. "That certainly changes things, but love doesn't just turn itself off so easily, Rand. Even if he . . . he broke my heart."

Rand nodded and turned soft eyes on me as he did so. "I understand," he said simply and started for the door.

"Rand," I stopped him even though I wasn't sure what more I should say. It seemed as if the damage was already done. "Eventually this won't be a problem for us."

"I understand," he said again, and before he turned to leave, he faced me again, worry gnawing at his features. He bit his lip as if he didn't want the words to come out of his mouth, but eventually, he opened his mouth and asked me: "Did you sleep with him?"

I swallowed hard and that was enough for Rand. He sighed and opened the door, disappearing into the cold fae night.

Seventeen

I couldn't sleep.

For the last four hours since Rand had left me, I'd been tossing and turning, wondering whether or not I should have been so forthcoming with Rand regarding my feelings for Sinjin. I mean, the last thing I wanted to do was hurt him—and by the look in his eyes before he walked out of my room last night, he'd been hurt and then some. If those thoughts weren't enough to keep me wide awake, reflections of Sinjin continued to plague me.

I kept replaying memories of Sinjin over and over in my head, wondering how he could have been so cold and calculating when he appeared to have really cared about me. The things he said, the way he acted—I fell for his whole charade hook, line, and blood drinker.

"Ugh," I groaned as I forced myself out of bed. I was in my house again, but only after insisting that I needed to go home to sort out my thoughts. Rand, acting as his normal overly protective self, argued with me, of course, but in the end my donkey obstinacy won out.

Figuring sleep would continue to elude me and needing a diversion for myself, I decided I was thirsty. I threw on my robe and stepped into my slippers, plodding off to the kitchen. Today I would head over to Sinjin's house to see if he was still there. If he was, I'd let Rand know so he could arrange to have Sinjin's casket, or whatever it was that the vampire slept in, moved . . . as in, into the future with us. And if Sinjin wasn't around, as I'd imagined he wouldn't be, I was just going to continue living my life as usual and basically wait around until he found me.

When he eventually did come to me, I was going to play dumb and act as though I had no idea where I'd been for the past day or so. Like I had amnesia. Then, of course, he would have to enlist the help of the "benevolent Bella" to ascertain just what in the hell happened to me. Then the two of them, like the Bobbsey Twins, would try and figure out whodunit.

Well, that was the plan, but I didn't feel like sticking to it. No, I didn't feel like playing some idiotic game with Sinjin where I had to pretend I wasn't livid with him and that I had no idea there was a huge knife in my back, thanks to him. Instead, I had my own plan. And that plan revolved around demanding answers from him—as his Queen, I had the position as well as the authority to do so.

There was no reason for me to wait until tonight to put my new and improved plan into action. As it was, I couldn't sleep and had nothing else to do . . .

With iron resolve, I forgot about the glass of water and, instead, hightailed it back into my bedroom. I pulled open my dresser drawers as I searched for a pair of jeans and my pink UCLA sweatshirt. I threw both on in record time and, eyeing my disheveled hair in the mirror, opted for my white baseball cap.

"All right, you bastard," I whispered. "The time of reckoning is here."

I grabbed my purse and keys from the kitchen counter before starting for my garage. Yes, it did occur to me that it was probably a better idea to wait for Sinjin to come to me, but I didn't care. He probably wouldn't be there anyway. At the moment, I just had to escape for a little bit, to get out of the house. And I couldn't wait any longer to demand Sinjin tell me what he really wanted from me and why he'd altered the course of history to get it.

Opening the door to the Jetta, I buckled myself in and turned on the engine, waiting for the garage door to lift. Then I started getting nervous.

What if Sinjin is at his house? What are you going to say to him? I thought to myself. *Are you just going to blaze in there with your guns drawn? Or are you going to be more subtle about it?*

I don't know, but it doesn't really matter. Whatever happens, happens.

Chances are, he won't even be there anyway.

Well, he'd better be because it's going to drive me crazy to have to sit and wait for him to come to me! No, I need to get this done and out of my system, and pronto!

I'd been so involved with my mental conversation, I nearly missed my cell phone ringing from deep inside my purse. I reached over and played treasure hunt for a few seconds before I finally grasped my phone and pulled it out. I recognized Christa on the caller ID immediately. I also realized it was past midnight but figured she'd just gotten home from a date or the fact that I was missing was keeping her up late.

"Sorry, Chris," I said as I answered. I suddenly realized that I'd virtually disappeared off the face of the planet for the last couple of days and hadn't gotten in touch with her at all. Bad friend.

"Um, where the hell have you been?" she asked, her tone heated.

I sighed as I put the car in reverse and, while balancing

the phone on my shoulder, attempted to back out. "It's a really long story, Chris, and I don't have time to tell you now."

"Where are you?"

I took a deep breath, putting the car in drive as I started down my street. "I'm on my way to Sinjin's."

"God, I thought he'd finally eaten you," she said as she exhaled a pent-up breath. "I figured you caught him on a bad day, when he was really hungry, and I was this close to calling the police. Good thing for you the only thing stopping me was that I would have sounded like a whacked-out, crazy bitch."

Even though she was completely serious, I couldn't help my laugh.

"This isn't a joke, Jolie!" she railed. "You need to reconsider dating him! He's a vampire, for crying out loud!"

"You're just now realizing this?" I muttered. She was still so caught up in her tirade, she didn't even hear me.

"I mean, it's not like the pig dates the farmer or the slop dates the pig."

"What?" I asked, shaking my head, as I turned on Sinjin's street. The familiarity of the pepper trees caused a sadness to root in my gut.

"Food hierarchy, Jolie," she said, the essence of *duh* in her tone. "You don't date your food."

"I'm not Sinjin's food," I pointed out. "Well, not yet, I hope."

I cleared my throat as I figured I ought to tell her the truth about Sinjin and me. "And anyway, Sinjin and I broke up."

"Then why are you on your way to his house?"

"Like I said before, it's a long story and one I can't tell you right now because I'm already here."

She sighed, long and deep, and fake for emphasis. "Okay, but promise me you aren't going to go all psycho

on him and beg him to take you back or some crap.
Remember to stay strong, Sista Sledge."

I shook my head at the very idea of begging him to
take me back. No, things were beyond over between us.
"I promise."

"Okay. Be safe, Jolie." She paused for a second or
two. "I've invested a good twenty years into you, you
know? Don't go and die on me now."

I laughed, thinking Christa had the strangest way of
expressing herself. But if anyone stuck by me through
the good and the bad, she did. "I'll be safe, Chris, don't
worry."

Then we said our goodbyes and I hung up the phone,
taking a deep breath as I faced Sinjin's house. None of
the lights were on, but that wasn't what snatched my
attention. It was the FOR SALE sign out front with a picture of the real estate agent who'd sold him the house.

So I was right: Sinjin had already moved on.

All hope inside me sank. As soon as I spotted that
sign, something in me suddenly became heavy; it almost
felt like I was drowning. I'm not sure why I didn't just
turn around and go home, but I didn't. Instead, I just sat
there with the motor running as I stared at Sinjin's house
and allowed the happy memories of our time together to
suffuse me.

That was when I promised myself I would beat this; I
would beat this depression, or at least the feeling that a
part of me was suffocating, dying. Yes, I would beat
this—I was already on my way. The love I felt for Sinjin
would crumble into nothing and eventually be blown
away, dissolving into the air like the unused molecules in
one of Mercedes' spells.

"Goodbye," I whispered to the house. But somehow,
I felt the driving need to turn off the car and walk up to
the house, just to see if it was completely vacant, or still
full of furniture. I wanted to ensure that Sinjin really

had given up the house in the same way that he would soon abandon me once he learned I had all my memories back.

Stop trying to kid yourself. The only reason you want to go up there is to feel close to Sinjin again and it's a stupid thing to do.

I ignored that voice and turned off the engine. Now I was just sitting here, in the dark, arguing with myself.

You might as well just go up there. I mean, it's dumb just sitting here and staring at his house like a lovesick dumb-ass.

He's already gone, so what's the point? You're just going to freeze your ass off.

You're still sitting here . . . Crap and a half!

"Ugh," I said at last as I undid my seat belt, throwing open the door. The cold night air assaulted my legs through my jeans and I shivered.

I stood up, not wanting to dally any longer. I was just going to go look through the living room window and see if there was any furniture. The only reason was to report back to Rand and Mathilda.

Okay? I asked my inner voice.

Okay.

Good. Fine. Done.

I ran across the street and felt my heartbeat pounding in my throat as I started up Sinjin's walkway. I felt a general depression again as I glanced around myself, thinking how everything had appeared in such a different light the last time I ventured up this path. Before, things seemed fresh and promising; and now, this was the beginning of the end.

I pushed my melancholy thoughts aside and tiptoed over the grass as I leaned against the living room window, cupping my hands on either side of my face, hoping to ward off the glare from the streetlights.

His house was empty.

I'd been expecting it, but the sight depressed me all the same. Sinjin had really packed up and moved out. He was just as aware as I was that whatever existed between us was dead and gone.

"Funny meeting you here."

I almost didn't believe it was his voice; but somehow, I knew I hadn't imagined it. I felt like I was stuck in sand as I turned around to face him. I didn't say anything right away, mentally begging my heart to calm down, but it adamantly refused. Sinjin looked more beautiful than I'd ever seen him. He seemed taller somehow, and broader. His hair was just as wavy as it normally was, with the ends curling up over his collar; and there was that wicked gleam in his beautiful blue eyes. He was every inch the devil's henchman.

"Sinjin." I said his name as if it were a curse and tried to shake myself out of my dreamlike stupor. I wasn't sure if I was seeing him in a different light because I now had multilayered memories of him, which allowed us a much deeper connection, or if I'd merely missed him. Either way, I couldn't help the breath that was stuck in my throat or my unabashed stare. Yep, I was standing there like a complete idiot.

And that was when I remembered: I remembered that Sinjin had been using me all along, that he'd thwarted my pursuit of a happy life with Rand by changing the course of history, that he'd worked tirelessly to ensure that I would fall fast and hard for him, and that the whole thing had been completely calculated, entirely choreographed, and utterly false.

I reminded myself that Sinjin Sinclair never cared for me. But most of all, I remembered that he'd broken my heart.

Something inside of me erupted, and fueled by his ass-holish smirk, I unleashed the palm of my hand against his cheek. His head turned to the side with the impact and, when he faced me again, his left eyebrow was elevated as if to ask, *What else do you have up your sleeve?* But his fangs were indenting his lower lip, indicating that he wasn't exactly happy. I mean, I had to imagine it wasn't every day that a master vampire got bitch-slapped.

"Why did you do it, Sinjin?" I demanded, my voice hollow.

"Do what, love?" he asked as he continued to eye me with that look of amusement. There was no trace of pleasure, however, in the depths of his eyes. There was no trace of anything, actually.

"Spare us both the lies," I spat back. "I know what you did but I want to know why you did it."

"I have nothing to confess," he said resolutely, before his eyes turned hard as he studied me. "Perhaps you would care to tell me where you have been the past day and a half?" His voice was angry as he inquired, as if I were the perpetrator, the one who'd broken our bond.

I shook my head. Two could play at this game. "Answer the damn question."

He glanced at me with surprise showing through his gaze, as if he hadn't expected such vitriol, as if my anger was unwarranted. Then his eyes narrowed. "You seem different."

"*Different* is a good word for it," I said crossly. "Or another good way to describe it is that every memory I've ever had has finally been restored to me." His eyes widened only a fraction; if I hadn't been paying attention, I might not even have noticed. "Including the one when Rand first walked into my store two years ago."

Sinjin nodded as if he weren't alarmed by the news in the least, but he seemed to be struggling to appear indifferent. By now, I knew him well enough to know that he was anything but indifferent. How could he be when the control he sought so intensely was now dripping through his fingers like water? "And your current memories?"

"I have those too."

He chuckled without humor. "I should say Randall has matured into quite the warlock, do you not agree?"

I shook my head—I wouldn't be derailed. "Stop beating around the bush, Sinjin. You owe me the truth."

"The truth about what?" he demanded, suddenly dropping the charade of civility. He took a step closer to me until we were separated by nothing more than two inches. I could feel the chill of his body seeping into my bones.

"I want to know why you manipulated time to meet me before Rand did," I said fervently.

He shrugged. "Is it not obvious?"

"Say it."

He shrugged again, acting like this wasn't a big deal, like I had no reason to question him. "I merely wanted to meet you before Randall had the opportunity."

"To what end?"

He didn't respond right away, but smiled at me lazily. "That would be giving away my hand, love."

That was when I lost any patience I might have had. "You are a son of a bitch, Sinjin," I seethed and started to pivot on my toes and walk to my car. It was useless even talking to him—he'd never admit to anything. I didn't know why I had bothered to come here in the first place; it was a huge mistake.

"What difference does any of this make now, poppet?" he asked. I stopped walking and turned around to face him. "Your memories have been returned to you and you have a lovely life to look forward to with the warlock."

I shook my head, pain burning through me at his words. He was just so . . . cold. Tears began to flood my eyes, but I forced them back.

I would not cry. I would *not* cry. *I would not cry!*

"Do you really think it's that simple?" I managed to squeak out. I closed my eyes, taking a deep breath. "Maybe you've been alive for too long and you've forgotten what it is to feel; or maybe you're an absolute cold, manipulative fuckwad . . ."

Sinjin's icy chuckle interrupted me. I glanced at him furiously, watching him shake his head as he laughed, crossing his arms over his chest. Just as quickly as he started laughing, he stopped and stared at me through hardened eyes. "You think I cannot feel?" he demanded.

I took a deep breath but wasn't about to back down now. "I don't think you understand what it is to be human."

"Human? What will it take for you to understand that I am not human?"

"It's beginning to dawn on me," I grumbled.

"My humanity died the day I died," he snapped and his eyes were glowing red, incensed and angry. "But that does not mean I cannot feel."

That was when I lost it. A hurricane was building inside me that had finally gotten the thumbs-up to wage as much destruction as possible. I could feel the tears I was trying so hard to restrain suddenly come busting forward. Trying to avoid making a total ass of myself, I turned away from him and started walking toward my car, seeking nothing more than escape. I had to get away from him.

I should have known better. I should have known Sinjin would never allow me to retreat when I most wanted to. No, he got some sort of sick pleasure out of making me uncomfortable. So I wasn't surprised when I suddenly walked headlong into his chest and felt his hands grab my upper arms.

"I feel," he whispered, gravely. I made the mistake of glancing up into his face, which was so angelically beautiful—even if it hid a monster. He remained a creature of the dark that preyed on the weak not only for his sustenance, but to dehumanize them.

"You feel nothing," I said, narrowing my eyes and glaring at him. Tears were rolling down my cheeks, but at this point I didn't care.

His eyes were white.

His hold on my arms tightened as he gazed down at me. There was a curious expression on his face that I'd never seen before, something that seemed pensive, haunted, maybe even pained. "Look into my eyes and tell me again I do not feel anything," he demanded.

I swallowed hard and glared at him. "You manipulated me. You wanted nothing more than to exploit me so you could control the monarchy." I swallowed down a lump of regret and closed my eyes, willing my tears to subside. I opened them and found his gaze still riveted on mine. "You never cared about me. And the worst part of the whole stupid thing is that I thought we were friends, Sinjin. I thought you cared enough about me as a friend to never even consider doing everything you did."

"No," he started and emphatically shook his head.

"Don't belittle me, Sinjin, it's too late," I said, trying to free myself from his grasp. He refused to release me.

"I am not belittling you," he started but I wouldn't listen to him.

My eyes burned as I glowered at him. "I know you now for exactly what you are and I . . . I hate you."

For the first time ever, I saw a look of shock on Sinjin's face. He dropped my arms and I stepped away from him. He said nothing more. And there really wasn't anything more I either needed or wanted to say, so I started for my car. The tears were pouring from my eyes, and I felt like I needed to throw up.

"Did you think I would allow you to leave on that note?" he asked and I felt the coldness of his body right behind me. He gripped my arms again and yanked me around until I was facing him. I felt the air catch in my throat because there was just something . . . off about him. It took me a few seconds to recognize the expression in his eyes as desperation. That was when it struck me—Sinjin knew everything he had worked so hard for was about to fall through the proverbial cracks.

But I didn't care. I refused to care.

"Let go of me," I seethed.

"Jolie, you do not understand," he said, his tone unequivocal, as his grip on my arms tightened. "You do not understand my reasons for what I did."

I shook my head and tried to extricate myself from his grasp, but his hands were like manacles. "You aren't going to talk yourself out of this one, Sinjin," I spat at him. "I know you for what you are, what you've been all along. I was just too stupid to pay attention even when you warned me yourself." I laughed incredulously. "I won't make the same mistake twice."

"Allow me to explain," he began.

"I'm not about to listen to you try to make this into something it isn't and never was." I took a deep breath, and when it appeared he had no intention of releasing me, I decided to pull rank on him. "As your Queen, I demand you release me."

He gritted his teeth and said nothing.

"I order you to release me," I repeated, realizing this errand had been a total waste of time. Sinjin would never admit the truth. If I were lucky enough to even get an explanation out of him, it would be biased, spun to make him out to be the good guy. I'd completely wasted my time.

"Is this how it will be between us, then?" he demanded, his fangs suddenly growing longer.

I held my chin up high and nodded. "Yes, Sinjin, this is how it will be between us. I am your sovereign and you are my subject." I never relished saying anything more than I did those words.

Sinjin said nothing but nodded and released me. I rubbed the blood back into my arms and caught my breath as I stared at him. There was one more piece of business we needed to discuss. And I wasn't about to back down now. "As your Queen, I order you to return with me to the present time—the time before Mercedes sent you back here."

He swallowed hard. "And how will you execute that without the prophetess?"

I smiled. "I have my ways."

He remained silent for a few seconds, just staring at me with an expression that defied description. It was like he was holding back—whatever words were on the tip of his tongue were stifled by his mouth.

"And when will our journey begin?" He glanced at the sky. "Dawn is near."

I nodded and hoped Rand and Mathilda would be ready. "Tonight."

"Very well."

"I want your word, Sinjin," I said. "I want your word that you won't skip out on your responsibilities and you'll show up tonight at my house as soon as the sun goes down."

He eyed me forlornly but then simply nodded. "You have my word."

I wasn't sure why, because I shouldn't have trusted Sinjin even remotely, considering the facts, but I believed him.

Figuring my mission was accomplished, I exhaled a pent-up breath and turned on my toes, heading for the Jetta.

"Everything that happened, every decision I made was to protect you," he said to my back.

I stopped walking and turned around to face him. "I would think you'd respect me enough not to feed me such a line of bullshit."

Sinjin's face was unreadable. "That is the truth. I never wanted to control or manipulate you. I merely acted as my role as sentry dictated. I was, am, and forever will be your protector."

And that was when all the anger and sadness hit me with the force of a truck. "You never wanted to manipulate me?" I said, my voice dripping with sarcasm. "Then why the hell did you make me fall in love with you and why the . . . fuck did you sleep with me?" I shook my head, hating the reminder.

Sinjin's expression didn't change. "Both events were logical outcomes of our closeness."

I shook my head. "Logical outcomes? Listen to how cold that sounds." I took a deep breath. "Sinjin, I wish you would just admit the truth for once and stop acting like I'm stupid."

"I am telling you the truth," he answered, his voice sounding suddenly tight.

"Please, Sinjin," I said, my voice cracking. "I'm not an idiot, contrary to what you obviously believe." Then I started for the car again.

"Whatever you think of my motivations is not true," he called out after me. "Everything I did was for you . . ."

But I didn't stop; I didn't even falter.

Eighteen

When I returned home, it was still dark. I probably had two hours of night left, and then the sun would crawl into her rightful place in the sky and I'd have one day left of what I now considered the present time. Was I worried about returning to the future? Yes, of course. As much as I trusted in Rand's and Mathilda's powers, abilities, and knowledge, there would always exist that undercurrent of doubt. That was just human nature.

When I pulled into my garage and turned the car off, I found myself zoning out again—as if I couldn't motivate myself to unbuckle my seat belt, open the door, and make my way into my house. I just felt exhausted, but at the same time adrenaline was pumping through me. Why? Because of Sinjin. I just had a sea of emotions roaring through me—anger and betrayal and, as much as it pained me to admit it, love. But all in all, seeing him had been good for me because it had, in a way, granted me closure. Even though he hadn't satisfactorily explained the reasons he'd manipulated both time and me, it didn't even matter, at this point. Maybe there was just a part of me that needed him to know I was completely aware of everything that had happened and there was no way I'd let him get away with it. And now that he knew, I felt like I could lick my wounds and heal. I could return to the future and be the Queen I needed to be.

And what was even more important, I could be the woman Rand needed me to be.

Sinjin, without even realizing it, had allowed me to get on with my life.

Jolie.

It was Rand's voice in my head.

I am so glad to hear your voice, I thought in response, feeling an overwhelming sense of warmth suffusing me. Rand was the one man whom I could openly trust, the one man who would never harm me. And it was his face that I pictured now and his face that I suddenly yearned to see.

I know you wanted some alone-time but I could feel that your mind was awake so I just wanted to make sure you were all right.

I felt myself beam. Rand had the ability to send mental mind feelers, as he called them, to see when I was awake and asleep. But that wasn't what made me all gushy inside. It was just nice to know that there was someone out there who genuinely cared about me, who wanted to ensure I was safe. Someone who sincerely loved me . . .

Thank you, Rand.

Thank you? And I wasn't sure how he did it but somehow his laugh transferred over our mind connection. His chuckle was deep and hearty and I loved the sound of it.

Thank you for always protecting me and believing in me and . . . for loving me just as I am.

He was silent for a few seconds. *Jolie, you don't have to thank me for any of that. It just is.*

Well, I'm thanking you anyway.

Is everything okay? he asked and then paused. *I'm worried about you.*

I quietly considered the question. *Things are as good as they can be, given the situation.* And as I finally unlocked the seat belt and opened my car door, I realized I was walking into my dark and lonely house, a thought that depressed me more than it should have. *Rand?*

Yes?

I paused, wondering exactly where he was. *Are you still in the fae village?*

No, I'm in a Hyatt up the street.

Up the street? I asked in surprise as something incredibly happy burst inside me. He was so close . . .

You know my worrisome nature; I didn't want to be so far from you in case something happened and you . . . needed me.

You should have just stayed with me, silly, I started.

No, you needed your space and I was happy to oblige you.

Oh, I thought and then took a deep breath, asking, *Well, I've had enough of my space for the time being. Do you want to . . . come over?*

I'd be happy to, he answered automatically, as if he'd been waiting for me to ask all along.

I smiled and, shutting the car door behind me, started for my house, feeling suddenly elated again. *Thank you,* I whispered in my mind. I absolutely meant it.

When I heard the knock on the front door twenty minutes later, I wasted no time in opening it. I just needed to see Rand, to throw my arms around him and tell him how much he meant to me, how much he'd always meant to me. I needed to wipe away the fact that I'd wounded him deeply and let him know how much I loved him.

I threw open the door and felt my breath catch when I beheld him. He was just so beautiful, so good. I stood there for a few minutes, staring at him, not able to say anything. He was wearing an off-white pullover sweater and dark blue jeans. His hair looked as if he'd just gotten it cut and he was freshly shaven, revealing the incredible lines of his jaw and the dimple in his chin.

"I never get used to how amazingly beautiful you are," I whispered.

"Me?" he said, smiling in surprise. "You're the one who makes my heart speed up every time I see you." He held his arms out and I rushed into them, wanting nothing more than to feel his warmth, inhale his spicy scent, and relish the sense of safety I always felt in his embrace. I rested my head against his chest, feeling like I was home, that Rand's arms were the only place I ever belonged or wanted to be.

"You don't know how much I've missed you," he said as he kissed the top of my head.

I pulled away from him and took his hand as I led him into my house, closing the door behind us. "I'm so sorry for everything that's happened, Rand," I said, shaking my head, loathing the guilt that was nearly choking me. "I never meant to hurt you, and I hate myself for doing it."

He glanced at me and took a seat on my sofa. "Jolie, you were honest with me. That's all I've ever asked of you."

I sat down beside him and took his hand in mine. "I know, but it kills me when I think about how you must be feeling."

He smiled sweetly, shaking his head. "It is what it is. It's not your fault that Sinjin used you to further his own ends."

I felt my stomach sink at his words, but they were the truth—Sinjin *had* used me to further his own ends, and that was exactly what I needed to focus on to heal the pain that still pulled me apart. Putting my anger aside for the moment, I focused on Rand again and noticed he was quiet, wholly focused on his hands, watching them knot into fists.

"I've dealt with my issues with Sinjin," I said softly, suddenly realizing how angry Rand was over the whole situation. As much as it pained me to hear that Sinjin exploited me for his own benefit, I was suddenly aware that it hurt Rand just as much to say it.

He glanced up at me, a question in his eyes. "What do you mean?"

I took a deep breath, knowing he wasn't going to like this part. "I saw him earlier."

He sat up straight, his eyes piercing as he stared down at me. "We were going to wait until daylight, I thought?"

I shook my head and stood up, walking to the kitchen to get a glass of water. I got one for Rand as well. After I filled each glass with ice and water, I braced myself and confronted Rand. His eyes were imploring, as if it was taking all his patience to sit quietly while I worked up my nerve to tell him what happened. "I couldn't wait, Rand," I admitted and then added, "I also didn't follow our plan."

Rand smirked as if he found the information as amusing as it was frustrating and raised a brow. "Why am I not surprised?"

I smiled at him in response and carried the glasses of water back over to my coffee table, putting mine down on a coaster while I handed Rand his. "I just couldn't pretend that I didn't know what he'd done," I rationalized. "I just couldn't give him the luxury of believing I was still ignorant, Rand. I wanted him to know that I was fully aware of what a total and complete asshole he is."

He nodded as if he couldn't find fault with the situation. "So what happened?"

I shrugged, memories of a few hours ago returning in a deluge of images. "I asked him why he did it but, of course, he refused to tell me."

"So he now knows you have your memories?"

I nodded. "Yes."

Rand stood up and ran his hands through his hair, showing that he was agitated, and started pacing back and forth. It was the same thing he always did when he was upset or frustrated. "Then he's going to try to leave town, now that he knows what our agenda is."

I shook my head even as I realized he wouldn't believe what I was about to say. "He gave me his word he wouldn't."

Rand turned to face me and there was surprise and irritation etched on his face. "His word, Jolie? His word is meaningless!"

I nodded, but I was steadfast in believing Sinjin wouldn't pull a fast one on me, on us. "I believe him, Rand. I told him to come to my house tonight at dusk and we would make our attempt to go home."

He glanced at me and exhaled, shaking his head at my apparent naïveté. "Then there is nothing left to do but wait and see if he keeps his word. I absolutely intend to be here, if and when he shows up," he said and took a deep breath. He was obviously being incredibly sweet for my sake; I could tell he thought I'd just made a huge mistake. "Or perhaps we should go after him in the daylight and just take him with us, as originally planned."

I shook my head, well aware that the time for that plan was long gone because Sinjin was also. "No, he isn't living in his house anymore, and I don't know where his daytime resting place is."

Rand nodded and took a seat on my couch again, drumming his fingers along the top of his knee. "Then we will stick with your plan," he said and offered me an encouraging, hopeful smile. But I could tell he imagined it would take a miracle for Sinjin to actually keep his word and show up. Well, we'd have to see . . . "So it wasn't a wasted trip then?"

I shook my head as I considered it. "No, it wasn't. I got what I needed." I glanced at the glass in my hand, watching as the ice cracked in the water, beginning to melt. I looked up at Rand again and noticed that his eyes were narrowed on me. "I got closure."

His jaw was tight as he studied me. "I could kill him for hurting you."

I took a sip of my water, swallowing down any residual pain with thoughts of Sinjin. "What's done is done. It's in the past and we have an incredible future to look forward to together," I said with a smile.

I now wanted to focus only on what could be instead of what wasn't. Rand was absolutely the man for me. I knew we could be happy together.

He nodded and returned the smile but I could tell his mind was elsewhere, probably still on Sinjin if I had to guess. Then something must have occurred to him and he glanced up at me resolutely. "We could spare you all this pain, Jolie."

"What?" I asked, eyeing him with surprise. "What do you mean?"

He nodded again, as if the idea were becoming more appealing to him. "Mathilda and I could erase your memories of what Sinjin did. You would never remember you were ever . . . in love with him." He said the last four words like they caused a sour taste in his mouth.

I thought about it for a good few seconds because it did sound attractive—erase the anger and the pain and be able to think about Sinjin the way I always used to— as nothing more than a flirt. But then I knew I could never agree to it. I shook my head. "I can't. I need to know, I need to remember what Sinjin did, so I never trust him again. I need to recognize him for what he is."

Rand smiled at me as if to say he understood. "I just hate seeing you in pain."

I patted his hand. "I'm going to be okay, Rand. I just need time, that's all. And what's more, now that I know what Sinjin is capable of, I know the risk he poses."

"Keep your friends close and your enemies closer," he said and nodded.

That was when it hit me. Was Sinjin my enemy? I guessed in some ways he was. I mean, he had completely acted out of his own self-interest and could not have cared less where mine was concerned. As his Queen, would I have to punish him when we returned to the future? Of course, I had to impose some sort of punishment; it wasn't like I could just let him go. And, really, it wasn't like I even wanted to let him go. At times like these, I was glad I had the help of Mercedes.

Do you really have the help of Mercedes? I asked myself. *If she was in on this the whole time, then isn't she your enemy too?*

No, you have to listen to Mathilda on this one. Mercedes isn't to blame. You need to find out her motivation and trust in her. Remember that she will always protect the kingdom first.

"Was it painful to see him?" Rand asked.

I glanced at him, thankful to be pulled away from my inner dialogue as I considered his question. "It was painful," I answered and thought about how ridiculous this whole thing was because Rand had warned me about Sinjin so many times. He warned me never to get close to him, never to trust him, and I foolishly disregarded his advice. I once thought Sinjin was just misunderstood, that maybe I could break through his tough exterior to find some sort of goodness within him. I glanced up at Rand and smiled regretfully. "I should have listened to you all along. You were always right."

"It was your lesson to learn, Jolie," Rand answered. "And it just goes to show how good you are—that you give everyone the benefit of the doubt."

"Well, look where that got me."

He smiled at me and grabbed my shoulder, pulling me

into the cocoon of his embrace. "It's one of the reasons I love you," he whispered.

"Has this whole thing . . . changed your feelings toward me at all?" I asked, suddenly afraid for his answer.

He pulled me into him more closely and held me, allowing me to listen to the beating of his heart as he ran his fingers through my hair. "Jolie, nothing could ever happen between us that would make me love you less."

And that was when I realized how incredibly lucky I was, how lucky I was to have this unbelievable man in my life. I didn't say anything but leaned up and cupped his cheek as I brought my lips to his. I didn't close my eyes—I wanted to see him, to soak in his male perfection. And he didn't close his eyes either; we both stared at each other as our tongues mingled. It soon became clear to me that kissing wasn't going to be enough . . . Sinjin had been the last man to make love to me, and that needed to be rectified.

I sat upright as I pulled the sweatshirt over my head and threw it on the sofa beside me. Rand glanced over at me in surprise, but I didn't miss a beat as I started removing my shirt. When I began to unhook my bra, Rand stopped me with a hand on my wrist.

"I don't want you to feel like you have to do this," he started.

But I interrupted him with a shake of my head. "I need to feel your claim again, Rand. I need for you to make love to me."

That was apparently all it took. He bolted forward and grabbed me in his arms, standing up as he carried me into the bedroom. I wrapped my arms around him and felt a shudder of excitement pulse through me at the thought of what was about to happen.

Once in my room, he gently laid me down on the bed and reached around my back, unclasping my bra. He slid it down each of my arms and seemed to take forever as he freed me from it and then he merely stared at my breasts as if he'd never seen them before, as if he were completely enchanted, mesmerized.

"You are the most beautiful woman I've ever seen," he whispered as he glanced up at me. "You have no idea how much you turn me on, how much you always have."

I just smiled at him in response and started to remove my jeans, unbuttoning them and pulling them down my legs. I wasn't interested in taking things slowly. No, now was the time for action. There was a fire burning within me that demanded fuel. I smiled up at him and grasped the bottom of his sweater, standing on my tiptoes as I wrenched it up and over his head. I was almost disappointed when I met his black undershirt rather than his gloriously naked chest and made a low grumbling noise in my throat to express my frustration.

Rand smiled down at me and, shaking his head in apparent amusement, removed the shirt himself, lifting it over his head as he gifted me with the view of his incredible biceps and even more incredible chest.

"When God was handing out muscles, you must have been in line twice," I said, awed.

Rand just chuckled and started unbuttoning his jeans. I watched him as he pulled them down his long legs and something became very clear. "But apparently you missed the line for boxer shorts."

He chuckled more heartily and I suddenly wished I had a camera so I could have recorded his stunning smile. He was just so incredibly gorgeous and genuine. What was more, he was mine.

"I was so eager to see you, apparently I forgot a few things," he admitted under his breath and seemed slightly embarrassed by the admission.

"A few things?" I repeated, cocking my eyebrow in question as I smiled.

He took off one shoe and held up his foot, revealing that he'd forgotten his socks as well as his boxers. I giggled and then took a deep breath as I glanced down the line of his incredible body, feeling him watch me as I did so. My gaze fixated on his erection and I dropped to my knees, grasping him in one hand while I took him in my mouth.

"Jolie," he moaned.

I watched him the entire time, watched him throw his head back as his eyes drifted closed, watched him undulate his hips against me. And he was pure masculine beauty to behold—utterly and impossibly powerful and strong and yet under my control, subject to my manipulation. He opened his eyes suddenly and pulled away from me.

"Your turn," he said quickly, but I shook my head. There was an urgency now rampaging through me that wouldn't allow any more time to go by without him inside me.

"No," I said. Freeing myself from my panties, I simply climbed onto the bed on my hands and knees and turned my head around to face him. "I need you now."

"My God," he whispered as he stared at my backside and swallowed hard. Then in another second, I felt the head of him at my entrance, threatening me with intense pleasure. I moaned against him and pushed back, encouraging him to seek shelter inside me, encouraging him to thrust.

And when he did, I was prepared for it even though it still took me by surprise. I moaned out and closed my eyes, feeling him pushing even deeper as he then withdrew and thrust again. And that was when I felt it, an unleashing of feelings deep within me. It was like every door to all my emotions was suddenly blown open; all the stores of sorrow and mourning from the time when I hadn't recognized Rand were now intermingling with the heightened feelings of love and absolute dedication that I felt toward him.

Like an explosion, it rained down within me, something emanating from the middle of my body and spreading at warp speed through the entirety of me. I clenched my eyes shut tightly and felt heat suddenly bubbling up within me—like the feeling you get when you drink something really hot on a cold day.

I opened my eyes and glanced down at myself, almost afraid that I was on fire, that something was happening to me. A thin, almost imperceptible white glow seemed to reverberate from my hands, climbing up my arms. When I glanced back at Rand, it was encompassing him too. I realized he had stopped moving within me, apparently having felt the same thing I was experiencing. The white glow encompassing us both began to grow, blinding as it emanated through the room. In another split second it was gone.

I pulled away from him and turned around until I was sitting on my knees, facing Rand, and was about to speak when I heard Rand's voice as clear as day in my head.

She's mine. She will always be mine.

That was when something occurred to me . . .

"Rand," I started, knowing what this meant and hoping we were ready for it, that he was okay with it. At that point, I also knew it didn't matter whether we thought we were ready for it, because it had already happened. It just *was*. This was nature's way of telling us that we were each other's soul mates—not even time would keep us apart.

It was suddenly incredibly clear that Rand and I were meant to be together.

"We're bonding," I said.

"I know," he whispered as he ran his finger down the side of my cheek. "I love you, Jolie. I've always loved you."

That was his way of saying he was okay with the fact that we were bonding. He was imprinting within me his indelible mark. We were joining in the ultimate fashion and would never, ever again be separated unless by death.

"I love you, too," I said and smiled as he reached for me and kissed me, pushing me back down against the bed as he settled himself between my thighs. At the feel of him thrusting within me, the subtle white glow began to return, bathing us both in its radiance. Rand thrust even harder as his emotions continued to feed into me and mine into him.

Nineteen

Rand and I were once again bonded, and all I could feel was happiness. I knew now, more than ever before, that Rand and I were meant to be together—we always had been. As for Sinjin? It was strange, but whenever I thought about the vampire or our brief time together, it was as if the feelings of pain and betrayal were replaced with numbness—as if I couldn't feel anything at all. I wasn't sure if the magic of Rand and my bonding had done something to eliminate any residual pain or angst that I felt toward Sinjin or if the numbness was due to my being completely head over heels in love with Rand. But I guess it didn't really matter anyway—what did matter was that I was no longer stinging from Sinjin's betrayal. Because of that, I could look at things clearly—without the taint of anger and pain that I'd felt before. I could see the situation and Sinjin for exactly what he was without the bias of unrequited love. It was important because as Queen, I needed to remain impartial and make decisions based purely on facts rather than emotion. I could now clearly recognize Sinjin for the manipulative and underhanded person he was without any of my emotional attachments getting in the way. And for that I was thankful.

Rand and I held each other for the remainder of the night and into the dawn, discussing our future together and how happy we were to have found each other again. The sun broke over the horizon and announced the next day was upon us. And that whole day moved like molasses. Rand returned to the fae village to escort Mathilda back to my house so she could help us with the time-traveling spell that evening. I decided to spend the day at my store so I could catch up with Christa. It was strange, but I felt I needed to say goodbye to her even though I knew we'd meet again in the future. It was probably silly, but something inside me wanted to see her before I attempted to time travel, to seek some sort of closure before I left.

For the entire day, I felt as if an enormous rock had taken up permanent residence in my gut. It made total sense, considering that the events this evening would change everything I knew, everything I'd ever known. Even though I had time-traveled before, those memories somehow seemed foreign to me, probably because I hadn't actually experienced them, even if the me of the future had. They just felt as if they weren't my own memories even though, of course, they were.

I didn't tell Christa anything about Rand, about our bonding, or that I was planning on traveling a couple of years into the future tonight. I just figured it would be too hard to explain and, furthermore, it would cause her undue worry. What did it matter anyway? Once I was back in the future, Christa wouldn't even know anything had happened. And what she didn't know definitely couldn't hurt her.

So we spent the day just making small talk, laughing about her myriad bad dates. When she finally asked me what happened between Sinjin and me, I just said I didn't want to talk about it; once I felt like I was over it, I'd explain. Luckily, she bought my excuse and left me alone.

That evening, I let Christa leave early for a date and closed up the shop just like I'd done a thousand times before. But, of course, tonight was different. Tonight would mark the last night I'd be in my store, in Los Angeles, in the United States! I must admit, however, there was something inside me that yearned for the tranquility of my home, Kinloch Kirk, nestled among the Scottish moors, perched high above the Eyemouth cliffs and pastures of wild heather. I couldn't help but feel as if I were saying goodbye to the life I had now. It was a feeling of sadness that deflated me, albeit tempered by excitement for the next chapter of my life, but sadness all the same.

As I swept the floors of the shop that had been a second home, I felt heavyhearted. I glanced around myself, taking in the worn sofas where my clients awaited their appointments, the Swiss cuckoo clock above the door that Christa had given me, the lettering across the window proclaiming my psychic abilities . . . It wasn't much, but it was mine. And my little business had allowed me to earn a decent living. It had paid for my home and a decently nice car. I'd really made something of myself here and it was hard to say goodbye. Even though I knew I was destined for much bigger and better things, it was hard to leave that part of me behind. I felt like I was saying goodbye to the old Jolie—the person who had no idea just who and what she was and the incredible things she'd soon experience.

The more I thought about it, the more I realized I was about to leave a much simpler time, a much simpler life. A life that was not only slower-paced but also safer, because I was more than aware of what awaited me in the future . . .

The Lurkers.

The realization frightened me. I'd be putting myself back into a dangerous situation. I was firmly aware that the Lurkers were an unknown; that was what made them such an absolute menace. Did they possess magic? Based on my visions of the throne and the battlefield, which attacked my magic twice, both in the future as well as the present, it seemed they did. That was a scary thought because we only ever thought of them as some form of pseudo-vampire and, as such, non-magical.

Vampire . . . Of course, my thoughts then turned to Sinjin and I stopped sweeping as I pictured him in my mind. Yes, there was still something sad in me over what had happened between us. I'd always been fond of Sinjin and now, more than ever before, I wished we could go back to how things used to be—when we were friends and cared about each other in our own awkward way. When I knew Sinjin to be nothing more than a harmless flirt.

He's anything but a harmless flirt, I reminded myself.

I know, but that doesn't mean I can't wish things were different.

I imagined the sadness I harbored over the deterioration of my friendship with Sinjin would always be there. It was a mere hiccup, though, compared with the agony I'd experienced when I first became aware of his manipulation.

I was healed. I wasn't sure how or why, but I was healed all the same.

I leaned the broom against the wall and took one last glance around me. Then I turned the lights off and opened the front door, stepping out into the burgeoning darkness. I faced the door and locked it, wondering what would become of my little store after I moved on. Maybe someone would open a donut shop or some sort of new-age boutique.

"Goodbye," I said as I took a deep breath and turned around, eyeing the stars twinkling in the night sky. The moon was full and already starting its journey over the earth.

"Poppet."

I turned at the sound of his voice and watched Sinjin

walk up the sidewalk toward me. He appeared out of nowhere, almost as if the darkness had suddenly delivered him. The moonlight created a soft haze around him that made him seem like some sort of heavenly creature. But his dark attire, black hair, and piercing blue eyes said otherwise. The smirk on his full lips warned he was trouble and then some. At that point, more than ever before, I really regretted what had happened between us. I wanted to like Sinjin. But I had to repress those feelings because I couldn't like Sinjin; not anymore.

"I thought I told you to meet me at my house," I grumbled as I offered him a raised brow to say I wasn't amused.

His smile widened as he stopped directly before me. Then he merely glanced down at me and I was suddenly struck by how incredibly tall he was, and how much stronger than me. It wasn't a feeling that caused me any sort of fear, though, mainly because I was firmly convinced Sinjin would never hurt me. Why? I had no clue. Probably because I was an idiot.

"I beg the privilege of your company . . . alone," he said in a soft, deep voice.

"Why?" I asked as I started for my car, not wanting to encourage him in the least. "There's nothing left to say."

"Ah, that is where you are quite mistaken," he said, keeping pace with me.

We reached my car and I unlocked the doors with my remote. I opened the driver's door and took a seat, watching Sinjin as he continued to stand on the curb just beside me. "Well, are you coming?"

He smiled and materialized on the other side of the car, opening the door and climbing into the passenger seat as he beamed over at me. "I did not realize it was an invitation."

I turned on the engine and glared at him, not wanting him to think he was in any way forgiven. "I wanted to make sure you weren't going to skip out on your responsibilities."

"I do recall giving you my word," he said and seemed rather put out, as if I should never have second-guessed him. Yeah, well, I was the new Jolie—the one who wouldn't trust as easily as the old one had.

I frowned. "Well, you're here so I guess that means you're good at keeping something." I glanced behind my shoulder to ensure no one was coming. When I found the coast clear, I pulled into the street.

"I never intended to hurt you," Sinjin said, and I could feel the weight of his gaze as it rested on me. I was never happier to be driving—to have an excuse for keeping my full attention on the traffic and pedestrians around me rather than the flagrant beauty of his eyes.

"I'm well aware of that, Sinjin," I said without offering him a sideways glance. "You wanted nothing more than to manipulate me, and making me fall in love with you was just part of your plan. So, no, hurting me was never your intention."

"You are wrong," he said tersely, never removing his eyes from me. "I have only ever wanted to protect you, to ensure your safety."

I stopped at a red light and glanced over at him, letting him know with one look that I was in no way amused and, furthermore, that I thought he was full of it and then some.

"I had taken a vow to protect you, in case you did not remember?" He was referring to a time in the future when Mercedes had appointed him as my bodyguard.

"Of course I remember," I snapped back at him. "And don't think for one second you're going to resume that role," I added.

He didn't say anything but cleared his throat in a way that said he wasn't happy with the news. "Regardless, I will forever be your protector."

"Sinjin, let's cut through the shit. Just admit that you were a complete and total asshole. Rand was right when he said you were selfish and had to manipulate every situation so that you always came out on top."

He gritted his teeth at the mention of Rand but then, just as quickly, assumed a more stoic expression. "I never denied that I seek situations of benefit to myself."

"Okay, now we're getting somewhere," I said, relieved. The light turned green so I faced forward and stepped on the gas. "So why continue with this line of bullshit about protecting me?"

"I merely stated the truth."

"Protecting me against what?" I demanded again, shaking my head with irritation.

"The Lurkers."

"What?" I glanced over at him. I couldn't help it.

"A car," he said simply and motioned ahead of us. I turned to face forward and had to brake hard in order to avoid the car stopped at the light ahead of me.

"Sorry," I muttered.

"Defending you from the Lurkers was why I went to the prophetess and requested that she send me back in time," he finished.

The shock of this news really jarred me. Sinjin, as a rule, never explained his reasons for his actions, so this was a huge surprise to say the least. "Why would you have asked that?" I turned left onto the freeway on-ramp and gazed over at him casually.

He was staring at me. "Have you not listened to a single word I have told you?" he demanded. I didn't respond so he continued. "I took a vow."

"So let me get this straight," I started, my tone relaying the fact that I wasn't buying his story. "You told Mercedes that you needed to go back in time to save me from the Lurkers? How does that even make sense? Why wouldn't you just send me back in time, instead of yourself?"

"It makes perfect sense," he said stiffly. "I intended to re-create history—knowing the future with the Lurkers and the threat they would pose, I told the prophetess that I would gain your trust and quash Bella's rebellion, thereby saving you from death."

"Which would also preclude me from saving Mercedes," I pointed out, none too nicely.

"That was merely a complication," Sinjin responded indifferently. "It was the reason I had Isabella tutor you, if you recall. Your power is enough that you could have saved the prophetess yourself, without her calling you into the past."

"Okay, so you wanted to save me from Bella and then what?"

"We intended to train you much faster to become Queen, to teach you what it meant to be the leader of the Underworld."

"And Rand?" I asked, my voice hollow.

"It would have spared you all the back-and-forth with him. The prophetess recognized the pain you suffered at the warlock's hands and was convinced it would have been better for you as well as the kingdom if he never ventured into your store that fateful day."

I remembered one of the last conversations I had with Mercedes before she sent Sinjin back in time. When I had begged her to send me back to 1878, so I could live out my life with Rand in a time when he loved me freely and I him. I felt my heart drop as I remembered how I'd told her how unhappy I was, how my relationship with Rand was coming undone . . .

It made perfect sense. Mercedes would always protect the kingdom, and that meant she would always protect me. Everything Sinjin said was true—Mercedes sent him back because she thought it would strengthen my allegiance to the crown instead of to Rand. She'd thought she was doing me a favor.

I felt like I wanted to be sick. I'd come so close to losing Rand—to never knowing him. I'd come so close to living a life I was never meant to live. But somehow, I couldn't be angry with Mercedes. I just accepted the fact, like Mathilda did, that Mercedes existed for the betterment of the crown. And she was the first to admit it.

Sinjin, on the other hand . . .

I exited the freeway and came to a stop sign before I was due to turn right. Once I braked, I glanced over at him. "I understand Mercedes' motivations in all of this, but you can't expect me to believe for one second that you were merely acting to protect me."

He swallowed hard and eyed me speculatively, a smirk playing with his lips. "Of course not."

Well, apparently this was diarrhea-of-the-mouth day for Sinjin because he was confessing things to me that I never, in a million years, would have imagined he would. "So?"

"I wanted to be first to meet you, poppet, for my own selfish reasons."

"Why?"

His eyes narrowed as he studied me. There was no traffic ahead of me, but I didn't make my turn. Instead I just stared at him, waiting for the moment of truth.

"I wanted you to love me."

I felt my heart rate increase, and something that felt like panic began stirring in my stomach. "Why?"

He was completely silent as he stared at me. It was as if he wanted to tell me but couldn't, like his voice went on strike or something.

"Why, Sinjin?" I prodded.

In a blink he was gone. He was there one second and a second later he dissolved into nothing, leaving me sitting in my car alone.

When I reached my house, there was a black Suburban I didn't recognize parked in my driveway. I pulled up behind it and turned off the car just as Rand stepped out of the driver's side and offered me a large smile.

I could feel his emotions as soon as we made eye contact. He was relieved to see me—in true Rand form, he was worried over the fact that I wasn't home and it was already dark.

We're going to have to work on your worrisome nature, I thought with a smile. He didn't respond but cocked a brow and regarded me with a grin.

"Hi," I said once he was in front of me. He didn't answer, just engulfed me in his arms, leaning down to place a chaste kiss on my mouth.

"Where have you been?" he asked as he squeezed me.

"I, uh, I was . . ."

But I never got the chance to finish my statement because Mathilda was suddenly beside me. Which was just as well because I wasn't sure how Rand would react to the fact that I'd been delayed by Sinjin. Speaking of the vampire, he was nowhere to be found.

"Child, are you ready?" Mathilda asked as she eyed me.

I took a deep breath, separating myself from Rand's embrace, and thought about the task at hand. "Yes, I'm ready."

"Where's Sinjin?" Rand demanded, looking around himself in an irritated sort of way. I could only guess whether or not Sinjin would show up after our conversation in the car. It seemed like he was on the threshold of confessing something that weighed pretty heavily on him—hence the whole disappearing act. Now whatever that something was would forever live in oblivion.

"I don't know," I said sheepishly, worried that Sinjin wasn't going to come through.

He'll come through, I told myself. *He gave you his word.*

"We need him," Mathilda responded, glaring at me impatiently.

"I knew this would happen," Rand said, shaking his

head as he ran his hands through his hair. "We'll have to do this without him."

Mathilda shook her head adamantly, her silver tresses echoing her movements like ripples in a calm lake. "We cannot. Those who breached the laws of time to travel here must also return."

I felt something heavy settle within me as I thought about what a feat finding Sinjin would be. But it was pointless even contemplating it. If Sinjin didn't want to be found, he wouldn't be.

He gave you his word!

That was when I spotted him. He appeared at the end of the street, walking all nonchalant, as if he didn't have time—er, that is, history—waiting on him.

"Here he comes," I said, relief suffusing me.

He suddenly disappeared from sight, materializing just beside me. I breathed in my shock and felt my skin tingle with the cold chill that filled the air around him.

"Did you doubt me, my pet?" he asked and smiled, acting as if he were just now seeing me for the first time today, acting as if he hadn't nearly admitted to something . . . very important, only moments before.

"Sort of," I answered, thinking it was closest to the truth.

"Poppet, you seem irritated with me." I hadn't noticed until just then that he hadn't spared a glance to anyone else in our party.

I took a deep breath. "I was wondering if you were going to come."

"I would not miss this for the world," he said, offering me a cheery grin.

"Let me make something perfectly clear to you, Sinjin," Rand interrupted, stepping forward when it seemed Sinjin was not going to acknowledge him. As I glanced at Rand, I could see the anger coloring his features—it was there in the reddish tone that bled across his cheeks, his neck, and the tops of his ears. His aura was electric blue, tinged with purple—something that only hinted at the incredible anger cresting through him. That was when I felt an eruption deep within me like lava overflowing into my stomach. It was Rand's rage.

"Ah, greetings to you as well, Randall," Sinjin said, not missing a beat.

"I believe you should face death for what you did to Jolie, your Queen," he said and took a deep breath, his eyes burning. "You have Jolie and Mathilda to thank for your life."

Sinjin said nothing to Rand, merely regarding him with ennui. Then he faced Mathilda and me and smiled. "Much obliged, kind ladies."

"He is here, we can continue with the preparations," Mathilda said, completely dismissing Sinjin as she turned to face me. "Do you have a garden, child? We will need nature's magic."

I nodded and led the way to my side gate, which would take us around my little house and into the backyard that boasted grass, roses, a lemon tree, and gardenias. Hopefully, that would be enough "nature" to fill Mathilda's needs.

"I hope you realize that punishment awaits you," Rand said to Sinjin as he reached over and took my hand.

"We shall see, Randall, we shall see," the vampire answered lackadaisically.

Mathilda eyed her surroundings, seeming to inspect my garden for its usefulness in her spell. She took a few steps to her right, then a few steps forward, until she was dead center in the grass with the foliage surrounding her. She looked up into the sky and seemed to be studying the moon.

"The orb is full, ripe for magic," she said, turning to face me. "Child, you must stand here."

She waited for me to approach her and took my hand, placing my feet exactly where hers had been. She motioned to Rand, took his hand, and positioned him to my right. Sinjin occupied the exact opposite position, to my left. Then she stood directly in front of me. She turned to Rand and extended her hand. He took it and she then faced Sinjin, doing the same. Then she addressed both of them.

"You must take each other's hands," she said unemotionally.

Rand grumbled something unintelligible but extended his hand. Sinjin grinned like this was all a big joke. Then I realized no one had taken my hand. "What about me?"

Mathilda faced me with a grim expression. "You are not returning," she said simply.

"What?" I demanded.

"Not returning?" Rand said at the same time.

Mathilda shook her head. "The Queen already exists in the future, having never time-traveled to the past. Only Rand, myself, and the vampire made the trip."

I couldn't argue. I hadn't time-traveled so, technically, I still existed in the future. Who knew what the heck would happen if I tried to travel with them now? Maybe I'd end up being two Jolies in one place or, worse yet, maybe time itself would freak out and spit me back into the dinosaur era, or the Spanish Inquisition.

"I understand," I said resolutely, afraid for what would happen once they traveled into the future. I wondered would the future just pick up where it left off when Sinjin and Mercedes cast that spell? It was too confusing to even consider.

"Are you sure?" Rand asked, staring first at Mathilda and then at me with wide eyes. "I don't want anything to happen to her."

Mathilda nodded but said nothing more. Then she took a deep breath and faced me. "I will unravel the net of magic; but your powers, child, more than any of ours, will enable this spell to take shape."

I nodded, feeling pleased I had all my memories. In having them restored, my experiences and my knowledge had been reinstated along with my powers. "What do I do?"

"Imagine a portal opening wide, the same portal you experienced when Mercedes sent you back into the present. Focus on that portal and keep it open. Allow each of us to travel beyond its frame."

I nodded. Over the course of my instruction and education in everything witchy, concentration and I had become damn good friends.

I love you, Jolie. It was Rand's voice in my head.

I caught his eye and smiled, taking a deep breath, trying to keep the tears at bay. He didn't need my tears right now—he needed my strength. *I will see you soon,* I thought in response.

I gave Rand one last smile and then closed my eyes and imagined a portal opening above us, a large black void that dominated the sky. I clenched my eyes shut tightly and saw the gossamer strands of Mathilda's web encapsulating the portal. What looked like raindrops caught in the ethereal threads, which were actually the captured essence from Mercedes' spell.

I felt energy bubbling up from within me, building momentum. In my mind's eye, I could see light escaping from my body, bathing me in a magical haze, increasing as every second ticked by, mounting as I continued to focus. The light shone from within me until I couldn't contain it any longer and, like an immense spotlight, it suddenly poured out of me, encompassing Rand, Sinjin, and Mathilda.

Then there was nothing but darkness.

Did *The Witch Is Back* bespell your heart?

Get ready to fall in love with another
Jolie Wilkins adventure . . .

Something Witchy This Way Comes

On sale fall 2012

Read on for a special sneak peek!

One

I blinked.

I blinked a few more times, and even then my vision was still cloudy, like I was just waking up with a massive hangover in a room bright with sunlight. I covered my eyes with my hand, trying to ward away the garish attack of light, hoping that my sense of hearing might help me figure out where I was. But my heart was beating so fast, it sounded like waves crashing into my ears.

I dropped my hand from my eyes and forced myself to focus, to concentrate on the scenery around me so I could get some sense of where I was and what had happened. Once I was able to make out the rocks that interrupted the otherwise deep blue ocean before me, I realized it wasn't my heart that was echoing through my ears at all, but the actual waves. I glanced down at my shoes and took in the sand, feeling the sea breeze as it whipped around my ankles and caused me to shiver involuntarily.

"Jolie."

I felt like I was moving in slow motion as I turned to face Rand. His dark brown eyes showed concern for me as he smiled, and his dimples made him appear almost boyish. His deep chocolate hair was tousled, as if he'd just awakened from a restless night. He was breathtakingly beautiful, as always. At the sight of him, something warm began to grow within me and I recognized the feeling—relief melded with love.

If Rand was here, I was safe.

But the question remained: Where exactly was I?

I swallowed hard, trying to bridge the gap that was growing in my mind. I'd been home in . . . Los Angeles only moments ago and now I was . . .now I was . . .

I glanced around again, at the beach and then behind me. I took in the craggy hillside that led up to pastures of heather, dotted with enormous pine trees and a three-story white mansion, the plaque of which proclaimed it to be Kinloch Kirk. Somehow, the title resonated with me, and carried me to a place in my mind that I hadn't visited in a while.

Kinloch Kirk is the home of the Queen of the Underworld, I told myself. *It's my home.*

"We're back in Scotland," I whispered to Rand as I faced him again, the dawning realization forcing the clouds from my mind. He said nothing, just nodded and reached for me, engulfing me in his strong arms. I leaned my head against his chest and inhaled his spicy, masculine scent, relishing the feel of his embrace.

"You failed."

It was a woman's voice—austere and calculating—and I knew it well. I swallowed hard as I turned to face the prophetess, Mercedes Berg, who stared past us, her mouth angry. The prophetess was the highest of all the witches and also the Queen's chief ambassador, *my* chief ambassador. But what struck me was how upset that her plan hadn't succeeded. Actually, it had been a complete fiasco.

And that was when it all came back to me, like someone had just pumped memory juice directly into my brain.

Mercedes had broken the rules of time by sending the vampire Sinjin Sinclair two years back in time to meet me before I ever became Queen . . .hell, before I was even aware that I was a witch. And Sinjin's purpose? To get to know me before Rand did, thereby ensuring that I would never fall in love with Rand, which is what truly happened. Sinjin had wanted me to fall in love with him instead, and as much as I now hated to admit it, he'd succeeded.

But luckily for me, Rand hadn't given up. A gifted warlock, he had recruited the help of Mathilda, a fairy. They'd traveled back in time to beat Sinjin at his own game. Why Mercedes had orchestrated the whole thing, I still didn't know. And why had Sinjin agreed to it? Well, I also didn't know for sure, but I did have my suspicions. He undoubtedly wanted the power that went along with being the paramour of the Queen of the Underworld.

"I attempted."

At the sound of Sinjin's voice, I felt something within me constrict. I had to fight the feeling, though, because I promised myself I would get over him.

I refused to look at him because the power of his betrayal still felt like a knife in my back. Instead, I faced Mercedes and felt anger riding up my throat. She appeared so nonchalant, almost indifferent, as if sending Sinjin back in time and royally screwing up my life was no big deal. She acted like it was no more serious than if she'd just stepped on an unfortunate beetle.

"And apparently you failed," Mercedes said, facing Sinjin with an expression that was none too friendly. I didn't miss the fact that Sinjin had no comeback. But I still refused to look at him.

"Why did you do it?" Rand demanded of Mercedes. He took a step toward her, his shoulders tight. She turned away from him without answering. "Why the bloody hell did you do it?" he repeated, and his voice was rough, his English accent more pronounced and heated with his anger. I was suddenly afraid of a possible confrontation between the two of them.

"You must not doubt the prophetess," Mathilda suddenly piped up from behind me. I turned to face her, in surprise, not having realized she was there. The oldest and wisest of the fae, Mathilda was slight, maybe barely four feet tall. Her long, silvery hair flowed around her body. When I looked at her, I sometimes couldn't tell how old she was. She'd told me a long time ago that each person's perception of her was different—they see her however they choose to see her—and apparently my confused mind was unable to distinguish her age.

But back to the time-traveling thing . . . Right before Mercedes sent Sinjin back in time, I was looking for my cat, who had escaped the house. Instead of finding her, I stumbled across Mercedes as she was performing a time-traveling charm on Sinjin. It was on the beach, just below the bluffs of Kinloch Kirk. Knowing it wouldn't be long before everything I knew was whisked away from me, I used my telepathic connection to warn Rand—who was miles away at the time—about Mercedes' intentions. Then, boom! When I woke up, it was two years in the past, in Los Angeles. I was completely unaware of the fact that I was officially Queen of the Underworld. Truth be told, I hadn't even met Rand or Sinjin because they had yet to venture into my life.

To make a long story short, Rand, Sinjin, and Mathilda were able to return to the present (I hadn't traveled back in time to begin with, so I didn't have to make the trek back.) I was surprised that everyone had returned to the same place—right here on the beach where Mercedes had first sent Sinjin on his merry way into the past. I wasn't sure why, but I had guessed that upon returning, each person would reappear wherever he or she had departed. Well, clearly that wasn't the case. 'Course, I also couldn't say I understood the hows and whys about time travel, so maybe I shouldn't have been surprised.

"Damn not doubting her," Rand raged.

"I had but one goal," Mercedes answered in her same level tone, fixing her gaze on Rand and then on me.

"What was it?" I asked, my voice sounding hollow and drained, which wasn't surprising considering everything going on around me.

"I made the decision to ensure the safety of our Queen and sovereign," Mercedes finished, raising a brow at Rand as if to say, *How can you argue with that*?

"Her safety against what?" Rand asked as he wrapped his arm around me, pulling me close. It seemed as if just the thought of a threat to my safety bothered him.

Mercedes didn't alter her straight-lipped expression. Instead, she stared at him vacantly for about two seconds. "The Lurkers," she finished succinctly. "Sending the Queen back in time would give us another two years to train her in an environment free of Lurkers." I was about to respond when she held up her hand. "I never told you, Jolie, but I could sense something was coming, something dangerous."

"So you decided to send Sinjin back in time to avoid it?" I asked.

She nodded. "It was the only way I could protect you, to give us more time to plan our retaliation."

"Fat lot of good it did," I muttered. The Lurkers, a breed of half-human/half-vampire creatures who had a vendetta against all Underworld residents, had done as good a job of attacking me in the past as they had in the future—well, now my present. Shit, this time-travel stuff was going to get confusing fast.

"What do you mean?" Mercedes pressed.

"She means that the Lurkers found her even though you upset the balance of time. So your reasoning was completely flawed," Rand finished, his eyes burning.

"The Lurkers found you?" Mercedes asked slowly, spearing me with her eyes.

I nodded, reliving my fear as I remembered my brush

with the Lurkers and how they had poisoned my dreams.
"Yes."

"How?"

"They sent me a dream," I answered, remembering
the images—a battlefield littered with bodies, an image
of a throne unattended. It was a dreamscape that appeared to me twice in my sleep. The first time, I awoke
with the realization that the Lurkers were not only half-
vampires, but also possessors of magic. The second time
I had the dream, I was back in Los Angeles, two years
ago, and the images resulted in an attack on my psyche.
"My magic wasn't strong enough to fight the images
and I became very sick."

"She could have died," Rand finished for me, his lips
tighter than before. I could feel his hands fisting around
me, and I glanced up at him and smiled, loving the fact
that he was so protective.

It's going to be okay, Rand, I thought the words,
knowing he could hear them. Even though I didn't believe my own words, it felt good to say them. I wanted
to trust that this was all going to work out just fine that
the Lurkers weren't such a huge threat after all. Wishful
thinking.

Instantly, I felt pride and love welling up within me, a
feeling that threw me for a second because they weren't
emotions that belonged to me. No, they were Rand's
feelings making themselves known to me. That was
when it dawned on me—Rand and I were still bonded,
which meant we were soul mates, for lack of a better
description.

I wasn't sure why I was surprised. I mean, we had
bonded after he, Sinjin, and Mathilda traveled back in
time. I guess I hadn't thought the bond would survive
when Rand traveled forward in time, but apparently it
had. And I had to admit I was elated. We've always
known Rand was the only man for me. I love him like

no other, and now I knew our bond had cemented us permanently. With it, we could hear each other's thoughts, and feel each other's emotions. Bonding is like the ultimate union achieved between two witches, and it's forever. The only end to a bond is death.

Mercedes and Sinjin manipulated you, Jolie, and that is not okay with me, he responded, shaking his head as he thought the words. But I couldn't say I sincerely agreed with him. Things were not as black and white for me as they were for him. And knowing that Mathilda trusted Mercedes so wholeheartedly spoke volumes, because I trusted Mathilda.

"We will discuss the dream later," Mercedes said resolutely as she faced me. I noticed she was careful not to glance at Rand, who probably looked furious.

"So that was your plan?" I asked her, trying to decide if I believed it. "To send Sinjin back in time to avoid the threat of the Lurkers?" She just nodded. "Then what about saving yourself?"

Mercedes was the prophetess, yes, but not all Underworld creatures believed in her existence—mainly because no one had ever seen her. She had imprisoned herself in the year 1878. Why? Because she'd received a vision that if she didn't relive the year 1878 repeatedly, she'd be killed by Lurkers. Luckily for her, she was able to harness my power to bring me back to 1878, and we returned to the present together. Thus, in sending Sinjin back and changing the course of history, she would also have changed the course of her own history, possibly sacrificing herself . . .

"I gave the vampire express instructions on how to train you until your powers were strong enough to send for me yourself," Mercedes answered.

"So you had it all planned out," I said, swallowing down the lump in my throat as the pieces began to fall into place. Did I actually buy her explanation? Any way

I looked at it, I couldn't think of another reason why she would have bothered with such a grandiose plan. And I had to admit that I did believe Mathilda when she said every action by Mercedes was intended to protect the kingdom, and likewise, to protect me. So, in a way, I guess I had to believe her.

Yes, I was still angry about the whole thing, but when I thought about it in this new light . . . well, it offered an angle I hadn't yet considered. And it also meant something else—that Sinjin had been telling me the truth. He'd insisted that he'd done Mercedes's bidding because he wanted to protect me. Prior to the whole time travel thing, Sinjin had been a guardian to me, the Queen. He'd insisted that he was and always would remain my loyal protector.

Even though I didn't want to, I turned to face him.

Sinjin Sinclair is in a word . . . stunning. He's about six-foot-four and lean, with broad shoulders and long legs. His hair is the color of midnight—so dark that it sometimes appears almost blue, and his eyes an even lighter blue—like the color of alpine water. He is the quintessential rogue, a real Casanova, and six centuries old.

I felt something inside me rise up. It was a sort of numbness that quickly gave way to anger and pain, then feelings of betrayal. I refused to give in to them, though, and instead took a deep breath. "Is that true?" I asked him.

"Of course," he answered simply. "It was to protect you." His eyes bored into me as if he could see into the depths of my soul. I felt myself swallow hard. "As I told you earlier."

"Jolie, don't believe a word from his mouth," Rand interrupted. "He's done nothing but lie to you, and he will continue to lie to you," he spat, staring at Sinjin.

"Poppet, I have only ever spoken the truth," Sinjin

continued, not even sparing a glance at Rand. It was the same as always between them—Rand wore his emotions on his sleeves, and where Sinjin was concerned, those emotions were usually anger, protectiveness, and jealousy. Sinjin, on the other hand, while he probably did experience the same emotions, was always even-keeled and levelheaded. I attributed it to the six hundred years he'd had to master his art.

"You conniving—" Rand started.

Sinjin merely cocked a brow in his direction and turned to face me again, wearing a smirk. "I have always been and will always be dedicated to the protection and longevity of my Queen."

Okay, so I was willing to suspend my disbelief for the moment and lend a little credence to Mercedes's and Sinjin's story, but there was one part of the whole thing that still didn't sit well with me. Well, aside from the fact that they both attempted to change the course of my life without my permission. I faced Mercedes and took a deep breath. "Was it your intention for me to develop feelings for Sinjin?"

I suddenly felt deeply depressed, and recognized that I was experiencing Rand's reaction to my words. I glanced at him quickly and smiled, letting him know exactly how much he meant to me. Even though Sinjin had in a way tricked me into falling in love with him, it wasn't something that would ever be long-term. No, I would beat this. I knew I would because I loved Rand and always had, and ours was the type of love that was forged by fate, set by the fires of destiny.

"That was not my intention," Mercedes said as she eyed Sinjin suspiciously. "But apparently it was a by-product?"

A by-product.

If only my feelings for Sinjin could be dissected and archived as nothing more than a "by-product." I said nothing, though, since I recognized the situation for what it was. Mercedes just didn't understand the language of emotions—she was one of those people who lived only for the facts; there were moments when I envied her for that.

"I do not believe any of this," Rand spat out at last. "And I have never trusted you," he finished, glaring at Mercedes. "What you did was in no way defensible. You changed Jolie's life when it was not your right."

And Rand was correct. One hundred percent. Whatever their reasoning, I couldn't deny that the wool had been pulled right over my eyes, that I'd had no say whatsoever.

And then something interesting happened. Mercedes' eyes narrowed as she faced Rand, and I could see heat building in her face, staining the apples of her cheeks to a handsome shade of cherry. Mercedes is very pretty—she has long dark hair and the most gorgeous green eyes you've ever seen. At the moment, though, those eyes looked like they were about to resurrect World War II.

"Perhaps there was one other reason I sent the vampire back in time, warlock," she said between gritted teeth. I couldn't remember the last time I'd seen her so upset.

"And what was that?" Rand persisted, seemingly unconcerned that she was so angry, which hinted at his courage. The prophetess could have made a peanut butter and warlock sandwich out of him in two seconds flat.

"It was a test," she finished squarely.

"A test?" he repeated, and I felt my heart rate increase. Tests are never good, particularly when you haven't studied.

"What do you mean?" I demanded.

She glanced at me and frowned. "You have admitted yourself that your feelings for Rand have caused you pain. As far as I was concerned, your feelings for him were getting in the way of your duty to your kingdom and your people."

I swallowed even harder. This was going to end badly. I could see it already. "That was not your place—" I started.

"It was and is my place," Mercedes interrupted, her eyes ablaze. "I am responsible for your safety and your happiness. And as far as I could tell, Rand has caused you nothing but agony."

"But—" I started, but she wouldn't be silenced.

"Do you recall the time when you begged me to send you back to 1878 because, in your own words, you 'hated your life'?"

Damn, I did, and now those words were coming back to haunt me. But it's not like I'd really meant them. I mean, at the time, Rand was being his usual obstinate self and I was having a pity party for myself, remembering 1878, when he and I had loved one another openly. But it wasn't like I really wanted Mercedes to send me back . . . or was it?

You asked her to send you back to 1878? Rand's words echoed through me, but I couldn't face him. His voice sounded too hollow, surprised in its sadness.

Yes, but I didn't . I didn't mean it, I responded, feeling guilty. Looking back on it, I was happy that Mercedes hadn't sent me back. Somehow I hoped all those thoughts translated over to Rand.

"I wished to spare you the heartache inflicted upon you by this man," Mercedes finished. She crossed her arms against her chest as if daring any of us to argue with her. I couldn't really find it in myself to be that angry with her because I did believe her. And somehow it's hard to be super irate with someone when they can't see the full picture, since they probably had good intentions. As it was, I actually felt sorry for her.

"That's just life, Mercedes," I said, shaking my head. "You can't control people's destinies. You aren't God."

She swallowed hard. "I was only doing what I thought right."

"Well it wasn't right," Rand insisted. "And Jolie is much more forgiving than I'm willing to be." He gritted his teeth. "Because of you, I nearly lost her."

"But you didn't," Mercedes snapped. "I had to ensure your worthiness to court my Queen," she continued. "This was a test of your loyalty and affection for her and of whether you were the ideal recipient for her love."

I watched Rand swallow hard as his arms tightened around me, his anger suddenly consuming me.

"Then you knew I would go after her? That I would time-travel just as Sinjin did?" he asked.

Mercedes glared at him for a few seconds before responding. "I did not know, but I suspected, or rather, hoped you would."

"And?"

She cocked a brow and frowned. "Obviously, you passed the test. This is proven not only by the fact that you are standing here, but also that you are bond mates again."

There really wasn't anything Mercedes didn't know. I'd reached that conclusion a long time ago. She had an uncanny ability to detect things, our bonding status a prime example. I mean, it wasn't like bond mates had to wear matching shirts proclaiming themselves bonded. It was just one of those things Mercedes knew.

"You are bonded?" Sinjin asked, turning to me. His expression was tight, his fangs indenting his lower lip. He didn't look happy. Instead, he seemed surprised, yes, but more than that—hurt.

"Yes," Rand responded before I could. "You lost, Sinjin," he said, his eyes angry as he took a few steps closer to the vampire. "Even though you did everything in your power to ensure that I would lose Jolie, you failed."

Sinjin said nothing, and I faced forward again. I didn't want to see pain in his eyes. I just couldn't believe it—couldn't believe that he'd ever cared for me.

You know he cared for you, a small voice piped up from within me. *Don't try to kid yourself, Jolie.*

Sinjin tricked me, I responded. *I don't care what Mercedes says or what excuses Sinjin makes—he isn't being honest. Yes, he wanted to protect me but he also hungers for power, and I've always known that. Everyone knows that.*

"At any rate," Rand continued. "Punishment must be doled out to those who transgressed against the Queen. I will not allow this to be swept under the proverbial rug."

I swallowed hard as I considered it. It wasn't like Mercedes could be punished, Or could she? She was like this supreme being—way more powerful than any of us—so how could we hope to punish her? I wasn't sure. Which left one person. I couldn't help it—I glanced back at Sinjin, only to find his eyes trained on me.

"I await my punishment with bells on," he said as he disappeared into the cold night air.

Are you Team Rand?
Read on for an exclusive short story told from
the point of view of your favorite enchanter.

Be Witched

One

Sinjin Sinclair was a bloody bastard.

"I am just attempting to point out the obvious," he said and shrugged as if his interests in Jolie were merely casual, nonthreatening. Clearly he'd overheard my most recent conversation with her—the one where I'd told her in no uncertain terms that I would not allow her to fight in the Underworld civil war. No, Jolie was too valuable, too precious . . . she meant entirely too much to me for me to allow her to risk her life.

I glared at him as he leaned against my desk and acted the part of unconcerned. I wanted nothing more than to evict him from my home but that was an impossibility— not with our legion of Underworld soldiers currently stationed at Pelham Manor, my home. And as much as I disliked the vampire, he was fighting for our side and, therefore, a comrade, so here he would remain . . . until further notice.

"I will not allow Jolie to take part in the battle." I took a quick breath. "And that is the end of it. This conversation is over."

I glanced outside at the throngs of our soldiers as they sparred against one another in the moonlight, practicing for a battle that would be much more black-and-white— either they would survive or they wouldn't. The only thought that caused me any comfort was the fact that *if* our side prevailed, Jolie and I would see to it that every soldier who perished would be reanimated. It was Jolie's gift—the ability to bring the dead back to life.

"Is it?" Sinjin asked, reminding me that he was still there, fastidiously attired in his customary black. In the one hundred fifty years he and I have been acquainted, what I've realized, aside from the fact that Sinjin is anything but likable, mostly due to the fact that he believes the world revolves around him, is that he is more than popular with the ladies . . . he always has been. Whereas I have always found myself to be a bit too cynical, too reserved and introspective, Sinjin is the opposite. He's garrulous and confident, witty, and with what most women consider striking good looks, he's easily navigated the waters of feminine attraction and laid stake to any woman he wishes to call his own.

My biggest fear was that he'd set his sights on Jolie.

"I have nothing more to say," I finished and even attempted to leave the vampire behind me as I started for the door, but the undead seem unable to grasp the concept of subtlety. In Sinjin's case, I imagine propriety perished alongside morality when his mortal body died and he became the bastard corpse with whom I'd unfortunately just spent the better half of a fortnight.

"She is stronger than you imagine," Sinjin called out, his accent suddenly sounding more British than it previously had. His English beginnings were a reality that irked me—in no way did I want to share any similarities with the vampire, not even our British ancestry.

I turned on my heel and scowled at him as heat began to bubble up within me. Who the bloody hell did he think he was, telling me Jolie was stronger than I imagined? I knew her far better than he did and I was more than mindful of her magical proficiencies. "I am quite aware of Jolie's abilities." After all, I had been the one to bloody well discover her!

"Then you must also be aware of the fact that she will not respond well to your patronization?"

Given the fact that I was convinced Sinjin had eavesdropped on the entirety of my and Jolie's conversation regarding the battle, he was already well aware that Jolie hadn't reacted well to the news that I would not allow her to put herself in danger. The conversation had ended in a minor argument and although Jolie was most definitely angry, I wouldn't budge.

I took a few seconds to respond, chiefly to talk myself out of my anger. Sinjin thrived on his ability to upset me. I would not allow him that small victory. When I spoke, my voice was even, calm. "I am not patronizing her. I am merely protecting her."

"Perhaps she does not care for your protection?" He elevated a brow in practiced form. "Perhaps Ryder . . ."

Ryder . . . just the mention of the bastard's name turned my blood to venom. If I had one goal, it was to kill Ryder. The vampire had kidnapped Jolie and delivered her to Bella, the witch with whom we were now at war. But his kidnapping of Jolie was not the reason I detested him—my loathing was reserved for the fact that he'd also attempted to force himself on her.

And for that, he would die.

"I will destroy Ryder myself," I spat out.

Sinjin's jaw tightened. It was the only sign that perhaps he wasn't quite as untouched by the conversation as he would have me believe. "The vampire will die, no doubt."

He said it as if he and I shared the goal of slaying Ryder, as if he would see to the vampire's execution himself. As long as there was breath in my body, such would not be the case. I'd reserved that honor for myself. "Then problem solved."

"Doubtful." He tapped his fingers against his lips and

seemed pensive. "Have you not considered that Jolie wishes to seek her own revenge against Ryder?"

"I don't care."

He shrugged. "Perhaps you should?"

While I certainly recognized Jolie for the powerful and talented witch she was, she was still a novice. Having only been introduced to this life a year earlier, there was so much she still didn't know. Furthermore, there was no way anyone would change my mind regarding her fighting in a battle where she would be up against more practiced witches, werewolves, vampires, and even demons. The idea was purposeless—a fool's errand. I glanced at Sinjin and eyed him suspiciously. "You claim to care for Jolie . . . would you want to put her in harm's way?"

Sinjin shrugged before a grin lit up his mouth, a grin that said the entire conversation had been an act, a mere farce. "I would never put our lovely witch in harm's way. In actuality, I quite agree with everything you have said, my dear Randall."

I didn't bother to point out the fact that Randall wasn't my name—it was Rand. And as to correcting him . . . that was also useless. He thrived on irritating me. "You have a funny way of showing it."

"I find I enjoy playing the part of devil's advocate on occasion."

I shook my head, tired of his games. "I have neither the interest nor the time to engage you any longer, Sinclair." I glanced outside again, catching the glint of metal in the moonlight—of blades and shields interspersed with magical bursts of fluorescent light as my men sparred against one another. It was a cold English night—evident by the frost settling on the window frame. The sound of a werewolf's howl interrupted the still air of my office. "I need to return to my men," I said and narrowed my eyes at the vampire as if to say he'd outstayed his welcome.

"Spoken like a true gentleman." He finally stood up from where he'd been leaning against my desk and started for the door. At the promise of his departure, I felt a pressure begin to lift from my shoulders. "Perhaps I should check on our ward?"

And just like that, the pressure returned. "Stay away from her," I barked. "She's sleeping and needs to heal." In order to win the loyalty of the fairies for our side, Jolie had recently bested a fairy in a tournament of magic. While that might sound inconsequential, the fairy, Dougal, had nearly destroyed her. But Jolie had prevailed, seemingly by the skin of her teeth, and in return, the King of the fairies had been forced to agree to fight alongside us, against the tyranny promised by Bella. I smiled inwardly as I remembered how small and insignificant Jolie had appeared against the mammoth powers of Dougal. And yet, she had bested him. She had proven her own strength, her own power. It was a moment I will never forget—how frightened I'd been for her, how close to losing her I'd come, and how proud of her I'd been when she'd prevailed.

And now? Now she was weak and needed to heal.

"I am well aware, Randall, but I do worry about the beautiful woman." He smiled again and then inhaled a quick breath, which was all just for show because vampires don't breathe. "To allay my fears . . ."

I took the few steps that separated us until I stood just before him. He was an inch or two taller than I, but I wasn't intimidated. I was broader. His ice-blue eyes blinked wide with surprise. "Keep away from her."

Sinjin frowned. "I do not believe you lay claim to her?"

I shook my head, although what he said was technically true. "Jolie might be taken in by your charm but I recognize you for who and what you are." I had to remind myself that I wasn't saying this out of jealousy, only to protect Jolie against Sinjin's advances. He didn't deserve her and I'd be damned if I stood casually by and allowed him to hurt her.

"And what is that?" he asked in a bored tone.

"Scum, Sinclair. You are scum."

He smiled without a trace of humor. "Well, I must admit that I am disappointed in your categorization of me, Randall, but I am quite pleased to learn that you believe Jolie is taken in by my . . . hmm, how did you phrase it again? Ah, yes, by my charm."

I grabbed his lapel even though I'd sworn to keep my temper in check. Nothing upsets me more than the ill treatment of those I care about. "Jolie is an innocent, Sinjin. If there is an ounce of goodness in you, leave her alone."

He glanced down at my hand in an amused sort of fashion, as if a trespassing ladybird, or ladybug as the Americans call them, had stopped for a quick respite on his shirtfront. He made no motion to free himself. "How do you know I harbor ulterior motives where our witch is concerned?"

I tightened my grasp. "Because I'm not a fool."

"Fool, no, but you do quite enjoy playing the role of hero, I daresay?"

There was something in his eyes that was angry, that belied his flippant comments, that hinted at feelings that were anything but trite.

"I have no idea what motivates your fascination with Jolie although I have a good idea it has to do with her abilities and powers . . ."

"Really, Randall, do you imagine me to be that shallow and self-serving?"

The expression on my face told him just how shallow and self-serving I thought he was. "What I do know is that if you ever hurt her, you'll have to answer to me."

"I do not intend to harm her." The smirk fell off his face. "You do not intimidate me, Randall."

"I want you to realize in no uncertain terms that you are playing with fire."

Then he laughed and the sound dripped with sarcasm. "Your warlock abilities are nothing to me."

He was referring to the fact that witches and vampires were immune to one another's powers. Before I could respond, he continued. "And although you are quite convinced that I harbor an evil plan where our beautiful one is concerned, I can assure you that your supposition could not be further from the truth."

I stood up straight and dropped his lapel. He arched a brow and offered me a quick smile. "Explain," I demanded.

He shrugged and smoothed away the nonexistent wrinkles on the front of his shirt. "I will not argue my attraction to Jolie. I find her alluring, irresistible . . ." He faced me again and smirked. "Sexy."

"Attach your sights on another woman, Sinjin," I bit out. An image of the two of them in a heated embrace flashed through my mind and the air caught in my throat, felt as if it were constricting my lungs. It was a mere fabrication sent from my mind's eye but it felt concrete, real enough that I could reach out and touch it. I wanted nothing more than to crumple it in my fists, to ensure I never subjected myself to the visual again.

"I find myself quite enamored of her." He paused for a few seconds. "Perhaps it is love?"

Love? I felt my stomach drop and then realized he was playing me for a fool. Sinjin Sinclair did not have the first idea what love was. "Love" did not exist in his vocabulary. "This isn't a fucking game!"

"Such language, Randall!"

Heat was now penetrating me and I had to hold myself in check, force myself to calm down even as my hands fisted at my sides. "I care for Jolie and I will not see her hurt, do you understand?"

"Do not pin your frustrations over the fact that you have not claimed her on me," he shot back fiercely. "You had your chance."

His words echoed through me, and though I didn't want to admit it, there was something inside me that agreed with him—a small, backstabbing voice that reiterated the fact that this was my fault. If I had just acted on my feelings for her, taken her when she was mine to take, perhaps Sinjin would never have been a concern, would never have been a player in the contest for her affections . . .

"Jolie is not anyone's to claim," I said in a low voice, my eyes scanning the wall until they rested on the clock as it lazily ticked the seconds away. It was three forty in the morning. "And the difference between you and me is that I respect her and I genuinely care for her." I exhaled my pent-up aggression. "I want only what is best for her."

"Do not assume to know what thoughts permeate my head. You know nothing of me, warlock," he spat the words at me, as if his tongue were choking on them. His irritation bled away a moment later and was replaced with a blank expression. He cocked his head to the side, as if he were listening for the faintest sound. Apparently feeling he needed to rely on another of his senses, he closed his eyes and opened his mouth, inhaling as if he were tasting the air the way a cat would. When he opened his eyes, they were glowing white.

"What is it?" I insisted.

Sinjin glanced at me for a mere second and then in a flash, he was gone. Before I had the chance to ponder his bizarre actions, a feeling difficult to explain descended on me. It started in the very pit of my stomach, something that felt like the beginnings of panic. I swallowed hard and tried to focus on the feeling as it permeated my core, building in intensity until I could recognize it as terror. But it wasn't my own terror and the only other person I shared a close enough connection with in order to feel her fear as my own was Jolie . . .

Rand! Her voice suddenly infiltrated my head.

"Jolie!" I exhaled her name and before I could take another breath, I was already through the office door.

Rand, I need you now!

I'm coming! I thought the words in return, hoping they would reach her, hoping they would give her some ounce of relief. Relief from what, though, I didn't know and the thought sickened me.

If something were to happen to her . . . I wouldn't let myself continue the thought. *Nothing was going to happen to her.*

I took the steps that led from the second floor of Pelham Manor to the third floor two at a time, running hell-bent for her bedroom, which was at the end of the corridor. My heart pounded in my chest as fear beat a destructive path through me.

Nothing was going to happen to her . . .

At the mouth of the corridor, I was met by the sound of wood splintering, of someone bursting through a door.

I yelled something unintelligible but pained all the same and tore down the hallway, afraid of what I would encounter in her bedroom. It was difficult to categorize the sounds that emerged—groans and fists meeting flesh, the lone cry of a wolf. I could only hope Jolie wasn't in the midst of it.

It felt like I was running through sand, that my feet couldn't move fast enough. It was as if time stood still as I forced myself down the corridor. When I reached the doorway, half the wooden door was discarded in the hallway and the other half was still hanging by a whining hinge. My eyes trailed from the splintered wood fragments cluttering the floor to the still lump of a naked man, bleeding in the corner of the room. He must have been the wolf whose howl I'd heard only moments before. My gaze continued up and rested on the small form of Jolie as she lay in her bed, Sinjin bending over her.

They were both covered in blood.

"Sinjin, it bit me!" Her voice was panicked, her body shaking.

"Jolie," Sinjin started and reached down to touch her face.

And that was when something inside me erupted, something laced with panic and anger, something protective and primitive. Sinjin was touching her, he was covered in blood . . . her blood and he was a vampire.

"Get the fuck away from her!" I screamed as I threw myself into him. But he must have been expecting me because I blinked and he was gone, using his power of excessive speed to sidestep me. I felt myself hit the post of Jolie's bed and when I turned around, Sinjin was standing before me, wearing an irate expression.

"She has been bitten by a wolf!" he roared as I realized he'd killed the wolf and it was the wolf's blood covering him, not Jolie's. "She will turn!"

"What?" she shrieked and attempted to lift herself up from the bed but I was immediately beside her, holding her down so she wouldn't elevate her blood pressure and spread the canine virus through her body quicker.

She felt so small in my hands, so fragile. Her sweet face was now flushed, sweat breaking out along her forehead and dampening her long blond hair. And her cornflower blue eyes were wide with fear, an expression that stabbed me in my very core. She glanced down at herself and inhaled a quick breath when she took notice of the large and bloody gash below her collarbone. The wolf had bitten into her chest and torn her flesh, obvious from the puncture marks made by his fangs. Blood covered her chest and stained the linens beneath her, spreading in a large arc until I wondered if she'd succumb from the blood loss.

I felt a cry sounding in the depths of my body as the reality of what was happening dawned on me.

If I were to lose her . . .

"Christ," I whispered as I inspected her wound. At the feel of my fingers, she winced and pulled away from me. She was just so frail, so frightened.

"Rand, it hurts!" she cried and I forced myself to smile down at her, hoping my expression would convince her that everything was going to be okay, even when I could recognize my smile for the lie it was. I put my hand on her forehead and she was scalding hot, which meant one thing. I wasn't certain why but I turned to face Sinjin.

"She's turning," I repeated the obvious and nearly choked on my own voice.

"Stop it from happening!" she squealed and began to shake. Tremors seized her middle until it looked as if she were suffering from a self-induced earthquake. It was a sign that the canine virus was taking hold of her, morphing her blood cells, asserting its control as it stampeded through her. I took her in my arms and wanted to curse myself for the fact that she was turning too quickly— that I had been too late in reaching her. It was possible that she was going to transform into a wolf right before my eyes—that is, if the change itself didn't kill her first.

"I can suck out the toxins," Sinjin said in a calm voice, as he took a step closer to the bed.

"No," I said, shaking my head, unable to stomach the idea of Sinjin drinking from her. I was a warlock, a master of witchcraft; my powers would be enough. "I can heal her myself."

"You do not have time," Sinjin continued as he glanced at her. "She is turning too rapidly."

Jolie gripped my hand and her eyes were wild, frightened. "Please, Rand."

I gulped hard as I weighed my options. Sinjin was correct—there wasn't time for me to charm her, to conjure up a spell that would reverse her metamorphosis. As a rule, I deal in black and white and the reality was that Sinjin was the only option we had. Without him, she would succumb, possibly to her death. It was a chance I wasn't willing to take.

I faced him and narrowed my eyes. "Do it quickly."

Sinjin smiled and it was the expression of victory. "You must charm her so she will not feel it."

As I mentioned earlier, vampires and witches are immune to one another's powers—Sinjin's ability to bewitch his prey, to remove any pain associated with his attack, would be useless on Jolie; his bite would be excruciatingly painful. While it might seem that Sinjin's request was innocent enough, such wasn't the case. I knew what it meant for a vampire to bewitch his prey and I'd be damned if I allowed the same to happen to Jolie. What was more, I imagined she would never forgive me.

I gritted my teeth and shook my head. "No, I can't allow her to succumb to you," I said, tightlipped. "My magic will . . ."

"Very well but this will be incredibly painful," Sinjin interrupted with an unconcerned shrug and sat down beside her, leaning over as he inspected the wolf's bite. He watched her and his eyes focused on the blood still pumping from her wound. His fangs lengthened. She closed her eyes as another eruption of shaking seized her. Time was now an extravagance we couldn't afford.

"Please, Rand, please do what he's asking!"

I couldn't watch her hurt. That's what it amounted to.

I couldn't watch her writhe in agony before me when I could stop her pain. Yes, I also knew what would happen once Sinjin bewitched her but I would just have to suffer through it and hopefully she would understand why I made the choice I did.

I knelt down, taking hold of either side of her face, forcing her attention to me. "Look at me, Jolie, and don't break eye contact."

She nodded and although another spasm seized her, she forced her eyes open. She was strong; she always had been. I didn't say anything as I gazed at her, but focused on the charm in my head, focused on the words that would allow her to submit to Sinjin's powers. I imagined a shell of white light surrounding her, sinking into her, sending its potency to every inch of her body to bathe her in my magic.

Seconds later, I released her head and stood up. "It's done."

Sinjin grasped her hand. "Look at me, poppet. This will not cause you pain, do you understand?"

She nodded and I could see her losing control of herself as she gazed into the vampire's eyes. I watched him too; I wanted him to be fully aware of the fact that I was standing over them, that I wouldn't allow him any transgressions with Jolie. His pupils dilated until the black swallowed the ice-blue only to immediately return to blue again within a blink. And, instantly, a smile spread across Jolie's face as her eyes took on a heavy-lidded appearance. She was relaxed now, even though her body continued to shake, continued to attempt to fight off the canine virus; it was as if her brain were not aware of the fact. Her pain had subsided, that much was obvious.

Sinjin smiled as his fangs sparkled in the moonlight. He grasped her neck and maneuvered her head to the side. All the while my heart beat frantically in my chest and it was all I could do to not pull him off her. The breath caught in my throat as I watched him sink his fangs into her already torn flesh. She inhaled slightly as if there were just the smallest hint of pain, but then her shoulders relaxed and her eyes glazed over as if she were feeling . . . pleasure.

Sinjin squeezed her shoulders as his fangs sank deeper and more blood began dripping from her wound. His hands palpated her arms, plying her flesh as he continued drinking her. As if that weren't enough for me to grab him and throw him off her, a moan escaped his lips. And Jolie responded to him immediately, groaning when he withdrew from her. She wrapped her arms around him as if begging him to return.

I felt sick.

I had to remind myself this wasn't real. Jolie didn't feel this way for Sinjin—it was merely his powers of persuasion working on her confused mind. Whatever she felt for him was of his doing, not hers.

She didn't want him. She couldn't want him . . .

"Jolie," I said but she wouldn't look at me. It was as if I wasn't even in the room. I felt my hands fist at my side and I had to close my eyes against the image of Sinjin above her with her bare legs wrapped around his waist.

If he didn't get the toxins out of her, she would turn into a wolf or worse yet, she would die. I had to keep reminding myself of that.

I opened my eyes to find Jolie running her fingers through Sinjin's black hair as she pushed his head back onto her neck. He pulled up from her and his eyes were bright with an unnatural light. He licked his lips, which were covered in her blood, and sank his fangs into her again. She screamed out in pleasure and it was the sound of someone in the throes of an orgasm.

"Stop, goddammit!" I yelled and took a step forward. "What the bloody hell are you doing to her?"

Sinjin didn't respond but merely withdrew his fangs again. Blood dripped from his mouth onto her face and he licked it off before apparently remembering me. "Do you want her to turn?"

I was panting, torn between killing him and realizing he was saving her. "No."

"Then let me finish."

Sinjin turned back to face Jolie and his eyes dilated again, weaving another round of bliss within her. She tilted her neck to the side and closed her eyes. "Please, Sinjin, please," she begged in a breathless voice.

I wrapped my arms around myself and tried to force the sound of her voice from my mind, tried to banish the image of her begging Sinjin. What was she begging him for? To bite her, to heal her? To touch her, become one with her?

It was a memory that would never leave me, a memory that would haunt me from here to eternity.

Sinjin bit into her with renewed zest, sucking her blood feverishly. She wrapped her legs around him again as her body writhed with pleasure beneath his. He groaned slightly as she screamed out another orgasm. I turned and faced the opposite wall, not able to watch anymore.

"I want you, Sinjin, please," she moaned.

And that was when I lost control. There was only so much I could willingly take, so much I could witness and this was too much. I felt anger encompass me, a mad rush of jealousy and pain washing over me until I thought I'd suffocate on the still air. My fists were so tightly clenched, I could feel my fingernails digging into the palms of my hands. I glanced down and before I could stop myself, I smashed my fist into the wall, feeling pain ricochet up my hand and into my arm. I turned around to face Sinjin. "Enough!"

Sinjin pulled away from her and his body heaved as he

licked the blood off his lips and closed his eyes, as if he were savoring the taste of her, as if she were the sweetest nectar. *He had no right . . . he had no bloody right!*

When he opened his eyes, he glanced at her again and it was the expression of someone hungry, of someone who had gorged himself on her blood and still wasn't satisfied. Then it occurred to me that perhaps it wasn't blood he was seeking. *Over my dead body . . .*

I took a step closer to him, my chest rising and falling as I tried to prepare myself for the fight that would surely ensue. There was no way in hell I would allow him another touch, another feel of her. And what was more, he was now in the throes of blood lust—the most dangerous moment for a vampire because it meant he was on the brink of losing himself to the power of his victim's blood and, possibly, draining her entirely.

If he so much as moves another inch closer to her . . . I couldn't finish my thought. I was too focused on his body language, paying close attention to whether or not he would defeat his primordial urges to drain her.

After another few seconds in which Sinjin did nothing but watch Jolie as a hawk would a field mouse, his fangs suddenly retracted, revealing the fact that he had bested the blood lust, that he was in command of himself. Jolie seemed to protest, grasping his head and trying to bring his face back down to her wound.

He chuckled. "No, pet, you must keep the rest."

"Get away from her," I said in an exhausted voice and grabbed his shoulder, pulling him back.

"I want more," she whimpered, still refusing to even so much as glance in my direction.

"No, Jolie, you're going to be all right now," I crooned in her ear. "These feelings are just temporary."

Sinjin chuckled from behind us; he'd already started for the door. It was as if he knew he was no longer welcome, that he'd done the deed to save her and now I wanted him gone. He paused just before the door and narrowed his eyes as he watched me. "Randall, do not outstay your welcome. It is clear whom she prefers."

"I don't have the patience to deal with you now, Sinjin," I said and faced him, anger beginning to boil up within me again. I was at the end of my tether and if Sinjin so much as looked at Jolie, I would burst.

Jolie suddenly began writhing before me, acting as if she was in the throes of pain. I grabbed hold of her flailing arms, afraid that perhaps Sinjin hadn't sucked enough of the poison from her.

"Did you get all the toxins out of her?" I demanded, glancing over my shoulder at him.

"Yes," Sinjin responded. "She will heal."

She opened her eyes and clutched me, trying to pull me down toward her. "I need you, Rand, right now!"

Although there was something in me that wanted nothing more than to feel her lips on mine, feel her body bucking beneath mine as I claimed her for my own, I ignored it. Jolie needed me, she needed me to see her through this, and dammit, that was what I intended to do. I would be her beacon. I faced Sinjin again. "When will this wear off?"

Sinjin smiled. "Another ten minutes or so. I had to charm her twice to ensure she would not feel pain."

I grumbled something unintelligible as Jolie continued to wiggle beneath me, rubbing herself against me as if she were a cat in heat. "Rand, please."

Sinjin's chortle was deep. "Apparently I awakened some dormant feelings in her. If you are not up to the challenge, I can satiate her."

Sinjin took a step toward us as if he would make good on his offer but, breaking Jolie's hold, I stood up, facing him. "I've had enough of you and your ulterior motives."

"Ulterior motives?" Sinjin questioned, feigning innocence.

I inhaled deeply. "Don't think I'm unaware of your interest in Jolie and it extends past mere physical attraction. I'm not a fool, Sinjin."

Sinjin shrugged. "I never accused you of being anything other than a gentleman."

"Just be aware that I'm on to you," I finished in a constricted voice. "Now leave us and send someone for him," I said and motioned to the lifeless corpse in the corner of the room. It was the first time I'd spared a thought for him since entering the room and noticing him lying in the corner.

Sinjin bowed and left the room and I breathed out my relief. Just being near him caused my blood pressure to escalate. And now with a new batch of memories that sickened me, I wondered how I'd ever rid myself of the bloody vampire. But Sinjin wasn't the one who deserved my attention. No, Jolie needed me and it was Jolie I wanted to focus on. I glanced down at her and watched her exhale. She closed her eyes wearily as the beginnings of a smile took control of her mouth. I held her more tightly, suddenly only too aware of the fact that I'd nearly lost her . . . again. Granted, there was a good chance she would have survived the transformation but the idea of Jolie as a wolf left me nothing but cold. No, she was a witch . . . she was my own kind.

She was mine . . .

"I think I might be back to normal," she said as the whiteness of her pallor began to give way to her ordinarily rosy hue and the vivaciousness that was Jolie began to come back, little by little.

I smiled as I held her in my arms. "You feel okay?"

"Physically, I feel better than okay, actually," she admitted shyly and I realized she was embarrassed. No doubt she was remembering everything she'd said and done with Sinjin. And as if those memories weren't awkward enough, I'd witnessed the entire episode. I didn't say anything but gave her an understanding smile and tightened my hold around her.

"I can move again," she announced, in an obvious change of subject, as she focused on her legs and wiggled her toes. Jolie's battle against the fairy, Dougal, had left her basically paralyzed. That is, until Sinjin had come along . . .

I nodded, none too comfortable with the realization that I now bore a deep debt to him. It was entirely because of him that she was lying here in my arms, that she wasn't canine or dead. "It's Sinjin's saliva. It must have healed not only the wolf's bite but the rest of you as well."

"It's that strong?" she asked and glanced up at me with her doelike eyes. The freckles that decorated the bridge of her nose gave her a youthful essence, a purity that was so uniquely hers. She'd seen and experienced things that would have caused a lesser person to crumble, would have ripped away any innocence they possessed. Yet Jolie was still the same woman I'd first encountered when I'd wandered into her fortune-telling store a year or so earlier. Well, she wasn't exactly the same. She'd learned so much, experienced so much, she'd come so far and yet her eyes were wide with a virtuousness that surprised me.

"Yes."

She seemed to suddenly remember the wolf and glanced toward the dead body heaped in the corner. "Do you know who he is?"

I shook my head, not wanting to be reminded of the fact that I'd failed in my part to keep her safe. Jolie was wanted—her ability to reanimate the dead had garnered attention from all creatures of the Underworld. It was no surprise that Bella, eager for power and domination,

had desired Jolie for herself. I'd been so foolish to think
Pelham Manor was secure—granted I'd employed guards
and, with the help of fairy magic, constructed invisible
magical nets along the tree line, designed to keep our enemies away. I'd still failed and in the process, I'd nearly
lost Jolie . . .

"No, but I do know he's one of Bella's."

"He was?" she almost choked. "But how did he get
through the fairy nets and all your soldiers?"

"Inside job," I said with a sigh, my mind elsewhere—
on the fact that I'd nearly lost her, for example. "This is
her way of saying she's agreed to our war."

We were both interrupted when one of my men appeared in the doorway. "Apologies for disturbing you,"
he started in a deep southern accent. Even though we
were in England, our soldiers were from every section of
the globe. This one, like Jolie, was from America. "I'm
here for the wolf."

I cleared my throat, slightly embarrassed by the fact
that he'd stumbled upon Jolie and me in an intimate moment. "No worries," I said and motioned to the corner
of the room. His eyes followed my lead and he merely
went to the wolf, picked him up, and hurriedly exited.
Not wanting any other visitors, I focused on the splintered remains of the busted door and, narrowing my
eyes, imagined the door mending itself, pictured the
wood seaming itself together again. When I blinked, it
was as if Sinjin had never destroyed it in the first place.

I glanced down at Jolie and found her watching me. "I
imagine that whole situation with Sinjin was difficult for
you to watch?" she asked.

I exhaled, not wanting a reminder. "More than you
know."

"Rand . . . thank you for doing what you did." She
glanced away and exhaled, as if remembering what had
just occurred. "I really don't even know how to verbal-

ize what I'm feeling. I'm just . . . very grateful to you and Sinjin."

You and Sinjin . . . I didn't allow myself to complete the thought. Without Sinjin's assistance, Jolie wouldn't be here, in my arms, as if she hadn't just skated over extremely thin ice.

"Yes, well . . ." I started, not exactly certain what my point was.

"I'm sorry you had to witness what you did," she interrupted. "I'm a little foggy on what happened but every time I think about it, I get embarrassed, so that must mean something . . ."

If she couldn't remember the details, I wasn't about to remind her. It was better for us both that she not recall exactly what went on. "It's better that way."

She nodded and tried to hide a yawn behind her hand. I smiled down at her and stroked her forehead. "You're tired," I said, pointing out the obvious.

"Yes."

I started to move, to stand up, but she clung to me and the fear I'd seen in her eyes moments earlier returned. "You need to sleep, Jolie," I said, just as I noticed the blood still staining her bedsheets and body.

"Would you prefer to sleep in another room?" I asked, thinking this one might now bear bad memories.

"Yes," she started and then dropped her gaze to her fidgeting hands. "I'm afraid, Rand. Will you stay with me?" There was urgency in her tone.

Really, I was needed outside with my men. I was more than certain that word of the wolf attack was now spreading through our battalions and it was my duty to announce exactly what had happened, that there had been one among us who betrayed our trust. And, furthermore, what I intended to do to ensure the rest of us were safe. But, at the moment, my men could wait. Jolie needed me and she was my priority.

I tilted her head up and smiled. "Of course." Then I reached down, secured her in my arms and lifted her. She rested her head on my chest and I started for the door.

"Which bedroom do you prefer?" I asked.

"Yours," she said with no hesitation.

I wasn't certain why but her answer caused a sense of warmth in me and I smiled to myself. "Very well."

I walked the few paces to my bedroom and opened the door with a thought. Once inside, I imagined the lights turning themselves on and they flickered in acquiescence, dimming themselves until they sent a slight yellowish glow throughout the room.

"I love it in here," Jolie whispered. "It smells like you."

I chuckled and kissed the top of her head but said nothing as I approached my bed and pushed the duvet to the side. Jolie clung to me as I bent down, intending to settle her against the pillows.

"I need to shower," she argued.

"Do you have the strength?"

She cleared her throat and dropped her gaze, as if she were embarrassed. "I need your help."

At the realization of what that meant, that she and I would be naked together, I felt a bolt of energy, of excitement pulsing through me. I immediately dampened it down, though, realizing this would be anything but sexual. She was hardly in the right frame of mind . . .

"Okay," I said and my voice was constricted, deep. It had to be more than obvious that I was battling with myself, forcing my desire to abate.

"Can you help me?" she asked and brought my attention to the fact that she was attempting to free herself from her "jammies" as she termed them. Her top was mostly ripped and already falling off her shoulders, thanks to the wolf's attack. I merely looped my finger underneath one strap and slowly pulled it up and over her wound, ensuring I didn't accidentally brush up against it, even though Sinjin's saliva was already in the process of healing her. Then, forcing my eyes to hers, I pulled the strap further down her arm until the fabric dropped away from her entirely, revealing her breasts.

Keep your eyes on her face, man! I reminded myself. It was a difficult task because Jolie's breasts are simply— awe-inspiring. I've only had the pleasure of witnessing them on a few occasions but if I had to, I could delineate them on paper flawlessly. Although I've never made love to her, we have come close. And as to why we've never become lovers . . . it's quite complicated. I began our acquaintance as her employer and fiercely promised myself to act the part of her guardian and protect her rather than seduce her. And now? Although I still consider myself her protector, she no longer works for me, so I suppose I could free myself of that promise. Perhaps.

"You can look at me, Rand," she whispered.

I swallowed but didn't respond, merely took advantage of the opportunity she was offering and allowed my gaze to move slowly down her face, to her neck and further south still. Her breasts were just as beautiful as I remembered them—full enough to fill my hand, with nipples that were alert and flushed pink.

"Do you want to touch me?"

I cleared my throat and forced my attention back to her face. "Yes."

She smiled and that was when I realized that perhaps she was still under Sinjin's power, there was a chance that this wasn't what she really wanted. And even though I could have been making a mistake, if there was even an inkling of doubt as far as where her feelings were coming from, it was a risk I was not willing to take.

"Jolie," I paused as I searched for the proper words. The last thing I wanted to do was upset or insult her. "I'm afraid the feelings Sinjin spawned in you have not yet abated."

She seemed taken aback, the smile dropping right off her lips. "Oh," she said and flushed with what appeared to be embarrassment.

And that was when I realized I had to make her understand that I wanted her, absolutely, but not like this. "I would never do anything to hurt you, Jolie, or take advantage of you when I don't believe you to be in the right frame of mind."

She nodded and dropped her gaze, crossing her arms against her chest. "I understand."

I ran my hands through her hair, imagining the sweat and blood fading into nothing and watched as the sheen of her hair returned. As I traced the incredibly soft skin of her temples and cheeks, the smudges of blood disappeared, leaving only the radiant beauty of her face. I could attempt to heal her wound but I already knew I'd be unsuccessful as not even Sinjin's saliva could heal it completely. Due to the virility of the canine virus, the healing process would need to run its own course. My warlock magic would not be able to hurry it along.

"You are beautiful," I whispered and brought my lips to hers. I only intended to kiss her chastely but she opened her mouth and before I knew it, my tongue had entered her mouth and now mated with hers. I groaned against her, felt my hands traveling up the line of her waist until they found her breasts. She wrapped her arms around my neck and I pulled her into me, needing to feel her against me. She moaned and something inside me yelled that I was taking advantage of the situation. She was still not in her right mind and I was seducing her? I was as bad as the bloody vampire!

I pulled away from her and took a few steps back. "I . . . I apologize. I should not have . . ."

"Rand, I want this."

I shook my head. "You need to sleep and heal, Jolie." I paused. "It's not right for me to do this with you . . . now."

Her eyes narrowed and she frowned, pulling away from me. "One of these days I wish you would just give in to your feelings for me and not find some excuse as to why you can't," she said and her voice was angry.

"There is a chance that you might rethink anything we do here and now," I rebutted. "I don't want that to happen."

She sighed and suddenly appeared exhausted. "It's hard to be angry with you or get disappointed when you're just so . . . honest and . . . and good."

I chuckled even though I wasn't sure how to take her comment. I wanted her; she had to know that. But I respected her and cared for her enough that the moment had to be right.

She faced my bed and sighed. I pulled the duvet back and, lifting her, delicately placed her against the pillows and pulled the cover up as if she were a child and I were tucking her in. Imagining gauze and tape, I closed my eyes and focused until I could feel them materialize in my hands. Then I set to bandaging Jolie's wound.

"Will you stay with me?" she asked. "Just until I fall asleep?"

I smiled. "Of course."

I sat down beside her and watched her roll onto her side until she was facing me. "Thank you," she said with a small smile.

"For what?"

"For always looking out for me and driving me insane with your infallible sense of honor."

I chuckled. "It doesn't sound very good when you put it that way."

She smiled as her eyes closed, revealing her incredibly long eyelashes as they dusted her cheeks. "It's good, Rand, it's good."

I stroked her hair and smiled, even as I realized she was drifting off, boarding the ship to the Isle of Sleep. "I promise to keep you safe, Jolie. I promise that this will never happen again."

"Mmm hmm," she muttered.

I shifted a long and silken strand of hair behind her ear, not able to tear my gaze from the tranquil beauty of her face. "You mean the world to me."

But she was already asleep.

Two

Sinjin was in my rose garden. The milky rays of moonlight reflected against his hair and bathed him in an eerie glow.

As I glanced out my window and watched him pick one of my red roses, I felt anger slowly winding up my body. Sinjin should have been out sparring with his men, training them for the battle, not playing the role of gardener.

I strode out of my bedroom doors, onto my balcony that overlooked the manicured garden and was about to yell at him to get back to his men when I caught sight of someone darting out from the shadows of Pelham Manor. She was wearing a cloak that obscured her face but somehow I knew who it was.

Jolie.

At her appearance, Sinjin smiled and once she was directly before him, he pushed the hood from her face, the moon's rays highlighting her blond hair. I felt my stomach turn. Why was she meeting Sinjin in the cover of darkness? And why the cloak? What was the secrecy about?

Feeling as if I couldn't move, I merely watched them, watched as Sinjin offered her the rose he'd pilfered from my garden and she accepted it with a demure smile. As soon as she touched it, though, she pulled away. She held her hand out before her and I could see the velvet crimson of her blood contrast against the paleness of her hand.

My pulse began pounding, causing a headache in my temples. I wanted to scream at her to get away from him, that she was bleeding and he was a vampire but I found I had no voice. I opened my mouth and nothing came out. Thinking I could jump over the balcony and use magic to soften my landing, I attempted to do so but found my feet rooted in place. I couldn't speak and I couldn't move. And I didn't even have the wherewithal to wonder why. Instead, I was transfixed by the sight of the two of them. All I could do was look on helplessly as Sinjin took Jolie's finger and sucked it, throwing his head back in ecstasy as the flavor of her blood hit his tongue.

Jolie, get away from him! I thought the words, our mental connection the final opportunity I had of reaching her. But she never turned to face me, never broke away from the vampire. Instead, she allowed him to drink from her, allowed him her finger, allowed him to enjoy her.

Jolie! I screamed inwardly again but as with the first time, nothing.

Was she under his spell? Had he somehow managed to bewitch her again? Had my charm not worn off? I pushed against the invisible shackles that kept me in place but realized I wasn't going anywhere. I was stuck.

I painstakingly brought my eyes back to the visual of Jolie and Sinjin and felt the breath catch in my throat. Sinjin had untied her cloak and it dropped to her ankles. Beneath the cloak, she was naked. The rays from the moon delineated every line of her body, the way her small waist flared into her hips, which tapered into her long and beautiful legs. Her back was toward me and I could barely pull my gaze from her plump and shapely rear. She was just so beautiful, so feminine, so . . . helpless when under Sinjin's power.

I opened my mouth to yell again but as with the first attempts, nothing. And that was when I remembered I was a warlock and had the advantage of magic. I held my hands out before me and focused all my energy between them, waiting for the telltale sign of light to bubble up between my palms. I watched as the faintest beginnings of a bluish glow began to grow from between my hands and doubled in intensity until it was humming with electricity. Facing Sinjin, I hefted my left arm backward and hurled the ball at him. It merely blinked and fizzled before it even touched the ground. Sinjin must have seen it, though, because he glanced up and when he recognized me, the bastard smiled.

And it was a smile that said he knew I was immobile, that there was nothing I could do to stop him from having his way with Jolie. As if to prove the point, he grasped her, none too gently, by the nape of her neck and rotated her around until she was facing me. It was as if she was a puppet to his puppeteer. There was a mask of vacancy on her face; she was playing the part of captive; she was under his spell. She was his to do with as he would and there was nothing I could do to stop him.

He grabbed a fistful of her hair and yanked her head to the side as if to prove that he could be as rough with her as he chose to be. That I was powerless to come to her defense. That I could do nothing more than watch.

He brought his hands up and stroked her naked breasts, his smile one of conquest, of triumph. Then, before I could so much as blink, he sank his teeth into her neck. She bucked against him either in shock or pain or possibly both but said nothing, merely closed her eyes as a smile took control of her mouth. He was going to seduce her, force her to his will, and I would have to watch every second of it.

Blood spilled from the wound he'd inflicted on her neck and when he pulled away from her, throwing his head back as he savored her taste, the blood came pouring from her neck faster, spiraling down her breasts, spreading at her nipples where it dropped to the ground beneath her.

Jolie, break away from him! Use your own magic to escape from his trance!

I don't even know why I tried; the situation was hopeless.

Sinjin's hands left her breasts and began caressing her stomach. He gripped her waist and pulled her into him, only to bury his face in her neck again. She didn't respond to his attack but glanced up and even though she was under his spell, she recognized me. I could see it in her eyes. She smiled as if we'd just met one another in the street under normal pretenses, as if she wasn't standing there stark naked with Sinjin feeding from her.

I glanced down at myself, at my immobile feet and focused all my attentions on moving them, on using my magic to break whatever spell had been inflicted on me. I closed my eyes and imagined light penetrating me, brightening in energy as it encountered whatever incantation I'd been plagued with.

When I opened my eyes, the breath caught in my throat. Sinjin's hand was between her thighs and what was more, her head was thrown back and her eyes were tightly closed. She was enjoying it!

I felt a scream tear at my throat and I sat bolt upright, glancing around myself in bewilderment. I recognized the mahogany furnishings and dark hunter green of the walls, which meant I was in my bedroom.

It had been a dream, just a horrible vision concocted by my subconscious mind. It wasn't real. Thank God.

I stood up, the adrenaline still rushing within me. I couldn't wipe away the image of Sinjin pleasuring Jolie, of her eyes rolling back in her head as he touched her, as he learned how to manipulate her body.

I shook my head and tried to quell the images even as they rampaged through me. Reaching for my pants, which I'd draped over the chair just beside my bed, I pulled them on, following with a white T-shirt. The pounding energy within me needed to be expended. The best way to work off the steam was to spar with my men, throw myself into practicing for the battle. Allow the testosterone that had been building within me a release.

I took the stairs two at a time and ran down the hallway leading to the kitchen that would, in turn, lead me outside to the training grounds behind the manor. All the while, images of Jolie and Sinjin continued to plague me, continued to play within my mind's eye like a film that couldn't be turned off. I stopped running and clenched my eyes shut, willing myself to stop the instant replay, pleading with my brain to quit bombarding me with images I couldn't take. When I opened my eyes, the memory of the dream was gone. My magic had done its job for now, at least.

Once outside, I hurried through the throngs of battling soldiers, finding a sense of peace in the war cries, flashes of steel, and snarling of vampires and werewolves. I could honestly say I would much rather witness the pain and anguish of battle than witness another vision of Sinjin touching Jolie, pleasuring her.

I spotted Odran, the King of the fairies, as he acted the part of leader and instructed two fae soldiers in the art of magic, and more specifically, how best to attack an opponent with a lightning bolt.

Physically, Odran is the essence of power. Jolie once remarked that he resembled a lion and I think it's a very apropos statement. Odran is both broad and incredibly tall. I would guess he's over six-foot-five. His mane of hair is the color of gold and long enough to reach his lower back. His eyes are amber and match the golden tone of his skin. And the King of the fae wears only kilts, either in blue or purple—the colors of majesty, the colors of the King. Although I feel very fortunate to call the fairies allies in our war against Bella, I cannot say that I care for Odran. He is too much a womanizer.

"Odran, spar with me," I called out. Even though it was an invitation, it came out as more of a command.

Odran faced me and dropped his chin quickly in a silent greeting. Then he smiled. "Aye," he responded in his deep, Scottish brogue.

The two fae soldiers stopped fighting one another and turned to watch us, probably pleased by the break.

Odran and I stood perhaps six feet apart. I nodded in silent recognition of the fact that our sparring was about to begin. Odran didn't respond but closed his eyes as his body began to emit a subtle yellow glow. He held his hands out at his sides, his fingers spread as the light began to build. He was buffering his magical stores, using energy to produce more energy. I could have done the same but the nightmare images of Sinjin and Jolie I'd just had the misfortune of concocting for myself were enough to see me through this fight.

I glanced down at my hands and holding them out before me, palms facing one another, I watched as a bluish light glimmered from between them until it appeared I was holding a blue fireball. I glanced up at Odran, found he was no longer focused on building his magical reserves and, therefore, was ready to begin. I turned to the side and unloaded the fireball, hurling it into Odran's stomach. It sizzled a few times and then disappeared. Odran chuckled as if my first attempt were mere child's play.

Child's play no, warm-up yes.

"Chan ann leis a'chiad bhuille thuiteas a'chraobh," Odran yelled. It was Gaelic, the old language of his people, and meant: It is not with the first stroke that the tree falls.

Not giving me adequate time to chuckle over his witticism, he charged me, all the while glowing a bright yellow. I braced myself for the impact—feet shoulderwidth apart and core tight. When he collided with me, it was as if I'd been struck by a train. The yellow of his glow sizzled against me and I could smell the rancid odor of burning hair. I hit the ground and glanced at my arms, realizing his energy had singed my arm hair. Even though I was down, Odran continued his attack. He fell on me and his energy continued to burn me, continued to scald me with its intensity. I clenched my eyes shut against the pain and focused on my warlock abilities, focused on pushing Odran away from me. When I opened my eyes, I realized my hands were glowing purple. I was ready. I thrust my palms onto Odran's chest and pushed. A jolt bolted through him and in a matter of seconds he was sailing through the air, landing in the dirt perhaps ten feet from me.

I took a moment to catch my breath and glanced over at Odran, realizing he was doing the same. Magically, I'd say we were both of the same degree. We were a good match. Before either of us had the opportunity to stand up and resume our jousting, Jolie suddenly appeared on the sidelines. She jogged the few paces separating us and stood between Odran and me. I felt something jealous and angry start in the pit of my stomach and the images of her with Sinjin began to flood my mind again. I fended them off, reminding myself they weren't real and, more so, that I was acting like a jealous fool.

Jolie smiled at me and reached down. I looked up at

her and nodded with a quick smile as I took her proffered hand. "Jolie," I said

"You're a sight for sore eyes."

I grabbed a towel lying on the ground and blotted my forehead, suddenly feeling slightly self-conscious about my appearance. I was certain I looked a mess—with smudges of dirt and mud covering every inch of me along with sweat.

I glanced at her and felt the breath catch in my throat. She was wearing her workout gear—stretch pants and a fitted T-shirt. It wasn't a revealing outfit by any means and yet I could see the curves of her body as if she were naked. "It's good to see you too."

She giggled and it was a sound that pleased me immensely. I draped my arm around her, suddenly needing to touch her, to feel her beside me. I pulled her closer and kissed the top of her head as we started toward Odran, who was now nearly upon us.

"Good job," I said to him.

"Aye, ye too," he responded and glanced at Jolie in question, as if he didn't understand what she was doing on the battlefield. I, too, wasn't certain why she'd decided to visit but I was happy to see her all the same.

"Hi, Odran," she said.

"Lass," he answered and slightly inclined his head. "What are ye doin' oot here?"

Jolie released herself from my hold and faced me, the girlish smile dissolving from her face. "I was hoping I could spar with you." I didn't say anything but I was sure my expression belied my curiosity. She continued. "I thought it would be good to take advantage of all this Underworld power and work on my magic too."

I nodded, not finding fault with her reasoning. "That sounds like a good idea."

I glanced out at my throng of warring soldiers, scanning them until I could find someone I could trust with

Jolie. Someone who wouldn't hurt her, but would challenge her, all the same. My eyes settled on John, who
happened to be a werewolf and the beau of Jolie's best
friend, Christa. Christa had relocated to England and,
more pointedly, Pelham Manor at the same time Jolie
had—when I'd taken them both under my wing to offer
protection against Bella and anyone else who would
seek to do them harm. Now Christa acted the part of my
assistant.

"John!" I yelled. He glanced over at me at the same
time Christa, Trent (a werewolf), and Sinjin did.

"Yessir?" John responded and began approaching us.

"Are you interested in training with Jolie?" I asked
and offered him an expression that said he better go
easy on her and if he hurt her, he'd have to answer
to me.

John frowned as if he wasn't comfortable accepting.
"But I thought you said she wasn't fighting Bella's . . ."

"She's not," I interrupted, glancing at her as if to reit-
erate the point. Yes, it had crossed my mind that her sole
intention had been to prove her abilities in combat in
the hopes that I would give her my blessing to attend the
battle. Well, that wasn't going to happen. I didn't care if
she hog-tied Odran, John, and Sinjin and did so all at
the same time. I would not risk her safety.

I looked back at John and shook my head. "It'll be
good practice for you to defend yourself against her
powers."

John obeyed with a quick nod and approached Jolie.
I stood on the sidelines next to Odran, Christa, and
Sinjin. I couldn't help but look at Sinjin askance. He was
the last person I wanted to see and the visual of him biting Jolie's neck seemed to return with a vengeance.

"I could not miss this," Sinjin said in response to the
quizzical look I offered him.

"John, go easy on her!" Christa yelled and then added, "I've got a twenty on Jules."

"Hey!" John yelled back. There was an ease between the two of them that caused pangs of envy in my stomach. I wanted the same between Jolie and me. I wanted to be with her; I always had but there was always some obstacle keeping us apart.

"Give me all you've got. I can defend myself," she said to John. I felt a smile break out across my face. She could defend herself and then some.

"You got it, girl." John ripped his shirt off and tossed it aside, then slowly walked around her, as if sizing up his competition. That or he just liked the image of her in her tight workout pants.

"Mind if I cut in?" Trent, the other werewolf who had followed us and who also happened to be Jolie's ex-boyfriend, interrupted.

Trent is far from making my favorite people list. He's a braggart, narcissistic, and he didn't treat Jolie well during their short romance. Truth be told, I can't stand the bastard. "Trent, mind your own bloody business," I called out and took a few steps closer, as if to say he'd have me to deal with if he didn't back down.

"It's okay," Jolie countered as a smile that wasn't quite sweet spread across her face. "I'd be happy to fight him."

"Okay," I said, chuckling to myself as I realized maybe Jolie was going to exact some retribution. I backed off at the same time that John returned to Christa on the sidelines.

"Don't hold back," Jolie said as she faced Trent and narrowed her eyes.

Trent shook his head. "Never do."

And without further warning, he lunged at her. I took a step forward, wanting to call interference but Jolie was faster than I. Using her magic, she disappeared in a split second, only to reappear a few feet from where she was just standing. Trent fell, face-first, at her feet. Jolie and I both laughed at the same time. She then held up her hands, palms facing each other and set to creating a fireball of energy. Yes, it could have seriously injured Trent but I could only imagine Jolie hadn't charged it with much more than a mild sting. Of course, depending on how angry she was with the bloody bastard, maybe she'd given it full strength. She aimed the fireball for Trent's stomach and released it. The wolf darted to the right to avoid it and the ball merely disappeared into the earth, blinking a few times before it popped and fizzled away.

I watched as Trent grabbed Jolie's ankle and yanked until she lost her footing and fell. She landed as I'd instructed her, with her weight thrown into her middle as she braced herself evenly between her arms. It was the best way to delimit physical injury. Once on her hands and knees, she rolled over in a split second but Trent was waiting for her. He pushed her down and jumped atop her, pinning her with his weight.

"I always wanted you in this position," he said, causing my stomach to sour. I knew Jolie could take care of herself but it didn't change the fact that I detested the way she was constantly receiving sexual innuendos. She deserved more than that. She deserved their absolute respect.

She just smiled, as if Trent's comment meant nothing to her, and began manifesting a handful of sand. She wasted no time in throwing the sand into his face, which allowed her ample opportunity to create another energy ball. Her ability to create energy was improving every time she tried it. I'd instructed her well. And I enjoyed playing the part of impressed instructor. I watched her hurl the orb into Trent's chest and he fell over, moaning as he gripped his stomach. I clapped, enjoying every moment of his pain.

"Nice!" Christa yelled.

But apparently the fool hadn't tasted enough defeat because he stood up and snarled, anger over the fact that he'd been bested by a woman no doubt driving him on. He charged her. I wanted to call out and warn her but I didn't. This was Jolie's fight. But I never took my eyes from her, wondering how she would counter him, what she would do. I watched as she magicked a heavy silver dagger and lashed out with it. I must have been on autopilot because the next thing I knew, I'd grabbed Trent's arm and pulled him backward, just shy of Jolie's blade.

"Bloody hell!" I yelled at Trent as soon as I released him and gave him a push that said in no uncertain terms that he'd made a fool of himself. "You weren't paying close enough attention! Don't let your personal issues get in the way."

"I have no issues with Jolie," Trent spat out.

We all were more than aware that there was no truth to that statement. I glanced at Jolie and noticed she hadn't responded other than to shrug while Trent continued to glare at the silver dagger in her hand. She glanced down at it and watched it disappear into her hand. When my gaze returned to her face, I found her studying me, perhaps to glean whether or not I was upset with her. I was nothing but proud, confident that she could defend herself should the need ever arise. I merely nodded and offered her a smile that said exactly what I thought. She responded with a great smile that spread across her face and made me want to kiss her.

Trent, apparently still irritated that Jolie had beaten him, trudged off while John patted her on the back. "Nice going, Jules," he said with a laugh. "I didn't realize you were so good."

"She's better than good," Christa said, beaming. "I didn't doubt you for a second."

Jolie smiled and quickly glanced at Sinjin before she turned toward me again.

"I want to fight Sinjin," she said in a matter-of-fact sort of way. I glanced at the vampire who was now smiling and licking his lips as if he'd just been served a bowl of O Negative. And all of a sudden, the memory of his hands all over her breasts returned. I shook my head, trying to free my mind from the recurrent images. *When would these visions end?*

Sinjin stepped forward and his eyes narrowed as he studied her, followed the contours of her body from head to toe. "Nothing would please me more."

"Jolie," I started, wanting to talk her out of this foolishness. Not only was Sinjin entirely too powerful for her but I also didn't want him to be so close to her, to be able to touch her. "Sinjin is centuries old . . ."

"I don't care," she said in that stubborn way of hers that absolutely drove me to madness. She walked the ten feet that separated her and the vampire, then she braced herself and motioned to Sinjin that she was ready for him. He laughed as if the context were completely different, as if it were just the two of them behind closed doors. I felt my throat begin to constrict.

Sinjin disappeared and reappeared seconds later directly in front of her. He could have reached out and touched her easily. I watched her gasp, watched her expression of shock as she realized how close she was to a creature who could kill her instantly.

"I will not go easy on you," Sinjin warned. I didn't expect that he would hand her a victory but, at the same time, if he so much as harmed a hair on her head, he would answer to me.

"I'm not asking you to," she countered and her voice faltered as if she was worried. Whether she was nervous about the fact that she was going to spar with a master vampire or whether that anxiety was a response to the fact that he was standing so close to her, I didn't know. As to what Jolie thought about Sinjin? I didn't know that either and perhaps that was why I tended to get so frantic concerning the two of them. Perhaps she had feelings for him? It would not be unusual—Sinjin could give Casanova a run for his money.

"Very well."

I watched Jolie close her eyes as she focused on her magic. In response, a sheen of light reflected around her, revealing the walls of a protective barrier she'd constructed around herself. But magic would not work against Sinjin. Granted, Sinjin's abilities to bewitch her would also fail so it would become a match of brawn against brawn. And physically, Sinjin was much stronger than she was.

He materialized directly behind her and pulled her into his chest, as if to show her she couldn't even defend herself when he was being gentle. "Your magic does nothing to deter me."

"Then how do I defeat you?"

He smiled. "You do not."

He turned her around to face him and then pushed her as she stumbled backward, falling down on her back and hitting her head against the dirt. She didn't fall as I'd instructed her and she'd pay the price later if she didn't already have the beginnings of a headache. I started forward but held myself back, allowed her to find out for herself what happened when she was ill prepared in battle. Sinjin must have knocked the wind out of her because she merely lay there for a few seconds.

"Sinjin!" Christa reprimanded and took a step nearer Jolie but Jolie held her back with a shake of her head.

"I'm okay," she muttered.

"I apologize," Sinjin said.

He stood above her, glancing down at her with what appeared to be apology and regret. He extended his hand and the thought of him touching her, spurred me onward. I wanted nothing more than to push him away from her, let him know that I was her protector. I side-stepped him and leaned over Jolie, offering her a smile. "He's just too strong."

She nodded but still made no motion to stand. "How is anyone supposed to defeat them?"

I didn't want to answer the question so I said nothing as Sinjin took the onus of answering it himself. "Only the oldest and strongest can battle against us, poppet."

"So that means everyone else is doomed?" She propped herself up on her elbows, apparently still too winded to stand. I wanted to pull her into my arms but I knew bet-ter. Jolie was not the type who wanted to be saved. She was independent, a modern and sensible woman.

"Not exactly," I said, rubbing the back of my head.

"The other creatures have been drinking our blood," Sinjin answered nonchalantly, crossing his arms against his broad chest.

"What?" she demanded and appeared to be horrified by the thought.

"It's the only way we can fortify ourselves to fight them," John responded, sounding defensive.

"Your blood?" she asked Sinjin.

"Of course not," he spat out, clearly insulted by the idea. "I am a master vampire and I do not share my blood."

She nodded, as if she weren't surprised by that and then turned to face me. "Rand, have you . . ."

"No!" I said quickly, offended that she would even consider the thought. I would never stoop so low as to ingest anything vampire. The mere thought of it sick-ened me. "I don't need it."

She offered me a quick smile of apology and reached

out her hand. I relished the feel of her soft and warm skin as it met mine. Before I could comprehend it, I felt an incredible wind come up from behind me. Not prepared for the gust, I felt myself wobble, lose my balance. I landed just beside Jolie but braced myself for the impact and was about to leap to my feet, to face whoever had been responsible for toppling me when I heard the sound of her giggling and I realized exactly what had just happened.

I faced her and smiled. "Is it like that then?"

"Come on, warlock, let the apprentice parry with the master," she answered in her most flirtatious voice. Warmth spread throughout me and I wanted nothing more than to grab her and climb atop her, to kiss her and yell to the world that she was mine. I watched her stand up and there was something giddy in her, something that said she wanted nothing more than to best me, to prove her skills.

I wouldn't give in.

I stood up and smiled at her.

You will regret that. I thought the words, reveling in our secret connection, loving the fact that no one else could speak to her in such an intimate way.

So come and get me.

I didn't. I wanted to take her by surprise. Instead, I focused on her lovely body and imagined her floating above the ground and gliding backward. Her eyes widened as she felt herself lift. She glanced down, as if to ensure that she was, in fact, floating. Smiling, I walked behind her while she closed her eyes and struggled to extricate herself from my power. I continued to focus on the charm, on the fact that I wanted to subject her to my control while she continued to struggle against it. I held my hand up and stopped her backward momentum as soon as a tree interrupted her path. She was still floating a foot or so off the ground, just suspended against the tree, exactly where I wanted her. Then I suddenly re-membered we still had an audience.

I turned around and faced the others, wanting only to be alone with Jolie.

"Get back to work, all of you."

Odran must have already grown tired with our games because he was nowhere to be found. John and Christa vacated the premises first. Sinjin made no motion to leave and merely switched his gaze between Jolie and me. I cleared my throat as if to tell him to hurry and be on his way. Seconds later, he disappeared into the air.

Which meant it was now just Jolie and me . . . and I had every intention of permanently wiping away the im-ages of her with Sinjin that had now been plaguing me for over an hour.

And as for you . . . I thought the words as I faced her.

You never taught me how to paralyze someone, she responded, still trying to free herself from my power.

I didn't respond, but allowed my eyes to consume her body from head to toe, pausing at her bustline. I could feel myself growing heavier. I wanted her. No, I needed her.

"There's a lot I haven't taught you," I said in a gritty voice.

"So do you plan to keep me stuck to this tree all night?"

I shrugged, enjoying the fact that she was helpless against me. Or, at least, was pretending to be. "I could."

I took the few steps separating us, the need to touch her overwhelming me, and said nothing more as I trailed my fingers down her face and neck. She shuddered. "It might be fun . . ." I said, allowing my fingers to continue down her neck, into her cleavage.

"Aren't you supposed to be commanding the troops instead of teasing me?" Her voice was breathless.

"Yes," I answered, although I could honestly say I

didn't give a damn about my men at the moment. Instead, carnal thoughts and feelings raced through me. *Claim her. Take her.*

Kiss me. It was her voice in my head.

It was all the invitation I needed. I gripped both sides of her face and forced my mouth on hers, wanting her to feel just how badly I wanted her, how much she excited me. My tongue was demanding and rough as it lapped at hers. And she met me with the same urgency, the same burning need. I pulled away from her, suddenly needing to see her face, wanting to witness the flush that had already stolen over her cheeks.

"Guess it doesn't take much to get you excited," she said with a jittery laugh, and pulled her knee up between my legs, rubbing her leg against the erection that was already straining against my pants. The breath caught in my throat. "Ah, I'm no longer frozen," she added.

I'd actually forgotten about maintaining my control over her for a while now. It was too difficult to focus on magic when all I wanted to do was bury myself in her.

"It doesn't take much to get me excited around you," I answered and absolutely meant every word. In fact, I couldn't remember the last time a woman had excited me this much.

Jolie beamed as if my words had pleased her immeasurably and threw her arms around my neck. I pulled her into my chest, wanting nothing more than to feel her against me, to relish her smell, feel her heat. "Rand, when was the last time you actually slept?"

Well, I'd slept just recently but due to the fact that I hadn't exactly slept well, visions of Sinjin arresting my mind, I didn't suppose that counted. "A week ago. I plan to sleep this evening."

"Come to my bed tonight," she answered coyly.

I shook my head and her expression dropped, replaced

with one of disappointment. "You come to mine," I finished with a smile and kissed her again.

"So this will be on your terms?" she asked with a flirtatious laugh.

I nodded. "Yes."

"And what should I expect will happen?"

I trailed my fingers down the small of her back. "Just be open to the possibilities."

She pulled away from me and I suddenly felt cold, wanting nothing more than to feel her lush body pressed up against mine. "Give me twenty minutes."

Before I could argue, she waved and turned on her heel, jogging for the house. I watched her until she disappeared through the back door. Then it was just me and my thoughts. Tonight was going to be a night that I had looked forward to since I first met Jolie. Tonight I would exercise all the fantasies I'd been storing in my head. Tonight I would make love to Jolie. Tonight I would make her mine.

It's quite interesting how twenty minutes can exist as a mere flash when you find yourself busily occupied or it can seem an eternity. I found myself pacing back and forth in my room. I'd already scoured the perimeter, ensuring the surroundings were clean and there wasn't anything out of place. All my clothes were hung up, my shoes put away, the bed made . . .

There was a nervousness within me that wouldn't abate. How long had it been since I'd been with a woman? I couldn't recall. I'd lived the life of a solitary man, focused entirely on the governance of the Underworld, not bothered with subjects such as romance and intimacy. It was a bit of an epiphany, really—the fact that I hadn't invested at all into my own personal life. That is, until I met Jolie.

Feeling as if my nerves would be the death of me, I

searched for a distraction, something to take my thoughts from my own anxiety. Was there anything Jolie might need? Food or drink? Hmm, perhaps a bottle of water? Deciding that was a good enough reason for me to quit my room, I started downstairs.

I didn't encounter anyone on my trip to the kitchen, which was just as well. The last thing I wanted was an interruption—a question about battle tactics or an invitation to play the part of referee. No, tonight was about Jolie and me. It was our night—something that had been in the making for entirely too long.

I opened the refrigerator, grabbed two bottles of water, and started for the stairs again. My heart hammered within my chest and I suddenly thought how ridiculous it was that I was nervous. Me, a grown man! A man who was in charge of hundreds of soldiers, a man who never backed away from challenge, and, instead, thrived on it. What would my men think of the fact that I was anxious about spending the evening with Jolie? I couldn't help but smile to myself as I considered it. I'd been with countless women over the one hundred sixty plus years of my existence and yet I couldn't remember the last time I'd actually felt this way, the last time I'd actually cared about someone . . .

Reaching the top of the stairs, I noticed the door to my bedroom was already slightly ajar. Jolie had arrived while I was in the kitchen, on my silly mission to keep myself occupied. I approached the door stealthily, not wanting to alert her to the fact that I'd arrived. Instead, I wanted to merely observe her like an artist viewing his subject. I never tired of Jolie's easy beauty or the way she talked to herself when she didn't think anyone was around.

I opened the door without making a sound and allowed myself to enter, immediately taking note of her on my bed. She was wearing blue-and-white-striped pajama shorts that happened to be incredibly short and showed off her lovely legs as, I'm certain, they were meant to. And on top, she wore a white camisole that strained against her ample breasts. Her nipples already stood at attention and I wondered if perhaps it was too cold in my bedroom.

She sat cross-legged with a book in her lap. It was the one I'd left unattended on my bedside table, Charles Dickens' *Great Expectations*. I didn't say anything for a few seconds, just enjoyed the visual of Jolie wearing next to nothing while sitting on my bed and reading my book. And it felt right to have her there. Somehow she just fit. I swallowed hard as I realized I could apply that statement to my life as a whole. In fact, I couldn't imagine my life without her; she had become such an enormous part of it. Really, there wasn't a day that went by that I didn't think of her, didn't laugh with her or, if apart, wonder what she was doing, what she was thinking. The realization frightened me because much though I cared for Jolie, I'd never really considered where these intense feelings would lead.

"How do you like Dickens?" I asked, no longer wanting to focus on what the future might hold for us both. The future would work itself out.

Jolie screamed in shock as she jumped and grabbed her chest, the book falling to the bed beside her. "You scared me to death!"

I chuckled and locked the door behind me, then approached the bed. I focused on her, taking her in, reveling in the fact that she was just so lovely, so natural. She wasn't a skinny woman—there was just the right balance of softness and muscle tone to her curves. I'd never before considered myself a man who had a "type" of woman he was attracted to, and yet Jolie was the exact embodiment of everything I wanted in a woman. "You look delicious."

"Thanks," she answered as her cheeks colored. Apparently I wasn't the only one with short-circuiting nerves.

I nodded and took the few steps separating us, taking the book from beside her and carelessly dropping it back on the night table. She stood up and moved closer to me, making a motion to drape her arms around my neck but I was suddenly all too aware that I'd been sparring with Odran and I hadn't yet showered. All that time I'd wasted in my bedroom, aimlessly searching for something with which to occupy myself, and the one thing I'd forgotten to do was bathe! Sometimes I surprised myself.

"I need to shower. I'm disgusting," I said.

Jolie smiled. "Okay, I'll just be right here." She lay back against the mound of pillows at the head of my bed. She never took her eyes from mine and I had to stop myself from jumping on top of her right then and there.

She belongs in your bed. The thought penetrated my head and I couldn't argue it, didn't even try.

I pulled my T-shirt off, still watching her as she reclined there like a cat, just waking up and indulging in a long stretch. I watched Jolie's eyes widen as she took in my naked chest. Her mouth dropped open as she scanned me from head to waistline.

"God, you are so gorgeous," she whispered.

I smiled but the sudden need to tell her that my appearance paled in comparison to hers almost strangled me. Jolie needed to know how lovely she was, how absolutely beautiful, how I cherished her. I reached out and ran my fingers down the side of her face. "No, Jules, you are the gorgeous one."

It was the first time I'd ever called her by her nickname. I wasn't sure why I had, perhaps because I wanted to be close to her, wanted to be accepted into her inner circle. She beamed as soon as I touched her but remembering my shower, I dropped my hand.

"I'll just be a second," I said and slipped into the bathroom. I turned the water on and felt myself beginning to hum the old Beatles song "Norwegian Wood." Yes, I was a shower singer. I always had been.

I lathered myself quickly, not wanting to keep Jolie waiting. After I'd rinsed, I turned off the water, combed my hair, dried myself, and then wrapped the towel around my middle. I gargled some mouthwash and, looking in the mirror, told myself I was ready.

I stepped into the bedroom and Jolie glanced up at me with a smile. "Have you been listening to my Beatles CD again?"

I merely smiled in return as I couldn't deny her accusation. She stood up and approached me, throwing her arms around my chest as she rested her head against me. I held her, loving the feel of her warmth, loving the fact that she was so petite and feminine. I pushed her away from me and tilted her chin up, kissing her as I lifted her into my arms. I would go slowly with her, I wanted to relish every moment we had together, be able to recall every second, every minute, every hour. I laid her on my bed and being careful not to crush her, settled myself atop her.

"Rand, make love to me," she whispered.

A shudder coursed through me at her words and I could feel myself responding, growing larger and heavier. I smiled down at her, thinking that was response enough.

I was absolutely going to make love to her and what was more, I was going to do so repeatedly.

I kissed her again, moving her arms above her head. Starting at her fingers, I caressed her palms, moving down her arms until I reached her camisole. Gripping the fabric, I shifted it upward until her breasts were bare. I couldn't tear my gaze from her alert nipples but my tongue grew envious, so I allowed my mouth to find purchase on one of them. She smelled like some exotic and sweet perfume and I grew heady on the scent and taste of her. She sighed, running her fingers through my hair.

"I don't know how long I can wait," I whispered, feeling as if I might explode if I didn't claim her quickly. "I'm not feeling especially patient."

"We've already waited too long." Her voice betrayed her urgency, her need.

Still sucking on her breast, I moved my other hand down her stomach and paused above her thigh.

Slow down, Rand, I told myself.

But there was something within me, something within both of us, that didn't want me to slow down. Jolie was correct—we had waited too long. And now was not the time for delay, now was the time for action.

I pushed her shorts to the side and, feeling the moist heat of her, pushed a finger inside her. She bucked against me, arching her back as she moaned in surprise and pleasure. I pushed a second finger inside her and started an eager dance of pushing in and pulling back out again. She felt so incredibly eager, so excited. I wanted nothing more than to fill her with myself.

"Rand," she moaned and suddenly it was as if someone had driven a blade right through my eye.

I clenched my eyes shut and pulled my fingers from her, cradling my head as I willed the feeling to go away.

"Are you okay?" she asked.

I opened my eyes and forced a smile as the pain began to fade away, leaving a mere imprint of itself. I was clueless as to what had just happened but I also wasn't about to let it ruin my evening. I glanced down at her almost naked body again and wanted nothing more than to taste her, to replace my fingers with my tongue. I pulled

her shorts down her legs, discarding them on the floor.
"I'm more than okay."

The pain returned but it was more of a dull ache, now
relegated to the back of my head. It was something I
could live with though. I slid my fingers into her again
and she arched beneath me, pushing her pelvis down
against my hand as if trying to encourage me to push
deeper. I could feel her fingers running down my back,
the sharp sensation of her nails biting into my flesh as
she braced herself for the impact of my fingers. Shivers
broke out over my skin.

God, how I wanted her, how I had to have her.

"Rand, I need you now," she pleaded.

I pulled the towel away from my midsection and nestled myself between her open legs. I glanced down at her
flushed face and smiled. She was the epitome of feminine
beauty and there was nothing I wanted more than to feel
her from the inside. I didn't have to look at myself to
know I was fully engorged, ready to take her. I held my
erection at her opening and made no motion to enter
her. I wanted to tease her, to drive her to the point at
which she begged me.

She pushed her hips down against me. "Don't tease
me," she pleaded.

But I wasn't teasing her at this point. Instead, I was
reeling with the pain that had, again, attacked the space
between my temples. I clamped my eyes shut, trying to
magically ward off the frantic ache but, if anything, it
hit me even stronger. My hands were now in fists at my
side and I opened my eyes to find I was clutching the
duvet cover.

"Rand?"

I stood up so suddenly, I nearly lost my balance. There
was an inferno erupting in my head and the most frightening part was that I now knew exactly what was happening. It had dawned on me as soon as I'd come so

close to entering her. I gripped my head and fought against the tide that was now reeling within me. I couldn't allow this to happen—I had to fight it. And the ever increasing pain was due to the fact that my body was rebelling against me. The pain hit me doubly hard and I clenched my eyes shut again, feeling as if blades were going to come through my retinas.

All I knew was that I needed to get away from Jolie. It was her body that was doing this to me, her body that was responsible, and I couldn't fight it much longer. "You have to go now, Jolie," I managed.

I opened my eyes and watched her sit up in shock. I knew my sentiment hadn't exactly come out correctly and I hated the fact that I couldn't explain to her what was happening but the pain was just so intense, I could barely even focus on my words, let alone speak them.

"What?" she demanded.

"You just . . . you just have to go," I said again as another bout of stabbing agony ricocheted through my head. I had to get away from her. I lumbered toward the washroom and closed the door behind me, thinking I needed a cold shower. Something to shock my senses, something to pull my mind from the fact that Jolie was in my bed and I wanted, no, I needed to have her.

I heard the door open but I refused to look at her. I couldn't. She would dissolve everything I'd just fought for.

"Rand, are you okay?" she asked.

The cold water actually helped to calm me and when I glanced down, I noticed my erection was completely gone. The pain in my head had since abated into a steady but dull ache. I breathed out a huge sigh of relief but continued bracing myself against the shower wall with both hands stretched out before me. I didn't trust that I could stand up on my own. I leaned into the water and allowed it to splash off my head.

"We almost bonded," I answered, finally feeling as if I could string a sentence together.

"Bonded?" she repeated. I could see the wheels in her head spinning as she realized what had almost happened, what it meant that we had come so close to bonding. When witches bonded, it was akin to marriage in the Underworld. Marriage, really, paled in comparison to bonding because bonding was forever. There was no divorce in the Underworld. But that wasn't why I'd fought so hard against the bond. What I'd fought against was the fact that when two witches were bonded, if one of them died, it could mean death or insanity for the other. And in these uncertain times of battle and war, the last thing I was going to do was jeopardize Jolie's life.

"How?" she insisted and I could see the fear registering in her eyes. I wasn't sure why but I was suddenly disappointed. I shook the feeling away, though, thinking I was ridiculous for even feeling it in the first place. I would never leave Jolie in the predicament that I had once been in—my lover had died and I'd nearly succumbed myself. If it hadn't been for the magic of the fae, I never would have survived.

"I just couldn't restrain myself . . ." I said and sighed, still supporting myself against the shower wall. "The bonding pheromones were coming off you so strongly and my body was aligned with yours. I tried to resist . . ."

"And did you?"

"I think so; I don't feel bonded now." I turned the shower off but stayed inside the glass stall, waiting for my heartbeat to regulate again.

"Rand, are you going to be all right?"

I glanced at her but immediately looked back down again, feeling a stirring of emotion within me as soon as I met her eyes. Dammit all but I still wanted her, my body still wanted to claim hers, wanted to mark my territory. "Can you return to the bedroom? I'm afraid of what might happen if I look at you right now."

She shook her head and I could see disappointment in the sag of her shoulders. And I didn't blame her, not one bit. If I'd been in the proper frame of mind, I too would have felt disappointment. As it was, though, I was still in a mad rush to defeat the increasing bonding tide that was already welling up within me again. Thankfully, Jolie did as I requested and returned to my bedroom, dropping herself back on my bed even though she left the door to the bathroom open. I took a deep breath and stood up straight, feeling my strength returning. I opened the shower door and stepped out, being careful not to look at her.

"And what's so bad about bonding with me?" she asked.

"If we're bonded and I don't . . . survive this war, it could kill you."

"I understand that part; I mean in the future."

"I don't know," I answered and it was an honest response.

"Why did you even ask me up here tonight?" she demanded.

"Because I wanted to be near you and thought I could restrain myself."

She nodded and closed her eyes. She was quiet for a few seconds. "I don't know how much longer I can deal with this, Rand."

I pulled on my blue bathrobe and walked into the bedroom. I glanced at her and found I could look upon her beauty and yet not feel as if I were being struck in the head with a pitchfork. Even so, I didn't want to risk it happening again so I reached behind me for the other dressing robe hanging behind my door and handed it to her. "Do you mind covering yourself with this dressing gown?"

She grabbed the robe and dropped it on the floor. "I can't do this anymore," she announced and, standing, started for the door.

"Jolie . . ." I didn't want her to leave; I didn't want the evening to end this way. Everything had turned out miserably.

She turned to face me and tears started in her eyes. "I'm done, Rand. Either you want to be with me or you don't."

She just didn't understand . . .

Yes, I wanted to be with her! Yes, I cared about her but I wasn't about to risk her life for my own selfishness.

"Jolie, if something happens to me, it could kill you—do you understand what I'm saying?" I repeated again, not entirely certain she'd comprehended my point.

"Yes!" she blared. "I'm not an idiot!"

I shook my head and glanced down, realizing I wasn't using the right words, I wasn't getting across the feelings that were bottled up inside me. I'd never been good at expressing my emotions. I suppose I was just like every other man in that regard. "I'm not willing to risk your safety."

"I'm talking about when the war is over," she persisted. "What then?"

"Either of us could be imprisoned or dead . . ."

"Let's say we win. Then what?"

I shook my head and sighed. I couldn't answer her because I didn't know what the future would hold, what I wanted and what she wanted. "I don't know, Jolie. The idea scares me to death." I paused and took a deep breath. "Bonding nearly killed me once before. I don't know that I want to enter into it again."

She shook her head and I could see her tears building, causing her beautiful blue eyes to shine. I reached out to touch her because I wanted to console her, but afraid the bonding pheromones might start again, I thought better of it and dropped my hand.

"If you aren't willing to allow things to progress naturally to where they seem to be headed, where does that leave me?" she asked, her voice hollow.

I ran my hands through my hair and didn't respond right away. I knew I couldn't give her the answer she wanted at the moment. I glanced up at her and found she was crying, tears streaming down her cheeks.

"Don't think of it like that, Jolie," I started, wanting nothing more than to comfort her. I hated it when she cried. And for me to be the reason for her tears . . . it was even more upsetting.

"And how should I think of it?" she insisted. I couldn't respond so she continued. "You won't answer my question so I will—it leaves me in the same place you always leave me . . . with nothing!"

"Jolie . . ."

She held up her hand as if to silence me. "This isn't fair to me, Rand. I need to get over you and I need to move on."

Bonding was only part of it, though. The situation between us would never be easy and I figured now was as good a time as any to inform her of just how difficult things between us could and would be. She needed to see the whole picture, to understand exactly what she would be getting into. "You should also realize it's difficult for witches to . . . procreate."

She rejected that argument with a wave of her hand. "I already knew that. Mathilda told me. But I would have sacrificed that if it meant we could be together."

She was too dismissive. She hadn't fully weighed the fact that she would never be a mother, that pledging herself to me would mean she'd never have the joy of watching her own children grow up, of having a family. And, really, Jolie was meant to become a mother. There was a softness and kindness to her that screamed it. "It would eventually destroy me if I wasn't able to give you a baby."

She turned toward the door again and twisted the doorknob. "I just can't do this anymore, Rand."

"Jolie," I said and focused on the door, magicking it to stay shut. "Don't leave."

"Open the door," she demanded and turned her angry eyes on me.

I closed the gap between us, needing her to understand where I was coming from, that this was no picnic for me either. "God, don't you see this is just as difficult on me?"

"Difficult on you?" she scoffed, jerking away from me. "You're the one who won't give in to the possibilities, not me. So, no, I don't see that this is in any way as difficult for you."

"I haven't said no to bonding . . . in the future," I corrected in a small voice. She just didn't seem to understand that I was doing this for her. That I didn't want to ever hurt her or disappoint her. She was everything to me.

"But you aren't exactly welcoming the idea either." She paused and wiped the tears from her eyes. "And that's not good enough for me."

"I thought our relationship was coming along nicely, why can't we just go back to how it was?"

She shook her head and looked at me as if I was a fool. Granted, I wished I hadn't said what I just had but I was reaching, reaching for anything that would mean I wouldn't lose her.

"Rand, we can't have sex. What kind of relationship is that?"

"Perhaps . . ."

"There's no point in discussing this anymore."

I slammed my hand against the door, not able to keep

my frustration at bay. Why did it have to be all or nothing? "Unless I commit to bonding with you?"

"Yes, well no!" she yelled. "I don't know, dammit."

"If we attempt anything sexual, it will bond us."

She dropped her fingers from around the doorknob and faced me. "You need to decide if I'm worth it to you."

Yes, she was worth it to me but she wasn't seeing the bigger picture—that it didn't matter if she was worth it to me because I would never risk her life for my own happiness. "Even though the war . . ."

Her hands fisted. "Screw the war; I'm talking about after the war—about our future together. You need to think about what will happen between us if we survive the war, because I won't want to go back to how it is right now."

"Is that an ultimatum?" I asked, my jaw clenched. I didn't like the direction this conversation was headed. I didn't like ultimatums.

"Yes, I'm tired of waiting around for you. Yes, there's a probability we will bond ourselves and that's a chance I'm willing to take, but if you aren't, I need to . . . get over it." She paused and faced me, her expression full of determination. "Now, open the damned door."

I grabbed her hand and pulled her into me, needing and wanting to touch her, to hold her. God, couldn't she see that this was killing me? Couldn't she see how much I cared about her, how much I wanted to be able to give in to my carnal feelings and make love to her? I leaned down and started to move in to kiss her but she jerked away from me. Apparently realizing I'd released the doorknob, she grabbed it and threw the door open, disappearing into the hall.

I don't know how long it was that I stood there in my bathrobe, merely staring at the empty hallway. But once I heard voices from downstairs, I closed my bedroom door and threw myself into a chair beside the empty fireplace.

Had I just lost her? And if I had lost her, were my reasons good enough? Yes, I couldn't tear myself away from the thought that I knew bonding wasn't an option—that I would never risk her life. But was there another way? Perhaps if we took a break and then tried to make love again? Perhaps it was just this evening, the order of events that had led up to the attempted bonding?

I shook my head as I realized how absurd my thoughts were. I knew in my heart of hearts that if Jolie and I were to attempt to make love again, the same situation would ensue. And if we ever did bond and Jolie were to suffer because of it, I would never forgive myself. And those were the feelings I focused on.

If anyone understood the dire predicament between two separated but bonded parties, it was I. I'd been the one who had nearly died when my lover had died. And even now I carried something within me that was hollow, a void. After Mathilda, the fairy, had nursed me through the darkest moments, I'd emerged alive but not whole. I was a mere shell of the man I'd once been.

When I tried to remember something, anything about the woman with whom I'd bonded, there was a blankness there. I couldn't recall her name, her face, her laugh or the way she smiled, how she felt in my arms. I couldn't remember any specifics about our lives together: how we'd met, things we'd laughed and cried about, arguments we'd had, the love we'd shared.

No, Jolie meant entirely too much to me for me to ever put her in this predicament. And, try though I did, I could not find fault with my stance on the situation. I might lose her but I would live out the remainder of my years knowing the sacrifice I made had been for the greater good.

The sacrifice I'd made had been for the woman I loved.